George Walter Prothero

The Life of Simon de Montfort, Earl of Leicester

With Special Reference to the Parliamentary History of His Time

George Walter Prothero

The Life of Simon de Montfort, Earl of Leicester
With Special Reference to the Parliamentary History of His Time

ISBN/EAN: 9783337155704

Printed in Europe, USA, Canada, Australia, Japan

Cover: Foto ©Raphael Reischuk / pixelio.de

More available books at **www.hansebooks.com**

THE LIFE

OF

SIMON DE MONTFORT

EARL OF LEICESTER

WITH SPECIAL REFERENCE TO THE

PARLIAMENTARY HISTORY OF HIS TIME

BY

GEORGE WALTER PROTHERO

Fellow and Lecturer in History
Kings College, Cambridge

WITH TWO MAPS

LONDON
LONGMANS, GREEN, AND CO.
1877

TO

MY FATHER AND MOTHER

I DEDICATE THIS WORK

PREFACE

If the attempt to go over ground already trodden by a historian of the power and learning of Dr. Pauli should carry with it an appearance of presumption, I may plead by way of excuse, and, as I hope, of justification, that in the first instance I had thought of confining myself to the office of a translator, and of asking permission of Dr. Pauli to reproduce his history in English. But as I went further into the history of the period, I found myself unable to agree with many of his conclusions, while the necessity of fuller treatment in certain portions of the subject, especially the constitutional aspect of it, forced itself upon me. I therefore began to study the history of De Montfort's time afresh, and the present volume is the result.

I have no fear of being charged with any wish of superseding the work of Dr. Pauli, or any others which may be the fruit of conscientious toil, for it is generally admitted by historical scholars that the student can derive nothing but benefit from carefully studying the views even of a large number of independent writers on the same subject. I trust, therefore, that the following pages may be found to contain matter, not to be found elsewhere, which may deserve the attention of the historical inquirer.

As regards the personal life of Simon de Montfort I have been able to add but little to the admirable account of Dr. Pauli. Still even here I have seldom relied on my predecessor, but have based my conclusions almost entirely on the records of the time. I say this however with no idea of casting a veil over my obligations to this eminent historian. The readers of this volume cannot fail to see the value which his work has for me.

The other book to which I owe most is, I need scarcely say, the 'Constitutional History of England,' by Professor Stubbs ; and here, again, if it should be necessary to anticipate any charge of not acknowledging my obligations, I may say that the portion of my book which has special reference to the constitutional struggle was written before the second volume of Professor Stubbs' work appeared. In that part of the volume some of my conclusions involve a slight dissent from his views ; but it was with hearty satisfaction that on reading his pages I found I was in the main in agreement with the greatest of living authorities. My obligations to him are, however, not only such as appear on the surface : I cannot sufficiently express my gratitude for the invaluable aid he has given me, especially in the correction of the sheets as they passed through the press. My best thanks are also due to Dr. Hort, to the Rev. H. R. Luard, and to Mr. Henry Bradshaw, for their kindly assistance and encouragement.

The references in the notes to *Rish. Chron.* are to the Chronicle of Rishanger, edited by Mr. Riley for the Master of the Rolls; those to *Rish. de Bellis,* &c. are to the other Chronicle attributed to the same author, edited by Mr. Halliwell for the Camden Society.

KINGS COLLEGE, CAMBRIDGE:
January 1877.

CONTENTS.

Contents.

MAPS.

SIMON DE MONTFORT.

CHAPTER I.

INTRODUCTION.

§ I. RISE OF PARLIAMENTARY GOVERNMENT.

THE Norman kings of England, in their efforts to found an absolute monarchy, made good use of every opportunity to crush the power of their mightier vassals, while, as a balance to that power, they kept alive, if they did not actively encourage, the remnants of national feeling and popular government. This community of interest, however slightly developed under his predecessors, bore fruit under Henry I ; in the struggle between him and his nobility the people stood by their king. Under his successor the pent up spirit of feudalism burst forth; it had its day and proved for ever its incapacity for government. The exhaustion of the older baronage, and a natural reaction against the anarchy of the preceding reign, enabled Henry II to rebuild the edifice of monarchy on foundations deeper than those which had been laid

B

by his forerunners. A strongly centralised administration of justice and finance made the king practically
independent of his barons, while it revived the ancient
popular institutions, and brought every class into
contact with the throne. A new aristocracy arose,
mainly dependent on the monarchy, but far more
national than that which sprang from the Conquest.
The union of king and people was stronger than
before ; it bore the strain of oppressive taxation and
religious struggle, of war without and rebellion within.
But the strengthening of the monarchy was not
the only result. When the sovereign supported himself by aid of the law, the thought was sure to occur
that the chains he forged for others might be used to
bind himself. The nobility he had done most to
raise, the people he had educated into a belief in law,
would be the first to cry out against a violation of
that law by the authority which gave it. Henry was
wise enough to avoid this danger : Richards personal
character and his long absence from home prevented
an outburst ; but Johns folly, tyranny, and vice
united all elements against him. The process of
amalgamation, which had been going on for a century
and a half, was now complete ; more than a generation
before it had been said that English and French-born
were no longer to be distinguished. The universal
pressure of a strong government, the tendency towards equality inherent in the rule of law, had helped
to complete the union, the last obstacle to which was
removed by the loss of Normandy ; and under a
sense of common wrong the new-born spirit of nationality sprang into consciousness of its power. There
was no longer an alliance between the king, the

Church, and the people, against the feudal nobility;
it was now for the first time an alliance of the Church,
the barons, and the people against the king. The
newer nobility, in whom the political sense was
strongest; the remnants of the older baronage striving
to recover their position ; the smaller barons, the subtenants, and others, who eagerly grasped the occasion
to make their complaints heard ; the towns, with
London at their head, in the first freshness of municipal and mercantile importance ; and above and
embracing all, the Church, with its broader notions of
justice and its popular sympathies—these were the
forces to the union of which John had to give way at
Runnymede.

Such in a few words was the general course of
national development, such the relations between
king and people, before 1215. Along with and dependent on the growth of the nation, grows the idea of
a Parliament, or representative council. In a people
composed of elements so different as those of which
England consisted immediately after the Conquest
there was no possible centre, no representative of
national unity, but the monarch. As the different
elements coalesced, a representative body became
possible ; no sooner was the national unity complete
than Parliament in its modern form began to appear.
But between the baronial assemblies of the Norman The National
Council
under the
Norman
kings.
kings and the Parliaments of our own day there is
very little similarity, though there is a distinct and
unbroken connexion. Many attempts have indeed
been made, chiefly by ardent supporters of Parliamentary rights, to trace back those rights to an antiquity
equal to that of the monarchy ; but regularity of

CHAP.
I.

1066—1215

The Na-
tional
Council
under the
Norman
kings.

composition and consistency of authority do not seem to have belonged to the earlier councils of the realm. On certain regularly-recurring occasions the Norman kings were in the habit of gathering round them their vassals. The king wore his crown, his greater barons appeared in all their state, with long trains of attendants, who heightened the splendour of their lords. Such an assembly was calculated to overawe a subject people, and to inspire respect in strangers who visited what was then perhaps the most splendid court of Europe.

At such times state business was sometimes discussed if the king willed it; sometimes there was no discussion; if it appeared inconvenient to hold the assembly, there was no scruple in omitting it altogether. The subjects discussed were only those which the king chose to bring forward; with him rested all initiative; until Stephens reign there seem to be no records of such discussions as could have led to a division.[1]

Next to the object of displaying a somewhat barbaric magnificence, the purpose of these assemblies was primarily judicial. But justice resided only in the king, or in those to whom he delegated his authority; there is little trace of a great feudal court of justice; the tendency was more and more to look on the king alone as holder of the scales. The prejudices of the barons in favour of judgment by their peers were satisfied so long as the Curia and the Exchequer were recruited from their ranks.[2] Although important trials were sometimes carried on before the Great

---

[1] Stubbs, *Const. Hist.* i. 357.
[2] Gneist, *Verw.* i. 241 seq.

Council, yet the permanent courts, and commissions named at will by the king, usurped more and more its claim to judicial functions. Further, there is no trace of any constitutional authority which might be supposed to be conferred on legislative acts by the fact that they were made by the king in council. But here a different tendency at once appears. The moral force which such acts would gain if backed by the magnates of the realm was too evident to be neglected. Thus the heading of the so-called Laws of William I, which in their oldest extant form are said by Professor Stubbs to date from the reign of Henry I,[1] states that the said laws were made by the Conqueror, 'with his chief men,' although the terms of the statutes themselves hint at nothing but an act of the kings sovereign will.[2] So too the charter issued by Henry I on his accession speaks of the laws of Edward having been granted by his father, with additions made by him, 'with the counsel of his barons;' and in the Act separating the ecclesiastical and civil jurisdictions, 'the one authentic monument of Williams jurisprudence,'[3] the king declares it to be done 'in common council and by counsel of the higher clergy and all the great men of the realm.'

Whatever argument may be deduced on behalf of parliamentary authority from these enactments of the Conqueror is considerably weakened by the fact that there are said to be no traces of legislative assem-blies under his successor.[4] On the other hand, the

Margin notes:
CHAP. I.
1066—1215
Legislative power of the council,
under William I :
under William II :

---

[1] The form given in *Fœd.* i. 1 is said by the same author to be a fabrication of the 13th century.

[2] Volo, interdicimus, hoc præcipio et volo, ego prohibeo, and the like are the terms used.—Stubbs, *Sel. Chart.* 80.

[3] Stubbs, *Const. Hist.* i. 213.   [4] Lords' *Report* i. 36.

CHAP.
I.

1066—1215
The Na-
tional
Council
under
Henry I :

charter of Henry I attributes his coronation to 'the mercy of God and the common counsel of the barons of all England ;' and it is just this right of coronation and the form of election, still kept up, which seem more than anything else to have preserved the notion of constitutional rights from complete oblivion. The ' consent of the barons ' is stated to have been given to the kings tenure of forests ; while concessions were made by the 'kings free gift,' and assemblies summoned ' by royal authority and power.'[1] Florence of Worcester declares the queen to have acted in Henrys absence ' with common counsel of the great men,' but the vague use of terms by the chroniclers renders such testimony very unsafe. It is evident however that the theory of assent to legislation was partially recognised, even if it be true that Henry I never called together a legislative assembly except at his acces-

sion.[2] Of Stephens reign it is scarcely necessary to speak. His election is said in his charter to have been made ' by assent of clergy and people ;' we hear of a General Council in 1136, at which the bestowal of temporalities on a bishop was made ' in the hearing and with the acclamation ' of certain vassals ; and at the end of his reign ' a convention of bishops and other chief men of the kingdom' swore to the terms of peace made between Stephen and his successor. But except on these and a few similar occasions constitutionalism was dormant.

Influence
of the Na-
tional
Council in
taxation
under the
Norman
kings :

There is the same scarcity of proof that the Great Councils had any real weight in the matter of taxation under the Norman kings. William the Conqueror and his sons, owing to their immense revenues, were

---

[1] *Fœd.* i. 8.   [2] Cf. the Lords' *Report* on this head.

tolerably independent of the assent of their tenants-in-chief, and would seldom have required to tax them beyond the regular feudal aids. Personal service took the place of a war budget ; the taxation of socage tenants, the tallage exacted from towns and other royal demesne, were limited by nothing but the kings will and the length of the purses to be emptied. The Conqueror was lord of both nationalities, and used both systems—the feudal, which he brought with him and improved ; the native, which he found and adapted : he needed the aid of neither party to tax the other, and was thus independent of both. The royal power in this respect was somewhat limited, or at least reduced from the dimensions to which it had grown under William II, by the charter of Henry I ; but even here the limitation is 'the kings own gift.' The same king speaks of 'an aid which the barons have given me ;' but not much stress can be laid on the use of such a word to imply that the barons were entitled to withhold the gift. We find no instance in which the right to a share in the taxation is stated ;[1] no parliamentary opposition to the king on this head or that of legislation, in the declaration of war or the regulation of the Church, appears in the records preserved to us. The difficulties to be met by the king are such as spring from the isolated resistance of feudal barons, not from a Parliament with traditional rights to defend. The Peers' Committee thinks that the consent of military tenants-in-chief was considered necessary in the case of extraordinary taxation ; but the theory, if it existed, seems to have gone no further than this, that the levying of such

somewhat increased under Henry I,

but hardly more than nominal.

[1] Stubbs, *Const. Hist.* i. 370. Anselm was not supported by the Church.

CHAP.
I.

1066—1215
Slight in-
fluence of
the Na-
tional
Council
under the
Norman
kings.

taxes without the form of approval by a council was held to be in some way or other unjust. As to legislation, the rights of the baronage seem to have been confined to that of being present and supporting, but not opposing, the kings acts. New laws, properly so called, during this period there were none ; royal edicts and charters, of so fleeting a character that it seems to have been considered needful to confirm them at the beginning of each reign, supplied their place. Sir John Fortescue says, some three centuries later, that it never was a maxim in England that ' that which the prince wills has the force of law ; ' but it is very much to be doubted whether it did not hold good during the first century after the Conquest.

Composi-
tion of the
National
Council
under the
Norman
kings.

It is very hard to decide, owing to the constant variation of terms, what were the component parts of a Great Council under the Norman kings. The elements and size of the councils vary according to circumstances, time, and place, from the small councils, or rather courts, consisting of the higher officers of the realm and the regular attendants of royalty, with whose aid the king transacted the ordinary business of government, to the great assemblies of all feudal tenants, whether tenants-in-chief or subtenants, possibly of the whole body of landowners, such as that of 1086, at which the Domesday survey was ordained. Such great assemblies were however very rare, and even those that occurred can hardly have been attended by all who might have been expected to be present. The ordinary Great Council appears to have been attended by archbishops, bishops, abbots, earls, and persons called, sometimes alone, and sometimes in conjunction with the rest of the proceres or magnates, by the name Barons. This word seems generally to include all who held by military tenure of the king in chief, except those who held of him by escheat, that is, those who by the death of their mesne lord were no longer subtenants but tenants of the king. It was however used in many different senses, and its meaning is very obscure. The distinction between earls and others, called especially barons, is already evident under the first Norman kings; and in the charter of Henry I a distinction is made between barones and homines, the former alone being recognised as members of the council, and apparently including earls and those barons who are called Majores Barones in Magna Carta. There naturally grew up a distinction between those who habitually attended and those who did not ; the number of military tenants-in chief was even under William I far too large ever to have met practically for the purpose of consultation ; the smaller barons would not have received the special summons directed to the greater and better known ; and thus a precedent was gradually established by which a distinction not originally existing was introduced and confirmed. Included in the list of barons would doubtless have been some of the inhabitants of London and the Cinque Ports, but such would have attended as barons in their own right, and in no way as connected with those towns. Corporate tenure, such as that obtained gradually by most great towns, conferred no right of membership, nor could such right have been exercised until the system of representation was introduced into politics. Ecclesiastics who were present, even if they kept at first the position they had held in the Witenagemot,

CHAP.
I.

1066—1215
The Barons
greater and
smaller :

origin of
the distinc-
tion.

Towns and
church.

Limited
nature of
the Na-
tional
Council.

must soon, in a feudal assembly, have been looked on primarily as feudal tenants, obliged to do military service like any other tenants-in-chief.

Thus the whole great class of freeholders, including all tenants not holding by military tenure, that is, all socage tenants, tenants of royal demesne and others, were left entirely without share in the government, and were subject to tallage and other exactions at the kings will. The class of subtenants, gradually rising to greater power, some of whom were superior in importance to many tenants-in-chief, while others were at the same time tenants-in-chief themselves, were considered, fallaciously enough, to be represented by their mesne lords. In the time of Henry II the number of such tenants holding by knight-service of their lords was nearly equal to the whole number of knights fees in the kingdom. The force of such a body may be imagined when they first became con-

The smaller
tenants-in-
chief theo-
retically,
not actu-
ally,
members.

scious of their political needs. The smaller tenants-in-chief who, from inadvertence, from fear of expense, very often perhaps because they were not summoned, had ceased, except on rare occasions, to attend the Council, were theoretically perhaps members but had no real power. It cannot have been pleasant for them to attend merely to be overridden by the physical force of the greater barons ; and the latter were not likely to encourage those who, nominally their equals by similarity of tenure, were in reality so far their inferiors in strength. Even in the case of the greater barons, that the king could abuse his privilege of summoning the members so as to keep out an obnoxious noble, is shown by the provisions of Magna Carta on that point.

This constitution of the national council as a feudal assembly lasted after the accession of Henry II up to and long past the date of Magna Carta. With regard to this point the utmost demanded in that charter is that all tenants-in-chief shall be in some way or another summoned. Unsettled as it may have been before, the theory that this was the legitimate form seems to have grown up during the reign of Henry II.[1] The importance of the council had meanwhile been growing in no small degree. In right of legislation, it is true, not much advance was made. The Charter of Liberties issued by Henry II confirms that of his grandfather, and the same form, that of a donation or concession, is kept up. The Constitutions of Clarendon are the report of a body of recognitors made in the presence of the great men, lay and clerical, and confirmed[2] by archbishops, bishops, earls, barons, and the nobler men and elders of the realm ; the latter seem to have been the great officers and men of experience connected with the kings courts, who would naturally attend such a council. The Assizes of Clarendon and Woodstock were made 'by assent of ' a similar body ; but the authority by which other assizes were issued during this reign is not stated to have been any other than that of the king. How little is to be inferred from this action by common counsel of the great men is evident from the fact that, when in 1177 Henry II assembled his whole army for an expedition to Nor-

CHAP.
I.

1066—1215
The National
Council
under
Henry II :

its influence
in legislation but
slight.

---

[1] Stubbs, *Const. Hist.* i. 356 : cf. *Vita S. Thomæ*, quoted in *Sel. Chart.* 123, where ' omnes qui de rege tenerent in capite,' are said to have attended at Clarendon in 1164 ; this can hardly, however, include any but military tenants-in-chief.

[2] ' Recognitus' is the word used.—Stubbs, *Sel. Chart.* 131.

CHAP.
I.

1066—1215
The Na-
tional
Council
under
Henry II :
mandy, he is said to have postponed the attempt 'by their counsel,' though how the advice of so vast an assembly could have been taken we are not told.[1] Still, although documents fail us during this reign, it appears from the chronicles that Henry II was accustomed to consult his council on a great variety of topics, as might indeed have been expected from so wise a king. From the first to the last years of his reign this habit was kept up ; in some cases the king appears to have yielded to the advice given.[2] Although no general opposition is said to have been offered to the kings wishes on questions of legislation, yet this increasing habit of consultation must have greatly strengthened, if it did not create, the theory that the assent of the national council was necessary to give

authority to law. During the reigns of Richard I and John the principle seems to have been kept up,[3] yet so little was it recognised that no legislative power is claimed for the council in Magna Carta.

Its influ-
ence in
taxation
much in-
creased
under
Henry II :
On the other hand, the theory of a right to assent to taxation struck firm root during this period. The commutation of military service for scutage introduced by Henry II, while it made the king at first more independent of his vassals, seems in the end, partly because it was an innovation on feudalism, partly because it was so much more liable than the older system to abuse under a tyrannical monarch, to have rendered opposition easier and more justifiable. It

---

[1] *Ben. Abbas* i. 178; the text implies the counsel to have been that of the whole army.

[2] 'Quorum (sc. episcoporum) consilio rex adquievit.'—*Ben. Abbas* i. 311.

[3] *e.g.*, at the Assize of Measures in 1197 (but see Lords' *Report* i. 49 here), the Assize of Bread in 5 John ; summons to barons, &c., 'nobiscum tractaturi de rebus arduis,' in 6 John.

was to this tax that resistance was first offered by Archbishop Theobald in 1156; his opposition seems not to have been successful, but a precedent was set up. There was possibly in this case nothing more than a mere denunciation of the tax, and that not in the council. The refusal of Archbishop Thomas to consent to a change in the system of taxation proposed by the king in 1163 was more serious; it was made in the presence of the great men of the realm, and an example was set that could not be forgotten. During the next reign the government was carried on for the most part in a constitutional manner by men trained up under Henrys rule of law, but signs were not wanting to show the growth of a popular party. Not much evidence on this head can be deduced from the opposition to Longchamp, whose offences were probably much exaggerated by John for his own ends; but the rising under Fitz-Osbert makes it clear that the lower classes had begun to feel their needs and their strength. The noble position of the Church as the champion of national liberties was maintained in 1198, when Hugh, Bishop of Lincoln, refused to make a grant from his lands for a war beyond the shores of England.[1] Under Richards successor constitutional feeling was to win its first great victory, but during the time of the Interdict the mind of the people was divided between indignation against Johns tyranny and unwillingness to submit to papal dictation, while until the arrival of Langton there was a want of leaders to give expression to the popular discontent. The resistance of the Archbishop of York in 1207 to the

---

[1] 'This event is a landmark of constitutional history.'—Stubbs, *Const. Hist.* i. 509.

levying of a thirteenth was overridden, and the archbishop exiled. This tax had been voted, however, 'by common counsel and assent of the kings council,' which might perhaps be taken to imply that the opposition of the archbishop was illegal.[1] The opposition of the laity, which ended in Magna Carta, began with the refusal of the Northern barons in 1213 to serve abroad, and their example was followed by the rest of the baronage.

Growth of parliamentary opposition.

Thus the idea of parliamentary government grew and strengthened during the first century and a half after the Conquest. The opposition to absolutism, offered at first by isolated individuals, became gradually the policy of a class, though it was not yet universal or really parliamentary. At the same time its character changed: it was no longer solely prompted, as in the first years of Henry II, by feudal anarchy, but was more and more the outcome of the tendency towards constitutional liberty. The principles upon which it acted, first distinctly laid down in Magna Carta, were checked for some time by the reaction which followed, and left to formulate themselves anew in the reign of Henry III. A general account of the charter would be out of place here, even if it were not impossible for me to throw any new light on a subject exhausted by the ablest writers; but a few words will be necessary to sum up the results of that famous document from a political point of view, inasmuch as the constitutional struggles of the following half-century would to a great extent have been anticipated had it retained its original form.

---

[1] *Fœd.* i. 96 ; see Stubbs, *Const. Hist.* ii. 240.

§ 2. THE GREAT CHARTER.

John was surprised, not crushed, at Runnymede : Result of Johns death. he contemplated and nearly succeeded in effecting a complete abrogation of the concessions extorted from him. After such a breach of faith his subjects could hardly again have come to terms with him except by some such method as was applied fifty years later to his son. His opportune death cut the knot. The greater part of the opposition would hardly have been induced by anything but despair to seek foreign aid, though the Pope had set an example by calling in Philip against John. No sooner therefore was the immediate cause of fear removed, than the national impulses regained their sway. From a child of nine years old there was little to dread ; the sins of the father could not with any justice be visited on his son. His representatives republished the charter, at least the greater part of it, with promises that the disputed points should be settled after fair deliberation. The retreat of the French removed the last obstacle to a pacification; this was followed by a third issue, again with considerable alterations, in what was, as far as concerned the charter itself, its final form.

The differences between the charter of 1215 and Differences between the original and later forms of the charter. that of 1217 were many and important, and involved, at least if construed literally, a great constitutional retrogression. The struggle afterwards to be related was a struggle to regain the ground lost in those two years. Magna Carta was in reality a treaty of peace, an engagement made after a defeat between the vanquished and his victors. It was not intended

CHAP.
I.

1215
Modifica-
tions intro-
duced into
the charter.
so much to bind the monarchy as a particular monarch : when he disappeared, it was but natural that
the other side should abate their precautions. That
spirit of compromise, which seems innate in Englishmen, together with a misgiving on the part of the
barons that they might have gone too far, a natural
unwillingness on the part of those in authority to
bind themselves, and a conviction that the elaborate
machinery of government needed strength and unity
at so critical a time, induced the one side to propose
and the other to accept certain modifications.[1] What
these were will perhaps be most easily understood, if,
instead of analysing Magna Carta according to modern
ideas of a specialised political system, we regard it as
containing, on the one hand, a recapitulation and confirmation of existing rights, and of such rights as
were directly deducible from these, and, on the other
hand, an enactment of certain provisions and the
establishment of certain machinery for the better
preservation of those rights.

Compari-
son of Mag-
na Carta
with the
Charter of
Henry I.
Of these constitutional safeguards some were
merely temporary, some were intended to be permanent. The latter were little more than statements
of political convictions which had grown up during the
last sixty years, but which had as yet received no
recognition in law. The Great Charter was thus based
on that of Henry I, but went far beyond it. That
charter had been mainly of a feudal character ; it
contained no provisions for, and scarcely even hinted
at, a constitutional form of government : the general
enactments were summed up in a promise to keep peace
in the land, and to observe the laws of Edward. The

[1] Cf. Stubbs, *Sel. Chart.* 330; Gneist, *Verw.* i. 290.

modes of oppression to which the Church was subject
were somewhat more clearly defined and denounced,
while the rights of the vassal alone were minutely laid
down, his protection carefully ensured, and the same
rights extended to the subtenant. These ancient
rights were therefore amplified and proclaimed anew
in Magna Carta, and with slight alterations reappear
in the subsequent editions of 1216 and 1217 ; the subtenant was in all cases as scrupulously protected as
the tenant-in-chief. But this was not all ; the advance
made in other ways since 1100 had to be recorded
and confirmed. We find therefore the judicial and
administrative system established by Henry II
preserved almost intact in Magna Carta, though its
abuse was carefully guarded against. The limitations
introduced were somewhat strengthened in subsequent
confirmations, and point, on the one hand, to an excessive growth of royal power, and, on the other, to
the necessity of concession to the feudal spirit. So
too were confirmed the rights and liberties of the
Church, including, at least in the charter of 1215, the
newly-granted freedom of election ; the liberties of
the towns were recognised, and London and the Cinque
Ports specially mentioned ; finally, the great progress
made in the forest legislation was recorded, and, having
been somewhat vaguely stated in the charter of 1215,
was incorporated two years later in a separate charter.
But the greatest advance made in Magna Carta,
and that which gives it its most lasting fame, is the
regard paid to the liberties of all subjects.[1] The same

---

[1] It is worth while to notice that the words in which these liberties
are stated in §35 of the charter of 1217 are considerably fuller and
clearer than the corresponding declaration in the charter of 1215.

Simon de Montfort.

CHAP.
I.

1215
Univer-
sality of
Magna
Carta.

spirit is visible in the charter of Henry I, and is inherent in both charters, as engagements in which the most powerful class promises to extend to others the benefits it claims for itself. But whereas in 1100 this spirit did not go beyond the bounds of feudalism, in 1215 it embraces the whole nation. The people, the 'communa' of the land, are called upon to undertake with their leaders the defence of their newly-won liberties; while the barons, the representatives of a foreign system, of the feudal invasion, acknowledge their fusion with older elements by a special extension to themselves of a right more ancient than feudalism, the right of judgment by their peers.

So far then existing rights, whether they trace their origin to immemorial usage, or to the ancient law of the land, or to charters and edicts of the kings, were stated, amplified, and confirmed. A great advance had been made since the last important charter, but the advance had been made on the same lines; that part therefore of the charter which embodies those rights with their logical extensions, and confirms the established system of government, was kept almost intact in the subsequent confirmations and in the final

form. Now the recognition of public rights, of universal liberty, was a great step, but how was it to be secured? The word of an absolute monarch was not a sufficient guarantee. But the constitutional ideas of the time were vague, and the measures in which they found expression were incompatible with the existing conception of monarchy. The spirit of nationality, of which the chief portion of Magna Carta was at once the product and the seal, was a fact that could not be gainsaid; but the principle of self-taxation and the other constitutional principles announced in 1215 had not yet struck so deep a root. The constitution of the Great Council seems indeed to have been at least in theory such as it is stated to be in the charter; the clause concerning its composition and the summons to it is merely a statement of usage in danger of becoming obsolete. Further, the right of self-taxation had already been asserted, as we have seen, and that too successfully: it was connected with the existing appliances for self-assessment: it was deducible from other and more general rights. When it was once allowed that the person and property of the subject were not to be liable to excessive punishment or tyrannical caprice, it was not hard to argue that his purse must be protected from financial exaction, even in the name of the State; that the taxpayer must have a voice in the levying of the tax; that his assent must be secured in regular form and after due deliberation; that the great officers who administer the law under which he lives must be men of the same blood as those whom they govern, and must be instructed in the law of the land. These objects then were provided for in the Great Charter of 1215, but further than this its compilers dared not go. Not a word was said of any share in general legislation, of any control over the executive, of the appointment by Parliament of the great ministers of the Crown.[1] The right of consent to taxation was claimed only in the case of an extraordinary tax, and that only for the tenants-in-chief;[2] the regular feudal aids were looked

CHAP.
I.

1215
Political
principles
of Magna
Carta :

their limi-
tations.

---

[1] Cf. Gneist, *Verw.* i. 288.

[2] It seems doubtful whether the clause 'simili modo &c.,' in § 12 of the charter of 1215 implies more than that the aid taken from London shall likewise be 'rationabile'; cf. Lords' *Report* i. 65.

on as a matter of course, though confined to three special occasions; the only limitation to their amount was that they were to be 'reasonable,' and to London alone, besides the great vassals, was even this vague privilege extended.

Reaction
visible in
subsequent
issues of
Magna
Carta.

So little appearance was there at this time of a Parliament according to modern ideas, and from even so moderate a statement of principles its authors seem to have shrunk back in alarm at their own boldness. The omission in succeeding confirmations of the clause in the charter of 1215, which granted liberty of election to the Church, is regarded by Professor Stubbs as showing merely the reluctance of the clergy to receive the privilege as a royal favour, the right itself being included among the liberties confirmed by the opening words of the charter. But there is no such way of accounting for the omission of the clauses bearing on the composition and rights of the national council. A promise was given in the issue of 1216 that certain 'serious and doubtful matters,' touching scutage and aids, the holding of the council, and other questions, should be treated of with due deliberation,[1] but even this promise disappeared in the issue of the next year. The charter of 1216 made no promise as to the appointment of fit persons to the high offices of the realm; the clause [2] concerning this important point was omitted without comment in that and later issues. Further, in the charter of 1217, it was provided that scutage should be levied as in the days of Henry II, a provision which probably secured against the arbitrary increase of the amount which had taken place under John, but which deprived the council of any

[1] § 42 of M. C. 1216.　　　　[2] § 45 of M. C. 1215.

CHAP.
I

1215
Other
differences
in subse-
quent
issues.

legal influence in the levying of the tax. The omission of the clause protecting the tenants-in-chief brought with it of course the omission of the clause protecting subtenants from similar arbitrary exactions.[1]

Besides this retrogression in those points where constitutional legislation might have been expected to be permanent, those articles which put a check, probably never intended to be lasting, on the royal power. were naturally omitted. The clumsy expedient intended to secure the execution of the charter, the establishment of a committee of government of twenty-five, did not reappear. It would have been a mere drag on the executive, for its powers were so unlimited that it could have interfered on almost any pretext, while its numbers almost precluded the possibility of united and energetic action. In spite of its failure, we shall see how the experiment was repeated, with almost equal want of success, in later years. Other occasional articles, whose objects had already been carried out, were also omitted ; one important addition was made in 1217, the order for the destruction of the adulterine castles built since the outbreak of war between John and the barons, a provision which shows how far the country had relapsed into a state of things similar to that of seventy years before. This clause was found to be no longer necessary in 1225 ; with this exception, the issue of that year is almost identical with that of 1217. There is however an important difference in the way in which the charter was issued. It is said to be granted of the kings own good-will,[2]

---

[1] It is observable that § 14 of M. C. 1215, concerning the composition of, and the summons to, a Commune Concilium, was not contained in the articles presented by the barons on which the charter is based.

[2] 'Spontanea et bona voluntate nostra.'—Preamble of M. C., 1225.

a statement recalling the charter of Henry I ; but as the price of this concession, and for the gift of these liberties, the people of the realm grant the king a fifteenth of their goods.[1] These two points are closely connected ; they contain from one point of view a great advance in theory, but from another the reverse.. If the liberties granted do not belong of right to the people, as is implied by the conception of the grant as a royal gift, it is obvious they can be withheld by the king at will, and only granted in consideration of a certain payment. To acknowledge this was to give up a great point of vantage, the argument from the abstract and inherent justice of the peoples claims. On the other hand, the recognition that property belongs to its possessors and not to the king, and that therefore the tax to be levied was a concession on the part of the people, was a great step gained, and as the king was sure to want money, it showed his subjects a way of enforcing their claims, of which they were not slow to take advantage.

The Great Charter then, as it stands in its final shape, is, with the exception of its appendix the Forest Charter, little more than a definition, extension, and confirmation of the charter of Henry I, with the judicial and administrative changes and the grants of privilege made since. This, it is true, forms the surest basis of political reform, but the attempt to formulate and legalise such reform was, as we have seen, no sooner made than it was allowed to fall through. The improvement on the earlier charters is indeed so great that the later one quite supersedes them ; hencefor-

---

[1] 'Pro hac concessione et donatione libertatum istarum, &c.' M.C. 1225 ad fin.

ward it is the Great Charter, and no other, to which
all appeal is made ; it is the Great Charter which is so repeatedly confirmed. But it too, like other early codes, was mainly negative ; feudalism and class-interest were still strong in it, though it contained the germs of a broader and nobler spirit. The constitutional prin- ciples advanced in it were legally thrust aside, legally, but not really, for they were too closely connected with existing custom, too much engrained in mens minds, for their memory to perish ; the very advance made in Magna Carta was likely to urge the sons of those who made it to outdo their fathers. The prin- ciple of self-taxation underlies the whole struggle of the succeeding reign ; other demands, such as that of the appointment by Parliament of the great officers of the Crown, were strictly connected with it; the right to dispose of the tax when paid is a corollary to it ; and exactions, favouritism, and administrative con- fusion only made the necessity of its recognition more patent. Yet it was not till the resistance became cor- porate instead of individual, universal instead of par- tial, constant instead of spasmodic, that the practical difficulties in the way of collecting a tax without support of Parliament became so great as to render the assent of that body indispensable. The attempt to introduce the principle was as yet premature. There was also a glaring inconsistency visible in the partial expression given to it in 1215. It was not only the tenants-in-chief, but the subtenants, the freeholders, the townsfolk, who paid the taxes. For these however there was as yet no adequate means of representa- tion, except in so far as the subtenants were repre- sented by their lords. If the principle was to be

The princi- ple of self- taxation :

as yet pre- mature, and par- tially applied.

recognised, these classes must be admitted to a share
in the government; but the magnates were unwilling
to admit them, nor was it perceived that the necessary
machinery already existed. This was understood
later, and the principle received due recognition; but
the issue of the struggle through which this point
was attained shows at once the prematurity and the
essential justice of the ideas which prompted the
charter of 1215.

§ 3. THE EARLY YEARS OF HENRY III.

Govern-
ment under
a regency.

The first sixteen years of the reign of Henry III
did not introduce any new principles, though the
kings minority naturally strengthened the idea of
parliamentary rule, and the cloud of popular discontent rapidly formed after he had taken the government upon himself. It was about the year 1232 that
parliamentary opposition began to take a more solid
form, and thenceforward it continually increased, together with a corresponding development of constitutional ideas, in spite of interruptions and temporary
relapses, till it culminated in the events of 1265.
There was at first, as we have seen, a considerable
reaction. The want of a more elaborate constitution
was not immediately felt. Copious legislation is not
a feature of an infant state, and the condition of the
country was such that a strong government was far

The
regents.

the most pressing need. Henry was on the whole
fortunate in those who represented him during his
minority. The great Earl of Pembroke and Archbishop Langton steered the country through the most
critical period, and with the help of Cardinal Gualo

got rid of the French, and conciliated, at least out-
wardly, most of their partisans. The influence of the
legate, backed by the strength of the spiritual arm, was
at this crisis most beneficial. It was unfortunate that
gratitude to the papacy for the saving of his crown led
Henry, in his devout subservience to Rome, to forget
the interests of his country. The year 1219 saw a
change for the worse. The Earl of Pembroke died,
Cardinal Gualo was recalled, and the legate Pandulf
took his place. Soon afterwards the struggle between
Hubert de Burgh, the justiciar, and Peter des Roches,
Bishop of Winchester, Henrys tutor, began. For a
time Hubert, supported by the archbishop, was practically supreme. He ruled well and strongly, but his
severity produced much ill-feeling. In 1222 he suppressed with no little cruelty disturbances that had
arisen between the citizens of London and the Abbot
of Westminster ; the rebellion of Falkes de Breauté
in 1224, which was countenanced by the Earl of
Chester, the head of the opposition, was directed
against, and to some extent excused by, his determined policy. The rebellion was put down, and with
it the troubles originated by John seemed to be over.
As a kind of seal to this happy consummation the
Great Charter was again confirmed, in the final form
spoken of above. Aided by the lull at home, by the
fifteenth granted to the king, and by the confusion
consequent on the death of Louis VIII, the English
succeeded in regaining Gascony and Poitou, though
the issue of the war, so much less favourable than it
might have been, added but little to the reputation of
the Government.

At this conjuncture the king, though not yet

Hubert de
Burgh.

Tran-
quillity
restored.

CHAP.
I.

1215-1232
The king
declares
himself
of age.

Unpopular
measures.

National
discontent.

twenty years old, declared himself of age, and took
the government into his own hands (January 1227).
He dismissed the hated Peter des Roches and his
following, but another of his first steps did not promise well. He began his reign without the issue of a
charter of liberties. The custom had been dropped,
it is true, since the accession of Henry II, but it must
have been expected as a prudent measure of reconciliation after the recent troubles. A further declaration, that all charters issued during the kings minority
would require renewal, was thought at first to en-
danger the Great Charter and the Charter of Forests;
but even if Henry, as is probable enough, thought of
breaking loose from all restrictions, his action seems
to have resolved itself into a mere threat. We are
told indeed that he actually cancelled the Forest
Charter, as 'made and signed when he was not his
own master, wherefore he was not bound to keep
what he had been forced to promise.'[1] The proceeding, whatever it was, was calculated to alarm all lovers
of liberty, and was a blunder in which it is hard to
acquit de Burgh, with his innate tendency towards a
strong government, of all share. It was naturally
attributed to him, and did not raise him in popular
estimation. The temper of the country was already
disturbed, and many of the nobles alienated from the
Government. The papal exactions from England as
a fief of the Church continued to be paid; the number

---

[1] *Matt. Par.* 336, 337. Gneist, *Verw.* i. 300, quotes *Matt. Par.*, as
given by Parry, to the effect that the king cancelled both charters; but
Matt. Par. mentions only the Forest Charter, stating that the magnates
under Richard demanded its restoration, though he does not say whether
this took place. For a solution of the difficulty see Stubbs, *Const.
Hist.* ii. 39.

of foreigners promoted in the country was already beginning to cause discontent ; only the year before, the
clergy, with the archbishop at their head, had refused
a demand from Honorius III for two prebends in
every cathedral. The position was difficult, and required first of all things in the ruler a strong and
steadfast policy. But that was not to be. Whatever
had been the faults of her princes, England had not
since the Conquest felt the want of a king with a will
of his own ; but this king was all his life the plaything
of his favourites. It was a bad omen when, in July
of this same year, an injustice done to his own brother
Richard, Earl of Cornwall, for the sake of one of his
creatures, produced a general rising of the great barons,
with the Earl of Cornwall at their head, who with
sword in hand compelled the king to make restitution of his brothers rights.[1]

It was not long before the other great cause of
dissatisfaction, the kings subservience to the Court of
Rome, made itself felt. Gregory IX had been made
pope the year Henry came of age, and the excommunication of the Emperor Frederick II, which soon
followed, showed that the policy of Innocent III, a
policy so disastrous to England, was to be resumed.
Next year Stephen Langton died, and in him the
staunchest bulwark of English freedom disappeared.
The Pope kept up the precedent of his appointment
by quashing the election of one of their own number
by the monks of Canterbury, and choosing Richard le
Grand, Chancellor of Lincoln, who was proposed by

CHAP.
I.

1215–1232

Weakness
of the king.

Growing
influence of
Rome.

---

[1] *Matt. Par.* 337. Several names, conspicuous thirty years later,
appear here : the Earls of Gloucester, Warenne, Hereford, Derby,
Warwick, and others.

CHAP.
I.

1215-1232
Papal ex-
actions,

opposed by
the laity.

Henry
quarrels
with
Hubert de
Burgh.

the bishops of the province[1] ; a man of energy and high principle, but without the broad views and commanding ability of his predecessor. His firmness was soon put to the test. The Pope demanded a tenth of all moveables from laymen and clergy throughout England, to prosecute his war with the Emperor. After showing great reluctance the clergy yielded, Henry having, it was said, consented through his proctors at Rome ; but the laity obstinately refused, and the old Earl of Chester went so far as to forbid any of the clergy in his County Palatine to pay the tax. The baronage was not inclined to pay for the quarrels of Rome, especially those with the Emperor, with whom negotiations had been entered into five years back, to end in his marriage with the kings sister six years later. The whole story throws a remarkable light on the position of the parties concerned : the use which the Curia made of English gold ; the subservience of the king ; the reluctant concessions of the Church ; the opposition of the laity. It was a mournful foreshadowing of the evil to come.

Still Henry might have staved off much trouble had he had the wisdom to cling to his faithful minister. It was at the outset of the unfortunate expedition to France that his fickleness and ungovernable temper led him into what seems to have been his first quarrel with Hubert de Burgh. Irritated, it appears, by the want of transport, the king, in one of those sudden bursts of passion which characterised him, called him ' a hoary traitor, who had betrayed

---

[1] The theory that the right of appointment to the archiepiscopal see rested with the pope was still more strongly illustrated in the choice of his successor, Edmund Rich, in 1234, after the rejection of three other candidates.

his country for French gold,[1] and, drawing his sword, would have rushed upon him had he not been prevented by the Earl of Chester. The expedition was only postponed, to be taken up next year (1230). The complete want of success which attended it, in spite of the disadvantages under which the French laboured, showed the want of administrative power in the Government, and the incapacity of the king as a commander. When he returned, after much loss both of honour and money, he found difficulties on all sides. He had with some trouble obtained an aid before starting. It was voted by the clergy only after deliberation, and with mention of their rights. At the close of the war they refused altogether, on the ground that their assent did not depend on that of the laity, but in spite of their opposition the king got the money. Up to this time the efforts of the clergy were mostly confined to resisting the king, while the lay barons made it their business to oppose the Curia ; it was not till many years later that the coalition of the two exactors rendered a hearty alliance of clergy and laity inevitable.

It was however already felt that the great contest between the papacy and the empire was draining the life-blood of England. A kind of secret society was established, which affixed letters to the doors of monasteries and other ecclesiastical buildings, threatening speedy punishment if the clergy gave way further to the exactions of Rome. Armed men with masks on their faces pillaged the granaries of Italian dignitaries, and gave away or sold the corn cheaply to the neighbourhood. Meanwhile financial difficulties, caused by the

[1] *Matt. Par.* 363.

war with France and thoughtless liberality towards continental favourites, pressed heavily on the king. In the midst of these troubles his evil genius, Peter des Roches, reappeared. He regained his influence over the king by persuading the magnates to grant a fortieth, and shortly afterwards succeeded in ousting his old rival Hubert de Burgh, who was dismissed by his sovereign with undeserved contumely and ingratitude. With him went the only remaining security for good government, for the Earl of Chester died about this time ; and the king delivered himself hand and foot to the ruinous counsels of his favourite. At this point may be said to begin a new period in the history of the reign : Henrys worst tendencies, till now somewhat kept in check by his minister, ran their course without restraint ; collisions between the monarchy and the baronage became more serious and more frequent ; the claims of the latter and their constitutional ideas became more definite. Henry had held the reins of government for five years, and the sketch I have attempted to give of that period will perhaps suffice to show that all the elements of future disaster were already distinctly visible. It cannot have needed very great political insight to foretell that with such a king a rupture was inevitable. But before 1232 the man who was destined to play so important a part in the struggle had already appeared upon the scene.

Dismissal of Hubert de Burgh,

the mark of a new period.

CHAPTER II.

FAMILY AND EARLY LIFE OF SIMON DE MONTFORT.

SIMON DE MONTFORT was the descendant of a family which took its name from a stronghold known still as Montfort l'Amauri. The little town so called is situated on the high ground between the valleys of the Eure and the Seine, in the south-east corner of Normandy. At a point on the northern slope of this ridge, whence the eye ranges freely over the broad valley of the Seine below, and a little river hastens down from the wooded uplands of Rambouillet to meet the larger stream, lies the village which perpetuates the family name. Close by this village is a ruined castle, whose weather-beaten remnants crown a hillock, probably the natural fortress, the 'strong mount,' which attracted the attention of the first Amalric. Montfort l'Amauri lies just half-way between Paris and Chartres, and the railway joining those towns now passes within a short distance. On the same line of railway, about ten miles to the south-west, at a point where three streams meet and flow towards the Eure, lies Epernon, the other principal possession of the house of Montfort before they acquired the county of Evreux.

CHAP.
II.

1028–1128
Origin of
the family
of de
Montfort :

Tradition connects the family of Amauri with imperial blood, for the first of the name is said to have been the grandson of Judith, daughter of Charles the Bald, and Baldwin Bras-de-fer, Count of Flanders;[1] his son William married the heiress of Montfort and Epernon, and their child, Amauri II, gave his name to the family possession. Another legend however declares this Amauri to have been an illegitimate son of King Robert, and thus makes the blood of the Capets to run in their veins.[2] Be this as it may, in this Amauri II the family first emerges into the light of history; we find him among the vassals of France

in the year 1028. His son, Simon I, appears, like others of his race, among the truest supporters of the French Crown; and to him chiefly the family owed their power, through a fortunate marriage with Agnes, daughter, and after her brother Williams death heiress, of Richard, second Count of Evreux. This important place is situated on the Iton, a tributary of the Eure, about thirty miles to the north-west of Montfort l'Amauri. The castle had been built by Duke Richard I, the great-grandfather of William the Conqueror, and given by him to his son Robert, whom he made first Count of Evreux, and shortly afterwards Archbishop of Rouen. This prelate however, in his secular quality as count, was married and had three sons, the eldest of whom, Richard, was father of Agnes. By this marriage therefore Simon I not only gained a noble property, but enabled his descendants to claim an equality in point of birth with the kings of England themselves.

[1] These details are mostly taken from *L'Art de Vérifier les Dates*, vol. iii, pp. 675 seq. and 803 seq. See Appendix I.
[2] *Recueil des Rois de France* (Du Tillet), p. 65, quoted by Pauli.

CHAP.
II.

1028-1128

The family
of de Mont-
fort in
France.

But this new dignity brought with it some evils in compensation, for the traditions of the Montfort family were those of adherence to the crown of France, while Evreux was decidedly Norman, and both Richard of Evreux and his son William had fought for their duke on the field of Hastings. Nevertheless William, when he came to be Count of Evreux, showed himself a troublesome subject, and was frequently in open revolt against the Conqueror and his sons. He went so far as to aid Duke Robert against his brother; but a little later we find him fighting on the side of Henry I at Tenchebrai. His fickle character was a constant source of disturbance, and, when he died without children in 1118, Henry thought to relieve himself from further trouble by seizing and garrisoning his castle of Evreux. But his nephew, Amauri IV of Montfort, claiming Evreux in right of his mother, took the place and expelled the garrison. His occupation was short; he was speedily driven out again, and for ten years was in constant opposition to the king of England, at one time a prisoner, at another free, now in open warfare on the side of France, now intriguing with discontented Norman barons; till at length, in 1128, Henry converted him from foe to friend by putting him in possession of Evreux and all his inheritance. Under his second son, Simon III, began a closer connexion with England.[1] His difficult position, on the frontiers of France and Normandy, must have

---

[1] The persons of this name who are found before this in connection with England, e.g. Hugh de Montfort, one of the most powerful allies of Duke William in his invasion of England, and Robert de Montfort, one of four Barons who tested the charter of liberties issued by Henry I, seem to have been members of another though possibly related family, the Montforts of Risle.

brought into play the state-craft which was so notable in his son and grandson. In spite of a divided allegiance, and the hostilities between Henry II and France, he seems to have managed to keep well with both sides, although compelled in 1159 to give up his castles, Evreux included, to the king. From that time, though the title remained, Evreux itself ceased to belong to the family; it was in the hands of the English king till ceded by John to Philip as part of the dower of Blanche of Castile.[1]

The earldom of Leicester.

But Simon gained more than he lost. He was fortunate enough, about the year 1160,[2] to win the hand of Amicia de Beaumont, sister and coheiress of Robert Fitz-Pernell, Earl of Leicester. From this marriage sprang three sons and three daughters. The eldest son, Amauri, seventh and last Count of Evreux, married Mabel, daughter of William, Earl of Gloucester, and became earl himself in right of his wife. The second son, Simon IV, who took the de Montfort estates, was the famous warrior, zealot, and crusader, 'the scourge of the Albigenses,' and became Earl of Leicester in right of his mother. A daughter, Bertrade, married Hugh, Earl of Chester, and was mother of Earl Ranulf, the great leader of the opposition in the early years of Henry III. It would have been hard, at the opening of the thirteenth century, to point to a family of greater force of character and pretensions than that of de Montfort. Simon IV, the crusader, married, about 1190, Alice, daughter of

Simon the crusader.

[1] *Fœd.* i. 79.
[2] Pauli says 'not later than 1173;' it could not well have been later than 1160, for the husband of his daughter Bertrade, the Earl of Chester, died in 1180. How it was that Amauri of Evreux did not become Earl of Leicester before his brother does not appear, nor is Dugdale clear as to how he gained or lost the earldom of Gloucester.

Bouchard V, Sire de Montmorenci, a woman noted for her piety and wisdom,[1] and in courage and energy no unworthy companion for such a husband. Simon himself, if we are to believe the report of an enthusiastic admirer,[2] combined with great intellectual ability, and the power of leading men, personal beauty and all the knightly virtues. Of his orthodoxy and ambition he gave only too terrible proof. His wife accompanied him on his crusades, and gave him valuable help in the foundation of his transitory dominion,[3] built up with bigotry and cruelty that have rarely been surpassed, and supported mainly by the terror of his name.

His connexion with England was little more than nominal. Robert, Earl of Leicester, died in 1204, and Simons right to his mothers heritage seems to have been recognised almost immediately. In August 1206 we find him spoken of as Earl of Leicester;[4] and on March 10, 1207, the king confirmed to him half the Barony of Leicester, with the third penny of the Earldom, and the High Stewardship of England.[5] This great office had become hereditary in connexion with the Earldom of Leicester before the end of the reign of Henry II, though even then the

Simon IV, Earl of Leicester.

---

[1] *Hist. Albig., Recueil* xx. 22, quoted by Pauli.
[2] *Id.* 23.
[3] *Chron. Guill. de Nang.* p. 156.
[4] *Rot. Lit. Claus.* 28 Aug. 1206. 'Comitissa mater comitis Leicestriæ.' In *Rot. Lit. Claus.* of the year before she is called 'Amicia Comitissa de Montford.' The author of the article in *Quarterly Rev.* cxix. calls Simons mother Petronilla, but in *Fœd.* i. 96 Petronilla is said to have been mother of the late Earl of Leicester (i. e. Robert), and therefore was grandmother of Simon IV.
[5] *Fœd.* i. 96. Hudson Turner (*Household Expenses* vii.) says there is no charter of his creation in existence, but it seems to have been lost, for, besides the mention of him in the writ of 28 Aug. 1206, we read in that of March 10, 1207, 'comitatus Leircestr' unde ipse comes est.'

CHAP.
II.

1207–1218
Simon IV,
Earl of
Leicester ;

dignity seems to have been shared by several persons at once. It had long ago ceased to have any political importance, the official functions connected with it having mostly passed to the Chief Justiciar, at a time when hereditary officers were being replaced by others over whom the king had more power.[1] The other half of the earldom was conferred by the king at the same time on Saer de Quenci, with the title of Earl of Winchester. The division was to take effect on the deaths of Petronilla, the mother, and Laurentia, the widow, of the late Earl of Leicester. Simon seems to have held the title until the position he had won for himself in the south of France made the mere name comparatively worthless, or until, as Pauli thinks,[2] the reconciliation of his backer, the Pope, with England, induced him to resign his claim. It is very doubtful whether he ever set foot in England ; it is certain he can never have reaped any pecuniary advantage from his earldom, for in the very same year,

1207, we find that the king deprived him of his possessions.[3] Though we are not told the reason of this change, it cannot be far to seek. Simons strength lay in Normandy, his family traditions bound him to the French court ; in the very next year he was appointed Captain-General of the French forces in the crusade against the Albigenses.[4] The conquests of the French king in Normandy would have in any case made the position of such a subject in England very doubtful, apart from the feeling with which he

---

[1] Stubbs, *Const. Hist.* i. 343, 345.   Gneist, *Verw.* i. 235.
[2] Pauli, *Simon de Mont.*, 25.
[3] *Rot. Lit. Claus.*, 27 Dec., 1207.
[4] Raymond of Toulouse was Johns brother-in-law.

seems to have been regarded by the baronial party. Whether the statement of one chronicler,[1] that the barons in 1210 conspired to elect him king of England, be true or false, it shows the repute in which he was held, and a possibility which John would not have been slow to take advantage of. The pretext for his degradation was apparently a debt to the Crown, for the custody of his lands of Leicester was given to Robert de Ropeley, in order to satisfy the king's claims.[2]

Simon was however too busy in the south of France to pay any attention to his English estates. His successes there made him a dangerous foe, and for some time there was good prospect that he would fully compensate for his losses by conquest from the continental possessions of England. Philip Augustus was not sorry to see the rise of his great vassal in that quarter; and the Pope, at least while England was under interdict, strongly favoured the ambitious advances made under the plea of religious enthusiasm. But when Innocent and John were reconciled, the tide began to turn; and the change seems to have brought with it a reconciliation between Simon and the English king. One of the last acts of John was to restore the count to the possession of his English estates, the custody of which, for his use, was given to his nephew, the Earl of Chester.[3] This seems to have been continued by Henry III, at least till the death of Simon before Toulouse, in 1218, after which the custody of the earldom was given to Stephen de Segrave, and in

---

[1] *Ann. Dunst.* 33.
[2] *Rot. Lit. Pat.* 1207, quoted by Hudson Turner.
[3] *Rot. Lit. Pat.* 17 Joh. m. 19.

CHAP.
II.

1218–1231
Descen-
dants of
Simon IV.

August 1218 to Peter des Roches, Bishop of Winchester.[1]

With the death of its founder fell the short-lived power of the de Montforts in the south. Amauri, the sixth de Montfort of his name,[2] eldest son of the crusader, continued the war a brief while, but, being of very different stuff from his father, gave it up after his mothers death in 1221, and, two years later, ceded his claim on the conquered lands to Louis VIII. He continued, however, to retain the title of Earl of Leicester, and was raised by St. Louis to the dignity of Constable of France. He died in 1241 on his return from crusade. Through his great-granddaughter, Yolande, the family estates came, at the end of the thirteenth century, into the possession of the Dukes of Brittany, with whom they remained until the union of Brittany with the crown of France completed the absorption of the once princely domains of Montfort into the royal treasury.[3]

Renewal of
claim on
the earl-
dom of
Leicester.

The hostile relations between England and France, which were almost continuous during the first fifteen years of the reign of Henry III, seemed to destroy all hope that the earldom of Leicester would ever return to the family of de Montfort. The peace however which was concluded in 1231 made it possible for Amauri, eldest son of Simon the crusader, to push his claim. It was doubtless the prospect of gaining so important an ally, as well as Henrys general taste

---

[1] *Rot. Lit. Claus.*, 28 July and 26 Aug. 1218.
[2] Amauri, elder brother of Simon IV, held the title of Count of Evreux. Simon IV seems to have been the first Count of Montfort, his predecessors having been called Barons.
[3] For this and many of the preceding details see *L'Art de Vérifier les Dates*, vol. iii, pp. 675 seq.

for foreigners, which gained the suppliant access at the English court. But the English nobility regarded the matter with eyes different from the kings. To them the de Montforts were aliens, though fifty years before Amauri would have seemed no more foreign than the great Norman earl whose possessions his father had shared. A divided allegiance was now no longer possible. Amauri therefore preferred the request on behalf of his younger brother Simon, the second and third brothers, Guy, Count of Bigorre, and Robert, being apparently dead.[1] When and where Simon was born we do not know, but since he is called an old man in 1264, it cannot have been long after the beginning of the century; nor, on the other hand, can it well have been before 1195, since he was the fourth son. He was probably, in any case, some few years older than his future sovereign.

Of his early life and education we know nothing; but since his brother Amauri had for teacher Master Nicholas,[2] according to Roger Bacon one of the best mathematicians of his day, his schooling was probably not neglected. He is said to have been unable to speak English on his first arrival, which indeed is no wonder. He was however well skilled in the use of arms, and, like his father, tall and handsome.[3] He may have first seen service under the elder Simon at Toulouse, and there laid the foundation of that knowledge of Gascony and Aquitaine of which he made so good use in later years.

[1] Guy died in 1218 or 1220, in the war against Toulouse; Robert died about 1226.—Nichols' *Hist. of Town of Leicester*, 104.

[2] Probably the brother Nicholas, who was afterwards confessor to Innocent IV, and Bishop of Assisi.—*Mon. Francisc.* 61.

[3] *Chron. Lanercost*, 39, 77.

CHAP.
II.

1231–1232
Simon
obtains the
earldom of
Leicester.

The first news[1] we have of him is characteristic of his stirring nature. We are told[2] that he embraced the English side, and fleeing from the displeasure of Queen Blanche, then regent, made his way to England, and was kindly received by the king. He had certainly visited England before April 1230, when Henry conferred upon him a temporary pension of 400 marks, with promise of the earldom;[3] but he seems to have returned to France again, whether with the king or not we do not know. In 1231 he obtained a grant of his fathers share of the honour of Leicester, and did homage for it in the same year. In 1232 the king confirmed to him all the land, with appurtenances, which belonged to Simon de Montfort, late Earl of Leicester, in England.[4] It is stated in the writ that this was done at the request of Amauri; but it seems probable that Simon had pushed his own claim at first without his brothers knowledge, and that it was only when Amauri found that the younger one had been before him that he withdrew in his favour.[5] With the formal renunciation of all claims on his fathers property in England made by Amauri in June 1232,[6] Simon de Montfort took his place among Englishmen.

---

[1] There is a report given in *Matt. Paris* that in 1226 he claimed restitution from the King of France of the fief of Toulouse ; but it seems to rest on but slight foundation, and is probably owing to a confusion between him and his brother. See Nichols' *Hist. of Town of Leic.* 105.

[2] *Chron. Will. de Nang.*, ed. *Géraud*, p. 191. *Nic. Triv. Ann.* 226.

[3] *Royal Letters*, i. 362, 'cum essetis apud nos in Anglia.'

[4] *Rot. Lit. Claus.* 1231 ; *Royal Letters* i. 401, letter announcing the homage, dated 13 August ; *Fœd.* i. 203. See too *Household Expenses*, p. xii.

[5] If not the letter of Amauri (*Fœd.* i. 202), in which he begs the king to give him the land, or, if not, to give it to Simon, must belong to 1231, and not 1232, as there given.

[6] Letter of Amauri (*Fœd.* i. 205). The deed however in which

But his difficulties were by no means over. He had to encounter the waxing opposition of the English nobility to foreigners, which seems to have been so far successful as to keep him for some years from the title, as well as the most substantial advantages of his earldom. It is probable that the Earl of Winchester refused to give up what he held of de Montforts moiety, the greater portion of which, in addition to his own share, his father Saer had held in 1206.[1] The meagre income yielded by the remainder[2] was by no means sufficient to support the state of an Earl of Leicester; for the next five years at least Simon does not seem even to have borne the title. He was still among the wealthy English barons little more than a penniless adventurer. Deeply in debt, his favour with the king procured him the gift of the Norman escheats within his fief, which were to be at his disposal 'till such time as our lands of England and Normandy be one again.'[3] A tardy recognition of his rights obtained for him the grant of four years revenue from the Leicester estates, to count from his fathers death, 'in order to pay his debts.'[4] It is no wonder that under these circumstances he, as other needy gentlemen have done, spent most of his time abroad. Of this period of his life we know but little. He does not seem to have been employed on any service of State for the first few years. It was during this

CHAP.
II.

1232–1236
but en-
counters
many diffi-
culties;

and lives
much
abroad.

Amauris resignation is made (*Fœd.* i. 203) appears to belong to a later date, since it was made in the presence of Cardinal Otho (cf. Pauli, *Simon de Mont.*, 34); if so, the resignation was probably renewed on the occasion of Simons marriage, or investiture with the earldom (1239).

[1] *Rot. Fin.* 7 Joh. m. 10, quoted by Hudson Turner.
[2] *Rot. Lit. Claus.* 8 and 9 Joh., quoted *ibid.*
[3] *Royal Letters,* i. 407.
[4] *Rot. Lit. Pat.*, 28 July, 1236.

time that he was foiled in two attempts to better his fortunes by marriage. He appears to have won the hearts of two noble ladies, the Countess of Flanders and the Countess of Boulogne ; but in both cases his hopes were shattered by the opposition of the French Crown, jealous of his connection with England.[1]

Simon, as a courtier,

The marriage of Henry III with Eleanor of Provence seems to have brought him home. At the nuptial festivities he performed the duties of Lord High Steward,[2] and from this moment his rise was rapid. He began to appear as a member of the kings council in the most important transactions of the day, although he still signed as plain Simon de Montfort, not as Earl of Leicester.[3] But his position at court made him an object of hatred to the national party. The Earl of Cornwall, who, as heir to the crown, was naturally head of the opposition, in remonstrating with his brother, alluded to him as one of 'the evil and suspect councillors' who were the causes of all the trouble.[4] · However, a way to much higher

woocs the kings sister Eleanor.

advancement was soon opened to him. His personal beauty, adventurous character, and a genius which raised him above his contemporaries, won the love of Eleanor, Countess of Pembroke, youngest sister of Henry III. This princess, who was born a year be-

---

[1] *Alber. de Trois Font.* s. a. 1237, quoted by Pauli.

[2] *Matt. Par.* 421, 'Comite Legecestriæ regi pransuro in pelvibus aquam ministrante.' He appears however to have had some difficulty in making good his title, which had been claimed by Roger, Earl of Norfolk. A compromise was arranged, Simon giving the earl the services of ten knights, in consideration of which Roger renounced his claim.—Nichols' *Hist. of Town of Leic.* 107.

[3] *Fœd.* i. 231, 233 ; he was present too at the confirmation of Magna Carta in 1237.—*Ann. Tewk.* 103.

[4] *Matt. Par.* 446.

fore her fathers death, had been betrothed, while still
a child, to William, Earl of Pembroke, the son of the
great Protector. The earl died suddenly in April
1231, in the midst of the festivities which the marriage of his sister Isabella to Richard of Cornwall had
occasioned. Although her affection for him must,
one would think, have had in it more of reverence
than of love,[1] yet so intense was her first grief, that in
the presence of the Archbishop of Canterbury and
the Bishop of Chichester she took the vow of perpetual chastity, and received the ring which bound
her as the spouse of Christ. But the spirits of a girl
of sixteen were too elastic to remain long under the
cloud of sorrow ; she never took the veil, but visited
the gay court of her brother, or kept up no small state
at her own castle of Odiham, in Hampshire, which
had been conferred upon her by the king.[2] Of the
great possessions which became hers after her husbands death she seems for some time to have reaped
but little advantage ; the quarrel between Henry III
and her brother-in-law, Richard, now Earl of Pembroke, gave the former an excuse to seize upon the
Irish possessions of the family. Meanwhile, though
she did not enter a convent, the Church claimed her
as its own ; but it seems probable that the ceremony
of her consecration cannot have been completely
performed, for it is hardly possible to conceive that
Henrys devoutness would have allowed him to sanction the marriage had not the omission of some for-
mality set his shallow conscience at rest. Be that as

---

[1] He was probably at least twenty years older than she.
[2] Greens *Princesses* ii. 59, 61.   This book contains many other
interesting details about the Countess and the Earl of Leicester.

CHAP.
II.

1238
Simons
marriage.

Opposition
of the
Church,

and the
baronage
headed by
the Earl of
Cornwall.

it may, the king, in spite of the warning of Archbishop Edmund, looked with the greatest favour on the match, and with his own hand gave away the bride.[1] The ceremony was performed on Jan. 7, 1238, in the private chapel at Westminster, in haste and in secret, lest it should come to the ears of the magnates and be prevented.

The secret however could not be long concealed. A general outburst of indignation followed the disclosure. The Church considered the marriage a violation of the holy bond by which Eleanor had bound herself; it was even supposed, though this was not the case, that the rejection of his advice had caused the archbishop suddenly to leave the country, and, according to one chronicler,[2] before he turned his back on London, he had paused on a hill whence he could see the city, and had solemnly cursed the marriage and its future offspring. The magnates were enraged at the sudden rise of a foreigner to a position only second to that of the Earl of Cornwall, and this proximity was so unpleasant to the latter that he headed the malcontents, and personally attacked the king with threats and upbraidings. 'Was this the result of all his brothers promises,' said the earl, 'that he removed his own countrymen from his council, to replace them by aliens, that he deigned not to ask the assent of his constitutional advisers before bestowing his wards in marriage on whomsoever he would?'[3] The whole

---

[1] *Matt. Par.* 465.

[2] *Chron. Lanercost,* 39. According to Hemingburgh and Knighton, the Bishop of Lincoln prophesied ill of the marriage; but this is evidently false, as he was Simons chief supporter about this time.

[3] He had at the same time married Richard de Clare to the daughter of the Earl of Lincoln.

kingdom was in an uproar ; the legate could not get
a hearing. The magnates drew their forces together ;
the citizens of London, twenty years later Simons
staunchest allies, joined in the cry. The king, over-
whelmed and confused, was only able to gain a short
respite for deliberation. It was hoped on all sides
that Earl Richard would avail himself of the opportunity to sweep from the land the hated plague of
aliens, and blessings were showered on his head. But, *The Earl*
by the time the barons were assembled, intrigue had *of Corn-*
wall ap-
done its work. By his submissive bearing, by pro- *peased ;*
not so the
mises and gifts, it was said, perhaps by his personal *rest.*
charm or his wifes intercession, Simon had won over
his brother-in-law ; and with the loss of their leader
the band of insurgents soon melted away, cursing the
fickleness of him who had been thought ' a staff of
strength.' [1]

But, in spite of the reconciliation with his most *Simon goes*
dangerous foe, the rest of the barons were not ap- *to Rome,*
peased, and the ecclesiastical opposition was as strong
as ever. To remove the latter obstacle, Simon set
off almost immediately for Rome, armed with letters
of recommendation from the king to the Curia,[2] and
with the still more necessary supply of gold, which
he extorted from his tenants for the purpose.[3] On *meets the*
Emperor,
his way through Italy he visited his brother-in-law
the Emperor, then engaged in war with the Lombard
League. He placed his sword for a while at Fredericks disposal,[4] and then went on his way with the

---

[1] 'Factus est suspectus qui credebatur baculus fortitudinis.'—*Matt.*
Par. 468.
[2] *Rot. Lit. Pat.*, 22 Hen. 3, m. 8, quoted by Hudson Turner.
[3] *Matt. Par.* 468.
[4] *Id.* 468, 471. Pauli suggests he may have fought at the siege of Brescia.

additional aid of imperial favour, if indeed that could
be considered an aid which was given by one so soon to
become the open foe of Rome. It is evident that he
made a favourable impression on Frederick, while the
bold ideas and antipapal policy of the latter may
well have influenced de Montfort for life. With the
and re-
ceives the
Papal per-
mission.
Curia he seems to have had no difficulty ; the Pope,
in spite of the opposition of the Dominicans, saw no
reason for interference. The friars quoted high authority in support of their opinion ; but, as Matthew
Paris, who never loses the chance of a sarcasm against
Rome, remarks, ' perhaps something more subtle than
is given to us to understand was in the minds of the
Roman Curia.' [1] Gregory IX bade the legate give
sentence in favour of the suppliant, [2] and with this
His return
to Eng-
land.
assurance Simon turned homewards. He seems to
have lingered on the way, probably in the imperial
camp, for he did not reach England till the middle
of October, when he was received with all appearance
of brotherly affection by the king, and then hastened
Birth of his
eldest son.
to Eleanor at Kenilworth. [3] Shortly afterwards his
wife, who had remained at home during his absence,
bore a son. The boy was called Henry after his royal
uncle. Early next year the king, in the presence of
the assembled barons, formally conferred upon Simon
the earldom of Leicester, and invested him with the
title. [4]

Simon in
his own
home.
In his home at Odiham or Kenilworth the sky of
Simons fortunes seemed without a cloud, when sud-

[1] *Matt. Par.* 471.
[2] Papal letter quoted by Pauli ; also *Matt. Par.* 471.
[3] This castle was formally bestowed on the earl in 1243. See a
description of it in Greens *Princesses*, ii. 81.
[4] *Matt. Par.* 483.

denly a change took place, unexpected in its arrival,
and most important in its consequences. A successor
to the throne, afterwards Edward I, was born on June
16, 1239. Simon stood godfather to the child, and
acted as High Steward at his baptism. The king seized
the opportunity to extort money from those to whom
he announced the happy event. If the presents he
received did not satisfy him, he sent the messengers
back for more, so that it was remarked, 'God gave us
this child, but my lord the king sells him to us.'[1] On
August 9 the earl came with his wife to attend the
churching of the queen at Westminster, when the
king turned suddenly upon him, called him an excommunicated man, and drove him from his presence.
Astonished and deeply hurt by these reproaches, the
earl and countess retired across the river to the palace
of the late Bishop of Winchester, where they lodged.
But no sooner were they arrived than the king sent
messengers to eject them. Thereupon they returned,
and made one more attempt to appease their sovereign ; but he, now thoroughly enraged, exclaimed,
' Thou didst corrupt my sister before her marriage, and
it was only when I discovered this that I gave her to
thee, unwilling as I was, to avoid scandal ;' and then he
went on in the same style to shower accusations on the
earl, declaring that he had bribed the Curia with gifts
and promises, and that, being unable to fulfil the latter,
he had deservedly fallen under sentence of excommunication ; nay more, he had made the king, without his knowledge, security for his bond and partner
in his fraud.[2] The earl, we are told, withdrew, blush-
ing with shame or anger, and as soon as night fell

[1] *Matt. Par.* 488.　　　　[2] *Id.* 498.

dropped down the Thames in a small vessel, with his wife and a few attendants, and made the best of his way to France.

Causes of
the quarrel.

What was the reason of this sudden and apparently unaccountable burst of temper? What truth was there in these violent reproaches? Dr Shirley,

Dr Shirleys
opinion :

in the 'Quarterly Review,'[1] followed by Pauli, ascribes it to the change in the politics of the English court, caused by the freshly-aroused hostility between Pope and Emperor. But surely it is hardly necessary to go so far afield to find a reason. The quarrel between the two heads of Christendom had indeed lately come to a climax. Frederick II had been excommunicated on Palm Sunday in this year, and the bull was published in England a fortnight before the scene at Westminster took place. It is said by the above-mentioned authors that the papal party at court, now in the ascendant, had probably urged his dismissal, owing to the friendship known to exist between him and the Popes greatest foe. De Montfort had therefore to be got rid of, and the same charge was trumped up against him which had been made against

reasons
against
this.

Hubert de Burgh a few years before. But was the papal influence in England at that moment so high, or the kings friendship for his brother-in-law so far cooled, as to account for this? Only last year Henry had sent Frederick men and money,[2] and letters of expostulation written by the latter this year, together with a very friendly one two years later,[3] seem to show that the good-feeling between them was never really interrupted, at least till the death of Isabella severed the

[1] *Quart. Rev.* cxix. 31, Pauli, *Simon de Mont.*, 36.
[2] *Matt. Par. Hist. Ang.* 408.   [3] *Fœd.* i. 236, 237, 241.

bond of relationship between them. And, even if the
papal party had been so strong, there is nothing to
show that Simon was in such bad odour at Rome. It
is true he was recommended by Frederick, and had
assisted him in return, but we do not know that he
had done anything since to change the feeling towards
him which had won from the Curia so speedy an
answer to his request. But what makes the idea of a
papal intrigue most improbable is the language used
by Henry himself with regard to the Curia; his allusions to the power of money at Rome, the avarice of
that court, and the venal suppression of truth, show
that he was by no means well-disposed towards the
papacy at that moment.[1] Further, it is more than
doubtful whether an excommunication was ever really
issued against de Montfort. Henry had no great
regard for truth, and it is at least strange that Simon
should have received the first news of it from the
kings mouth, and in so unofficial a form. On the
other hand, the king seems at the moment really to
have believed the first accusation to be true; even
he would hardly otherwise have dared to insult his
sister publicly; nor was his anger feigned, for, though
a hypocrite, he was not a good actor. The following
explanation may perhaps cover all difficulties.

The party which had opposed Leicester before Probable
was not likely to be pacified by the papal dispensa- cause of the quarrel.
tion. It would not have been difficult for any Iago
of the court to whisper in Henrys ear the insinuation
that there was only too good reason for the eagerness
with which the marriage ceremonies had been hurried

---

[1] 'Victa veritas Romanæ cessit avaritiæ,' &c.—*Matt. Par.* 498.

E

CHAP.
II.

1239
Quarrel
between
the king
and Simon.

on. He, with his strange mixture of credulity and distrustfulness, would have been easily persuaded ; and the sight of his late favourite would have kindled his resentment into flame. The fact, that a reconciliation so soon followed, seems to show that we need not look further than to Henrys character for the explanation of a scene which disgraced the monarch and alienated his most attached subject.[1] If this explanation is correct, it follows that the first accusation was false, and the facts, as far as they go, bear out this. Such a charge, twice made and utterly unsupported, bears its refutation on its face. It is evident at least that it cannot have occurred to Henry till immediately before the event, seeing that de Montfort was in high favour with the king for a year and a half after his marriage ; such a storm could not have been brewing in his mind all this time. Perhaps the strongest argument against the charge is the fact that Bishop Grosseteste evidently disbelieved it.[2] In a letter[3] written just after de Montforts disgrace, the bishop bids him bear his trouble patiently, according to the name he holds ; but he never so much as hints that he considers the punishment deserved. The point of the letter is, 'Whom the Lord loveth, he chasteneth,' not 'Be sure your sin will find you out.' Lastly, the date of the birth of Henry de Montfort, November 28, 1238, ought to be taken into account.

Falsity of
the first
charge.

Reason of
Henrys
anger.

The immediate reason of Henrys anger, which, once stirred, looked round for what might be considered less selfish motives, is probably to be discovered

---

[1] Cf. Hudson Turner, *Household Expenses*, xvii.
[2] This is urged by Dr. Shirley, *Quart. Rev.* cxix. 31.
[3] *Grosset. Epist.* 243.

in the latter part of his speech, in which he accuses de Montfort of bribing the Curia, and using his name as security for extravagant promises. The fact of the bribery seems undeniable. Payment for justice, especially at the venal court of Rome,[1] was so ordinary an occurrence that we need not wonder that Simon yielded to the custom. It was a dishonourable transaction, doubtless, and has therefore been considered by some writers so alien to Simons character as to make it impossible to attribute it to him.[2] This rests perhaps hardly on sufficient grounds. He was not immaculate, and the job would hardly have been considered dishonourable. Further, it is likely enough that he made more use of Henrys name than the latter liked; though this would almost be justified by the favour in which he stood with the king at the time, and by the terms of his credentials, which amounted to a general assumption of responsibility for the whole affair. When de Montfort failed to fulfil his engagements, his creditors, Italian moneylenders who transacted the Popes business abroad, would have applied to Henry, whose surprise and indignation burst forth in the way we have seen. They may also have hinted that if the money were not paid Simon might still be considered liable to excommunication. This will account for Henrys allusion to that danger.[3]

The earl and countess bowed before the storm, and avoided the consequences by a voluntary exile of seven months in France. Though the kings anger

Simon retires to France.

---

[1] This is borne out by frequent allusions in contemporary poems and chronicles.

[2] *Quart. Rev.* cxix. 31.

[3] Hudson Turner, *Household Expenses* xvii.

CHAP.
II.

1240

Simon
returns to
England,

and is
nominally
reconciled
to the king.

Prepara-
tion for a
crusade.

seems to have pursued them even there, it was soon mitigated, probably in a great degree by the efforts of the Bishop of Lincoln, who in the letter already quoted had promised to plead their cause; and in April 1240 Simon returned, and was received by king and court with all due honour. The countess remained for a time abroad, expecting the birth of her second child, who was named Simon after his father. The earl was now to all appearance safe, but the consequences of the late rupture between him and the king were not so easily effaced. Though he completely recovered his position at court, and continued to raise it in the country, his friendly relations with the king were irremediably shaken. Whatever confidence he can have had in Henry must have disappeared; the insult and the injury were such as a man of far milder temper and less haughty spirit could hardly have forgotten. He was forced to take up a more independent attitude. He would probably in no case have taken the kings side in the constitutional disputes, which were already becoming serious; but it is probable that the quarrel hastened the time at which he entered, as we shall soon see, on his long service in the ranks of the opposition.

Meanwhile, whether on account of a former vow, or in order to allow time for things to settle, he prepared, with Richard of Cornwall, and other English nobles, to go on the crusade, so eagerly preached throughout Europe by the court of Rome. He had indeed with Earl Richard and William Longespee

---

[1] *Royal Letters,* ii. 16, in which Henry bids his proctors at Rome do what they can to help Peter of Brittany in a dispute he has with de Montfort.

been released from this vow,[1] and it seems doubtful
whether he ever really started on the expedition. We
hear nothing of his exploits in the Holy Land, nor is
he mentioned by Matthew Paris as having joined the
army, though both the departure and return of William
Longespee, heir of the earldom of Salisbury, are
especially noticed.[2] It is possible he had no more
real intention of going than he had in 1261, when
he declared he would leave England for the Holy
Land.[3] The fact too, that he and his wife took
the cross in 1247, and that it was then supposed
to be for the purpose of expiating the sin of
his marriage, seems to show that he had not been
on crusade before.[4] On the other hand, it must
be said that he had a special incentive in the fact
that his eldest brother Amauri had been taken by
the Saracens, and was languishing with other noble
captives in prison in Cairo.[5] A letter written in June
1241 by the nobility of the kingdom of Jerusalem to
Frederick II,[6] asking him to allow Simon de Montfort, Earl of Leicester, to act as regent till the arrival
of the emperors son Conrad, has been considered
sufficient proof that he was in the Holy Land, and
had distinguished himself there so as to merit this
great mark of approbation. This seems to be the

CHAP.
II.

1240
Uncer-
tainty as to
whether he
went on
crusade or
not :

---

[1] *Letters of Greg. IX*, quoted by Pauli.
[2] *Matt. Par.* 536. 582.
[3] *Ann. Osney*, 129.
[4] *Matt. Par.* 742.
[5] *Id.* 530, (?) Babylon.
[6] Letter printed in *Household Expenses*, xix. dated 7 June, 1241.
It is obvious however that the letter might have been written, though
Simon should never have been there. Nichols seems to be wrong in
stating that the *Annals of Dunstable* say Simon went to the Holy
Land.

CHAP.
II.

1240-42
Richard of
Cornwall
in the East.

only ground,[1] though certainly a strong one, for believing that Simon took part in this crusade.

The little band of Christians was hard pressed at this time by the superior power of the Mohammedans, and Richards assistance, rendered perhaps even more valuable by his great wealth than by the troops he brought with him, was welcomed with the greatest joy on..his arrival at Acre in the autumn of 1240. There was however but little for him to do; a truce had already been struck, involving the release of the captives, and a special treaty was made between the earl and the Sultan of Egypt, which gave the former time to rebuild the shattered strongholds of the Christians, and otherwise to place their affairs on a better footing.[2] In May 1241 he re-embarked, and on his passage through Italy visited his brother-in-law the Emperor. He was entertained by him for two months with all that eastern luxury and elegance, which increased the fame and injured the reputation of Frederick II.[3] If Simon de Montfort was in the Holy Land he would probably have returned with Richard. He may have stayed to close the eyes of his brother, who died on his way home, at Otranto, in the summer of this year.

Whatever be the truth on this point, we find him in England early in 1242. He must have been present

---

[1] About the same time however Simon sold property to the Canons of Leicester to the amount of 1,000*l.*—Greens *Princesses*, 77.

[2] See Richards own letter, giving an account of the expedition.—*Matt. Par.* 566.

[3] Matthew Paris gives an interesting account of the musical and other entertainments, and especially of the performance of two Saracen girls of great beauty, who danced exquisitely on rolling spheres, and glided to and fro over the polished floor wherever they would, singing and clapping their hands, interlacing their arms, and bending their bodies to the tune of the cymbals and tambourines on which they played.

CHAP.
II.

1242
Prepara-
tions for
war with
France.

at the important council of that year, in which the king met with the most determined opposition to his demands for money, and had to submit to a sound rating from the assembled baronage for his wastefulness, and his unconstitutional action in breaking the truce with France without their consent.[1] The names of the barons are not given by the historians, but there is no reason to doubt that Simon took his place among them ; which side he took must however remain uncertain. Louis IX had made his brother Alfonso Count of Poitou, an insult to the English claims, and especially to Richard of Cornwall, who held that title. The Count of la Marche, Henrys stepfather, found little difficulty in persuading the king to undertake an expedition to France. He promised to find the men if the English would provide the money. Henry, with his usual rashness and short-sighted ambition, entered on the war with a light heart. In spite of the opposition of the magnates he collected a large sum of money, by means only too well-known to the financial policy of the day, the policy of attacking singly those whom he could not break when united together.

In May 1242 Henry entered upon his ill-advised expedition, attended by the queen, Earl Richard, and a few nobles, among whom was Simon de Montfort.

It is to this affair that we must probably refer a very interesting satirical song, written by a Frenchman, on a certain assembly held in England to discuss an expedition against France.[2] The writer, in sarcastic

---

[1] See below, p. 66.

[2] *Polit. Songs*, p. 63. Mr. Wright refers this song to 1264, and says it alludes to the mediation of the King of France. But nothing in

CHAP.
II.

1242
Song on
the expedi-
tion to
France.

and somewhat coarse language, paints the extravagant pretensions of the English king, the ardent wish of Henry and his brother Richard to recover Normandy, and the paternal pride which the former takes in his son 'Edward of the flaxen hair.' Henry thinks he has only to land and the French will run away ; he will march on Paris, will carry off the Sainte Chapelle just as it stands, for a trophy of his victory ; will have Edward crowned in St. Denis, and will celebrate the occasion with a great feast of beef and pork. But at the assembly in London, in which the king proposes the expedition, 'not a baron, from best to worst, will move.' Afterwards however the Earls of Gloucester and Winchester support the king, outdoing him in braggadocio ; upon which Sir Simon de Montfort starts to his feet, with anger in his face, and advises the king to let the matter drop, for 'the Frenchman is no lamb,' and will defend himself bravely. Thereupon ensues a quarrel between de Montfort and Roger Bigod, who is indignant at Simons freedom of speech, and vows, perhaps in allusion to his own name, by 'Godelamit' that the affair shall be brought to a glorious conclusion. The king appeases him, and there is an end of the matter. These events are of course not introduced here as undoubted matter of history, but, allowing for poetical treatment and a

---

the song agrees with this hypothesis. There is no allusion to an act of mediation ; invasion and conquest are alone spoken of. The opposition mentioned is just that of the Parliament of 1242 ; we know of no Parliament in 1263, or 1264, at which the events of the song would have been possible ; at the latter period there was no talk of an invasion of France, and Normandy was formally given up in 1259. The only difficulty is that Edward, then three years old, is called a bold knight ; but that is probably only a satirical exaggeration of his fathers pride in him.

foreign author, there is much probability in them. The attitude in which Simon de Montfort is represented is just that which he is likely to have taken; the traits of the other characters accord with what we know of them.

The expedition undertaken so lightly ended in a miserable failure. The Count of la Marche proved a broken reed. Deserted by him, the English suffered a severe defeat at the battle of Saintes, and the Earls of Leicester, Salisbury, and Norfolk, with a few other great barons, were hardly able to save the army from destruction, and the country from the penalty of a royal ransom. This doubtless increased the favour in which Simon already stood at this time with the king,[1] and which the Count of Toulouse and the King of Aragon, hereditary foes of the house of Montfort, tried in vain to undermine.[2] Henry bestowed upon him several marks of friendship;[3] he held a most important position in the royal council; and when the other nobles left for England, disgusted at the ill-success of the campaign, and at the idle frivolities in which Henry wasted time and money at Bordeaux, he and William of Salisbury, though much to their own loss, remained. Simon had a year to examine the restless party-spirit, the faithlessness, the hatred of authority, which characterised those who had been

Failure of the expedition.

Simon in high favour with the king.

---

[1] *Lettres de Rois*, 58, where Henry uses his royal privilege of taking possession of all prisoners in Simons favour : the letter is dated 3 July ; battle of Saintes fought 22 July.

[2] *Matt. Par.* 590, 596.

[3] Gifts mentioned by Pauli, *Simon de Mont.*, 46. A year later Kenilworth was finally conferred on the earl and countess ; the king became surety to Eleanor for 400*l.* a year, owed to her from her Irish estates ; Simon was made guardian of Leicester Castle, and had certain wardships made over to him.—Greens *Princesses*, 82, 85.

CHAP.
II.

1243
A truce
with
France.

once his fathers foes, and were now in nothing but name the subjects of the King of England. Henry at length concluded a disgraceful truce with France, in which he resigned all claim on Poitou, the original motive of the war. This was in September 1243. He returned to England with even less honour and in greater difficulties than thirteen years before; while Simon de Montfort had in the interval made good his position in the country he had adopted as his own.

CHAPTER III.

PARLIAMENTARY HISTORY, 1232-49.

WE left the king at the point when he had just
dismissed his old and faithful servant, the Earl of
Kent. In spite of the unpopularity of the justiciar, it
was an evil day for the country when he fell. It was
better to be fined by Hubert de Burgh, than to be
robbed by Peter des Roches. The bishop was now
completely master of the situation. He soon introduced numbers of Poitevins, his fellow-countrymen,
and others into England : many were placed in positions of authority, others served him as armed dependents. The expedition of 1230 had produced a
financial crisis. The clergy had already refused the
taxes demanded. In the council of March 1232 the
lay magnates declared they were already half-ruined
by the expenses of personal service in the war, and
were neither able nor in duty bound to give further
aid. The clergy evaded the question with the plea
that they could not vote in the absence of many of
their members. So soon then had men come round
again to the position taken up by the framers of
Magna Carta. Here were both the great principles
therein stated, the necessity for completeness in the
composition of the council, and the right of assent to

Opposition
to Peter
des
Roches.

an extraordinary tax, again clearly put forward ; here
were the clergy and the laity again simultaneously,
though not yet jointly, opposing unlawful claims.
Peter des Roches had already made the king believe
that it was his own fault if he could get no money
from his subjects. Henry now procured from the Pope
a dispensation from the oath to Magna Carta, on the
ground that he had sworn in youthful ignorance to things
injurious to the welfare of his realm and to his royal
prerogative.[1] The temper of the country was growing
dangerous. The barons refused to appear at Oxford,
and backed their refusal with the threat that, if Henry
did not dismiss the bishop, they would look to choosing another king. When at length, after a third summons, they made their appearance, it was in arms.
The Earl of Pembroke, against whom the chief efforts
of Peter des Roches were directed, and several other
great barons, were outlawed, and their properties confiscated and given to the Poitevins. Robert Bacon, a
Dominican, and a clerk in the Curia, when preaching
before the king, told him to his face that he would
have no peace till the bishop and his satellites were
gone. It was no opportune time for a foreigner like
Simon de Montfort to be claiming his rights, and
during all this period he was probably, as we have seen,
absent from England.

Danger of
civil war.

The declaration of Peter des Roches, when the
bishops tried to protect the outlaws, that there were
no peers in England as in France, and that the king
could punish rebels as he pleased, seems to have
brought matters to a crisis. Collisions between the

[1] *Letters of Gregory IX*, 1233 and 1234, quoted by Pauli, *Gesch.
von Eng.* iii. 594.

Earl Marshall and the kings troops followed in the winter; the Welsh, at the earls instigation, entered Wiltshire, and freed Hubert de Burgh from captivity. The Pope himself[1] wrote to ask mercy for the man who had worked with his legates to preserve England from a complete rupture with the holy see. At last, in the Parliament of February 1234, Archbishop Edmund, who had just been appointed by the Pope, took the lead of the opposition. In full council he reminded the king of the evil done by this same Peter des Roches in the days of his father John, and declared that he and his had incurred the ban for their violation of the law of the land. The king yielded to the voice of the Church. Peter des Roches was dismissed. Hubert de Burgh was restored to favour, but not to office; the other outlaws were pardoned. Stephen de Segrave, one of the most odious of the kings instruments, was also degraded from his office of justiciar; and this important post seems to have remained unfilled, or reduced to political insignificance, till the appointment of Hugh Bigod by the barons in the Mad Parliament.[2]

Dismissal of Peter des Roches.

Thus the first important constitutional victory of

---

[1] *Fœd.* i. 211.

[2] See Foss, *Judges* ii. 136, 151, ed. 1848. It has been implied, from a passage in *Matt. Paris*, p. 495, that Simon de Pateshulle held the office of Chief Justiciar in 1233, and his son Hugh in 1234; but this rests on a misinterpretation of the words. The latter was only one of the justiciars at this time, and was appointed, not to the office of Chief Justiciar, but to that of Treasurer. Foss is of opinion that the former office remained vacant from 1234 to 1258. He also believes the office of Chancellor to have been vacant from 1244 to 1261, though several persons are mentioned in the interval as Custodes Sigilli, a new title first used in 1255, whose holders seem to have taken the place of the Chancellor. Stubbs, *Const. Hist.* ii. 275, says, 'There (sc. in the exchequer) the treasurer stepped into the place of the justician, and became from the middle of the reign of Henry III one of the chief officers of the Crown.'

CHAP.
III.

1234-36
Import-
ance of the
dismissal
of aliens.

The kings
marriage.

Pecuniary
difficulties.

the reign was won ; thus was a great maxim of State, England for the English, successfully upheld. The dismissal of foreigners from office formed an important stipulation in Magna Carta ; there was no point perhaps which attracted so much attention all through this period. But it was not yet understood that such relief was only temporary ; that the evils abolished were noisome weeds, whose strength lay far beneath the surface, only to be uprooted by the ploughshare of a radical reform. Two events soon made this fact visible to all. The king, urged by his dynastic ambition, succeeded in 1235 in bringing about the marriage of his sister Isabella to Frederick II ; but, as if to neutralise any good effects which that alliance might have had, he next year united himself to Eleanor of Provence, whose sister had shortly before become Queen of France. For both these affairs much money was wanted. Henry bound himself to pay 30,000 marks as Isabellas marriage-portion. His marriage with Eleanor was celebrated with a magnificence [1] which, for the moment, all that was high and rich and splendid in England united in contributing to produce. But a Nemesis was at hand. The king could not claim the regular feudal aids in either of these cases ; he had therefore to collect the money under other names.[2] His difficulties are shown by the fact that he had to ask the Emperor for a respite, and did not pay the full amount of the dowry till 1237.[3] The demand, repeated in that year on

---

[1] See a detailed account in *Matt. Par.* 420.
[2] The *Annals of Tewkesbury* say that tallage was exacted ; in *Ann. Dunst.* 142 it is said scutage was taken.
[3] *Fad.* i. 228, 232.

account of the expenses of his own marriage, was probably the main reason of the opposition which produced another confirmation of the charters, a remedy
not yet seen to be hopeless with such a king as
Henry III.

Meanwhile the old cause of discontent had appeared again. With the queen had come over her
uncles, William, bishop-elect of Valence,[1] Peter,
Boniface, and Thomas of Savoy. It will be remembered that it was at the kings marriage that Simon
de Montfort, himself a foreigner, made his first public
appearance. Nothing in the history of that great man
is more striking than the complete unlikeness between
him and all those with whom he was at one time
classed, under the hated name of alien. The popular
feeling against foreign interference was not slow in
manifesting itself. At the Great Council which met
at Merton in 1236, shortly after the marriage, it was a
significant fact that the lay magnates, in resisting the
wish of the clergy to introduce the papal decision as
to the legitimacy of children born before marriage,
appealed to the law of England, and protested against
any alteration therein. The laws passed at this
council, which are regarded as the first statutes
passed by king and Parliament together, were little
more than a kind of appendix to the feudal regulations of Magna Carta ; but, as such, their tendency
was to protect the unprotected, to introduce law instead of caprice, to prevent unjust action on the part of
the kings officers. Moreover, the union of interests,
so remarkable in Magna Carta, was strengthened,

---

[1] To be distinguished from William of Valence, the kings step-
brother.

CHAP.
III.

1236-37
Constitu-
tional
advances.
as in 1215, by the extension to subtenants of the same privileges which the greater nobles extorted from the king. The statutes were indeed not altogether satisfactory to the barons ; they had in vain attempted to diminish the centralisation of power in the kings hands.[1] They had more success shortly afterwards, when they insisted on the privilege of meeting only at Westminster. This principle had been hinted at, though not exactly laid down, in that clause of Magna Carta which provided that the council should be summoned to meet at a certain place. It will be seen later to what use it was put by the constitutional party. In this same eventful year (1236) another great advance in constitutional principles was made. The king tried to force Ralph, Bishop of Chichester, to give up the great seal. The bishop boldly refused, saying that it had been given him ' by common counsel of the realm, and without assent of the same he would not resign it.'[2] This was a distinct improvement on the principle enunciated in Magna Carta, when it was only demanded that the great officers should be men acquainted with the law of the land, not that their appointment should depend on the authority of the National Council.

The principle, that national assent was necessary for taxation, received a confirmation next year (1237), when the council, according to the precedent of twelve years before, made the grant of a thirtieth dependent on a renewal of the charters. At the same time it was proposed that the council should have a share in the

---

[1] In the question of jurisdiction in cases of trespass.—*Ann. Burt.* 249.

[2] *Matt. Par.* 430. He had been appointed in 1233 for life.

disposal of the tax. The money was to be put into
the custody of certain of the magnates, to be spent
by their counsel for the good of king and country.
The barons also strengthened their hold upon the
lower classes, by special provisions ensuring a just
assessment by four men elected for the purpose, and
protecting the poorest class from suffering from the
tax.[1] The confirmation of the charters which was the
price of this concession is the first public document
to which we find the signature of Simon de Montfort
attached.[2] But he was not ready yet; had Richard
of Cornwall taken up with a good heart the position
to which the popular voice called him, he might have
rendered the labours of de Montfort to a great extent
unnecessary. But he had much of his brothers fickleness and want of purpose. He was not without insight and sympathy with the people, but allowed
himself to be led away by dynastic ambition and the
enjoyment of wealth from the performance of sterner
duties, and his temporising character led him constantly to appear as arbitrator and mediator when the
possibility of half-measures was long past.

After this second great success the constitutional
struggle seems to have experienced a slight lull.
The king took advantage of it merely to heap up
materials for a fresh disturbance. William of Valence,
the queens uncle, remained supreme; his brothers
and other foreigners were richly endowed with lands
and offices. To such an extent did this reach that
in 1238 even the Pope found himself constrained to

Richard of
Cornwall
as a leader.

Influence
of aliens:

extrava-
gance of
the king.

[1] *Fœd.* i. 232 ; *Matt. Par.* 436 ; Stubbs, *Const. Hist.* ii. 53.
[2] *Ann. Tewk.* 103 ; confirmation dated Jan. 28, 1237. The same
authority states that 'cives et burgenses et alii multi' were present at
the 'colloquium' in which the money was voted.

F

remonstrate with Henry on his ill-judged liberality to prelates and nobles, on the ground that such conduct was damaging to the Church, of which England was a fief.[1] To protect the papal interests the legate Otho had been sent to England the year before. The feeling against him may be guessed from the riot at Osney, the protection of the actors in which was one of the first steps by which Bishop Grosseteste won his universal popularity. The general state of the country was not likely to be happy under such a rule. Robbers were unusually numerous in different parts of England.[2] The grievances of the Church produced a strong remonstrance from the clergy, headed by the Bishop of Lincoln, in 1240.[3] But it was all in vain ; the legate, though appealed to, would not or could not protect them. The clergy, it is said, as a body, refused to pay ; but it is evident that many persons, principally the higher clergy, were forced separately to contribute.[4] On this Church, already losing all confidence in him as a protector, Henry had tried to force William of Valence in the place of Peter des Roches ; but before the struggle ended that prelate died. He was more successful in obtaining the election of Boniface of Savoy to the vacant see of Canterbury, in the place of the sainted Edmund.

During the absence of Richard of Cornwall and other magnates on crusade there was not much chance of parliamentary opposition ; but when, soon after their return, the king resolved on the expedition to France, financial difficulties revived it again. In the famous council of 1242, of which some mention has been already made,[5] followed the first instance of an

---

[1] *Fœd.* i. 234.   [2] *Ann. Tewk.* 115.   [3] See below, ch. vi.
[4] *Ann. Tewk.* 115, compared with *Ann. Dunst.* 154.   [5] See p. 55.

absolute refusal of aid,[1] the confirmation of the charters having usually solved the difficulty. So important was this refusal considered at the time, that a special report of the proceedings[2] was drawn up, in order that the barons' answer might not be forgotten. They enumerated the various occasions on which tax had been paid, and the conditions under which assent had been given. The king had not kept his promises ; his confirmation of the charters was worthless. They asked, pertinently enough, what had become of the money voted five years before, and declared moreover that the king used judicial means to amerce his subjects unjustly. As for the war with France, it would be time enough to discuss that when the King of France had broken truce. In this famous protest the right to know what had become of their money is clearly demanded, and the report incidentally proves not only that discussion on taxation was usual, and that a tax, instead of being merely announced, had come to be demanded, but it shows that the barons had begun to interfere even in the executive. The discussion of peace or war is a great step towards the actual exercise of executive authority. The summons to this Parliament, addressed by the king to the magnates, recognises the right, in stating that the object of their meeting is to discuss 'certain important business touching our State and that of our kingdom.'[3] One would much wish to know what part Simon de Montfort took in this debate. Many barons supported the

CHAP.
III.

1242
Opposition
of the
baronage :

political
principles
advanced.

---

[1] 'Contradixerunt igitur regi in faciem, nolentes amplius sic pecunia sua frustratorie spoliari.'—*Matt. Par.* 580.

[2] *Matt. Par.* 581, 582 ; Stubbs, *Sel. Ch.* 359.

[3] This was not however the first time the summons had taken this form, as Gneist, *Verw.* 302, seems to imply ; see note to p. 12.

CHAP.
III.

1242-44
Effect on
England
of the
struggle
between
Pope and
Emperor.

king in the field, though they had withstood him in the council-hall, and among them, if the song already mentioned can be relied on, was Simon de Montfort.[1]

From May 1242 till September 1243 the king was abroad. No sooner did he return than the constitutional difficulties began again. The year 1243 was an important one for England. It was the year of the accession of Innocent IV, under whom the gigantic struggle between the papacy and the empire came to its climax, and enlisted on one side or the other all the forces of the civilised world. The policy of the Church had a most important effect on the internal affairs of England, and more than any other single cause contributed to the outbreak of 1258. Innocent, immediately after his accession, made strenuous efforts to collect funds for a renewal of the conflict with the empire. The visit of the papal nuncio, Martin, who came armed with unusual powers, and enforced local contributions throughout England early in the year 1244, produced an indignant remonstrance

from the English Church.[2] The clergy, besides declaring the demand in itself unjust, in that the Emperor was not yet condemned by the voice of Christendom, set forth the evils produced by this constant drain on the national Church, whose funds ought to have been devoted to other purposes, and declared that without consent of the king and magnates, their joint patrons, they had no right to contribute at all. The spirit of the protest is intensely national ; the clergy were anxious to join with the laity to protect their

---

[1] See p. 55.
[2] *Ann. Burt.* 265. It is given also by *Matt. Par.* 535, under the year 1240, as coming from the rectors of Berkshire.

common rights. In another protest,[1] apparently drawn up about the same time, they appeal to the origin of the English Church and the objects for which it was endowed, while they point out the danger of an attack from the Emperor, which this subservience to Rome may cause. Nor were the laity backward in the struggle. The disastrous expedition to France, condemned even by the kings partisans,[2] had exhausted the private means of many. The inhabitants of the Cinque Ports had defended the coast at their own expense.[3] Individual contributions, extortions from the Londoners,[4] and the like had just sufficed to keep the Court from penury while the king remained in France. But the evil day could not be avoided ; Henry appeared again as a suppliant before his Parliament.

In the autumn of 1244 the magnates assembled for the usual Council at Westminster.[5] The king opened the proceedings by putting forward his demand for an aid, and received the answer that the question should be discussed. The clergy took counsel by themselves, and, having resolved on united action, proposed to the lay magnates that they should join their forces. The barons replied that they would do nothing without consent of the whole body. Thereupon they elected a committee of twelve, four from

CHAP. III.

1242-44

Pecuniary difficulties produce general opposition.

The council of 1244:

union of clergy and laity.

---

[1] *Matt. Par.* 622.

[2] *T. Wikes,* 90. 'Consumpta inutiliter, ut assolet, innumerabili pecunia.'

[3] *Fœd.* i. 250.

[4] *Matt. Par.* 600. 'Secundum voluntatem et æstimationem extortorum pecuniam civium mutilarunt.'

[5] The chronology is much confused here, but it appears probable that this council was held between the end of August and the middle of November—such at least is the verdict of Prof. Stubbs, *Const. Hist.* ii. 61, note 3. See *Matt. Par.* 639 seq.

CHAP.
III.

1244-45
Parlia-
mentary
opposition:

protest and
demands
of parlia-
ment.

The king
tries to
coerce the
clergy.

each of the three bodies into which the council appears to have been theoretically divided.[1] There were
four earls: those of Cornwall, Leicester, Norfolk,
and Pembroke. From the corresponding class of the
clergy there were four chosen: the Archbishop-elect
of Canterbury, and the Bishops of Winchester,
Lincoln, and Worcester. Of the baronage, lay
and ecclesiastical, appeared two abbots and two lay
barons. It was resolved that what the twelve thought
best should be explained to the whole body, and that
the twelve should enter into no negotiation with the
king but by consent of all. A formal complaint was
then drawn up, stating that the king had not kept the
promises made at the confirmation of charters in 1237,
that the public money was wasted, that for want of a
Chancellor unjust privileges and exemptions were conferred. They demanded therefore that a Justiciar
and a Chancellor[2] should be appointed, who should
uphold the Commonwealth.

The king, after repeated efforts which failed to
bend or weary out the stubborn resistance of the
baronage, prorogued the council till next spring
with certain vague promises, trusting that dis-
sension would cause a split in the enemies' camp.
Hoping to find the clergy more amenable than the
lay barons, he attempted to coerce them separately

[1] The committee is said to have been elected by the clerus, the laici,
the barones, four from each class. The usual division of the clergy
attending a council into bishops (including archbishops) and abbots,
answered to that of the laity into earls and barons; but here the clerus
are the bishops, the laici are the earls, and the barones are the rest of
the clergy and laity.

[2] The Chancellor, Ralph, Bishop of Chichester, was just dead
(Jan. 31, 1244); the last justiciar was dismissed ten years before (see
note 2 p. 61).

by exhibiting letters from the Pope, bidding them contribute to the support of a king, 'of all the kings of the earth, the dearest to the Holy See.' The clergy, unable to resist the pressure put upon them by king and Pope, were at their wits' end, and were beginning to yield, when the noble bearing of Bishop Grosseteste turned the scale. Persuaded by his words, 'Let us not be divided from the common council; for it is written, If we be divided, we shall all die,' they avoided the royal solicitations by a timely flight from London. They were however soon assembled again to hear the demands of the nuncio Martin, who had lately arrived, and, having been somewhat roughly repelled by the king, had made direct application to the clergy. Placed thus, as they themselves expressed it, like corn in the mill, they began to argue that they would have to choose between two evils, and seeing that the kings petition was supported by the Pope, and that it did not do violence to their national prejudices, they resolved to give way to the royal demand. Meanwhile the magnates had sketched out a plan,[1] in accordance with which the king should transact the business of government with the aid of four Councillors or Conservators of Liberties, as they were to be called. These were to be elected by the whole body of the baronage, and two of the number

The clergy inclined to yield.

Proposed plan of government.

---

[1] *Matt. Par.* 640, gives what appears to be a draft sketch of a scheme of government, to be presented to the king, his consent to which, with a confirmation of charters, was to be the condition of a new vote. It is inserted by Matthew Paris without any remark, and may possibly not belong to this year, but the ideas expressed in it make it appear improbable that it should come any earlier, while they are in accord with the demands put forward at this time. Prof. Stubbs points out (*Const. Hist.* ii. 63) that in several respects this scheme resembles the later plans of de Montfort.

CHAP.
III.

1244-45
Parliamen-
tary con-
cessions to
the king,
at least were to be always in attendance on the king ;
the Justiciar and the Chancellor were also to be
chosen by the council, and no writ not signed by the
latter and sealed with the great seal was to be considered legal.   It does not seem however that this
plan was ever presented to the king ; for although
the lay magnates, on hearing of the likelihood of de-
fection on the part of the clergy, besought them to
act only by common counsel of all, as they had agreed
to do, yet, when the council met, the king, by promises and solicitations addressed to individuals, persuaded the members to grant him what he asked.
Even so however it was given under the name of one
of the three feudal aids, that for the marriage of his
eldest daughter.   This is most important, as showing
that the principle of assent was no longer restricted
to the levying of extraordinary aids, but was now
extended even to those which in Magna Carta had
been allowed to belong of right to the king.   At the
same time a list was made and presented to the king
of all the taxes levied during his reign, as a reminder
that such a state of things could not be suffered any
longer.   The nuncio however, who, thinking to avail
himself of the appearance of concession, now renewed
his application to the clergy, received so decided a
rebuff that he is said by the chronicler to have howled
with rage and mortification.[1]

The money voted in this council went the way of all
the rest.   Even the staunchest royalists must have been
in despair.   The king, having undertaken an expedition

---

[1] 'Dicitur magister Martinus oblatrasse comminando.'—*Matt. Par.*
644.   The clergy were aided by the kings prohibition to contribute
from their lay fees.

against the Scotch in 1244, which was only prevented from leading to a war by the resolute bearing of the King of Scotland and his army, and by the mediation of certain nobles, proposed an attack on the Welsh in the autumn of the next year. These attempts were doubtless intended to stir up a warlike enthusiasm, and to open the purses of the refractory nobility. But the barons were not to be duped so easily. To Henrys renewed demands they returned a point-blank refusal, in contempt of a king whose self-indulgence and prodigality had reduced him to such a point that he could hardly appear in public for the crowd of debtors waiting to assail him.[1] It is evident that the feeling of disgust at such a government as this, and the consequent resistance to the king, were increasing rapidly.

But the popular party did not yet understand their true interests. Against a disunited enemy the king could still make head.[2] Ten years more were needed before the union became firm ; the frequent use of committees testifies to that jealousy which prevented the malcontents from joining under one mans headship. At this time Bishop Grosseteste was perhaps most capable of taking the lead ; but, as we have seen, he was not master even of his own class.

The above-mentioned council is especially interesting to us as being that in which Simon de Montfort formally took his place in the ranks of the opposition. He had now been for seven years a member of the royal council. Although nearly half that time had been spent abroad, he had had plenty of opportunities of seeing the way in which the government was

The kings request refused.

Disunion in the popular party.

Attitude of Simon de Montfort.

---

[1] *Matt. Par.* 650.
[2] The magnates are said to have been ' vacillantes et dissidentes.'— *Abbrev. Chron.* 292.

CHAP.
III.

1245
Attitude of
Simon de
Montfort :
carried on.   His early leaning towards the king, which was probably prompted by motives of personal ambition, and the necessity of gaining a safe footing in the country, had received a rude shock five years before, and the incapacity of Henry, evinced in the French expedition and its consequences, seems finally to have opened his eyes.   The king had, as we have seen, made great efforts lately to secure him as a partisan ; and that he did not as yet throw himself heart and soul into the opposite scale is shown by his appearance on this same occasion as a mediator between the king and the bishops.

Still his appearance among the twelve representatives of the community tells its own tale.   It is hard to see what opportunity he can have had of raising himself to that position, unless it were in the great debates of 1242, in the Court at Bordeaux, or in the preliminary discussions in the Parliament of this very year.   It does not however follow that he was at this time more decided in his opposition than Richard of Cornwall, who was also a member of the committee.[1]

Although the attempt at an alliance between clergy and laity broke down in 1244, they seldom presented a more united front against papal exactions than in the next year.   A protest from 'the magnates and the whole people of England' was sent in 1245

---

[1] Dr. Pauli does not seem to give sufficient weight to the appearance of Simon in this parliament, or to the part he took in 1246.   He says, (*Simon ae Mont.*, p. 46,) 'S. blieb stummer Zuschauer der Missregierung ;' and p. 48, 'fünf Jahre lang sah der Graf ohne Partei zu ergreifen diesem Treiben zu.'   It is very improbable that his mind was not made up before the year 1258, as Mr. Green too (*Short History*, p. 149) implies.   I now find however that Prof. Stubbs (*Const. Hist.* ii. 64) expresses a similar opinion : 'Simon . . . . must have led a quiet life on his estates till 1248.'   Comparatively quiet it was, no doubt.

to the Pope, then in council at Lyons. Frederick II had been excommunicated, and the Pope made yet more exorbitant demands on his fief of England ; but the English proctors withstood him to the face, and, knowing well the real object for which the money was wanted, refused to allow the pretext that it was to be applied for the liberation of the Holy Land.[1] The English nobility were directly injured by the transference of patronage from them to the Curia ; Italian ecclesiastics, it had been calculated, drew a larger revenue from England than the king. This last fact, which a commission appointed by Henry himself this year had brought to light,[2] seems to have restored him for a while to his senses.[3] He too was infected with the prevailing enthusiasm, and posed for the next two or three years as the head of the antipapal party in England. He had already last year forbidden the bishops to contribute from their lay fiefs. Now, when the Pope, after deferring his answer to the English proctors for some time, wrote to the bishops bidding them renew the oath of fealty, which involved the yearly tribute to the Holy See, the king in a rage vowed he would protect the liberties of England, even if the bishops would not. So strong was the opposition that Innocent had to resort to conciliatory measures.[4] The nuncio Martin was however driven from the

The king in opposition to the Pope.

The nuncio expelled.

[1] Walter de Cantilupe, Bishop of Worcester, and Roger, Earl of Norfolk, were two of the proctors.—*Ann. Dunst.* 167.

[2] The amount calculated was 60,000 marks yearly.—*Abbrev. Chron.* 294 ; cf. the protest from 'magnates et universitas regni Angliæ.'—*Fœd.* i. 262.

[3] 'Rex aliquantulum conversus ad se cœpit detestari curiæ cupiditatem.'—*Matt. Par.* 659.

[4] Bulls promising to reward English prelates with permission to enjoy plurality of benefices, and confirming to the lay magnates the right of patronage.—*Fœd.* i. 262.

CHAP.
III.

1245

The
nuncio
expelled.

kingdom. He had taken up his abode in the Temple, and thence sent his letters and collectors forth to drain the rich monasteries and chapters of all their wealth. His insatiable greed at length forced the baronage to take the law into their own hands. Fulk Fitz-War in was sent to bid him begone, and that within three days, or he and his would be cut to pieces. The terrified priest sought in vain for help from Henry. To his request for a safe-conduct, 'May the Devil give you a safe-conduct to hell,' was the reply of the pious king. He was however allowed the escort of a single groom, and lost no time in making his escape to Dover.[1] According to one authority, even the regular papal tribute was objected to in the council, on the ground that it had not been voted by the national assembly.[2]

Vacillation
of the king,

and the
bishops;

But, under this seeming firmness, weakness and vacillation were already apparent.[3] Orders having been given to prevent papal legates or letters entering England without permission, a papal bull had been seized at Dover; but the king was frightened by Martin into ordering its delivery. From this and similar proofs the nature of the opposition was soon seen. The bishops, utterly distrustful of the kings protection, and knowing his character as well as did the Pope, thought it hopeless to resist and less ruinous to conciliate. Under this idea they had agreed to the papal demands at the Council of Lyons,[4] in the hope

---

[1] See an amusing account in *Matt. Par.* 659.
[2] *Bart. Cotton*, 125.
[3] ' Anglorum nobilium corda mutantia, necnon et regis inconstantia muliebris.'—*Matt. West.* 208.
[4] These demands were a sum of 6,000 marks, and the first years revenues of vacant benefices in the diocese of Canterbury.—*Matt. Par.* 692, 707.

that the Pope would be satisfied. The Bishop of
Lincoln went so far as to send round the letters
authorising the appropriation of the revenues of
vacant benefices. This was a distinct invasion of the
royal privilege, in accordance with which the revenues
of at any rate the more important benefices when
vacant belonged to the Crown. On the publication of
these letters the king was at first much enraged, but,
thinking discretion the better part of valour, he soon
gave way, and the Pope at once increased his demands.
This abortive ebullition of wrath on the part of the
king was repeated several times this year. The list
of papal exactions is too long to relate. Henry resisted
for some time, but the Pope knew with whom he had
to deal. 'This petty king is recalcitrant,' said he,
'and must be chastised.' With that he instructed the
Bishop of Worcester, in case of further resistance, to
lay the kingdom under an interdict. The king yielded
and England was given over to papal avarice.[1] It
must be acknowledged as some excuse for the king
that the bishops at this time, actuated a good deal by
schemes of their own,[2] neglected the paramount duty
of resisting these unlawful aggressions, and even threw
their weight into the opposite scale ; but it was Henry's
own fault that they had lost all confidence in him.

Encouraged by this victory, the Pope seemed bent
upon trying how much the patience of the English
Church would bear. He put forward the almost incredible demand of one-third from all beneficed clergy,
one-half from all non-residents, and one-twentieth

---

[1] 'Impune hiatibus Romanæ avaritiæ satisfactum.'—*Matt. Par.*
709.
[2] See ch. vi.

CHAP.
III.

1246

Remon-
strance
against
papal
exactions.

from certain exempted persons.[1] The collection of this enormous tax was for the time postponed by the royal prohibition, which the bishops were glad enough to obey. But meanwhile the papal exactions, added to the expenses of a Welsh war, resultless as usual, had produced in the Lent Parliament of 1246 a summing-up of all the grievances which the English Church and nation suffered at the hands of the Pope. The Parliament was summoned expressly to discuss the state of the realm, at this time 'tottering and in urgent need.'[2] The remonstrance was sent by the magnates, the barons of the sea-ports, the clergy, and the whole people. Simon de Montfort signed his name on this famous document next after the Earl of Cornwall. In this letter, the last protest addressed by the representatives of the nation to their oppressor —for the letter sent in the spring of next year did not emanate apparently from the 'universitas'—the barons declared the discontent of the nation to have risen to such a height that, spite of the affection they bore to the Church, they would soon have to take active measures, and would help the Church and people of England to the best of their power. The danger both to Church and king was great, and only to be avoided by timely concession. They proceeded to state the results of the papal policy in England, and remonstrated humbly but firmly with the Pope on the injustice of his claims. The letter was supported by one from

[1] There are slight variations in the statement of this demand, but the amount is well substantiated by *Matt. Par.* 716 ; *Ann. Burt.* 276 ; *T. Wikes*, 94.

[2] *Matt. Par.* 696 ; in *Hist. Angl.* 4 it is said to have been the demand made in 1245 for one years revenue of vacant benefices which first produced the storm.

CHAP.
III.

1246
Failure of
the remon-
strance.

the clergy, confirming the justice of the barons' complaints, and introduced by one of similar tenour from the king. The only answer vouchsafed by the Pope was an increase in his demands as stated above.[1] The objections of the clergy, carefully drawn up, and their appeal to the general council, were equally ineffectual. One more despairing appeal from 'the clergy and people of the province of Canterbury' was sent next year, but the tone is that of a crushed and broken people, humbly praying the tyrant to leave them enough to support life.

The struggle seems for the time to have been given up as hopeless. Still this letter produced some effect, for the Curia, fearing to drive their petitioners into a desperate resistance, yielded so far as to commute their various demands for a lump sum of 11,000 marks, and gave up the claim on the personal property of ecclesiastics dying intestate, which the Pope had made the previous year. This seemed to the heads of the Church so advantageous an offer that they closed with it at once. The policy of the bishops had however produced disunion in the Church, and they became the object of so much suspicion and ill-

[1] The Popes letter (*Fœd.* i. 266) cannot be an answer to the remonstrance of 1246, and must really belong to 1247, not 1246, as given by Rymer, since (*a*) it is dated 12 June, in the fourth year of Innocent IV, he having been elected 24 June, 1243 ; (*b*) it is in answer to the kings request to give up the twentieth, whereas no such request occurs in Henrys letter of 1246 ; (*c*) the twentieth was not demanded, with the other exactions, till 30 April, 1246, while Henrys letter accompanies the barons' letter, dated 28 March. (The twentieth alluded to may be the 6,000 marks promised by the bishops at Lyons in 1245 ; cf. *Ann. Burt.* 280 seq.). Further the bull specially touching the half to be taken from non-residents, given in *Fœd.* i. 264, under 1245, belongs to 1246, being dated 29 Dec., in the fourth year of Innocents pontificate. The Popes letter (*Fœd.* i. 266) must therefore be in answer to a letter from the king, no longer extant, probably accompanying the remonstrance of 1247. But see Mr. Luards note on this letter (*Ann. Burt.* 285).

CHAP.
III.

1246-49
Disunion
in the
Church.

feeling that they absented themselves from Parliament, knowing that 'the hearts of men were sore.'[1]
On the other hand, the exemptions of several orders—
the Templars, Cistercians, and others—the special exemptions given to various branches of the regular
clergy, and the somewhat subservient proselytism of
the Franciscans and Dominicans, who were looked on
by the older foundations as the Popes jackals,[2] must
have produced a sense of unfairness, and sown the
seeds of distrust and discord among the leaders of the
English Church. Truly, as Ranke says, 'England appeared no longer a free country ; all her riches went
to serve the Pope of Rome, and the Crown itself became the tool of the hierarchy.'[3] And with the sore-
ness from these exactions came the bitter feeling that
English contributions produced not gratitude but contempt ; the Curia laughed at those whom they robbed,
the Pope called Henry a partisan of the Emperor, and
seemed to threaten him with a similar fate.

The affection of all classes towards the Church
began to grow cold.[4] The disappointment of all hope
of help from the king, and his want of faith in particular instances,[5] caused a suspicion that his resistance was merely pretended, that he was in reality
doing his best for the Pope. This, like the still vaguer
suspicion of collusion between the Pope and the

---

[1] 'Corda omnium sauciari.'—*Matt. Par.* 719.

[2] 'Seduli papalis pecuniæ collectores ;' 'omnia ad commodum
domini Papæ diligentes negotiatores.'—*Matt. West.* 245. Friars
Minors were sent to collect in 1247, among whom two Englishmen,
Alexander and John, are especially named.—*Matt. Par.* 722.

[3] *Eng. Gesch.* i. 57, quoted by Pauli.

[4] 'Tepuit devotio fidelium et filialis affectus charitatis.'—*Matt. Par.*
719.

[5] A flagrant instance of this is given in *Matt. Par.* 730.

Emperor,[1] which must have been dissipated ere this, shows the universal distrust, and partly accounts for the lack of effort which prevailed, and which would have resulted in complete despair had not the people found some one in whom they could confide. At this time even the news of a combination of French nobles to resist the papal exactions in that country failed to rouse the English baronage to a similar effort. Crime of course abounded. Money had deteriorated so much in value in consequence of mutilation that it was resolved to issue a new coinage ; the die was altered by the prolongation of the cross to the margin, the object being to make it no longer possible to clip the coin. The mint was handed over to Richard of Cornwall as compensation for the debt of 20,000*l.* which his brother owed him. The change of coinage was managed so badly as to produce great distress in the land.[2] In 1249 a terrible system of robbery and collusion therewith was discovered at Winchester. Several of the culprits belonged to the kings household, and pleaded that they had been driven to crime by the non-payment of their wages.[3] But while the king omitted to pay his lacqueys, he enriched his relations and favourites. The plague of aliens had broken out afresh. The king took pity on his half-brothers, who were now orphans, their mother having died in 1246. They came to England next year, and with them a swarm of hungry Poitevins. Noble English youths were married perforce to penniless and, as report said, ill-born and ill-favoured foreign maidens ; William of Valence received a rich heiress ; his brother Aylmer was raised to the bishopric

Bad state of the country.

New influx of aliens.

---

[1] *Matt. West.* 205.   [2] *Matt. Par.* 748.   [3] *Id.* 760.

G

CHAP.
III.

1246-49
Degrada-
tion of
England.

of Winchester, though he died soon after consecration without having enjoyed the see. Even Baldwin, the banished Emperor of Constantinople, came to England as if to the worlds poor-house.[1] No wonder that the English were despised and robbed by other nations; that the whole world acted on the new version given by the Pope of the saying, that of those who have much, much shall be required. The Emperor called the English weak as women, and even the opponents of papal arrogance likened this country to Balaams ass, spurred and beaten till she at length found a voice.[2] And soon the king, not to be behindhand in the race, began to give up all resistance, and joined eagerly with the spoilers in wasting the land committed to his charge. The English are indeed a long-suffering race, but the miseries they endured during this time leave only a feeling of amazement that the revolt of 1258 did not break out ten years sooner.

No ad-
vance in
constitu-
tional
principles.

The parliamentary history of this period is little more than a wearisome repetition of demands for money, and resistance generally made in vain. Since 1244 no new ideas made their appearance. It was the time during which the papal claims usurped every ones attention. Just at the close indeed a new turn was given to affairs by the kings desertion of the national policy he had, however feebly, pretended to take up. His renewed extravagance and favouritism

Parliament
of 1248.

caused the tide of opposition to begin to flow against

[1] *Matt. West.* 226, 227.

[2] ' Angli vilescunt et depauperantur.'—*Matt. West.* 249, under year 1251. ' Puteus inexhaustus est (sc. Anglia), et ubi multa abundant de multis multa possunt extorqueri,' words of the Pope, *Matt. Par.* 705 ; see the picture given by a certain cardinal, an Englishman, of the position of the papacy in 1246, when opposing the Popes intention of putting England under an interdict. —*Id.* 715.

him rather than against Rome. His demands for money at the Lent Parliament of 1248 met with a stubborn refusal. 'How was it,' the barons asked, 'that he did not blush to make such a request, in despite of all his promises?' A long list of complaints was brought forward, accusing him of extravagance and manifold injustice, and showing the fatal consequences of his acts; the old demand for the appointment of the high officers of State by the council was renewed. The king prorogued Parliament, but without effect. Finding the barons still refractory, he at last refused outright to allow the principle for which they strove, and argued that he was only claiming a privilege allowed to every free man in acting without counsellors and as he would.[1] The barons therefore unanimously declared their resolution not to submit to further spoliation, and the council broke up, neither party having gained its object, in mutual anger and disgust. The king seems however to have yielded at least in word, for Parliament met at Easter 1249 to carry out what he had promised as to the election of officers of State; but owing to the absence of Richard of Cornwall, who was still looked up to as the head of the opposition, nothing was done.[2]

It had been discovered by this time that the only means of checking the judicial abuses which prevailed, and the enormous power conferred upon the king by his command of the administration, lay in getting possession of the great offices under which the dif-

CHAP.
III.

1246-49
Demands
of Parlia-
ment;

resisted by
the king.

Appoint-
ment of
ministers
by the
council.

---

[1] *Matt. Par.* 748.
[2] *Id.* 765. The same reason is given in the original text of the *Hist. Angl.* 51; the later text, which states that Henry refused the demand again, seems to be taken from the account of the Parliament of 1248.

CHAP.
III.

1246-49
Appoint-
ment of
ministers
by the
council.

ferent branches of government were organised. The
system established by Henry II was, as has been
often said, a great bureaucracy. To keep such a
machine in order it was necessary that a man of
business like its founder should be at its head. It was
encompassed by many dangers, both to king and
people, though a blessing to the latter under an able
monarch. To the former the chief danger was that
the great offices should become hereditary in certain
great families, or that the baronage should get the
appointment to them into their own hands. A centralised government, though immensely powerful when
the centre is strong, is more open to assault when the
centre is weak. The barons were right in directing
their efforts on the citadel ; the king tried to hide his
weakness by leaving the chief posts unfilled, and ruling
through subordinates.

It seems hardly doubtful that Simon de Montfort
took a leading part in the struggle which I have attempted to sketch. Whenever any names are mentioned as taking the lead, though this, it is true, is
seldom enough, his is amongst them. He was present
at the Parliament of 1248.[1] How much is owing to
him it is impossible to say. But we have seen the
opposition growing stronger and stronger, and the
character of the last debate, the boldness of the accusations brought against the king, the emphatic
refusal of his demands, seem to point to the rapid
approach of a crisis. It is difficult not to connect in
some way the absence of Simon de Montfort on the
Continent with the sudden lull in the internal politics

[1] *Matt. Par.* 743. Pauli, *Simon de Mont.* 50, says he took no part
in the opposition on this occasion, but on what ground does not appear.

of England after his departure. If the opposition
flagged, it was not because the evils under which the
country laboured were less. They were gradually
accumulating, till the thought of them became a fixed
resolve that such a state of things must have an end.
Meanwhile the man who was to give that thought
expression had another work to do; and while the
way in which he performed his task is quite sufficient
to justify the choice, the tendencies he had already
shown, and the obvious dislike and jealousy with
which the king regarded him while he was in Gascony,
make it hard to avoid the suspicion that Henry was
glad to see him out of the country, and perceived in
him already his most determined opponent.

Of Simons private life during the period we know
but little. A young family was growing up around
him in his home at Kenilworth. We hear of his visit-
ing the monastery of Waverley in the spring of 1245,
in company with the countess and two of their sons;
an event recorded with much satisfaction by the
chronicler.[1] In the year 1247 he and his wife took
the cross, but the expedition to Palestine, if such was
contemplated, was postponed indefinitely by his appointment in Gascony. He lived in intimate friendship with the Bishop of Lincoln, in whose house his
children were for some time brought up; with the
Franciscan Adam Marsh, one of the most learned
men of the day, who seems almost to have filled the
post of confessor to him and his wife; and with John
of Basingstoke, Archdeacon of Leicester, a man who
had studied at Athens, and was deeply versed in the

[1] *Ann. Wav.*, quoted by Mrs. Green, *Princesses* ii. 87.

CHAP.
III.

1246-49
Attitude of
Simon de
Montfort.

literature of Greece and Rome.[1]   He studied Grossetestes political pamphlets, and interchanged with him
and other friends letters on the chief topics of the
day.[2]   At the same time he doubtless watched with
careful eyes the feelings of the less influential classes
around him, as he did those of the baronage in the
council hall at Westminster.   Knowing as we do his
character and after-life, it is hard to believe that he
remained idle all this time, or that he emerged from
obscurity into the daylight of public life when he
took upon himself the task of saving Gascony for the
English Crown.

[1] His death in 1252 caused the earl much sorrow.—*Matt Par.*
835.

[2] *Monum. Francisc.* 110 seq. 163, 170, &c.   Grosseteste sent him a
treatise, ' de principatu regni et tyrannidis,' which he returned through
Adam Marsh.   He was much struck by the bishops proposal ' de liber-
andis animabus,' and was prepared to support it ' cum complicibus suis,
si tamen inveniantur.'   This seems to show that Simons ideas were
too far advanced to find much support yet.

CHAPTER IV.

SIMON DE MONTFORT IN GASCONY.

IT was in the year 1248 that Henry resolved to send Simon de Montfort as his viceroy to Gascony. Henrys own experience, gathered in the expedition of 1242, showed how untrustworthy were his allies, how rebellious his subjects. At the head of the restless nobility stood Gaston of Bearn ; on the south the King of Navarre only waited for a chance of attack; on the north the progress of France was always a cause of anxiety.[1] Surrounded by jealous neighbours, and torn by internal faction, the rescue of the province demanded the best man that could be sent—a soldier, statesman, and diplomatist in one. The condition of England and the fickleness of Henry had had a bad effect on the dependency ; the seneschals had been changed nearly twenty times since Henry came to the throne. Many of the merchants were thinking of exporting their wine to Spain instead of England,[2] and the King of Aragon was ready, as we shall see, to bring forward a claim to the province. Henry knew the danger, and gave Simon extraordinary powers. He was called not by the usual title 'seneschal,' but 'locum-tenens'

CHAP.
IV.

1248
State of
Gascony.

Simons
powers.

---

[1] Pauli, *Simon de Mont.* 51.   [2] *Royal Letters* ii. 379.

1248-49
Simons
powers :

of the king.[1]   Henry made him a grant of money,
which however, like most of his promises, seems to
have remained unfulfilled ; and secured to him the
revenues of his earldom for eight years after his death.
Money was borrowed for his first expenses, and large
sums extorted from the Londoners.[2] With such funds.
hastily collected, and with royal authority for six years,[3]
Simon started in the autumn of 1248, and on his way
through France succeeded in prolonging the truce,
but only from September to Christmas 1248.[4]

he sub-
dues the]
the pre-
vinces,

He immediately set to work with such energy that
he brought Gaston of Bearn to submission, and compelled the King of Navarre to agree to the arbitration
of a committee of four, to be chosen by the opposing
parties.[5]   He had taken prisoner one of the most
prominent freebooters, Bertram of Egremont, and re-

and re-
appears in
England.

turned at Christmas, much to the joy of the king and
the whole Court, to bring the news of his success, and
take counsel as to his future proceedings.[6]

He returns
to Gas-
cony :

In February 1249 he returned to the Continent.
On his way through Paris he addressed a letter to
the king, which shows the difficulty of his position in
Gascony, and the uncertainty of support at home.[7]

his difficul-
ties abroad,

He tells the king he has received news of a conspiracy
of the Gascon nobles who had forfeited their estates,

---

[1] He was however afterwards generally called 'Senescallus Vas-
coniæ.'

[2] *Roy. Letters* ii. 380 ; *Matt. West.* 235.

[3] *Rot. Lit. Pat.* 7 Sept. 1248 ; *Matt. Par.* 838.

[4] *Fœd.* i. 269.

[5] *Ibid.*

[6] *Matt. Par.* 757 : 'Cujus (sc. Comitis) adventus Regem . . . non
mediocriter exhilaravit.'

[7] *Roy. Letters* ii. 52.   The letter is not signed or dated, but, as Dr.
Shirley says, it can hardly be from any one but Simon.   If so, it is especially interesting, as it is the only literary production of his which we
possess.

which would be certain to break out about Whitsuntide. His position is dangerous, since he befriends
the lower classes and defends the rights of the Crown,
and therefore is hated by the nobility. He wishes
to speak with the king again, and to get sufficient
forces, for of the royal rents he cannot get a penny.
Another difficulty is the guerilla character of the war;
the rebels move in troops of twenty to forty, burning
and pillaging as they go. But the most important
reason why he must speak with the king is, that his
enemies will accuse him at Court, and say he is the
man who set the province all aflame with civil war.
He then assures the king of the good state of his
castles and garrisons in Gascony, and says that he
will visit him as soon as his business in Paris is done.[1]
His fear of Henrys fickleness was only too well
justified. His position was indeed a hard one; no
money, no troops of the right sort—he probably
wanted some light-armed Welsh or Irish, such as
were found useful on a later occasion—a series of
isolated castles to take, secret foes at home, and the
constant danger of a war with France.

Whether he returned home or not seems uncertain;
at any rate he found time in the course of the summer
to bring the rebels again to subjection. This time he
sent Gaston of Bearn and others to England, and
proceeded to secure his conquests with a string of
forts. His success appears to have delighted the king,
for in June we find him renewing to Simon and his

---

[1] This business was probably a prolongation of the truce. It seems
to have been prolonged from Christmas 1248 to mid-June 1249, when
Peter of Savoy was sent out to prolong it to 1 Nov. of that year. In
1250 Richard of Cornwall went to prolong it for sixteen years.—*Lettres
de Rois* i. 82.

CHAP.
IV.

1249
The king
throws
difficulties
in his way.

son his former gift of the Norman escheats within his fief, and in November he allowed him the Irish revenues and the proceeds of the sale of the royal wine, to fortify and protect the province.[1] But Henrys weakness already threw difficulties in his way. Some of the rebels seem to have escaped from Gascony, and to have come of their own will to England to beg the kings mercy.[2] Of these Henry took hostages, and sent them back to be tried in Gascony, with injunctions that they were to be treated with moderation ; at the same time destroying the whole effect of Simons work by pardoning Gaston of Bearn and· Arnold de Hasta. 'Such a labour of Sisyphus was the service of Henry III.'[3] It may have been on this account that he returned to England, for he was again in the country some time this year. We find the citizens of London appealing to him

Appeal to
him from
the citizens
of London.

and other magnates for protection in their suit with the Abbot of Westminster—a sufficient proof that he had already won a reputation as a friend of the people. The magnates, among whom was the kings brother, immediately attacked the king and the abbot with threats and reproaches, and compelled the former to retrace his steps.[4] This intervention on the part of Leicester is not likely to have put him on better terms with the king. Nevertheless he went on bravely

He com-
pletes the
subjection
of Gas-
cony.

with his work. In the course of the year 1249 he took the castle of Egremont, and forced the Count of Fronzac, in accordance with his injunctions, to submit.[5]

---

[1] *Roy. Letters* ii. 55, 56, 380.
[2] *Fœd.* i. 271.
[3] *Quart. Rev.* cxix. 40.
[4] *Lib. de Ant. Leg.* 13 seq ; *Matt. Par.* 783.
[5] The Count of Fronzac had been accused before the king last year (*Fœd.* i. 271), and the latter had warned Simon of it.—*Roy. Letters* ii. 63.

Finally, on the first Sunday of Advent, he compelled
the citizens of Bordeaux to settle their quarrel,[1] and
with this his victory, in spite of the kings folly,
seemed to be complete. No wonder his praise was
in every ones mouth, and that he was said 'in all his
dealings to have followed nobly in his fathers steps.'[2]

In a task like his constant effort was needed, and Simon in need of
for constant effort constant supplies. But these it money;
was impossible to obtain; a well-regulated finance
was one of the most conspicuous wants in the England
of the day. The scanty aid from home was soon
exhausted; Simons private means followed. At returns to England,
Epiphany 1251 he was again in England. He seems
to have returned some time in the winter of 1250–
1251, arriving worn and travel-stained at his home,
with only three attendants. In February 1251 he
was with the queen at Windsor, endeavouring, it
would seem, to persuade his sister-in-law to use her
influence in his behalf.[3] But others had been there
before him, and though the king could not resist his and ap-
appeal when made face to face, the answer shows peals to the king,
what had been going on behind the earls back. He
had been accused of severity and injustice, and even
treachery, and it is evident the king more than half
believed the reports. Still, so bravely had he fought,
and so emphatically did he deny the charge, and remind the king of his own experiences in Gascony,
that Henry could not resist. 'By the head of God, who gives way.
Sir Earl,' said he, 'thou hast said the truth, and I
will not refuse thee aid, since thou hast fought so well.

---

[1] This peace, given in *Fœd.* i. 275, was confirmed by the king on
3 June, 1253.—*Lettres de Rois* i. 83.
[2] 'Per omnia patrissare diceretur.'—*Matt. Par.* 767.
[3] *Matt. Par.* 810 ; cf. *Mon. Franc.* 152.

CHAP.
IV.

1251

Simon
returns
with sup-
plies to
Gascony.

But grievous complaints have come up to me, how that those who came to thee, aye, even those whom thou summonedst as if in good faith, thou hast thrown into prison and allowed to perish in their bonds.' With this surly acquiescence the earl had to content himself.[1] The requisite men and money were raked together from all quarters, from the Leicester estates, from Flanders, and elsewhere. With them Simon returned to Gascony, accompanied by his wife, in the autumn of 1251, and put down the rebels for the third time. His expenses, doubtless, were great; Adam Marsh had to write to the countess, warning her not to increase them by luxury and display in dress, and to beware of giving way to licence of tongue, lest she should thereby increase her husbands difficulties; on the other hand, she was to help him in every way, to keep him to his engagements, to restrain him from lavish expenditure.[2]

His
enemies at
court.

It was a hydra-headed opposition that he had to meet. He might drive his foes before him in Gascony; it was only that they might reappear in more dangerous form in England. Fortunately he had friends at home, who kept him informed of the state of affairs. He had been encouraged during his last stay in England by news from Adam Marsh of a favourable change in the attitude of the king.[3] During his absence in Gascony, Adam wrote to him words of

---

[1] About the same time the royal favour was manifested in various ways, the acknowledgment of a debt, permission to build a castle, and so forth.—*Roy. Letters* ii. 382, 383.

[2] The letters of Adam Marsh (*Mon. Franc.* 294, 297, 299) are probably, with Pauli and Mrs. Green, to be referred to this year, though Mr. Brewer would refer the second to 1252, when the countess was however not with her husband.

[3] *Mon. Franc.* 281.

comfort in his difficulties, referred him to the example
of patience in the Book of Job, and added more
earthly consolation in the shape of reports of conversation held with the king, who showed himself at
heart well inclined, if it were not for the influence of
those about him.   But this news was soon followed
by worse; the king, wrote Adam, had been much
annoyed by certain utterances of Simon which had
come to his ears ; the earl is therefore warned to set
a watch upon his tongue, for 'the heart of fools is in
their mouth, but the mouth of a wise man is in his
heart.'   The good friar had however himself incurred
the displeasure of the king by boldness of speech, and
could no longer further the earls business at court.[1]
The more precious must have been the assistance of
his steadfast friend, Bishop Grosseteste, in whose care
he had left his two eldest sons on his departure for
Gascony.   It was evident however that his presence
was wanted at home, and shortly before Christmas
1251 he returned with his wife to England.

The feeling of the king towards him was by no
means favourable, and though Henry came to meet
him it was not to see him, but his half-brother Guy
of Lusignan, who came over with the earl.   Simon
had left behind him men whom he could trust in
possession of his castles ; but this did not prevent the
Gascons from rising again as soon as his back was
turned.   They pretended not to rise against the king,
but against the tyranny of his lieutenant.   He was,
they said, the real traitor, for he extorted from nobles
and worthy citizens money to enrich himself, and hid
the truth from the king ; they repeated the old accusa-

[1] *Mon. Franc.* 275.

CHAP.
IV.

1251
Letters of
Adam
Marsh.

Simon
returns to
England.

He is out of
favour with
the king.

Causes of
complaint
against
him.

CHAP.
IV.

1251
Henry
believes
the accu-
sations
made
against
Simon :
tions of false imprisonment, and the like. Henry, as
ever, at once distrustful and credulous, could not
altogether disbelieve the reports of Simons doings,
and doubtless his action had been violent and his
wrath severe enough to give some colour of truth
to these stories. Henry failed to see that the earl
ought to be supported to the utmost, that if he could
not grant him pecuniary aid, he could and should at
least give him his moral support. But jealousy and
ungenerous dread of greatness would not let him be
convinced. When the earl demanded why he trusted
traitors rather than him, his tried and faithful servant,
Henry only answered that, if he knew himself to be
honest, he ought to be thankful enough for an investigation. It is very probable, from what we know of

Simons temper, that he quenched rebellion sharply
and sternly ; he was not the man to bear gently with
the open and secret resistance he had to meet ; but
the castled brigands of Gascony could not be put
down by gentle means, and we should have heard
little of these complaints had not the kings suspicious
ear drunk in only too greedily all that the enemies of
his great lieutenant chose to pour into it. The voices
of the lower orders, and the merchants whom he pro-

tected by destroying the robbers' nests,[1] could not be
heard ; the way in which the peace was made between
him and certain of the citizens of Bordeaux [2] testified
in vain to the growth of those constitutional principles,
and that sympathy with the people, which characterised

---

[1] See the report of the citizens of Castel d'Uza, *Roy. Letters* ii. 57,
and the description of Egremont in *Matt. Par.* 810.

[2] *Fœd.* i. 275. ' Hæc fuerunt ordinata . . . in præsentia Baronum
. . . et totius communiæ Burdegaliæ, qui ad hæc audienda et appro-
banda fuerunt specialiter congregati.'

his later life. But the clamour of his enemies travelled
across the sea, and found easy entrance at the English
Court. Simon de Montfort and the rebels of Gascony
were regarded as having equal claims to respect.

Accordingly, in spite of the possibility of a war *Appoint-*
with Navarre,[1] and the certainty that such proceedings *ment of a commis-*
would put new life into the efforts of the malcontents *sion of enquiry :*
in Gascony, a committee of eleven English nobles was
appointed on January 4, 1252, to examine into the
justice of de Montforts demands for aid ;[2] while at
the same time two commissioners were sent out to
make enquiries into the matter in the province itself,
and in fact to supersede Simon in the settlement of
breaches of the truce with France. Orders were given
to the citizens of Bordeaux to send six delegates to
England to plead their cause . before the king.[3] The
commissioners sent to Gascony were Rocelin de Fos,
Master of the Templars in England, apparently of
Gascon extraction, and Henry of Wingham, a former
governor of Gascony.[4] The result of their investigations
was what might have been expected ; the Gascon gave *their ver-*
his verdict for his countrymen ; the Englishman, who *dict.*
knew what it was to be seneschal in Gascony, was
equally positive on the other side. The presence of
the kings half-brother, William of Valence, who, as
we shall see later, was no friend of Simon, did not
contribute to a satisfactory settlement. The com-

---

[1] *Roy. Letters* ii. 283.

[2] *Id.* ii. 68 ; cf. ii. 386. The constitution o this committee was afterwards modified (16 March) ; it seems at first to have been pretty equally divided between Simons probable partisans and enemies ; but in that part of it which eventually discussed the question, the Bishop of Worcester was the only one on whom Simon could have reckoned.

[3] *Id.* ii. 69, 70. *Matt. Par.* 832, states the commission to have been a secret one.

[4] Pauli, *Simon de Mont.* 60.

CHAP.
IV.

1252
Complaints
against
Simon.

missioners seem however to have been of one mind in refusing to accept the excuses of Gaston and his friends, who used a political quarrel among the citizens of La Reole as a pretext for occupying the citadel.[1] Meanwhile the citizens of La Reole, or some part of them, addressed a letter of complaint to the king, in which they inveighed against the treatment of their hostages by Leicester, and the taxes levied by him. It was these taxes that seem to have caused the disturbance, for the party that was inclined to the English entered the castle, where they were supported by Leicester, and attacked by Gaston and his associates. A truce was brought about by the Archbishop of Bordeaux, and according to him was broken by both sides simultaneously. Simons lieutenant, William Pigorel, acted energetically in the affair, and therefore had to bear the chief brunt of the attack.[2] Whether Simon was in Gascony at this time or not seems uncertain; he appears to have returned thither about the middle of March 1252. He was at Court shortly before, and had entered into

a solemn engagement with the king to lay all his pecuniary transactions before commissioners, the king promising at the same time to pay him whatever should appear from their decision to be due. At the same time he was to give up three castles into the kings hands before Whitsuntide, a step nearly equivalent to putting them into the power of his enemies. Although power was given him to raise two thousand marks for official purposes, to be accounted for before the commission, he does not seem to have taken any measures during this visit to Gascony

---

[1] *Roy. Letters* ii. 78.   [2] *Id.* ii. 77.

which were calculated to cause a fresh outbreak. The
object of his journey was probably to collect witnesses
on his own side for the approaching trial. These, it
must be confessed, he seems afterwards to have richly
rewarded.[1] He must have left England before March
23, for on that day the king wrote to him bidding him
not to go, but the letter arrived too late. He returned
to England shortly after his accusers, probably early
in May.[2]

The commissioners on arriving in Gascony had
commanded a suspension of hostilities, and shown
letters from the king inviting the malcontents to send
delegates to England. This they were at first unwilling to do, but agreed on the condition that peace
should be maintained during their absence. An
agreement which Simon had forced upon his enemies,
that they would not appeal against him, was cancelled.
This was of course a necessity, and it is hard to see
what can have induced Simon to insist on so untenable
a stipulation, and one which would be so likely to
prejudice mens minds against him. Be that as it
may, the cancelling of the agreement went still further
to undermine his authority, and prejudged the case
before it came before the court. The Gascon delegates
arrived in England towards the end of April ; but the
king, though every minute of delay was so much loss
to his power abroad, sent out another commission,[3] consisting like the first of a Gascon and an Englishman,
the latter, like Henry of Wingham, a former seneschal.

[1] So at least says *Bart. Cotton* 129.
[2] *Roy. Letters* ii. 81, 384, compared with *Matt. Par.* 836, and *Mon Franc.* 123.
[3] Nicolas de Molis, seneschal in 1244, and Drogo de Barentin. The three castles were to be handed over to the former. Pauli, *Simon de Mont.* 61.

H

CHAP.
IV.

1252
Royal
Commis-
sion in
Gascony.
They were but a short time absent, and on their return declared their opinion that, although Simon had in some cases dealt severely, it was no more than the delinquents deserved. Whereupon the Gascons vehemently demanded a trial, and a day was fixed. Meanwhile the earl had returned in great haste to England, and fortunately his partisans, with Richard of Cornwall, the Earl of Gloucester, and other chief men of the kingdom at their head, mustered in force to prevent the unjust action which it was feared the

king would take. The trial, if such it could be called, began early in May, and for a whole month the delegates, a numerous body, poured forth a flood of accusation against the earl. The king showed his incapacity as a judge by frequent interruption and contumely directed against the accused, all of which Simon bore with great moderation and self-command. Among his friends there are said to have been only three who were of real use to him, the Bishop of Worcester, Peter of Savoy, the queens uncle, and Peter de Montfort, Simons cousin. The rest were lavish in their praise, and in promises of assistance ; but these were little more than words.[1] The Bishop of Lincoln, who would doubtless have been his staunchest partisan, was not present. The Gascons brought forward their old accusations, and tried to support their case by a reference to the supposed prosperity of the country under former governments.[2] It was with

[1] 'In tam frequenti vocali benevolentia experiebatur perraram realem amicitiam.'—Letter of Adam Marsh in *Mon. Franc.* 124, from which this account is chiefly taken.

[2] *Matt. Par.* 838. The same writer states as a reason for the part that Richard of Cornwall took, that the king, having formerly conferred Gascony on him, afterwards resolved to give it to Prince Edward, and in 1242 insisted on Richards giving it up. The latter refusing, Henry

great difficulty that Simon and his adherents obtained
an audience, but, on this being granted, he related in
order all the events of his lieutenancy, proving his
assertions by trustworthy witnesses. After him, his
partisans from Gascony, armed with letters from the
commons of Bordeaux, showed to the satisfaction of
all present how well Simon had discharged his duty,
proving that the only reason of the opposition he
encountered was the energy with which he put down
sacrilege, murder, and crime of all sorts. ' It is very
possible,' said Simon, turning to his accusers, ' that I
have taken away from you privileges granted by Earl
Richard and my predecessors, but it is because you
got them by dissimulation and forfeited them by
treachery. Who is to believe you, whom the king
himself has found to be no friends, but foes and
impostors ? '

The earl and his party were ready to submit to
trial by combat, or any other mode of decision, in
England or Gascony, whichever their opponents
should choose ; but the latter would agree to nothing.
At length even the king was obliged to own that the
plaintiffs could not prove their case, and the whole
court chimed in with its approval. Leicester then
bade the king make good his word ; he had ruined
his estate, he said, in the kings service : the king
should at least pay his debts. The king gave vent

tried, though in vain, to get the Gascons to seize him. Richard fled to
England, and Henry then persuaded the Gascons by large sums of
money to exchange their allegiance. Richard and he had never been
on good terms since. In presenting Edward to the Gascons in 1252,
Henry said his brother did not care ever to see Gascony again ; the
sea-voyage was unpleasant to him, and the province cost more than it
brought in. This may have been true, though Henry got more than 1,000
marks a year from Bordeaux alone, but if so it was his own fault.

CHAP.
IV.

1252
Quarrel
between
Simon and
the king.

to his vexation at the failure of the trial in the hasty answer, that with a traitor and supplanter like him he thought it no shame not to keep his word. Thereupon Simon could keep his temper no longer; he sprang to his feet and gave the king the lie. 'And but that thou bearest the name of king;' he added, 'it had been a bad hour for thee when thou utteredst such a word. Who would believe thou art a Christian? Hast thou ever confessed?' 'I have,' said the king. 'What is confession worth without repentance?' asked de Montfort. 'Never did I repent of aught so much,' retorted Henry, 'as of suffering thee to enter England, and win honour and land therein, that thou mightest grow fat and kick.' The scene was cut short by the intervention of the bystanders; it remains as a valuable illustration of the two men, the weakness and vehemence, the injustice and imprudence, which characterised the king; the equally violent passions, the impatience of contradiction and control, which were the most conspicuous blots on the character of de Montfort. His moral superiority over Henry is evident throughout.[1] The

attitude of the rest of the baronage towards Leicester is very remarkable. Sixteen years before they had joined to thrust him from the country as an alien and an upstart, and it was all Henry could do to protect him from their wrath. The same body now assembled to defend him from the injustice of his sovereign, and when Henry again brought the subject before them, in the autumn of

---

[1] Compare the accounts in *Matt. Par.* 836–839, and *Mon. Franc.* 122–128. In this and other portions of the trial one may remark the sarcastic tendency of Simons oratory; the allusion to confession was a home-thrust at Henrys excessive but superficial devoutness.

1252, they turned upon him with reproaches, tauntingly alluding to his failures, and declared it was right well done if the earl had striven to destroy the whole pack of Gascon thieves.[1]

The trial was over, and Simon gave the king the alternative, of letting him return to Gascony with full powers, whether the matters in dispute were decided or not, or of allowing him to resign, on condition that he and his should be secured from loss or damage of any kind.   But the king, as usual, preferred half-measures ; he sought to prevent disturbance by a series of edicts, to hold good till he should appear in person ; guardians of the truce were appointed, being the two Gascons who had acted as commissioners in Bordeaux ; jurors were to be chosen equally from the two parties.   Meanwhile Bertram of Egremont had been set at liberty ; authority was given to the Bishop of Bordeaux to examine into certain questions in dispute ; the power of the kings lieutenant could hardly have been less had he been formally deposed.[2]   The province was given over again to its former state of anarchy.   Simon was then dismissed with the words 'Go back to Gascony, thou who lovest to stir up war ; there thou mayst find plenty, and get the same well-merited reward which thy father got before thee.'   This too before the Gascons, who, we are told, were highly delighted by the kings wit, and the taunting reference to the elder Simon and his fate.   But the earl only answered, 'Willingly do I go, and I will not return till I have subdued thy rebellious subjects, and placed thy enemies

[1] *Matt. Par.* 853.
[2] *Roy. Letters* ii, 86-90, 390 ; *Fœd.* i. 282.

CHAP.
IV.

1252
Simon
leaves
England,

beneath thy feet.' With that he retired, and crossing at once with his eldest son Henry to France, soon drew together in the country of his birth, by the help of his family and friends, a sufficient force, with which, burning for revenge, he marched upon Gascony.[1] He stayed some time at Boulogne on his way, and seems to have wished to see and consult Adam Marsh on affairs of importance. The Countess of Leicester went to Oxford, but failed to persuade the Franciscan to undertake the journey. A little later Adam wrote to the earl, announcing the approaching confinement of his wife, and rebuking him for carrying off the parish priest at Odiham to be his chaplain.[2]

The delegates returned to Gascony in high displeasure at the attitude of the English nobility, having first done homage to Prince Edward, on whom the king now formally conferred the province. But on their arrival they found the earl awaiting them.

The ridiculous precautions taken by the king in the hope of keeping peace were seen in a moment to be worthless ; both sides at once proceeded to hostilities. The Gascons had at first a slight success, and, routing an ambuscade set for them, carried off a certain knight, a dear friend of the earl. Thereupon Simon roused himself as if out of sleep. Asking him who brought the news whether the enemy were far off, he at once set spurs to his horse, and, without waiting for his followers, attacked the enemy with all the headlong vehemence which distinguished him in battle. He speedily

---

[1] *Matt. Par.* 844.
[2] *Mon. Franc.* 262, 336. These letters are probably to be referred to this date.

released the prisoner, but was unhorsed and surrounded. The Gascons turned all their force against him, and he was in the greatest danger, when the knight whom he had rescued clove his way through the press, and, mounting the earl upon his horse, brought him out unharmed. The battle lasted half the day, but ended in the complete rout of the enemy. Five of the chief nobles were taken, and the Gascons did not dare again to meet de Montfort in the field.[1] Soon after this the news of Henrys last attempt against him, alluded to above, was brought to the earl, who only remarked, ' I knew the king would make the attempt, in order to enrich some Poitevin or Provençal with my earldom.'[2] Meanwhile however strenuous efforts were being made at home by the countess in his behalf, and in her attempts to mitigate the kings anger she was supported by the queen, with whom she was on excellent terms.[3] Eleanors influence over her brother, that of a strong character over a weak one, had always been considerable, and doubtless contributed largely to the change we find taking place shortly after these events in the kings attitude towards the earl.

Towards the end of the year 1252 Simon retired into France. It is a striking testimony to his widespread fame, and the general respect for his character,

---

[1] *Matt. Par.* 845, ' nec sunt ausi amplius inimici ejus contra ipsum obgrunnire.'

[2] *Id.* 853 ; see above, pp. 100, 101.

[3] Mrs. Greens suggestion (*Princesses* ii. 106), that the letters of Adam Marsh (*Mon. Franc.* 393, 394) relative to the above are to be referred to this period, is most probable ; but that authoress seems to have no ground for saying that Simon returned to England this winter, though Adam expects he will next spring, and warns him to beware of danger ; the dismissal of which she gives an account on p. 107, appears also to be misplaced.

CHAP.
IV.

1252-53
Offer of
the High
Steward-
ship of
France to
Simon.
that the French nobility, after the death of the Queen Regent and during the absence of Louis IX on crusade, offered him a place among the guardians of the Crown, and the office of High Steward of France with all the honours appertaining to it.[1] It is a still more striking proof of the justice of that estimate that he twice declined this splendid offer, ' being unwilling to prove a renegade' from the service of him who had called him a traitor a few months before.[2]

Hardly had Simon turned his back on Gascony than the miserable country was again in uproar. Civil war broke out ; every mans hand was against his neighbour; Gaston of Bearn transferred his allegiance to the King of Aragon.[3] Some authorities
declare that the king deposed Simon in the autumn of 1252, and ordered the edict to be proclaimed in Gascony.[4] If this is true, it is probably the reason why he left the country. His last expedition seems to have been undertaken merely with the object of taking private vengeance on his foes, and not in his quality of seneschal. Even if he had not been formally dismissed, the events of the past year must have shown him that it would be impossible for him any longer to hold the province. At any rate he practically resigned his post in the winter of 1252-1253. He was afterwards compensated in a pecuniary

---

[1] *Matt. Par.* 863, 879. His brother Amauri, now dead some years, had been High Constable of France.

[2] ' Constanter comes, ne transfuga videretur, renuebat.'—*Matt. Par.* 865.

[3] ' Se transtulit ad regem Hispaniæ.'—*Matt. Par.* 864.

[4] *Matt. West.* 250 ; *Matt. Par.* 867 says it was in 1253 ; *Ann. Dunst.* 184, say the king deposed him, but he refused to obey ; *T. Wikes* 104 says the earl, enraged at his dismissal, gave up three castles to the enemy, these being probably the three he gave up to Henry (above p. 96).

point of view, at least to some extent, for the remaining two years of his term of office. He remained inactive in France some time, and looked on at the failure of all attempts to allay the disorder. The king arrived at Bordeaux early in September 1253, having placed the Regency in the hands of the queen and the Earl of Cornwall. As late as April he had, or pretended to have, the intention of going to the Holy Land ; when he was on the point of starting for Gascony the Pope excommunicated all who should disturb the kingdom during his absence in Palestine.[1] The crusades were a pretext which Henry and the Pope knew well how to use.

On his arrival in Gascony Henry succeeded in recovering his own castles, though at great loss ; his army suffered terribly from privations. At the same time he busied himself in furthering the marriage of his son Edward to the sister of the King of Castile, and of his daughter Beatrice to the eldest son of the King of Aragon. He hoped doubtless to anticipate any attempts on Gascony from that side. His efforts towards subjugating the country were confined to the destruction of vineyards.[2] He released his prisoners, who at once rejoined their companions. Soon after his arrival he had summoned Simon de Montfort to his aid, but apparently in vain. Matters were now looking so hopeless that he had to repeat his request in a humbler tone, begging the earl to come and treat with him, promising him a safe conduct and leave to return if he wished to do so. At the same time he

CHAP.
IV.

1253

The king
arrives in
Gascony :

his success
only
partial :

he applies
to Simon
for aid.

---

[1] *Fœd.* i. 289, 292.
[2] Which the Gascons 'pugnam anilem reputabant.'—*Matt. Par.*
877.

CHAP.
IV.

1253-54
Simon
comes to
the kings
aid.

made efforts to conciliate him by grants of money.
Simons influence in France was invaluable to the
king, and he was begged to bring with him all the
light troops he could find.[1] At length he gave way.
If he had seen with secret joy the kings distress, he
had now the serene satisfaction of returning good for
evil. The last words of the old Bishop of Lincoln
are said to have prompted him to this exercise of
charity ; he obeyed 'that dear friend who had been to
him as a father confessor,' and went with a large force
to the kings assistance.[2] The Gascons, 'who feared
him like a thunderbolt,'[3] gave way at once ; the Pope
opportunely excommunicated Gaston of Bearn and
his associates, and the province was again reduced

to order. Financial difficulties were settled between
the brothers-in-law, at least in some degree, and the
breach was for the time healed over. How long
Simon remained with the king we do not know. He
may have spent Christmas with the Court, and have
returned with Earl Richard and other magnates
immediately afterwards for the Parliament which met
in January 1254 to discuss the kings demands for
aid. He was in England at any rate by Easter of
that year. Whether it was want of money, or the
arrangements for Prince Edwards marriage, which
kept Henry at Bordeaux, is not clear ; at any rate

he remained there in wasteful idleness till the autumn
of 1254, and then returned by way of Paris, where

---

[1] *Lettres de Rois* i. 87, 90, 95, 96.

[2] 'Cui (sc. episcopo) comes tanquam patri confessori extitit familiar-
issimus.'—*Matt. Par.* 879.

[3] 'Tanquam fulgur formidabant.'—*Matt. Par.* 879.

the two Courts vied with each other in splendour and
extravagance, to England.   He landed at Dover
shortly after Christmas in that year.[1]

---

[1] His debts incurred during this expedition are said by *Matt. Par.*
913, to have amounted to more than 300,000 marks.   This is over and
above what he actually paid.

CHAPTER V.

PARLIAMENTARY HISTORY, 1249-1257.

CHAP.
V.

1249-52
Pecuniary
difficulties
continue.

The Pope
grants the
king a
tenth for
three years.

THE state of things in England had not improved during Simons absence in Gascony. The wearisome tale of oppression and futile resistance, of broken promises and disunion, need not be told in full. The king tried all sorts of means to get money, mulcted the Londoners and the Jews, and made spasmodic efforts to be thrifty, but all in vain. He did not give de Montfort much aid, but the contributions, which apparently nothing but Simons presence could obtain, small as they were, increased his difficulties. In 1252 there came a change. The king, who, as we have seen, had already given up the part of national leader which sat so badly on him, was now in close communication with the Pope, and had procured a bull granting him a tithe of the spiritual revenues of the Church for the space of three years, on the pretext of an aid for his expenses in the contemplated crusade.[1] An assembly of the prelates accordingly met in London in October 1252. The clergy appear to

---

[1] According to *Matt. Par.* 834, he had got the bull as early as April 1252, and had ordered the crusade to be proclaimed in London with great solemnity, vowing to start on it before 24 June ; but his intention was mistrusted from the first. The original bull appears not to be extant ; that given in *Fœd.* i. 280, under the year 1252, belongs to 1253, and alludes to an opposition to the grant of the tenth.

have been summoned separately at first, in order that they might be prevailed upon the more easily when deprived of the assistance of the laity. Both archbishops were absent. The papal bull, granting the three years' tithe, was then read aloud to them, and the kings proctors, assuming the grant as a matter of certainty, went on to ask that the money for one year, or at least half of it, should be paid before the king started. Upon which the Bishop of Lincoln exclaimed, in great anger, 'What is this, by our Lady! ye take things too much for granted. Think ye we shall consent to this accursed contribution? Far be it that we should so bow the knee to Baal.'[1] And when the Bishop-elect of Winchester, the kings half-brother, hinted that France had submitted, and England would have to do the same, Grosseteste retorted that for that very reason England should not yield, and so strengthen the exaction by a precedent. The great majority of the bishops supported him. The king then altered his tactics, and requested submissively that an aid might be granted him. But the bishops remained firm, and pleaded the absence of the primates of York and Canterbury as an excuse for avoiding a decision.[2] Henry then tried, as usual, to influence them singly, and began with the Bishop of Ely. The bishop still refusing to yield, he turned

CHAP. V.

1252

Opposition of the clergy,

headed by Grosseteste.

---

[1] *Matt. Par.* 849. 'O quid est hoc, pro nostra Domina? Absit hæc a nobis ad Baal genium incurvatio.' The account illustrates well the superiority of Grosseteste, and the vacillation of the majority of the Episcopate.

[2] The Archbishop of Canterbury returned 18 Nov. 1252 (*Hist. Angl.* 127). The clergy of the northern province had, it appears, already consulted on the matter, and had made answer to the king that, seeing that the interests of the whole English Church were at stake, they could not decide without their brethren of the province of Canterbury. — Stubbs, *Const. Hist.* ii. 67, quoting *Roy. Letters*, ii. 95.

CHAP.
V.

1252-53
The king
demands
money
from Par-
liament,

savagely upon him, and bade his servants 'turn out that boor.' Meanwhile the lay baronage had begun to assemble, though in small numbers. The season was very rainy, the roads were almost impassable, and when the travellers arrived, wet, dirty, and out of temper, they found London a sea of mud, provisions at famine prices, and the city so full of people that it was almost impossible to get a lodging.[1] And for what were they summoned? Only to hear once more the never-ending demand for money. The king however does not seem to have dared to lay before the laity the demand for the tenth, which indeed did not immediately concern them, but asked their advice in the matter of Gascony, laying the blame of the troubles there on the Earl of Leicester, whose violence, he said, had so disturbed the province.[2] At the end of his address, as if merely by the way, he requested money to help him on the crusade.

The magnates answered that their reply must depend on that of the clergy, and laughed in secret at the 'silly king who, without skill or experience in war, was going to make an attempt in which the King of France and all his chivalry had failed.'[3] The council broke up in the midst of universal indignation.[4]

However, in the spring of 1253, when de Montfort had left Gascony and was staying in France, affairs in the province had come to such a pitch as to necessitate active interference, and the Easter Parlia-

---

[1] *Matt. Par.* 852.

[2] Whether it was at this Parliament or at a smaller meeting held later in the year that Henry met with the rebuff alluded to above (p. 100), in his attempt to raise the baronage against Leicester, I am unable to say.

[3] 'Regulum istum,' &c.—*Matt. Par.* 852.

[4] 'Cum omnium indignatione.'—*Hist. Angl.* 126.

ment yielded to the kings request. After a discussion, which lasted more than a fortnight, the barons
granted him a scutage, and the clergy acquiesced in
the collection of the tithe. As the price however of
the concession they demanded that the king should
observe all privileges and liberties previously granted,
both lay and clerical, and, on his promising this, a
solemn excommunication of all those who should in-
fringe the charters was pronounced with book and
candle by the assembled prelates, the king and the
whole council taking part.[1] But the effect of this imposing ceremony was spoilt by a deed, which perhaps
caused more universal indignation than any other, and
made the name of the chief actor in it 'to stink in the
nostrils' of all Englishmen.[2] Peter d'Aigueblanche,
Bishop of Hereford, a native of Savoy, proposed to
the king a plan for getting money, to which the latter
consented, but which nowadays would send its perpetrators to the common gaol. The royal seal was
affixed to a schedule which was fastened so that the
inside could not be seen : the schedule was blank.
The swindlers then, under some pretext or other, obtained the signatures of several bishops and abbots to
the schedule, which was taken to Rome and filled up
with an obligation to pay certain merchants of Sienna
sums of money owed them by the king. The Pope
was duped into believing that the prelates in question
had signed with their eyes open, and threatened them
with excommunication if they did not act up to their
engagements. This story is given by so many authori-

---

[1] *Fæd.* i. 289 ; cf. *Matt. Par.* 865. The writ of excommunication,
with the bishops' signatures, is dated 13 May 1253.

[2] 'Cujus memoria fœtorem sulphureum exhalat.' — *Ann. St.
Albans.*

ties that in its main features it cannot be doubted:[1]
it fully accounts for the vengeance taken upon the
Bishop of Hereford ten years later than this.

Meanwhile the parliamentary struggle continued,
rising and falling with monotonous variation. The
magnates who assembled in January 1254, in the
kings absence, refused his demand for an aid, suspecting
that his pretext, the state of Gascony, was nothing
but a false alarm : they promised however to go in
person to help him should it appear to be necessary.
It is remarkable as a step in the theory of assent to
taxation that the bishops and abbots, while promising an aid on their own account, refused to bind
the rest of the clergy by the same obligation.[2] The
partial good-will shown by the magnates on this occasion was soon cooled by the discovery that the king
had been attempting to dupe them. They assembled
after Easter to hear his renewed requests. They
were made, as before, on the ground that an invasion
by the King of Castile was imminent. This was a
strange excuse, seeing that just at this time Eleanor
of Castile was formally betrothed to Prince Edward.
Unfortunately too for Henry, Simon de Montfort
was present, and was able to give the magnates information as to the real state of things in the province, which confirmed them in their decision not to
send aid till they were better certified as to the truth

[1] *Ann. Osn.* 107. In *Ann. Burt.* 360 it is said that the Bishop of
Hereford feigned himself proctor of several religious houses, and so
brought them into debt ; so too *Ann. Dunst.* 199 ; *Matt. Par.* 910.
Flor. Wigorn. 185 says that almost all religious houses in England were
bound for sums varying between 200 and 500 marks. Cf. *Ann. St.
Albans* 373–385.

[2] *Matt. Par.* 881 : cf. Richards report of this to his brother, *Id.
Additam.* 189.

of the Spanish invasion. It was strange, they said,
that they never heard of such a danger when the Earl
of Leicester was in Gascony. So the council was
dissolved, and Henrys ruse failed.[1] On the kings
return, after Christmas 1254, the council, which met
first at Portsmouth, was shifted to London, and then
to Winchester, and was finally dissolved without any
result.[2] At the Easter Parliament of 1255, which
was very largely attended, the barons answered the
kings request for money, this time in the shape of
horngeld, by a renewal of the demand for the power
of electing the three chief officers of the Crown. They
now supported the claim by a reference to ancient
custom, though history would hardly bear them
out on this head. They also laid to his charge fresh
violations of the charters, and, as the king would
not yield to their request, Parliament was prorogued,
in order that some change of feeling might induce
one party or the other to give way.[3] The names of
those who were present at this Parliament are not
preserved to us, so that we do not know whether
Simon de Montfort was there or not. He was in
England, at any rate, in the preceding autumn,[4] and
there is no reason to suppose, especially after his

[1] *Ann. Dunst.* 190 ; *Matt. Par.* 887, 'per comitem Simonem, qui tunc de partibus rediit transmarinis, edocti, &c.' From the context it is most probable that these words refer to the present council ; if not they can only refer to that of January. It was to the Parliament of April 1254 that four knights representative were summoned from each county, being the first certain instance of such representation since 1213 : see Stubbs, *Sel. Chart.* 367.

[2] *Ann. Tewk.* 155.

[3] *Ann. Burt.* 336 ; *Ann. Dunst.* 195 ; *Matt. Par.* 904, 'Exigebant . . . ut de communi consilio . . . eligerent, sicut ab antiquo consuetum et justum.'

[4] He was present at the burial of W. de Cantilupe, 30 Sept., 1254, and with the Earl of Hereford bore the body to the grave.—*Ann. Dunst.* 192.

I

CHAP.
V.

1255

The Sicilian
scheme ;

pressed by
the Popes.

nominal reconciliation with the king, that he absented himself. He had been so far reinstated in his former position as to be sent in the summer of 1254 on a confidential errand to Scotland, with a message for the king, so secret and important that it could not be trusted to paper.[1] What its import was one can only guess.

By this time the real cause of the kings renewed demands had become known. The late Pope, Innocent IV, had endeavoured to make Henry his firm ally by appealing to his dynastic ambition. He had first of all offered the throne of the Two Sicilies, as a fief of the Church, escheated after the death of Frederick, to Richard of Cornwall; and when that cautious and somewhat miserly prince drew back, he chose the kings younger son Edmund as the recipient of his favour.[2] The weak but ambitious father, with his usual imprudence, eagerly took the bait, and this was the crusade for which the tenth was to be granted. The enemies of the Church were the imperialists: the promised land was Sicily instead of Palestine. The great emperor and his two sons were dead, but the Ghibeline party did not perish with them, and Manfred, Prince of Tarento, natural son of Frederick, was not likely to yield without a struggle. But the king shut his eyes to all difficulties, and the death of Innocent IV in 1254 caused no interruption, for his successor, Alexander IV, took up the scheme with equal energy. Innocent had extended the grant of the tenth to Henry for a further

---

[1] It is strange that Dr. Pauli should declare Mrs. Greens allusion to this embassy (*Princesses* ii. 111) 'totally unfounded,' when the appointment appears in a writ, *Pat. Vascon.*, 38 Hen. III, m. 8, p. 2, quoted in the Fœdera. It was perhaps connected with the marriage of Margaret.

[2] Bull for Richard, 5 Aug., 1252; for Edmund, 6 Mar., 1254, in the Fœdera.

term of two years ;[1] he had bidden both king and queen to abstain from useless expenses, in order the better to prosecute the affair ; more than once he urged Henry to enter actively on it, and one of the last acts of his life was to bid him hasten to the protection of Apulia, or he would have to find some other more worthy of the throne.[2] Even Richard, though too cautious to undertake the conquest of Sicily, could not withstand the temptation of an imperial crown ; Henry urged his election, in the hope of an accession of strength against France ; the Pope eagerly promoted the same object, and he was crowned at Aachen, though only supported by a portion of the Electors, in 1257.   Henry, once started on this ambitious policy, could not stop ; and though unable to hold his provinces in France, accepted the worthless offer of half the lands belonging to the King of Castile in Africa as a dowry for Alfonsos sister.[3] The Pope, while allowing him to change his vow of crusade for the help to be given to the Church in Sicily, would not go so far as to let him dispute with the Saracens in Africa this chimerical possession.[4] The conditions on which the kingdom of the Two Sicilies was given to Edmund were embodied in a formal agreement in 1255, by which the future king was reduced to the position of a mere slave of Rome, restricted in a most degrading manner under terms which no feudal lord would have thought of imposing on a vassal. The obligations entered into by the king included the immediate liquidation of a debt of more than 135,000 marks, said to have been incurred

Ambition of Henry ;

his agreement with the Pope.

---

[1] *Fœd.* i. 303.
[2] *Id.* i. 302, 304, 312.
[3] *Id.* i. 301.
[4] *Id.* i. 304, 316 ; *Roy. Letters* ii. 112.

CHAP.
V.

1255

by the Pope in the conquest of the land. The negotiations connected with this engagement are the prominent feature of the next few years, and did more
than anything else to bring about the catastrophe.

The Sici-
lian scheme
checked ;

The attempts made by the Pope to expel Manfred
from Southern Italy were not successful. The papal
forces were almost annihilated by that prince, aided
by a large body of Saracens, whom Frederick had
settled at Nocera. Shortly before this event the
Bishop of Bologna had been sent with the ring of investiture to England, and on his arrival the king lost
no time in getting the ceremony performed, and in
addressing his son in public as King of Sicily and
Apulia. His paternal pride was however destined

its unpopu-
larity in
England.

to receive a rude check. The scheme was thoroughly
unpopular in the country ; the report that a papal
legate was on the point of arriving added greatly to
the general discontent, while the attitude of many of
the greater barons, at this time thought to have been
bought over by the king, brought the nation to the
verge of despair.[1] The Earl of Leicester, the one
steadfast friend of national liberty, was probably at
this time absent in France. He had gone thither on
business of his own, and was empowered to prolong
the truce, as it was a matter of great importance that
no obstacle should prevent the passage of the army
which Henry, with a childish sanguineness, hoped to
convey to Italy.[2]

[1] *Matt. Par.* 911. The Earls of Gloucester, Warenne, Lincoln, and
Devon are mentioned as having been thus corrupted, but not the Earl
of Leicester ; cf. *id.* 846.

[2] The truce was prolonged by S. de Montfort and P. of Savoy in
1255, according to the writs in *Fœd.* i. 324, for three years, though
from subsequent events the period seems only to have been one year.
Early in 1256 P. de Montfort was sent to France, to amend and con-

The papal ambassador did appear, though not, as was dreaded, furnished with the authority of a legate ; his name was Rustand ; he was a lawyer, and a Gascon by birth. On his arrival the Sicilian affair was brought forward by the king in the October Parliament, 1255, with pressing demands for money. Earl Richard headed the opposition, and declared he would have nothing to do with an engagement undertaken without his counsel and the assent of the baronage. The barons, returning in a remarkable manner to the original form of the Great Charter, complained that they had not all been summoned to Parliament, and, in the absence of so many of their peers, could, in accordance with the charter, assent to nothing.[1] At the ecclesiastical assembly held at the same time, the Bishop of London vowed he would lose his head rather than submit, and was supported by the Bishop of Worcester, who professed an equal readiness to be hanged. The hopes raised by these bold utterances were further encouraged by the proclamation of the Bishop of London, that no one in his

firm the truce already made by his cousin (writ dated 20 Jan., 1256), and with him J. Mansel and another (writ dated 24 Jan., 1256 ; cf. *Matt. Par.* 912). This staved off the danger for some time, but the election of Richard so much increased it, that in June 1257 a commission of three was sent over, consisting of the Bishop of Worcester, Hugh Bigod, and Adam Marsh, and they were empowered to act under the direction of the former ambassadors, S. de Montfort and P. of Savoy, who were to cross at the same time ('quos similiter ad partes illas transmittimus,' writs dated 22 June, 1257). S. de Montfort and J. Waleran were to have been sent at first (*Roy. Letters* ii. 121). It appears that the ambassadors did not start till the end of Sept. 1257, and did not return till 2 Feb., 1258 (*Matt. Par.* 955). Roger Bigod went out instead of Adam Marsh, who died about this time. Peter of Savoy and John Mansel were appointed at the same time to conduct the negotiations with regard to Sicily (see writs dated 28 June, 1257, in *Fæd.* i. 359, 360.) cf. below, p. 127, note 1.

[1] *Matt. Par.* 913. The allusion is of course to the suppressed constitutional clauses of Magna Carta.

CHAP.
V.

1256
Opposition
of the
church.

A crusade
preached.

Vain efforts
of Henry
and the
Pope.

diocese should obey the orders or instructions of Rustand. Upon this the king violently attacked him, and threatened to persuade the Pope to unfrock him. The bishop made the memorable reply, 'Let them take away my mitre, and I will put on my helmet.' [1] The clergy in general, in their diocesan assemblies, agreed on a single form of protest, in which they objected that the tenth had been granted without their assent, and that the previous concessions had been made for a specified object, which had not even been attempted.[2] Meanwhile Rustand and others vigorously preached a crusade, which, being directed against Christians instead of heathens or heretics, provoked more scoffing than enthusiasm.[3] Large sums had already been sent to Italy, and had been swallowed up by the war against Manfred, whose success, joined to a natural feeling of indignation against the way in which the Pope had handed over the country to an unknown foreigner, caused all Apulia to swear allegiance to him.

The opposition of all classes in England rendered the payment of the sums demanded quite impossible. The Pope sent letter after letter urging haste, and threatening with excommunication all who refused to pay the tenth. He even threatened to put the kingdom under an interdict, and left no stone unturned to get the money.[4] Next year the king instead of lowering raised his demands. He produced papal

[1] 'Tollant mitram, galea remanebit.'—*Matt. Par.* 915.
[2] *Ann. Burt.*, 360. In spite of all this the feeling with regard to both Pope and king was that they acted in ignorance, being led away by evil counsellors.
[3] 'Moverunt sannas et risum prædicatorum mutabilitates.'—*Matt. Par.* 914.
[4] *Fœd.* i., under the year 1256 passim.

letters in support of the claim for a renewal of the
tenth for five years, and other extravagant exactions.[1]
The prelates, assembled separately in February 1256,
hard pressed by king and Pope, bullied by Rustand,
were on the point of giving way, but for the support
of the lay magnates. They however remained firm.
It seems almost strange that they should have thought
it worth while to argue the point, or to give reasons
for their refusal. They urged however in self-defence
the state of the realm, the disturbances in Wales,
Scotland, Ireland, and Gascony ; pointed out the
difficulties of the Sicilian undertaking, the disadvantageous conditions offered by the Pope ; and finally,
since the contract was made without their knowledge,
refused the aid demanded.

Meanwhile the object of Henrys wishes was
rapidly falling from his grasp. He was sorely vexed
by the news he received of Manfreds successes. The
election of Richard to the German Crown raised up a
rival in the King of Castile, and a feeling of jealousy
in France which threatened every moment to burst
forth into war. This situation of course produced
disturbances in Gascony, which were fomented by the
Spaniards. The Welsh harried the frontiers, the
nobles of the northern marches were disaffected
towards the English king and his son-in-law of Scotland, yet the infatuated monarch would not give
up the struggle. He thought to impress his subjects
with a *fait accompli*, when in the Lent Parliament of

---

[1] *Ann. Burt.* 388, 390. Such were the demands for the first years
income of vacant benefices during the next five years, half the income of
non-residents, the revenues of all but one of benefices held by pluralists
(the right to hold a plurality was conceded by the Pope to the English
Church in 1245), &c.—Cf. *Ann. Osney*, 115.

1257 he produced his son Edmund, with the royal ring on his finger, and in the Apulian dress, as King of the Two Sicilies, before the assembled magnates. At the same time he confessed the enormous debt of 350,000 marks, which he owed on his return from Gascony,[1] and the full extent of which seems to have been hidden from the public hitherto. In answer to his appeal the laity remained obstinate, and the king

was forced to use the expedient of a scutage for an expedition against the Welsh, which probably could only be levied on the poorer and weaker tenants.[2] The clergy however, seemingly in despair, voted the king the large sum. of 52,000 marks, on consideration of that which ere now must have been seen to be the weakest of safeguards, a fresh confirmation of the charters, and the promise of redress of grievances which were to be embodied in a protest.[3] This was the last great contribution which went to swell the list of papal and royal exactions. Whether the money was ever collected or not seems uncertain. The king is said to have refused to accept so paltry a gift. The convocation which assembled in the follow-

ing August to draw up the list of grievances was dissolved prematurely on account of the Welsh war, and the grant was probably lost sight of in the confusion of the next year. The ravages of the Welsh drove the king in the summer of 1257 to summon all the forces of the kingdom against them, but the army,

---

[1] *Matt. Par.* 913.
[2] 'Ad maximum pauperum gravamen.'— *Ann. Tewk.* 158.
[3] *Matt. Par.* 947. The sum is said by *Matt. Par.* 951 to have been 42,000 marks. The sum of the unnecessary expenses which Henry had incurred since he began to be 'regni dilapidator,' was computed in this year to amount to nearly a million of marks, which, as *Matt. Par.* 948 says, is 'horribile cogitatu,' when we recollect that it is equivalent to about fifteen millions at the present day.

by wanton destruction of the crops in order to anticipate the enemy, did more harm to the country than
the Welsh. After suffering several defeats the famine
which they themselves had produced forced them to
return. The failure of the expedition, and the wound
it inflicted on the national pride, were apparently the
last thing needed to break down the reverence of the
people for their king.

At the same time a change occurred in Henrys
foreign policy, which shows incidentally the growing
strength of the opposition. It is remarkable that all
the ambassadors sent with Simon de Montfort in the
summer of 1257 to prolong the truce with France
were among the earls supporters, excepting Peter of
Savoy, who however had been one of his best
friends in 1252, and was after all but a lukewarm
royalist.[1] Hugh Bigod was the baronial Justiciar
next year. Adam Marsh was one of his oldest and
most intimate friends ; the mantle of Grosseteste had
fallen on Walter de Cantilupe, Bishop of Worcester.
Although the same cannot be said of the ambassadors
appointed to conduct the Sicilian affair in conjunction
with the earl, yet their instructions left no doubt as
to what must be the result of their embassy, and
coincided with what we find afterwards to have been
Simons policy. The king was still very unwilling to
relinquish the enterprise, and wrote to the Pope to
say that in spite of the opposition of the barons he
hoped still to carry it through.[2] The commissioners

[1] See note 2 on p. 116, where I have collected the details respecting
these negotiations.

[2] *Roy. Letters* ii. 126. This letter is said by Dr. Shirley to have
been written in Jan. or Feb. 1258. It is not dated, but it seems probable that it is rather earlier than this. The ambassadors who really

were entrusted with full power to amend the conditions on which the concession of the kingdom of Sicily had been made. They were to obtain a relaxation of the threat of interdict, and a further respite in the performance of the kings engagements. If possible, the matter was to be peaceably arranged by the marriage of Edmund with Manfreds daughter. If the Pope refused these proposals, they were to offer him a choice between three courses, which were such that he was extremely unlikely to take any one of them. In case of need they were empowered to renounce the whole scheme. It was evident that the Pope would hardly grant such conditions as would satisfy de Montfort, and that if he had the direction of the affair it would end in a complete renunciation. It was announced that the object of the embassy to France was to secure peace for the prosecution of the Sicilian scheme ; the best result of the embassy to Rome would have been that of securing peace with France by the removal of the cause of jealousy, the Sicilian scheme itself. Simon de Montfort did not go to Rome, nor did his colleagues ; they could ill be spared by their respective parties at this crisis. They did however go to France; but, though kindly received by the king, they got nothing but hard words from the nobility, and returned with small success.[1] As long as the English claims on Normandy were kept up, a lasting peace with France was impossible.

Both these embassies, though unsuccessful, were

went to Rome were the Bishops of Bath and Rochester, and the Archdeacon of Lincoln ; they seem to have only postponed the affair. See *Fœd.* i. 368, 369.

[1] *Matt. Par.* 955. Dr. Pauli is however of opinion that they did not go at all.

signs of a new foreign policy, which struck at the
roots of one of the great causes of internal discontent.
They are the first indications that the steady opposition of the English people to unwise interference in
foreign affairs was beginning to tell. It was the first
triumph of a tendency which the final cession of
Normandy two years later, when Simon de Montfort
was in power, shows to have been after the earls
own heart. The king in giving way so far as he did
seems to have had an inkling of what was about to
happen ; he may well have been appalled at the
temper of the country. He had just had a warning
of the fiery passions smouldering around him, only
waiting for an opportunity to burst forth in a great
conflagration. It was apparently at the time when
the magnates were assembled in London for the
Lent Parliament of 1257 that a violent quarrel broke
out between the Earl of Leicester and William of
Valence. The latter, trusting that his royal brother
would support him in his insolence, and not content
with humbler prey, had made an inroad on de Montforts lands, and carried off some of his property.
The earl seems to have brought the matter before
the king, and in the dispute which arose William
added insult to injury by calling Simon, in the
presence of the assembled barons, a traitor, which, as
the chronicler naïvely observes, is a great offence to a
knight. Whereupon Simon was so enraged that he
drew his sword, and would have revenged himself
upon his enemy then and there but for the intervention of the king, who, in fear for his brothers life,
threw himself between the disputants.[1] The incident

[1] *Matt. Par.* 950.

was probably soon forgotten, but it was enough to show what was to be feared. However, after the Welsh expedition, a moment of quiet ensued ; several of the chiefs of the opposition were absent in France ; the year closed without any indication that an outbreak was nearer than it had been any time within the last five years.

Meanwhile Henry found leisure to visit the Abbey of St. Albans, and means to make princely offerings to the shrine. These were indeed the occupations which best suited him, the only consolations which he still retained. Such a spectacle arouses feelings of a mingled nature. For while we condemn Henry as a ruler, and find him hardly less despicable as a man, yet, in the midst of such trouble as was shortly to burst upon him, some feeling of pity is mingled with our resentment. The death of his daughter Katharine, the illness of the queen, the triumph of the Welsh, the disappointment of his hopes in Sicily, threw him about this time into a violent fever.[1] He was now just fifty years old. The gaiety and conversational powers which had enlivened his brothers table at Wallingford, and astonished the monks of St. Albans, had given place to a violence of temper, to which indeed he had always been liable, but which had now reached such a point that when the fit was on him —and the slightest opposition sufficed to rouse it— his most constant attendants dared not approach him. He had hardly a man, beyond creatures like John Mansel, whom he could call his friend ; he had

---

[1] 'Rex audito infortunio, &c. . . . in tantam precipitatus est tristitiam, quod in febrem tertianam . . . est prolapsus.'—*John of Oxenedes*, 192.

alienated almost all his vassals in turn ; the English barons whom he tried to win took his gifts and opposed him in the council ; the 'foreigners whom he pampered sneered at him, and used him for their own selfish ends. But though no one loved him, his character was not such as to make him hated as his father was ; he was the object of dislike and contempt rather than of hatred and fear. With his brother Richard he was never on good terms ; even his eldest son, in whom a noble character was nearly ruined by paternal indulgence, had openly called him to account for his injustice. He had no claim on the affections of his people ; he had not added to, nay, he had diminished, English power abroad. He could not dazzle the nation with feats of arms like his uncle Richard, or enforce their respect like his grandfather with administrative reform. Affectionate he was, but his was too often the random affection which is worthless to its object ; liberal, but with other mens money; personally brave, but no commander; virtuous, but his virtues were of a negative kind. He was not cruel, but he looked on the traders and the Jews as sheep kept only to be shorn ; he was not by nature a despot, but he had no idea of political rights. He was ambitious, but short-sighted ; credulous, but distrustful ; sanguine, but timid. He was not resolute, but obstinate ; not selfish, but weak ; a man of great desires, but little will. He possessed a certain cunning, but not the astuteness and decision of John. He had the same want of political insight, but neither the nobility of character nor the power of inspiring affection, which characterised Charles I. To his credit it must be acknowledged that, with a father and grandfather who were notoriously licentious, Henry was a blameless husband ; but this very uxoriousness was no small cause of his troubles. In a superstitious age two traits in his character commanded some respect, however little they may win now. Although not grateful as a rule, but rather chafing under an obligation, he never forgot the debt he owed to Rome for saving him his crown. Although no oath was sacred to him, although he thought nothing of seizing without the shadow of an excuse the goods of a merchant, his devoutness was such that the pious King of France said, ' Whatever be his sins, his prayers and offerings will save his soul.' [1]

Of the character of his great antagonist it is harder to judge. Hitherto we have seen but little of him ; our view has been confined to the general course of the constitutional struggle, which I have traced, however imperfectly, up to the point where it suddenly enters upon a new phase in the Revolution of 1258. The history is a somewhat wearisome and monotonous one ; the contest seems endless and resultless ; the country is to all appearance as badly off, the chance of relief as distant, the deadlock in the government as hopeless, as ten years before. But in the interval parties have been forming, political ideas

---

[1] A striking illustration of his devoutness is given in an extract, to be found in *Lettres de Rois* i. 140. When Henry was in Paris, on a visit to Louis IX, on the way from his palace to the council-room he had to pass a number of churches. At each of these he heard mass, and in this way the whole day was occupied, so that the King of France and his nobles waited in vain till evening. This happened next day also, and on the third day Louis ordered all the churches on Henrys route to be closed. This time he appeared early enough, but asked, in terror, if the kingdom were under an interdict. Explanations followed, which resulted in Henry being allowed to satisfy his religious feelings without interrupting the course of political business.

CHAP.
V.

1257
Public life
of Simon
de Mont-
fort.

ripening ; the conviction that such a state of things must have an end has grown stronger and stronger. It is impossible to trace with certainty the part Simon de Montfort took in the preliminary struggle. The few allusions to him after his return from Gascony leave the impression that the king tried at one time to conciliate him, at another to keep him out of the way. We find him acting as ambassador to France and Scotland, though on no occasion does he seem to have stayed long away. With his public duties on one of these occasions he combined certain private trans-actions in France,[1] and such matters may have demanded his attention at other times, but we may fairly believe that during the greater part of the four years previous to the meeting of the Mad Parliament he was in England. He had increased the kings obligations to him by becoming his creditor to a large amount, not only for what was still owing to him from the Gascon accounts, but for a voluntary loan. Various more or less doubtful securities were given him for this debt : the money owed by the Earl of Norfolk to the Crown ; the debts of a certain Jew, Aaron by name ; lastly the castle and lands of Bigorre, in Gascony.[2] He took his place among the nobles who witnessed the writ by which in 1256 the title of the young king of Scotland to the earldom of

---

[1] *Roy. Letters* ii. 107.   Dr. Pauli says (*S. v. Montfort*, p. 71), ' Weder die freundschaftlichen Beziehungen zu dem Könige waren wieder hergestellt, noch trat er der Opposition der Englischen Magnaten bei. Er lebte vielmehr zurückgezogen mit den seinen in der französischen Heimath, u.s.w.' I can find no ground for this.   He was certainly in England the greater part of 1254; the countess was in England in 1255; the earl in 1256, and again in 1257.   I cannot find any proof of his being in France during this time except once in 1255.

[2] Mrs. Green (*Princesses* ii. 111) quoting from *Rot. Lit. Claus.*

Huntingdon was confirmed.[1]   In the next year several knights fees were conferred upon him, and he received a promise from the king not to dispute a will he intended to make.[2]

Was Simon in retire-ment dur-ing these years

With such scant notice of the public life of de Montfort we must be content.   Of his private life, since the death of Bishop Grosseteste, we know less than ever : the letters of Adam Marsh to him, if any, as does not appear probable, were written during this period, tell us next to nothing.   There seems no reason to believe, as has been suggested, that he sub-mitted to a voluntary exile in France, away from his fair lands of Kenilworth and Odiham.[3]   We need not suppose, and it is of itself very improbable, that a man who stood in the very first rank of the baron-age, nominally reconciled to, if not actually on friendly terms with, the king, should have left his country and abstained from politics at such a crisis. There were indeed during the last four years no such vigorous attempts to resist the oppressor as those of 1246 and 1248—the resistance had become rather sullen and passive—nor were there the like opportu-nities of personal distinction.   But are we therefore to conclude that the man who was so prominent in the period before he took office in Gascony, and who appears as the recognised leader in 1258, lived in retirement all this time?   If his name is not men-tioned by contemporary historians as a leader, no more is the name of any other.   Yet leaders there must have been even of such opposition as there was, and it is impossible to account for the position Simon

Probability that he to)k an active part.

de Montfort assumed immediately on the outbreak of the revolution, by any other hypothesis than that he was one of the foremost of those leaders. His opinions and character had long been known to a small body of liberal-minded men: a much larger party were now beginning to look up to him as the one man in whom they could trust.[1] I have already alluded to the change of Henrys foreign policy in the year 1257, as a proof that the principles embraced by the earl were making way. And by whose agency should they have made way, if not by his? He was not the man to hurry on a premature development in order to call attention to himself. It is no wonder if the chroniclers, noting down events year by year, failed to observe till the outbreak the steps by which he won the lead. His rise was gradual and unobserved by many. His was not the flashy liberalism of unthinking youth, but the settled judgment of a mature experience. We do not know that he ever theorised in politics; he certainly did not found a school; in statecraft there were probably living some, though not many, who were his superiors. The popular reverence for him was likewise slow in growing. A nation, especially perhaps

[1] Cf. p. 86, note 1, where the 'complices' of Simon de Montfort are alluded to. In *Mon. Franc.* 225 we read, 'Simon comes Leycestriæ, cujus et ad divinum honorem et ad utilitatem publicam flagranter anhelat desiderium, a quo plurimorum salus tam propter evidentes quam propter secretas causas pendere cognoscitur, &c.'; *id.* 277 (letter to the earl), 'super negotio quod nostis videtur mihi nihil scribendum hac vice, præsertim cum agatur de re maxima, et hinc speratur salus summa, illinc vero timeantur extrema pericula.' The warmth of the expressions in the former letter hardly warrant its being placed much earlier than this time, and it cannot be later than 1257, when Adam Marsh died; the latter was written before 1253 (for Grosseteste was alive), and appears to allude to some weighty consultation, when the Bishops of Lincoln and Worcester were with the earl, on a matter too important to be committed to writing.

K

CHAP.
V.

1257
Political
character
of de
Montfort.

the English nation, is slow to recognise its great men. The feeling which placed Simon de Montfort on the same pedestal with St. Thomas of Canterbury was not the growth of a day, but it had its roots in the heart of a people. That which gave him his strength, that which drew men to follow him to the death, was this : that the love of right, the feeling of sympathy with an injured people, became in him a stern resolve which no temptation could shake, no obstacle stay, no danger intimidate. As the men of an earlier day, the links between the gloomy present and the glories of the Great Charter, one by one disappeared, he stood forth alone. His peers were almost all more or less suspect : on him rested no stain of yielding. The friends and counsellors on whom he had depended were gone ; he was far past the prime of life. But his was not the nature to be daunted by the lonely heights , solitude showed him his strength. The time was come, and with it the man.

CHAPTER VI.

THE POSITION OF PARTIES IN 1258.

BEFORE we enter upon the final act of the drama, it will be better perhaps to pause and review the parties which were arrayed against the king, the steps in his policy and in that of the Pope which had led to the union of the national forces against them, the evils complained of, and the claims made. The national party may be said to have consisted of the whole body of the clergy, the greater portion of the lay baronage, including almost all the smaller barons, and London with the sea-port towns ; the other towns were perhaps rather on the kings side than on that of his opponents, and the lower classes cannot be said to have had much influence on affairs as yet. The kings supporters were at first, with the exception of a few lukewarm members of the baronage, and some still rarer exceptions in the Church, only his creatures, his foreign relatives, and the crowd of parasites whom he had introduced ; these however with their dependents made up no contemptible force. Later on, by the desertions from the opposition, by the aid he received from the foreign clergy in the country, through the moral influence of the Pope and the King of France, his party became far superior to that of

CHAP.
VI.

1258
The
national
party.

The kings
party.

K 2

CHAP.
VI.

1258
Compari-
son of the
movements
of 1258
and 1215.

his foes. It is observable that the originators of the revolt of 1215, the northern barons, had much less to do with that of 1258, and afterwards took up a neutral if not royalistic attitude. The strength of the opposition lay at this time in the great midland baronage, which had in the earlier struggle formed the second rank in historical order if not in importance. The weight of the smaller barons was now much greater, and the civic element had received an accession of strength in the south-eastern sea-ports. The influence of the universities must not be neglected, but, though morally great, it was not of much practical use when it came to blows. In the earlier revolt the national party, though more completely successful at first, and though it left behind it an imperishable monument, hardly preserved its superiority long enough to find time to disintegrate ; but signs were not wanting to show that, had circumstances permitted, had John been really overpowered, it would have broken up of itself, as it did after the victory it won in the Mad Parliament. It was a great disadvantage in the latter case that there was no churchman of the eminence and character which enabled Stephen Langton to take the lead of the whole party. Deprived of their natural head—for Archbishop Boniface was in no way worthy of the chair of St. Thomas—the clergy could only take up a subordinate position, and their ranks were less united than before. It was also a great drawback that there was no Fitz-Walter, no William Marshall. Simon de Montfort was by birth, and in the opinion of his peers remained to the end, an alien. The popular instinct saw as usual more clearly than the eyes which were

blinded by the prejudices of an exclusive caste. It
must be allowed that as a whole the baronage do not
come nearly so well out of the ordeal as their fathers.
True national feeling was not so strong in the most
powerful portion of society as it had been fifty years
before ; it had descended one step, and it received
expression at the hands of an individual rather than a
class. The kernel of the constitutional party, the band
of men that followed Simon de Montfort to the end,
was so small and comparatively so weak that it never
had any chance of ultimate success. The class that was
to win by his most advanced reforms was not ready
to enjoy, nor strong enough to hold, the benefits he
offered them. The movement of 1258 was only the
natural result of thirty years of bad government ;
its chief result was to show the incompleteness of the
political ideas of the time, and to throw the real leader
into clearer relief. The movement of 1264 was premature ; its budding principles were nipped by the frosts
incident to a too early spring, but they contained the
germs of a fruit which is far from having ripened yet.

Of the elements of the opposition above-mentioned Elements of the op-
the Church had probably most to complain of, and to position.
her we owe more than to any other body the protec- i. The Church : its
tion of our freedom in early days. It has been relations
already seen how for half a century before Magna with the Papacy;
Carta the opposition to unjust taxation was kept up
by the Church and by the Church alone. Edmund
Rich had not the courage or the power needful to
follow in Langtons steps, but he did his best ; the roll
of great names was continued by Grosseteste, Cante-
lupe, Sewal, Basset. It is impossible to say how much
we are indebted to the example of the Church, to its

CHAP.
VI.

1258
influenced
by the
general re-
lations of
England
with Rome;
broadening and anti-feudal influence, to its institutions, which kept the idea of universal equality combined with order, of authority and the popular voice, ever before the people. Still for a great part of this century the English clergy were thrust out of their right position by the general situation of the Church. The key to the papal policy in England during the first half of the thirteenth century is the struggle between the papacy and the empire; the immediate harm the struggle did was immense, and the papal power declined from the very moment of victory; but out of evil comes good, and it may be fairly said that we owe the constitutional advance of that century in a great measure to the ambition of Rome.

Fortunately for England, the simultaneous deaths of John and Innocent III gave her time to recover from the effects of the civil war and of papal interference. It was in opposition to king and Pope that the barons had won the charter; the leader of the opposition was the head of the English Church, and before the Reformation that Church was perhaps never nearer a schism than at that moment. Hon-

orius III did not lose the opportunity of influencing England through the monarchy; his protection of the youthful king was most hearty, and, on the whole, beneficial to the country, for his legates, avaricious as they were, exerted themselves in the cause of order, and order was what the country wanted at the mo-

ment. But the accession of Gregory IX, the policy of Frederick II, the coming of age of Henry III, gave a new direction to the relations of England and Rome. Henry was full of gratitude and devotion to the papacy; both temporally and spiritually he felt himself bound to support the Church ; everyone who could claim any connexion with Rome found a welcome at his Court. But his weakness allowed unscrupulous men to get him into their power, and under the evil auspices of Peter des Roches papal exactions reached an unprecedented height. Fortunately the national spirit of Langton rested, to some extent, on his immediate successors, and the fall of the Bishop of Winchester checked for a time the subservience of England to the Pope.

Still the growing vehemence of the conflict between Frederick, 'the wonder of the world,' and the papacy, a conflict in which not Christendom alone, but Mohammedanism too, was involved, prevented England from remaining aloof. The bond which had been signed by John, degrading England to the position of a fief of Rome, supplied the legal ground of exactions, which, apart from Peters pence and the regular feudal tribute of a thousand marks,. were limited only by the endurance of the English people. England had not remained untouched by the distant waves of the storm raised by Hildebrand and Henry, by Alexander and Barbarossa ; but it was under Innocent III, and still more under his successors, that she was drawn into the full influence of the hurricane. She was as yet untainted by heresy, and though the cruel deceptions of the Albigensian crusade obtained but little sympathy here, political reasons may be sufficient to account for the notable absence of Englishmen from the armies of the elder Simon de Montfort.[1] But although men from every part of Europe had contributed to crush the spark of free-

[1] Pauli, *Simon de Mont.*, 27.

CHAP.
VI.

1258
Feeling
towards
Frederick
II;

universal
change of
feeling to-
wards the
papacy.

thought that arose in a corner of France, it was a different matter when heretical opinions were, rightly or wrongly, attributed to the temporal head of Christendom. Frederick, the fascinating embodiment of the spirit of that early renaissance, drew all eyes upon him by the splendour of his youthful achievements, the vigour of his intellect, the novel luxury and eastern elegance of his Court, the air of mystery which at once attracted and repelled the vulgar gaze. His caustic epigrams went the round of Europe, and were treasured up against him in the note-books of the Popes. But what told more for him than all this was the fact that the battle against the temporal power was no longer fought by a pure Church, aiming at most at a complete spiritual independence, but by an arrogant hierarchy, organised and disciplined on feudal principles, aspiring to universal dominion. Gregory excommunicated Frederick for not going on crusade, and was enraged beyond measure because he went. The policy of Innocent, who used the voice of the Church assembled at Lyons to pull down one of the two pillars of Christendom, was condemned even by the saintly Louis. The restoration of the kingdom of Jerusalem, though not reckoned by Rome, was remembered to Fredericks advantage by the rest of Europe, and men shuddered, as at the worst of civil wars, when the forces of the Emperor, with the red cross still upon them, marched to meet the forces of the Pope.[1] The exactions of the Curia would have offended the national sense of Englishmen, even had they been devoted to the crusade against the infidel

[1] Cf. Milman, *Lat. Christianity*, bk. x. ch. iv.

for which they were noninally made ; but when it
was known that the crusade was against fellow-
Christians, the demands of Rome were felt to have no
ground.   The general feeling in Europe was expressed, though others dared not express it so boldly,
by the Paris priest, who, when bidden to publish the
ban against Frederick, declared from his pulpit that the
Pope excommunicated the Emperor, and the Emperor
the Pope ; which of the two were right he could not
tell, but ' in the name of God who knoweth all' he excommunicated him who was in the wrong.   In England the feeling is stated by Matthew Paris to have
been, as elsewhere, one of great confusion and uncertainty ; men knew not which side to take.   ' The
Church,' they said, ' and especially that most devoted
branch of it, the English Church, suffers daily oppression from the Curia, but never has she been oppressed
by the Emperor.   The Pope accuses the Emperor of
heresy ; but in his letters he writes as a humble
Catholic concerning God.'   Opinion thus divided
needed but little to throw its full weight on the antipapal side.

The papacy could hardly have won as it did but
for the aid of three things: first and foremost that of
the two great orders of Friars Preachers and Friars
Minors, noble instruments in the hand of an evil
policy ; that of the Lombard cities, whose liberties
Frederick vainly and foolishly endeavoured to crush ;
and that of English gold. With the first and last only
of these we are concerned here.   The enthusiastic
devotion, the self-denial, the early simplicity and
poverty, of the friars won them a hold on the lower
classes in England, which was a strong tower of

CHAP.
VI.

1258
Uncer-
tainty of
public
opinion.

Influence
of the
Friars in
England.

CHAP.
VI.

1258
Influence of
the Friars
somewhat
ambiguous;
support to the Church. How should the authority
which canonised St. Dominic and St. Francis go
wrong?. And not only among the lower classes did
their influence extend : the Franciscans became con-
fessors to the highest nobles ; they were the leaders of
education at the universities. Their chief enemies
were the older monastic foundations, who were
prompted by a kind of professional jealousy, added to a
feeling of shame at the work which the friars did
and which they left undone, and of envy at the
bestowal of papal favour, to revile the new comers as
slaves of the papacy, and to proclaim upon every occasion the growing corruption which too soon began
to eat into even the order of St. Francis. Thus the
friars held an ambiguous position, and those who
patronised them, as Bishop Grosseteste, were com-
promised in the eyes of the great body of the regular
clergy, who suffered most of all from papal exactions.
On the other hand, this connexion would not have
had any of the like disadvantageous effects on the
position of a layman like Simon de Montfort, who,
while on most intimate terms with Adam Marsh
and other leading Franciscans, did not appear in
the light of a public patron of the order. This long
friendship ·is however specially interesting to us, as
testifying to the serious and earnest character of
Simons mind, to his thirst for knowledge, and to his
deeply religious disposition, while at the same time
it may have originated, or at least matured, those
broad and popular sympathies which afterwards so
endeared him to the people.

But it was the last of the three supports above-
mentioned, and the outrageous demands of the Curia,

which did most to determine the position of the
English clergy in the constitutional struggle. This
position was not taken up at once. The attitude of
the episcopate during these years varied considerably,
and is full of apparent contradictions. It depended
chiefly on the changing relations of king and Pope, to
both of whom the good-will of the English Church
was of the greatest importance. In accordance with
these relations the kind of influence and the amount
of pressure brought by the Pope to bear upon his
ecclesiastical vassals in England varied considerably.
On what grounds did this influence rest, and how
was it applied? Innocent III had laid down the law
of episcopal elections ; they were to be free on the
part of the clergy, but subject to the consent both
of Pope and king. But he further extended the papal
claim. He asserted successfully the right of sanction-
ing the election to bishoprics, and John having given
up his share of the right, he became sole arbiter. It
was already evident from the case of Archbishop
Stephen, that this right was equivalent to that of appointment. Still this could hardly be extended to the
whole of the episcopate, and it did not give the Pope
sufficient hold on the English Church. The hierarchical
tendencies of the episcopate were a more real support
to the papacy than the right of appointment, and these
were more fully understood and more boldly used by
Innocent IV.* The question of the episcopal visitation
of monasteries and of episcopal rights over cathedral
chapters was that which most agitated the English
Church at this time. The most influential of the English
bishops, Grosseteste of Lincoln, Cantilupe of Worcester,
and others, were making great efforts to assert their

CHAP.
VI.

1258
Effect of
papal exac-
tions on
the position
of the
English
Church.

Papal
influence
exerted
through
episcopal
appoint-
ments ;

and the
hierarchi-
cal tenden-
cies of the
Bishops.

CHAP.
VI.

1258
Hierarchi-
cal tenden-
cies of the
Bishops :

how used
by the
Pope.

authority over the regular clergy within their dioceses ; and, on the whole, they seem to have been successful. Their attempts met with very strong opposition on the part of the regular clergy, and invectives on this head are constantly met with in the monastic chronicles of the time. Grosseteste appears to have visited his diocese yearly, and in his first visitation deposed seven abbots and four priors, while he made diligent enquiries into the rights of the beneficed clergy.[1] His example was energetically followed by the Bishop of Worcester. We find the latter enforcing rules of his own on the monks, and banishing the recalcitrant to other abbeys.[2] Innocent IV seems to have perceived that the bishops in England were more important to him than the religious orders. He therefore favoured these efforts, supported the Bishop of Lincoln in the question as to the right of visitation of the chapter, and sought to win rather than subdue the episcopate.[3] He listened favourably to their objections against archiepiscopal visitations, and laid down the mode of that visitation, and a regular scale of charges. He even went so far as to bribe them with a hint that he would allow pluralities,[4] and conferred on the bishopric of Lincoln the privilege that no one offered for preferment by the Pope should be provided for out of the patronage of that see without special recognition of the power to withhold the gift. It was not till near the end of his life, when he had a more facile ally, that the Pope turned against the Bishop of Lincoln, and refused to allow his appeal against the exemptions granted to the Cistercians and

---

[1] *Ann. Dunst.* 143 ; *Hist. Angl.* 69.   [2] *Ann. Tewk.* 146, 150.
[3] *Ann. Dunst.* 166, 168.   [4] *Fœd.* i. 262.

other orders.[1]   It was owing partly to this politic
action of Innocent IV, and partly to the conviction
that it was hopeless to depend on the king for protection,[2] that the bishops were induced to vote such
enormous sums of money for the support of the papal
see.   In the early years of Henry III they had
staunchly opposed royal claims for money,[3] and had
even resisted the encroachments of papal power ;[4]
but, as time went on, their resistance to the latter
had grown very weak.   Their opposition to the king
was always stronger, and they were never at one with
him ; it was only at one period, about the year 1247,
that even the lower clergy were on his side, and then
he was raving at the episcopate for conceding to the
Pope the aid they refused the sovereign.   These
causes then—the claim of visitation and the concessions made to the Pope by the higher clergy—were
chiefly instrumental in producing the split that for so
long a time divided the Church of England, and made
a firm defence of their rights impossible.   The episcopal policy will be best understood by a brief examination of the character and conduct of Bishop Grosseteste, the most distinguished churchman of his day.

Robert Grosseteste,[5] during the latter half of his
episcopate, and, in the absence of Archbishop Boniface, the real head of the English Church, was a
staunch churchman, a man full of belief in the ecclesiastical power, in its world-wide extension, its holy

CHAP.
VI.

1258
Effect of
this policy
on the atti-
tude of the
episcopate :

disunion in
the English
Church.

Episcopal
policy as
illustrated
in Bishop
Grosse-
teste.

---

[1] *Matt. West* 240.
[2] 'Ecclesia Anglicana quasi inter duas molas (sc. Papam et regem)
conterebatur: hinc Scylla inde Charybdis timebatur.'—*Matt. Par.* 709.
[3] In 1229, 1231.   [4] In 1226.
[5] See Mr. Luards preface to his edition of the *Letters of Grosseteste*,
and Dr. Brewers preface to the *Monum. Franciscana.*

CHAP.
VI.

1258

Opinions of
Bishop
Grosse-
teste;
office. He was moreover an ardent supporter of the papacy, a believer in rule and order; though sprung from the people, he was no democrat; in a word, he was as real a member of the hierarchy as Gregory or Innocent. But this high opinion of the Church brought with it a deep-rooted conviction of its great responsibility, its dangers, and its duties. This vast power must be exercised only for the glory of God; no taint of earthly motives must corrupt that dignity which is so high above the earth. It was this noble ideal which he defended alike against king and Pope. The

on the
papacy,
power of the Pope was unlimited, he thought; he allowed to Pope and cardinals the right of all presentations, but this right should not be abused to thrust Italians, unable to speak English, or relatives of the Pope with nothing else to recommend them, into English benefices. The last act of his life was to refuse Innocents demand of a canonry at Lincoln for

the
monarchy,
one of his nephews. The monarchy was ordained of God, he considered, but its duty was not to waste the people committed to it, nor to coerce the Church which was independent of it. Carrying this notion

the empire;
of spiritual superiority further, he placed the papacy above the empire, and therefore supported it in its struggle, which he regarded with somewhat of prejudice, as carried on by the Church and not by an individual. He seems never to have opposed a demand for a contribution to be made *bona fide* on behalf of the Pope. It was a different matter when the tenth was demanded for the king by the Pope in

his opposi-
tion to the
Pope.
1252. It was not till the temporal ambition of the Pope became fully apparent, and Innocent leagued with Henry for the prosecution of so worldly an

object as the Sicilian crown, that he set his face against the project with all the vigour of a character which remained strong as ever in spite of approaching death. This being his attitude, it is not surprising that he was misunderstood, and it must be confessed that his notions of the ecclesiastical power led him at first to sacrifice the national interests to this object. He would have said that he regarded the souls of his people rather than their pockets; but the mass of the clergy, whose laxities he visited so severely, and who had to bear the expenses to which he consented, were hardly likely to sympathise with him. We accordingly find him and the rest of the bishops becoming suspect throughout England, and considered weak and cowardly.[1] Grossetestes sympathy with the friars, and its effect on his position in the Church, have been already alluded to. The feeling of hostility which he stirred up could not altogether be obliterated by his constant support of national liberties against royal encroachment, and his unswerving refusal to appoint incompetent aliens to the dignities of the Church. There were few souls high enough fully to appreciate and love him; he was looked upon as an Ishmael, whose hand was against every man, and every mans hand was against him.[2] Still, the beautiful legends told of what happened at his death, and the miracles said to have been performed at his shrine, show that the classes in which his friends the friars had most influence revered him as a saint.[3] His last

CHAP.
VI.

1258

His position misunderstood in England:

hostility towards him.

---

[1] *Matt. Par.* 730, 'suspecti;' 951, 'enervati et meticulosi.'

[2] 'Omnibus adversans, Ismaeli similis.'—*Id.* 688.

[3] On the night of his death bells were heard in the sky by the Bishop of London; some friars, on their way to Bugden, where he died, heard heavenly music in the air, the music made by angels come down

CHAP.
VI.

1258
Antipapal
policy of
Grosse-
teste.
opposition to the Pope, on the question of presentation, seems to have obscured the true conception of his character, which is evident from his life as a whole ; Matthew Paris, constrained to find some ground of praise, calls him in terms which he would have been the first to reject, 'an outspoken opponent of king and Pope, the hammer of the Romans ;' while he goes on to acknowledge his many other virtues, and his fulfilment of all the highest duties of a bishop.[1] Such was the friend, the protector, the counsellor of Simon de Montfort.

Change in
the rela-
tions of the
English
Church
with the
papacy,
About the time of Grossetestes death a change occurred, which caused this split to heal, and united the clerical party. Innocent IV had, from the time of his accession, taken up a still more decided line of action than his predecessor. The fruits of this were soon felt in England. 'He laid aside all shame,' we read, and extorted larger sums of money than any before him, so that 'a murmur of complaint, loud though late, rose up from the heart of England.'[2] His opinion of England was expressed in the words, 'Verily it is an inexhaustible fount, and where there is much abundance, thence can much be extorted.'[3] But for some time, and especially during the heat of

---

to take his soul. I may mention here a story showing the close connexion of Grosseteste and de Montfort in the popular imagination. On the Sunday before the battle of Evesham a lad was brought to be healed, at the bishops tomb, of dumbness and contortions. He fell asleep, and slept long ; on waking he began to speak, and told his parents it was needless to wait longer, for the bishop was not present ; he was gone to Evesham 'to help Earl Simon, his brother, who was to die there.'— *Rish. Chron. Camd. Soc.*, p. 71.

[1] 'Regis et Papæ redargutor manifestus . . . malleus et contemptor Romanorum, &c.'—*Matt. Par.* 876.

[2] *Matt. West.* 180.

[3] *Matt. Par.* 705 ; see above, p. 82.

the struggle, when Innocent depended mainly on the episcopate, the kings opposition threw difficulties in his way. We have seen the warmth of Henrys youthful devotion and gratitude to the Holy See, which Honorius did not live to put to the test. Gregory IX stood towards him in the double relation of a feudal lord and a spiritual father;[1] while claiming the right of appointment, he recognised to a certain extent the ancient royal rights over the Church.[2] This policy bore fruit in the partial approval shown by Henry of his action against Frederick, as testified by the publication of the ban in England. But during most of his papacy, and the first part of that of Innocent IV, the connexion between Henry and his great brother-in-law the Emperor, the threats and entreaties of the latter, and the authority exerted by the Pope, without royal leave, over the bishops, did much to cool the ardour of Henrys devotion. From the first Innocent IV had paid considerable attention to him, and had issued bulls confirming his rights, declaring his intention not to interfere with lay patronage, bidding the clergy support their king;[3] such favours were however too cheap to win Henry completely. After the death of the Emperor and the collapse of the secular power he made greater efforts. Henry had now nothing more

CHAP. VI.

1258 caused by a change in the attitude of the king.

Policy of Innocent IV towards Henry.

---

[1] He sanctioned the marriage of Isabella to Frederick II ; he interfered on behalf of Hubert de Burgh ; he stood security for Isabellas marriage-portion ; he warned the king against extravagance and imprudent generosity.

[2] He forbade the election to a bishopric of anyone unpleasing to the king ; he commanded the Bishop of Lincoln, during the vacancy of Durham, not to interfere in that diocese to the prejudice of the kings rights.

[3] *Fœd.* i. sub annis 1244, 1245.

L

CHAP.
VI.

1258
Policy of
Innocent
IV towards
Henry

to fear from the indignation of the Emperor; his dynastic ambition could be utilised to its full extent. Innocent perceived that he could not win all interests, he therefore confined his attention to the king, and sought to make him his firm ally by more substantial favours. About the same time Henry, on his side, showed an inclination to come to a better understanding with the Pope. As early as 1250 we find him requesting the tenth. The Pope at that time declined to grant it, declaring it unconstitutional to do so without consent of the clergy.[1] He also refused

undergoes
a change.

to allow him the tenth requested from the Church of Scotland, a demand which he styled 'utterly unheard of.'[2] But such petty scruples soon gave way when it occurred to him that he might make use of Henry as a tool to uproot imperialism in Italy. The crusade from which he had formerly dissuaded him, as endangering the peace of his own country, was now urged upon him with the greatest eagerness; the unconstitutional tenth from England, and that unheard-of contribution from Scotland, were now granted

Effect of
this on the
English
Church.

willingly enough.[3] The move was a bold one, and at first appeared likely to prove successful; but the Pope had over-reached himself. It was this alliance of their foes which united the different sections of the English clergy, and welded them into the solid mass they had formed forty years before. Instead of the mutual support which king and Pope expected,

---

[1] *Fœd.* i. 272.

[2] 'Penitus inauditum.'—*Id.* i. 277.

[3] It was however not the tenth, but a twentieth, which was granted from Scotland. The feeling as to the tenth granted to the king is expressed in *Gest. Abb. St. Alb.* i. 369, where it is called a 'novitas a seculis inaudita,' that the Church should pay for the support of the laity, instead of the reverse.

nothing went further to undermine the influence of
both than this unnatural union of the temporal and
spiritual power, this coalition of the Pope who ought
to have been an emperor with the king who ought to
have been a monk.

Along with this process of union grew the political
ideas of the Church, and its clearness of political vision.
Nothing is more remarkable than the reverence dis-
played at first for the papacy. In the long lists of
grievances drawn up by the representatives of the
clergy, it is constantly suggested that the true state
of the case is hidden from the Pope and the Curia,
that if they knew the reality they would never
countenance such exactions. The convocation in
1255 declared their intention of appealing to the
Pope, 'who beyond doubt was a most holy man.'[1]
But the truth began to dawn upon them at last,
although as late as 1257 they resolved to claim the
papal protection against the king. Long before this
it had been darkly hinted that Pope and king were
intriguing merely to get money, and the temper of
convocation in 1257 showed that they were becoming
convinced of the fact. The deception by which money
was demanded as a subsidy for the crusade, while it
was intended for the Sicilian scheme, and the exposure
of the still grosser piece of trickery practised by the
Bishop of Hereford,[2] must have shown everyone
the truth. The crusades were in many ways one of
the chief supports of papal power during this age, and
the Popes knew well how to convert the crusading
spirit to their own ends. But at this time devotion to
the Church, we are informed, began to grow cold, and

[1] *Ann. Burt.* 265. [2] See p. 111.

CHAP.
VI.

1258
Theory of
a National
Church;
therewith the impulse towards crusades. Moreover, with the growth of national feeling in England had grown the idea of a National Church. In 1244 we find the theory of a distinction between Churches advanced ; the clergy in their remonstrance[1] say that as the Church of Rome has its patrimony, so other Churches have theirs ; that they are not tributary Churches, the Pope having indeed the care of all souls, but being in no sense the owner of all Church property. On the contrary, they recognise the right of lay patronage, and the consequent claim to a voice in the management of Church property which belongs to lay

patrons. Once too, in 1246, they recollect that there is an authority yet higher than the Pope ; they threaten to appeal to the General Council ; but they do not seem to have dared to carry out the threat. They replied to Rustands demands with the argument, that it is true in a certain sense that the property of the Church belongs to the Pope, but only inasmuch as it is under his protection ; he has no more right to the enjoyment or appropriation of it than a king has to seize the property of subjects whom it is his duty to defend.[2] The venality of the Curia, from which they had often to buy the confirmation of elections, the secular character of the struggle in which the Pope was engaged, scandalised many whom the mere amount of the papal exactions might not have offended.[3]

But the less ideal grievances they had to complain of—the vast number of Italian ecclesiastics in possession

---

[1] *Ann. Burt.* 265. [2] *Matt. Par.* 920.
[3] 'Gratiam ab illa venali curia obtinuerunt.'—*Gest. Abb. St. Alb.* i. 309; cf. *Ann. Burt.* 265.

of English revenues, amounting, according to one
calculation, to more than three times the ordinary
royal income ; the incompetence of these persons, and
the consequent neglect of their cures ; the summoning
of English ecclesiastics out of England to plead before
the Curia ; the pernicious effect of the clause ' Non
obstante,' so often introduced into papal decrees, and
thence imitated in royal edicts,[1] by which all confidence in agreements and grants was destroyed ; that
'most obnoxious statute,'[2] that all prelates must come
to Rome to be confirmed in their sees ; and, more than
all, the ever-increasing pecuniary demands—these
were doubtless more present to their minds than the
advanced theories mentioned above. The avarice of
Rome is a constant theme of the satirical poems,
whose punning verse assailed not only the Curia, but
many English prelates too. Certain bishops are said
to prefer lucre to Luke, marks to Mark, the bag to
the Book. But at Rome matters are at their worst,
and if the head of the world be foul, how is the rest
of the body to be clean ? Everything is for sale in
Rome : ' Give, and it shall be given unto you,' is the
rule ; he that gives most gets most favour from the
judges. Pope and cardinals lead the race for wealth,
all other dignitaries follow in their order ; all pillage
as they can.[3] If such were the feelings raised by

CHAP.
VI.

1258
Grievances
of the
English
Church
against the
papacy :

papal
avarice, '

'

and
venality.

[1] This provision was one inserted to cancel all existing privileges
which might interfere with the execution of any given decree. It was
specially mentioned in the remonstrance of the English Church as one
of the greatest evils.—*Fœd.* i. 265.

[2] ' Statutum cruentissimum.'—*Matt. Par.* 956.

[3] ' Sic lucrum Lucam superat,
Marco marcam præponderat,
Et libræ librum subjicit.
Polit. Songs, ed. Wright, p. 10.

CHAP.
VI.

1258

Effect of
royal con-
nivance at
papal ex-
tortion.

papal extortion, what was likely to be the effect when
the king joined hands with the extortioner, and
brought the whole weight of popular indignation on
himself, with far less dignity and reverence to defend
him than belonged to his ecclesiastical ally? It was
but natural, if the efforts of the English Church were
henceforward more heartily and more effectively directed against the encroachments of the king than
they had been against those of the Pope.

(b) Rela-
tions of the
English
Church
with the
monarchy:

It remains to consider the constitutional position
of the Church in England, and its relations to the
king. The new ideas concerning the independence of
the Church, as yet comparatively moderate and vague
in Lanfrancs day, had been recognised to a certain
extent by William I. The corner-stone of ecclesiastical
liberty, a separate lay and clerical jurisdiction, though
only partially granted by him, showed how far things
had advanced from the almost complete fusion of

Church and State before the Conquest. Yet under
the Conqueror the Church was full of Norman vassals,
and was little more. than an instrument of royal
despotism. It was revivified by the purity of Anselm,
but the successful tyranny of Rufus shows how
little able it was as yet to stand firm against the
king. The slight support which Anselm received
from Rome threw the English Church back upon
itself, and contributed to the growth of its nationality ;

Again,
> 'Roma caput mundi est, sed nil capit mundum.
> . . . Romanorum curia non est nisi forum.
> . . . Dabis aut non dabitur ; petunt quia petis.'—*Id.* p. 14.

Another poem quotes 'Cui caput infirmum cætera membra dolent,' and
'Quicquid delirant reges, plectuntur Achivi,' and the like.

but Anselm was and remained an Italian, and the
struggle for investiture which he fought had far less
of interest for England than the struggle which made
St. Thomas a popular hero.   It was not till Stephens
reign that the Church began to take up a really independent position. About the same time the religious
revival, and the increased study of the canon law,
gave the Church at once a hold on popular veneration
and a greater sense of its own dignity.   It began to
appear as the representative of popular liberties, at
least by force of example. By Beckets time England
had learnt to consider the English Church as its own,
and this feeling was strengthened by Beckets well-
known attitude towards the papacy. He was disgusted
by the compromising policy of Alexander III, who
dared not offend Henry : never would he go to Rome,
he swore ; let them go who prevailed in their sins. He
was less of an ultramontane than Robert Grosseteste.
His martyrdom was a victory for the English Church,
and frustrated the plans by which Henry had hoped
to subject it to the state ; it was also a great advantage for the papacy.   After that event papal
influence rose, and royal influence fell, till John gave
up the right of consent to election which Henry I had
formulated in law, and conceded to the Church perfect
freedom in the matter.   The omission of any special
mention of the right in subsequent confirmations of
Magna Carta was probably due to the same feeling
on the part of the regents which prompted the omission of the constitutional clauses.   Taking advantage
of this, Henry III constantly ignored the claims of the
cathedral chapters to the choice of bishops.   The persons selected by those bodies seem, it is true, to have

CHAP.
VI.

1258
Growth of
independ-
ence :

CHAP.
VI.

1258
Abuse of
the royal
power of
appoint-
ment.

been often so unworthy as to justify papal interference, and to the papal choice we owe some of the greatest ornaments of the English Church. But the same defence cannot be made for the king; Peter des Roches, Archbishop Boniface, Aylmer of Winchester, Peter d'Aigueblanche, are mournful illustrations of the use he made of royal power. It is evident that the theory of the independence of the Church had made but little advance in England, though it had received constitutional recognition in Magna Carta. The English Church was indeed less independent of the king in 1258 than in 1215, and far less independent of the Pope than in the days of Becket.

Opposition
of the
Church to
royal
power.

But this subjection to royal power was more and more resented. Ideas on this point were now further developed; ecclesiastical principles were more closely applied to the existing state of society than ever before. In the great manifesto of ecclesiastical rights which Grosseteste published about the year 1236, in the form of a letter to the primate,[1] he opposed the recent ordinance by which the king appointed abbots as itinerant justices, laying down the principle that no ecclesiastic can hold a secular office. The subjection

Theories of
Grosseteste
in 1236.

of ecclesiastical to secular tribunals 'in actione personali,' and especially in cases of supposed disobedience to royal mandate, was objected to on the ground that consecrated members are freer than lay members of the great body of the Church, just as the spirit rules the flesh, not the flesh the spirit. Ecclesiastical judges ought to decide in disputed questions whether a case belonged to the ecclesiastical or to the secular court,

---

[1] Grosseteste, *Epist.* lxxii. p. 205.

seeing that authority is delegated by the former, as by a superior, to the latter.   The king, it was alleged, violated this principle; nay, he went further, and often prevented ecclesiastics from deciding in purely ecclesiastical cases, or hindered their decision, sometimes even gave judgment himself. Bishops ought not to be compelled to give account of their right to presentation, or their reasons for refusing those offered for preferment; in cases of disputed patronage the ecclesiastical courts should decide; it might even be questioned whether laymen ought to have patronage at all. This last principle was not, as we have seen, the general opinion of the bishops, nor did Grosseteste make a dogma of it; but, even omitting this, the theory put forward was one which could not fail to bring the ecclesiastical into perpetual conflict with the secular power.   It is noteworthy that Grosseteste in this letter never appeals to Magna Carta: once only he appeals to the Oxford Council of 1222, in which Archbishop Langton excommunicated the violators of ecclesiastical liberties. His arguments are chiefly deduced from analogies from the Old Testament, from the primitive Church, or the writings of the Fathers.

The wrongs which the Church, like other bodies, had to complain of under Henry III were not so much consistent oppression as constantly recurrent molestation, an ever-varying infringement of privilege, a total want of sympathy with other mens opinions, an inherent love of irregularity. The king often interfered with elections; he strove, when unable to persuade the clergy *en masse*, to extort money from the prelates separately, he made monasteries pay for

CHAP.
VI.

1258
Grievances
of the
Church
against
Henry

a *conge d'élire*,[1] issued edicts affecting the Church without its consent, claimed the property of ecclesiastics dying intestate, and finally endeavoured to prevent discussion in the ecclesiastical assemblies altogether.[2] The great difficulty of determining the lay and ecclesiastical jurisdiction, which Grosseteste tried to settle, was constantly appearing. The clergy in 1240 complained of the interference of secular judges in ecclesiastical cases, and the articles[3] which the English Church in 1258 declared to be of the most pressing importance have special reference to the summoning of prelates before secular tribunals, the liberation by secular authorities of culprits condemned in ecclesiastical courts, as well as the punishment of the latter by loss of temporal property, and many other questions of a similar nature. An attempt was made by the king in 1247, at a time when he was on unusually good terms with the majority of the clergy, owing to his temporary opposition to the Pope, to settle many of the disputed points, and rather to the advantage of the Church :[4] but, if we are to believe the clergy, he did not regard his own enactments in this more than in any other matter.

We have a list of grievances, drawn up by Bishop Grosseteste, in which the same complaints were made, and many minor charges brought against the king and his sheriffs and bailiffs, of unjust action at law, interference with the testaments of priests, and the like.[5] It must, of course, be remembered that we have here only one side of the question ; still, grant-

---

[1] E.g. St. Albans paid 300 marks in 1235.—*Gest. Abb. St.Alb.* i. 307.
[2] *Ann. Burt.* 401.   [3] *Id.* 412–422.
[4] *Matt. Par.* 727.   [5] *Ann. Burt.* 422.

ing that there is some exaggeration, there will remain
a large residuum of truth, which must have weighed
very heavily against the king in the approaching
struggle. The list of privileges of the Church, compiled by Robert Marsh, under the direction of the
Bishop of Lincoln, contains theories still further
advanced than those in the protest already mentioned, with which he began his episcopate. The
principle of separate jurisdiction is maintained in this
document, even to the extent that no ecclesiastic
should be compelled to take an oath in a secular
court; and the theory of the sacredness of Church
property, of the servants of the Church, of property
under its protection, is expressed with great fulness
and vigour. 'As the father is not subject to the
son,' argues the compiler of this ecclesiastical Bill of
Rights, 'neither should the ecclesiastic be subject to
the layman.' Such then were the relations in which
the Church stood towards king and Pope, such its
internal condition, and the ideas that animated it,
such the grievances that aroused its opposition and
welded it together, till it grew to be the soundest
element of the party at the head of which Simon de
Montfort stood.

The other of the two great supports of the national party, the lay barons, had not so much to complain of as the Church, while they had more power
of resisting oppression. Consequently their resistance was more fitful and their principles less developed, though on the other hand their temporal power
made them more important when it once came to
blows. Their greatest ground of complaint, as it was
one of the greatest in the Church, was the ruinous

CHAP.
VI.

1258
Grievances
of the
baronage :
aliens.
influx of aliens into England. These persons, headed by the queens uncles and afterwards by the kings half-brothers, seized upon the posts of honour and emolument near the kings person, were thrust into important positions, as sheriffs, bailiffs, and castellans, and completely occupied the kings ear, to the exclusion of the rightful governors and councillors of the realm. ' England for the English' was the cry which raised the loudest response ; the expulsion of the aliens was the first step of the victorious barons in 1258, as it had been the first step of the reformers of

1215. Not only was universal jealousy stirred up, but enormous loss entailed upon the country by the influence of foreigners over the king, which they made use of to persuade him to war and other undertakings against the advice of his council; by their extravagance and the kings imprudent generosity to them;

and by the violations of feudal rights, especially in the matter of wards and widows, which were perpetrated for their advantage. It was chiefly to ensure against these that the Statute of Merton was passed. The breaches of trust committed by the king as guardian form a most important item in the baronial indictment, and the ground on which it was easiest to bring home to him direct violation of the law.[1] Another grave point in which the king in-

---

[1] A notable instance of this kind of injustice is the story of the widowed Countess of Arundel, who, appealing to the king for recognition of her right to a certain wardship, which the king unjustly kept in his own hands, was received by Henry with sneers and banter ; upon which, woman though she was, she delivered her testimony in the kings face in so masculine a manner, that Henry, utterly abashed, and acknowledging the truth of her statement, was forced to give way for the time ; yet she did not gain her plea, but returned, after great trouble and expense, without success.—*Matt. Par.* 853, s.a. 1252.

fringed the charters was in the matter of the Forest
Laws. Lands already disafforested were alleged to
have been planted again, and rights on lands not
within the forest bounds sold as if they belonged to
the king. But the chief grievances of the barons, the
hardest to formulate or to bring under any distinct
law, were the amount and the frequency of taxation,
the scandalous misuse to which the taxes were put,
the unjust action of sheriffs and bailiffs, as well as of
the itinerant justices, and the general misgovernment
and confusion of the country. From these grievances
are distinctly traceable the constitutional advances
made during this period.

The first grievance, that of taxation, did not
directly injure the great barons to any great extent ;
indirectly it did, by sapping the wealth of the
country, and diminishing in the case of their Church
patronage the value of their property. Direct taxation they were able to resist, and this the king knew
well, or he would not so often have requested their
assent. For a long time they did not take active
measures to prevent scutage and other taxes, to
which they refused to consent, from falling heavily on
the weaker barons and the great body of freeholders.
Aid was unconditionally refused by the barons several
times ; and from them the king could get nothing :
but often, when scutage was denied in Parliament, we
hear nevertheless that the king extorted it, and we
cannot doubt on whom the burden mainly fell. Thus
in the matter of taxation it was gradually seen that
though the king had a legal right, as the revised
charter allowed him, this right was rendered in a
great measure nugatory by the power of resistance

CHAP.
VI.

1258
Relations
of the
greater
with the
smaller
barons.

possessed by the principal taxpayers. The smaller, being unable to resist, were urged by force of ex· ample to win the same position by combination and an appeal to constitutional justice : constitutional principles were evidently still more important to them than to their superiors. On the other hand, the right which the greater vassals claimed and won, they won not only for themselves but also for the lower class. The latter were useful to their superiors, and while supporting them, gained strength and confidence in themselves, until, having at last got a leader, they were able to stand alone when the jealousy of the greater barons forced that leader to rest almost entirely upon them.

The right of withholding assent to taxation was constantly put into practice, but never distinctly formulated as it had been in Magna Carta. The feeling grew rapidly that what had once been granted could not be taken away by royal edicts or papal condemnations. The Great Charter in its first form became more and 'more the rallying-point, though in many respects an advance was made on it: for instance, in 1244 the right of assent was claimed, as we have seen, not only in the case of extraordinary aids, but also in that of the regular feudal contributions. The

theory of self-taxation was passing through the intermediate stage of a supposed bargain between the king and his subjects, confirmation of the charters being the price paid ; but this very arrangement shows that the older theory, that the tax was a charge made by the king on property in reality belonging to him, and levied for his own good and not that of the country, was still believed. The feudal notion still

possessed too strong a hold on the popular mind : the
remonstrances took the form of a protest against the
abuse of an acknowledged right rather than that of a
claim for legal justice. Still this very abuse was
rapidly undermining the older theory, and with the
claim for assent grew the secondary claim for a voice
in the employment of the money. This led very soon
to a demand for a share, if not in the legislation, at
least in the government, especially in its relations with
foreign countries. I have in passing remarked the
occasions on which different constitutional principles
first appeared ; it will be needless therefore to do
more than to sum them up here. We find the above-
mentioned ideas on several occasions strongly though
informally expressed. The clergy as well as the
barons declare that the object for which a certain tax
was granted has not been followed ; the king recognises the right to know what is to be done with the
tax, by telling them it is for a crusade, or a Welch
war, or an expedition to Gascony. Not only this,
but the barons ask the very pertinent question, what
has become of the money ? they enquire into the reasons of its disappearance, upbraid the king with his
private extravagance, his expenses in wine, robes, and
the like,[1] and display an inquisitiveness and a regard
for their own interests which must have been very
irksome to a spendthrift like Henry. To prevent
such misuse of public money it was proposed, as early
as 1237, that it should be paid into the hands of a
committee, and spent only by their consent—one of
the most advanced financial ideas that we meet with

[1] *Matt. Par.* 743.

1258
Baronial
claim on
general
control.

during the whole of this period. But, since it was necessary to strike at the root of the matter, the barons were led further to claim a general control over the kings actions, which would, if carried out, have amounted to a practical abolition of monarchical power. We find the aid for Sicily refused because the king had acted without the advice of his council ;[1] a decided objection was shown to the war with France in 1242, and aid refused by the barons because the war was entered upon against their will ;[2] ten years afterwards, the council insisted on the acquittal of Simon de Montfort, in direct opposition to the royal inclinations.

Claim on a
share in the
administra-
tion.

As the abuse of taxation led to a demand for a share in the guidance of the kingdom as a whole, so the decay of the bureaucracy established by Henry II brought about the claim on a share in the internal government and the administration of justice. We saw that the right of election to the high offices of State was not recognised either by the compilers or the revisers of Magna Carta ; even the one limitation on the freedom left to royal choice, namely, that the objects of that choice should be fitting persons, vague as this was, was dropped in the subsequent confirmations. The power thus given to the executive, especially in the matter of law, was immense. The system elaborated by the Court-lawyers had a levelling tendency, by which the old rights of jurisdiction exercised by the feudal lord over his tenants were

[1] *Matt. Par.* 913. Here Richard of Cornwall was the speaker.
[2] 'Responderunt Magnates . . . quod talia conceperat inconsultus ;' and 'admirantur Magnates quod sine eorum consilio et assensu tam arduum negotium est aggressus.'—*Id.* 580. So the clergy protested against paying the Sicilian debt as contracted without their knowledge. —*Ann. Burt.* 391.

gradually superseded. It brought the king and the lower classes together, to the detriment of baronial power. To get this machinery into their hands was therefore the object of the barons in claiming the right of appointment. The demand they put forward in 1215, though for a time allowed to rest, was not forgotten. As early as 1236 we find the Bishop of Chichester resisting the kings wish to deprive him of the great seal, on the ground that it was given with the assent of the common council, and not by the king alone.[1] In 1244 the joint committee of clergy and laity complained that justice was not done, and demanded that only such persons should be chosen to high office as should be willing and able to guard the interests of the nation.[2] It was seen however that the king was no fit judge of these interests ; accordingly, four years afterwards, the demand was directly made that the high officers should be appointed by, or at least through the co-operation of, the council of the realm, ' as was the custom under the kings predecessors.'[3] This demand was repeated in 1255, and again refused.

In the long interval, when there was neither Chief Justiciar nor Chancellor in England, the king was able, by means of his underlings, to inflict endless annoyance and damage upon his subjects, as well as in various ways to extort large sums of money. So lucrative a source of wealth was the so-called administration of justice, that he never really gave way on

Marginal notes: CHAP. VI. 1258 Appointment of high officers.

Government without ministers.

---

[1] *Matt. Par.* 430. The bishop had been appointed in 1226, and held his post till 1244: see above, p. 64.

[2] ' Justiciarius et cancellarius fierent per quos regni status solidaretur, ut solebat.'—*Matt. Par.* 539: see above, p. 70.

[3] ' Per concilium regni ' is the phrase used.—*Matt. Par.* 744 : cf. above, p. 83.

M

CHAP.
VI.

1258
Abuses of
the judicial
system.
this point till 1258, and appears only once even to have held out the hope that he would do so.[1] The barons, in their petition of 1258, stated some of the ways in which the king got money, and the evils thence ensuing. The visits of the justices, according to the petitioners, were so arranged that persons having property in different counties were summoned to several places at once, and were fined for non-attendance. Further, so many exemptions from service as jurors were granted, that is to say, doubtless bought, that in many counties it was impossible to hold the grand assize. The facilities which this would give for all sorts of injustice, the practical destruction of the jury system, and the consequent violation of the spirit of the Great Charter, need not to be enlarged upon. It was equally fatal when advantage was taken of the absence of a Chancellor to issue writs which thwarted the course of justice,[2] when persons living in different counties were prevented from impleading one another, when the laws on debt were abused by col-

lusion between the justices and the Jews. Closely connected with the question of jurisdiction was that of the appointment of sheriffs. The office, it appears, was generally farmed from the king, the consequence being that the sheriffs looked on their power as a means of making money. They levied excessive fines, and often on trivial pretexts : for instance, the holding of two acres of land in a county was considered sufficient ground for summoning the holder to the county court, and fining him for non-attendance. They took fines for the receiving of malefactors, and mulcted the neighbouring villagers

[1] In 1248.—*Matt. Par.* 765.   [2] *Id.* 639.

if they could not account for a traveller who had hap-   CHAP.
pened to die on the road. That the condition of law   VI.
and justice in the country was very low, is shown by   1258
the fact that in 1236 all the sheriffs had to be removed from office on account of their venality,[1] by
the disclosures at Winchester in 1249,[2] and by
stories[3] which illustrate the shameless use the sheriffs
could make of their power and the want of protection
from their toils. Such being the evils from which the   importance
people had to suffer at the hands of the royal officers,   of the office.
it is remarkable that the power of appointing sheriffs
does not seem to have been distinctly claimed
(though it may have been included in the general
demand for the right of appointing to the high
offices), till the Mad Parliament. As soon as the
idea of summoning the middle classes to the franchise began to gain ground, the political power possessed by the sheriffs, and their influence over the
county courts in the election of the four knights, in
sending out the summons to Parliament, and the like,

---

[1] 'Corrupti muneribus exorbitarunt,' &c.—*Matt. Par.* 439.
[2] See above, p. 81.
[3] E.g. the story told (*Matt. Par.* 931) of the sheriff of Northants,
who, coveting some oxen belonging to a respectable farmer, seized the
cowherd, accused him of having stolen the oxen for his master, and
carried him off, vowing ' he would make him sing,' i.e. accuse his
master and himself. By dint of torture he forced the man to plead guilty,
and put him in prison till the arrival of the justices. The man was
then brought forward to accuse his master, instead of which he related
the whole story. The justices being puzzled, a commission was sent
down, one of the members being Simon de Montfort. The result of
their enquiry was that worse things still were discovered, and the
sheriff would have been hung but for the intercession of the King of
Scotland (on part of whose earldom the offence was probably committed). The injured man and his servant were known, it is said, to
have been of excellent character, while ' the whole county and certain
of the justices were well aware that the sheriff was a rascal (cavillosus
avarus et conducticius) ;' yet the latter would have reaped the fruits of
his villainy but for the boldness of a farm-labourer.

made it very necessary that the national party should insist on their appointment by Parliament.[1]

1258
Regularity
of sum-
mons to
Parliament
insisted on:

Lastly, we find the provision that the Parliament should be regularly summoned, which was allowed to drop in the revised charter, insisted on certainly in one instance. In 1255 the barons based their refusal to act on the ground that they had not all been summoned ; and closely connected with this was the reason given, according to some authorities, for the interruption of business in the Parliament of 1249, namely, the absence of the Earl of Cornwall, just as in 1253 the clergy declared they could do nothing in the absence of the archbishops. It was felt that no decree or concession made by Parliament or council could be binding unless all members took part in it, or were at least invited to do so. With regard to another provision of the charter, that Parliament must be summoned to meet at a certain spot, we find the notion gaining ground that not only must it be summoned to a certain spot, but always to the same. This principle was however urged only when occasion seemed to require it. In 1236 the barons would not meet in the Tower, but insisted on assembling at Westminster, though they do not seem to have objected to being summoned to Merton just before.[2] For many years after that the principle seems to have been lost sight of. The national council met at various places, London, Oxford, Portsmouth, Winchester ; in fact wherever the king happened to be.

place of
meeting :

[1] The petition presented by the barons at the Parliament of Oxford in 1258 contains a long list of grievances, and demands for redress, including those above-mentioned, and others hardly less important.

[2] Pauli, *Gesch. von Eng.* iii. 624. The refusal to appear at Oxford in 1233 does not appear to have been made on the same ground.

But the principle was necessary to the separate and independent existence of a Parliament, if it was to be considered more than a mere offshoot of the Court ; and we shall find it in after-years insisted on with great earnestness. The provision, which was perhaps most important of all, that Parliament should meet at regular intervals, though not distinctly laid down during this period, was nevertheless usually observed. It met generally three times a year, about the beginning of Lent, shortly after Easter, and in the autumn. The exact time of meeting varied a good deal, but we find these dates fairly well kept. It seems impossible to determine whether sufficient notice was always given, and the Parliaments were, of course, interrupted when the king was at war, unless they were summoned by the regency ; but there was no lack of frequency in them. Under the existing system of government, the mere fact of the barons assembling in Parliament did not impose any considerable check on the king, and the refusal to summon them at all would have been a very extreme measure. It had become customary, when the king wanted a general grant of money, to announce the fact in a great council : if the barons conceded it, well and good ; if not, the king was not prevented by their refusal from levying taxes on the weaker barons, and on others who were still more in his power. An unconditional refusal was, as we have seen, very rare ; and, in spite of difficulties, the king always seemed to hope that he would be able to persuade or terrify into submission. There was therefore no great temptation to desist from summoning Parliaments, though Henry would probably have tried the experiment

CHAP.
VI.
─────
1258
Growing
importance
of Parlia-
ment.

had he seen how, through their regular assembling
and their almost continuous resistance, there was
built up a power which was to shatter that of the
monarchy. The statutes of Merton mark a great
advance in the history of parliamentary legislation ;
but though the summons ' to consult on important
business ' seems to become more frequent, and thus
the general right of Parliament to assist in the
government of the country was more and more clearly
recognised, this was confined to questions of external policy, or such as demanded immediate action.
The reign is very barren in legislation properly so
called, in administrative organisation such as that
which distinguished the reign of Henry II ; but what
there was was generally carried out in the old way, and
the common council of the realm had very little to do
with it.[1]   Still, all the advance that was made tended
inevitably in this direction; the initiative in legislation
is the last and culminating triumph of parliamentary
government.   One fact; though of small importance
in itself, yet deserves to be noticed : the name Parliament had already begun to be used, as it had in
France a century before.[2]   Already, as we have seen,
most of its privileges had won or were winning recognition, either in fact or in theory ; it was no long step,
though it was a very difficult one, to formulate or
systematise those privileges, and to perfect its constitution.

[1] Except perhaps the statute of Merton.
[2] 'Parliamentum Runemede, quod fuit inter dominum Johannem
regem patrem nostrum et Barones suos Angliæ' (*Rot. Lit. Claus.*
28 Hen. III) is the first documentary use of the word. It is used in
Ann. Dunst. sub anno 1244, and by Matt. Paris, sub anno 1246, for
the first time, but does not for many years come into regular use (see
Gneist. *Verw.* i. 293).

Of the particular evils suffered by that ill-defined class, the smaller barons and the freeholders, which formed the greater part of de Montforts own supporters, as distinct from the large and loosely-connected reform party of 1258, it is very hard to form an idea. They were the same, to a great extent, with those of which the great vassals had to complain, only in an exaggerated form. Taxation pressed much more heavily upon them; they were less able to combine, and quite unable to resist singly the oppression of the kings tax-gatherers, his justices, and his sheriffs: wards and widows from the class of small tenants-in-chief were completely in his hands. But the greatest grievance of the smaller barons, as well as that of the greater subtenants, the towns, and probably the more important freeholders, the evil the redress of which, had they had a voice, they would doubtless have demanded most loudly, was the want of representation. The possession of this privilege would have gone far to remedy all their other wrongs. The common council, though in a sense a representative body, failed entirely to represent the wishes and interests of the middle and lower classes; just as the prelates, as a body, seem often to have acted in a way contrary to the wishes of the mass of clergy. But the latter had a means of making their wishes known through their own assemblies; the chapters and monasteries were bodies which could easily send representatives. The like assembly for the smaller barons did not exist, for the county courts were not in a position to give force and expression to public opinion. The distinction between the special and collective summons shows the difference which had long ago

CHAP.
VI.

1258

iii. The
smaller
barons, the
freeholders,
&c.: their
grievances:

their want
of representation.

CHAP.
VI.

1258
Want of
representa-
tion for the
smaller
barons, &c.

crept in ; the power of the greater barons had grown, while that of the others had sunk. Their attendance had become for many reasons next to impossible, and political representation did not exist.[1] The example of the clergy could not fail to arouse in them a longing for at least an equal share in the government. And if this class felt the want, what must have been the political unrest of the large and important body of subtenants, who had not even the consolation, which the smaller tenants-in-chief had, of feeling themselves on a nominal equality with the great barons, nor the vantage-ground which this position presented for further political action ? But they had no means of making their wishes known at the time, or of revealing to us their feelings, for they had no chroniclers ;[2] the way in which they and the Londoners followed Earl Simon is almost the only proof we have—though it is a sufficient one—that he undertook to supply a real want.

Of the other two constituents of Earl Simons following, London and the sea-port towns, it is easy enough to see why the first was so staunch a partisan. The superiority of London to other towns was if possible more remarkable in those days than it is now.[3] It had a long municipal history to look back on already. It had long been connected with the cause of liberty, and had held a high place in the country. London was the first to recognise Stephen as king. The commune of London supported John, during his brothers

---

[1] See below, s.a. 1264, for a few remarks on the growth of representation.

[2] They never even petitioned, except in conjunction with the greater barons, till 1259.

[3] But see Stubbs, *Const. Hist.* ii. 218 on this point.

reign, in the revolt against Longchamp ; its adhesion
to the baronial cause was most important in 1215,
and it was rewarded by special mention in Magna
Carta. The population was more mixed than in
other towns, more mercantile and habituated to travel,
and consequently more open to new ideas. But the
city was by no means undivided. The monopolies
possessed by the guilds were doubtless very oppressive
to the poorer part of the population. Already we
find two distinct parties among the citizens ; the poor
are very democratical, they have great weight in the
municipal government, and elect a popular mayor ;
the richer citizens are on the side of the king, the
poor are for the barons. The city had already obtained important privileges, and if the remark is true
that English liberties have all been bought and paid
for, of no class is it so true as of the civic class. John
had granted the right of annually electing a mayor ;
the royal sheriffs had no authority within the town ;
the citizens even farmed the revenues of the whole
county of Middlesex.

But these privileges were of little avail against the
royal power. The history of London during this
period is a history of unparalleled exactions and
tyranny.[1] The right of apportioning and collecting
their own taxes did not lessen the total amount of
taxation to be borne. The city being looked on as
royal demesne, the king, whenever he was unable to
get money from Parliament, and often at other times,
extorted it from London, availing himself unsparingly
of the omission of the clause in Magna Carta which

---

[1] See the *Liber de Antiquis Legibus*, passim.

CHAP.
VI.
1258
Exactions
from
London;

had provided that the aids demanded of the city were to be such as were reasonable. It may probably be said with truth that the Londoners and the Jews together contributed more to pay the kings private expenses than all the rest of the kingdom together. Large sums were exacted almost every other year for the fifteen years before 1258, amounting in one case, in 1252, to 20,000 marks. These exactions were made by way of tallage, and without reason given, 'as if the citizens had been slaves of the lowest condition,' says a sympathising chronicler.[1] A source equally large was that of fines, which were imposed on every available pretext, for readmitting an outlaw—the permission for which was granted when the king was young and therefore was alleged to be null and void— for letting a prisoner escape from Newgate, for not keeping the assize of bread and beer, and so forth. We have seen into what trouble a quarrel with the Abbot of Westminster brought the citizens ; in like manner a disturbance between the Londoners and some young courtiers whilst playing at the quintain caused the former to be fined in a large sum of money.[2] The royal wish that they should exchange certain liberties they possessed for others belonging to the Abbot of Westminster caused them endless trouble : the authorities stood firm, but the king often renewed

the demand. It being found that the mayor and the chief citizens were emboldened by the outcry of the masses, who clamoured for a voice in the decision, they were summoned to Windsor, in direct violation

---

[1] 'Velut a servis ultimæ conditionis.'—*Matt. Par.* 852. 'Secundum voluntatem et æstimationem extortorum, pecuniam civium mutilarunt.' —*Id.* 600.
[2] *Matt. West.* 852.

of their charters. They had to pay to get their sheriffs appointed and their charters confirmed. A fair, lasting a fortnight, was decreed by the king to be held at Westminster, for the advantage of the abbey, and the citizens of London had to shut up their shops and carry their goods to the fair. The king frequently removed the mayor, for declaring that the royal command to elect a certain person sheriff was an infringement of their liberties, or for using indignant expressions at the withdrawal of an ancient privilege. The municipal authorities were sometimes deposed in the most arbitrary manner, and the city put under governors appointed by the king. New-years gifts were constantly demanded, and presents turned into precedents. Henry even added insult to injury. He was annoyed that in spite of constant draining the wealth of London increased. When he heard that the Londoners had bought up the plate he had sold to pay his private expenses, he exclaimed, 'They would buy up the treasures of Octavian, these boors who call themselves barons. London is an endless fount of wealth.'[1] Direct injuries such as these were sufficient to justify any measures of redress; it is impossible to estimate the damage to trade, the discouragement to manufacture, the loss of public confidence, from which the greatest mercantile city in England must have suffered.[2]

CHAP.
VI.

1258
other
grievances.

and insults.

---

[1] *Matt. Par.* 749. Octavian was perhaps Augustus, but more probably the Cardinal Octavian, who led the papal forces against Manfred, and to whom we find Henry writing on several occasions. The citizens had a right to the title of 'barones:' see charter of John to London, "sciatis nos concessisse . . . baronibus nostris de civitate nostra Londoniarum:' and cf. Stubbs, *Const. Hist.* i. 368.

[2] The following story illustrates Henrys way of dealing with the chief city of his kingdom. An anonymous letter was made use of

CHAP.
VI.

1258
The sea-
ports:
illegal
seizures by
the kings
officers.

These evils were probably also at the root of the discontent felt by the Cinque Ports and the other sea-port towns. The barons in 1248 complained that the king seized merchandise, in point of fact committed highway robbery by means of his officials, that he confiscated wine, wax, silk, and other goods, without thinking of paying for them. It was even alleged that his officials seized fish, and compelled the fishermen to transport it far inland.[1] The barons in 1258 complained that the kings agents at fairs and markets took twice or thrice as much as they were entitled to; the general result of all this being, as they said, that prices rose, that English merchants were ruined, and foreign trade ceased to flow into the country. A striking example of the kings arbitrary procedure in these matters is the prohibition of the export of wool, which he is said to have issued in 1244, in order to annoy the French.[2] It may be doubted if such an edict could have ever been fully executed, but the mere fact of its having been issued shows how little regard was paid to commercial interests. All these things would be the more resented by the sea-ports, owing to the importance which they felt themselves to possess; for on them fell the whole duty of sup-

• as the basis of grievous accusations against the highest municipal authorities ; the king, under the pretext of sheltering the poor, summoned these officers, refused to let them be tried by jury, as they demanded, and as their charters decreed, and threw them into prison. It was afterwards found that they were innocent, but they were not restored to office, nor was any reparation made.—*Lib. de Ant. Leg.* 30.

[1] *Matt. Par.* 743. This is supported by the accusation brought by Prince Edward against the king, of oppressing the Gascon merchants, and by the story (*Id.* 832) that the Friars Minors refused to accept certain fine robes offered by the king, knowing that he had come by them dishonestly.

[2] *Ann. Dunst.* 163. This was however repeated by Earl Simon, and, partially at least, by Edward I.

plying the navy, and of defending the coast in time

of war. This duty was common of course to London
with the Cinque Ports ; the latter however had also
an importance of their own. Instructions were issued
to Dover and other towns, to prevent the entry of
foreign emissaries without the royal leave ; the possession of Dover Castle was most important in the
barons' war, and it was entrusted by Simon de Montfort to his eldest son Henry, as the key of England
by which the invasion of foreign mercenaries was
to be prevented.

But while London was so far advanced in material *Other
towns not
so far ad-
vanced :*
prosperity and in political ideas, and while the other
sea-ports followed her example, the majority of the
towns were in a more backward condition.[1] Barons
of London and barons of the Cinque Ports we hear
of, but in hardly any other cities. The castles of
the great lords, the magnificent abbeys and episcopal
palaces, the homes of the smaller barons and other
landed proprietors, gave the country an air of wealth
and splendour which was totally absent from the
towns. They were still in many cases mere collections
of the poorest and weakest part of the community.
They had hardly any independent existence ; they *their dependence
on the king.*
were generally royal demesne, subject to tallage and
other exactions at the kings pleasure, or they were
equally at the mercy of some great noble. Many had
indeed got considerable municipal privileges, such as
York, Lincoln, Oxford, Winchester, but for these
they looked to the king and to the king only. Their
traditions, so far as they went, generally led them in

---

[1] See Prof. Brewers preface to *Monumenta Franciscana.*

CHAP.
VI.

1253
Contrast
between the
sea-port
and other
towns.

the same direction ;[1] Northampton and Leicester had' supported Henry II against his sons; Northampton had helped John against the barons. Their budding life naturally looked to the monarchy for protection against the tyranny of feudalism, and Henry III, like his father and grandfather, had shown them great favour. The evils from which London and the other mercantile ports suffered did not press so heavily on the inland towns; their trade was but small, and the spirit of liberty was not so strong in them as in the sea-faring population.[2] Not many towns had got beyond the wish for mere passive liberty, or at most for municipal authority. The municipal freedom of London had been completed by the liberty of electing its own mayor. The citizens were strong enough to protect themselves, and had nothing more to gain by connexion with the Crown, while they had everything to lose by its rapacity. They began to covet a share in the government of the country, from which they were, in their corporate existence, as completely excluded as the uncultured peasants outside their walls. The same idea was much later in presenting itself to the minds of the generality of townsfolk, and yet they had to be included when the franchise was extended to the sea-ports, however little gratitude they felt for the gift. From these reasons we find London and the Cinque Ports among the most active if not the most efficient supporters of Simon de Montfort ; while the other

---

[1] In 1258-65 Nottingham and Northampton seem to have been on the Baronial side, while Bristol, Worcester, Oxford, Winchester, &c. were decidedly royalist.

[2] Cf. the spirited reply made by the men of the Cinque Ports to Edward I in 1293.

towns were mostly neutral, if not actively on the side
of the king.

The only remaining element of the reform party, the Universities, did not perhaps add much practical weight, in a struggle which had to be decided by the sword, but their moral influence was great, and that was almost entirely with Simon de Montfort. The importance of Oxford had risen in this century to an unprecedented height, and the number of students is said to have reached 15,000.[1] The distinct existence of the University, with a Chancellor and a jurisdiction of its own, was recognised by royal edicts. Its fame was in all lands : many teachers at Paris were Oxford men.[2] The study of logic and the appeal to the understanding, so actively favoured by the Franciscans, had introduced a freedom of discussion which was applied to politics. The hatred of foreigners, which was so strong throughout England, found vivid expression at Oxford in the attack on the servants of the legate Otho in 1238 ; an anti-royalist feeling was probably at the bottom of the frequent collisions with the townsfolk which occurred at both Universities. The reforming tendencies of the younger portion of Oxford were sufficiently shown by the fact that in 1264 the students turned out *en masse* to join the national party ; and this event fully justified the king's suspicions if not his policy, when he issued orders for the temporary suppression of the University. Lastly, Bishop Grosseteste never relinquished his early connexion with Oxford, and stood forth as its protector on every possible occasion. Adam Marsh, its

[1] *Rishanger, Chron.* 22.
[2] E.g. Edmund Rich, afterwards Archbishop.

Universal
alienation
from the
king.

Disunion
in the
national
party.

The
country
ripe for
change.

Doctor Illustris, was a popular lecturer there, and at the same time an active politician. Which side these men favoured in the struggle we have clearly seen.

Thus it appears that almost all classes of society were alienated from the king, but they were not yet united against him. The two classes that were able to take the initiative had not acted in real unison since the time of John ; their interests were not so far interwoven nor mutually dependent enough to force them into alliance, till the grievances of each grew to such an extent as to convince them that they were necessary to each other. They had made attempts, as in 1244, to combine, but the combination failed to produce any effect ; we are told they were disunited and undecided. The disunion was kept up by the king, who often sought to win the great barons by favours, and, if we are to believe the historians, he was not unsuccessful in bribing several who seemed to have put their hands to the plough.[1] As long as the Pope confined himself to exactions from the Church the barons looked on comparatively unmoved, though protesting now and then ; but when he began to support the king, and to drag him into transactions which affected the whole realm, they began to be seriously alarmed. The result of this feeling was seen in 1256, when the clergy were on the point of giving way to Rustand, but were encouraged by lay support to resist.

But both parties might have waited long for each other, had not the man who by his character and connexions was best fitted to be the link be-

[1] See above, note 1, p. 116.

tween them seen the necessity of mutual support,
and formed the central point of contact for layman
and ecclesiastic, merchant and baron, rich and poor.
The temper of the country was by this time ready.
The 'divinity that doth hedge a king' had long ago
faded away from Henry.　More than twenty years
before this the barons had threatened to choose another
king, if he did not free himself and the country from
the hated Peter des Roches.　Men had begun to laugh
at his authority ; they had seen through his ruses, his
pretext of a crusade, or a war with France ; the incapacity he showed in the conduct of the Gascon wars
and in his expeditions against the Welch convinced
them that royalty and generalship did not always go
together.　He was the first English king since the
Conquest who had decidedly failed in the art of war.
Ill-omened comparisons between him and his father
became frequent.　'He takes the cross as John did,' it
was remarked.[1]　When he met with opposition from
the Master of the Hospitallers, he asked, 'Will ye
expel me like my father John ? '[2]　His ungovernable
temper had given bitter offence to many of the nobles,
and degraded him in the eyes of all.　In 1255 he
attacked the Earl Marshal, who was defending his
friend Robert de Ros, with violent language, and called
him a traitor before the assembled peers.　'Thou
liest,' replied the earl, 'and what couldst thou do if thou
wert in the right ? '　'I would seize thy corn,' said
Henry, 'and thresh it out and sell it.'　'And I,' retorted
Bigod, 'would send thee the heads of thy threshers.'[3]
When such a scene was possible, Henry must have

---

[1] *Matt. Par.* 849.　　[2] *Id.* 854.　　[3] *Id.* 917.

CHAP.
VI.

1258
Political
ideas on the
monarchy.
sunk very low in popular estimation ; but there were
still more dangerous indications of political ideas
which might be fatal to an arbitrary system of government.   On an occasion already alluded to the Master
of the Hospitallers, when Henry wished to cancel his
charter, said to him, 'As long as thou keepest justice
thou canst be king ; as soon as thou breakest it, thou
ceasest to be a king.'   And in the same spirit the
clergy, answering Rustand, had compared the Popes
rights to those of the king, declaring the duty of both
to be to defend and not to waste the goods of their
subjects.[1]

Political
poem on
the battle
of Lewes,
The political opinions of the day received their
highest development in the great poem, written a few
years later than the point we have reached, on the
occasion of the battle of Lewes.[2]   We find here put
forward a noble ideal of political duty, as incumbent
on king and subjects, and a thoughtful conception of
liberty in its relation to law, combined with a breadth
of rational feeling and a depth of political insight
which would alone be sufficient to raise the movement
we are examining far above the rank of a mere feudal
which ex-
presses the
ideas of
Earl
Simon.
revolt.   That the poem embodies the ideas which
animated Simon de Montfort there can be no doubt,
though it is possible he would have been unable, if
called upon, to formulate them so clearly ; for the

---

[1] 'Secundum quod dicimus, omnia esse principis, ac si diceretur
defensione non dispersione.'--*Matt. Par.* 920.

[2] *Polit. Songs*, ed. Wright, p. 72.   This poem is written in the usual
trochaic rhythm, of even and elegant flow, and in generally correct
Latin.   It consists of 968 lines, and is divided into two exactly equal
parts, of which the first is a defence of Simon de Montfort and a
summing up of the case against his enemies ; the second is a general
statement of principles and their application.   For the first half see
below, s.a. 1264.

first half consists of a minute and careful defence of his policy and actions, in a tone of so warm approbation that it could only have been written by one of the staunchest of his partisans. It seems likely on many grounds that it emanated from the pen of a Franciscan, but the authorship cannot be determined with any certainty.

The whole root of the quarrel is said to lie in this, that the king wishes to be free to rule exactly as he pleases. This, say his friends, is the only real kingship. The kings will is law. He merely acts as every great lord is entitled to do, dealing as he pleases with his own ;[1] if he mismanages his property, on him falls the loss, but no one interferes with him ; the king merely claims the same liberty, and moreover only that which his predecessors had before him. Therefore the barons have no right to interfere with the appointment of high officers, or the custody of castles and the like, which things concern only the king. The barons answer that, inasmuch as they are bound to protect the kingdom from foreign invasion, they are bound to protect it also from internal treachery. They do not attack the king, but his worst enemies, when they expel his evil counsellors. Those who rule the king for their selfish interests, and waste and impoverish the realm by introducing aliens and ousting the native nobility, do as much harm to the country as those who invade it with arms in their

CHAP. VI.

1253

Arguments for and against an absolute monarchy.

---

[1] This was actually argued by the king on one occasion (*Matt. Par.* 748) ; for a similar argument from the disobedience of his subjects. cf. *Matt. West.* 272. It is worth while to remark that the same argument was used in 1642 to support the kings claim to the town of Hull and its magazines, and was rebutted by Pym on the ground that the kings towns are his own no more than his people are his own.

hands. It is all one whether the king acts of malice prepense or is led away by ill advice ; the barons are equally bound to assert their position as defenders of their country.[1]

Political poem: the supremacy of law.

The king is not superior to the law.[2] He asks, 'Why am I to be limited in the choice of the officers by whom I rule?' The answer is that that is not true liberty which is totally unlimited. On the contrary, true liberty is not lost by wholesome restraint, true power does not disappear under regulated compulsion.[3] The law which limits royal power really enfranchises it, because it prevents it from being hurt by evil. Such a law is no slavery, but the saving of honour. It is not reckoned as impotence in God that He cannot sin. In like manner the king may do all that is good, but may not do what is evil ; and this is the gift of God. Moreover, his duty is, since his people are Gods people, and are entrusted by God to him, to love and help them. If he does so, he deserves

---

[1] ' Bracton reckons as superior to the king "not only God and the law, but his court of earls and barons, for the former (comites) are so styled as associates of the king, and whoever has an associate has a master ; so that if the king were without a bridle, that is, the law, they ought to put a bridle upon him."'—Hallam, *Middle Ages* ii. 331. In the first count of the indictment made against the Despensers in 1321 (*Statutes*, i. 182), an almost identical argument is said to have been used by the younger Hugh to get influence over Edward II.

[2] ' The king must not be subject to any man, but to God and the law ; for the law makes him king.'—*Bracton*, i. 8 ; and again, ' The king can do nothing on earth, being the minister of God, but what he can do by law.'—*Id.* iii. 9.

[3] The same idea is applied by Grosseteste to the Pope, who possesses ' potestatem in his quæ operantur ad ædificationem, non in his quæ ad ruinam.'—*Matt. Par.* 918 : cf. his sermon before the Council of Lyons, quoted by Stubbs (*Const. Hist.* ii. 301), ' præsidentibus huic sedi sacratissimæ in quantum indutis Christum et in quantum vere præsidentibus in omnibus est obtemperandum : sin autem quis eorum, quod absit, superinduat amictum cognationis et carnis . . . . obtemperans ei in hujusmodi manifeste se separat a Christo, &c.'

honour at their hands ; if not, he loses his authority,
and must be recalled into the right way by the people.
Mutual dependence therefore is right ; let a prince so
reign that he may never find it necessary to avoid
depending on his subjects. The prince that does so
will find it result in his own ruin.

But supposing such a foolish prince to exist, what
is to be done ? He will go wrong if he chooses his
own counsellors. What authority then remains ?
None but that of the community.[1] It is in the collective memory of the nation alone that the truth concerning the laws and customs of the realm can be
discovered. Tradition is alive in the people, for they
daily use the laws of their fathers. Appeal must
therefore be made to the community ; its opinion
must be ascertained. The community should choose
those persons as counsellors whose interests are most
wrapped up with those of their country : such men
will feel in their own persons the wrongs of their
country, as the limbs feel with the whole body.

Further, although it is pre-eminently necessary
that those who sit in office shall be just and wise, their
obligation does not stop short there. Subjects who
waste or abuse their property must be checked, for
the whole kingdom suffers if part be destroyed.
Thus the kings argument from the liberty allowed to
every subject falls to the ground.[2] No one can do

---

[1] The word used is communitas or universitas. Bracton writes, at the
close of this reign, ‘Cum legis vigorem habeat quicquid de consilio et de
consensu magnatum et reipublicæ communi sponsione, auctoritate regis
sive principis præcedente, juste fuerit definitum et præceptum.’—
Bracton, i. 1, expanding the definition given by Justinian.

[2] It is remarkable, as showing the obstinacy of the feudal idea of
property, that the kings argument is not met directly by the counter-
statement, that what is subject to him is not his own.

CHAP.
VI.

1258
Political
poem : the
king to be
ruled by
law ;

quite as he will, but is under authority. The ultimate authority rests with the whole community. Law
is light to him who would guide his steps and those of
his subjects aright. The law of the universe is well
called a law of fire, for fire lights, warms, burns. Such
a fire is the law to a king. He cannot change the
law. It is often said, ' the kings will is law.' Truth
says otherwise, for law stands if the king fall. · Law
is like fire, for it lights as truth, warms as charity,
burns as zeal : with these virtues as his guides the
king will rule well. He will then remember that he
holds office not for his own but for others' good. If he
so truly love his people, he will consult and inform his
counsellors, however wise he be, in order to make all
of one mind, even as the Lord told His disciples of
what He should do. Let the king seek the glory of
God, and learn to rule himself first : without that he
can never rule men.

From all this the conclusion is, first, that it is the
sacred duty of the barons, as representing the community, to look to and protect the welfare of the
kingdom, and to interfere in the government with
that object ; secondly, that this object is best secured
by seeing that the king have round him native counsellors, not strangers or favourites, who upset all law
and the venerable custom of the land.

Such are the political principles put forward by
an unknown writer, six hundred years ago, as those
on which the leader of the reform party acted. It was
·a pity that Simons most powerful supporters did not
understand them better. It is the great doctrine of a
General Council that is here laid down, the doctrine
that the voice of God finds its truest expression in

the voice of the people ; not the people acting on
mere impulse, or with unguided judgment, but acting
on the traditional and collective experience of ages,
as embodied in law. In this case law is not looked and of law:
on as a mere compact, but as a living growth, added
to and kept alive by each succeeding generation. It
is therefore not a codified law nor a collection of royal
edicts that is here meant, but rather an active tendency or principle, the resultant of ages of order and
rule, which will on any special occasion lead the
people by instinct to a right decision, and will supply
a constant guide to the ruler, as a sort of political
conscience, by giving him insight into the truth, love
for his people, enthusiasm for the right. It is to be
observed that this verdict of the popular voice is not
claimed on all questions, but only on those into which
an insight is given by popular interest and experience. Some little confusion is caused by the dif- interpreta-
ferent senses in which the word law is used : at one words
time it appears to be formulated and written law, the 'law,'
clearly-defined boundary of royal power ; at another
it is tradition or custom, living in popular institutions ;
at another—and this is the most general sense—it is
the national or the individual conscience. It is also and 'com-
difficult to see exactly what is meant by the com- munity.'
munity of the realm. There can hardly have been
present in the authors mind any notion of universal
suffrage. The barons are looked on as the rightful
supporters of and sharers in the government ; the existing theory of the constitution is kept in view ; it is
probable therefore that the word is used in its usual
sense, as implying not only the whole body of tenants-
in-chief, but also subtenants and freeholders and

1258
Contrast
between the
political
poem and
the policy of
Henry III :

his wilful-
ness and
imprudence
inexcus-
able.

probably all freemen. The composition of Simon de Montforts Parliament may throw some light on this.

Limited as is the political liberty claimed, and moderate as are the conclusions arrived at, nothing can be imagined more antagonistic to the system of government pursued by Henry III than the broad and liberal principles on which the poem is based. That system was essentially autocratic. The European position to which Henrys grandfather had raised the monarchy, his connexions with other sovereigns, the example of the Emperor Frederick II, and, most of all, the growth of royal power in France, induced him with his imaginative and sanguine, but weak and unstatesmanlike, nature to enter upon a foreign policy, which demanded for any chance of success the resolution of Henry II combined with the subtlety of Innocent III. His expenses were necessarily very large, and some excuse may be made for him in the fact that the regular royal revenues were probably far from sufficient for what he attempted. But it is obvious that he need never have attempted it—that he ought never to have attempted it. His French wars were unnecessary ; nothing could be more absurd than his Sicilian scheme. His grandfather had abstained from foreign interference as much as possible, yet he was far more respected abroad than Henry III. And even had he chosen to take up an active policy abroad, it is probable that with care and good government he would have carried the baronage with him. The aids which they granted him as it was would have been indefinitely increased, had he acted by their counsel, dropped his foreign favourites, and ceased from waste and illegal exaction. All they

asked him, until driven beyond endurance, was that
he should keep his word.   It seems impossible to
find any good defence for Henry, even though we
should attribute nothing but selfish motives to the
barons ; and this, though true to a great extent of
many, cannot be said of their leader, or of the party,
however small, which embraced the principles just
stated.   What could be expected of a struggle, in
which ideas of liberty were propounded with the clearness and power of the political poem, while Henry
had apparently nothing better to oppose to them than
the plea that he merely claimed a privilege allowed
to every one, that of acting as he pleased ; or the
argument that, as his subjects did not keep his laws,
he could not be expected to observe his charters ? [1]

[1] See note 1, p. 179.

CHAPTER VII.

THE REVOLUTION OF 1258.

CHAP.
VII.
——
1258
Miserable
state of the
country.

THE wet summer of 1257 had caused a very bad harvest; it was followed by a hard winter, and a late, cold spring. A terrible famine was the result. In the early part of the year 1258 so many persons died of hunger that their bodies were left lying on the roadside, and in London alone 15,000—probably an exaggerated reckoning—are said to have perished.[1] Corn was introduced from Germany, but the king, while his people were starving round him, could not resist the temptation of seizing the corn and selling it at famine prices. The attempt was stopped, but the wrong was enough to goad a gentler people than the English into rebellion. The Welch had harried the frontiers all the preceding year, and, emboldened by success, had made a league with Scotland,[2] and continued

Fresh
papal exac-
tions.

their attacks this spring. Lastly, as if there were not already misery enough, the papal legate, Arlot or Harold, came to England, armed with bulls threatening to excommunicate the English Church if they

---

[1] *Matt. Par.* 969. In *Ann. Tewk.* 166 the number is given as 20,000.
[2] The treaty, made by the barons of Scotland, not the king, with Llewelyn and the Welch chiefs, is given in *Fœd.* i. 370.

refused assistance to Pope and king.[1] On his arrival a convocation was summoned by the Archbishop of Canterbury, which passed resolutions far stronger than any hitherto made. It was resolved that the penalty of excommunication should be inflicted on any who violated ecclesiastical privileges, these being laid down with great exactness and detail. Even the king, if he wasted the revenues of vacant benefices, was to be placed under the ban.[2] The bold attitude assumed by the clergy seems to have caused the king to give vent to a violent fit of anger, for we are told that the prelates absented themselves from the Parliament that followed 'out of caution.'[3]

At this Parliament, which met at Westminster on April 10, to discuss Welch affairs and the Papal claims, the king demanded ' untold money,'[4] for the expenses incurred in Apulia. The unprecedented magnitude of the demand produced general consternation, and William of Valence began to lay the blame of all these evils on English traitors. The fear of provoking universal wrath caused him to specify the Earls of Gloucester and Leicester, which accusation he repeated before the assembled nobles, calling de Montfort in particular an old traitor and a liar. Simon retorted, 'Nay, nay, William, I am no traitor nor the son of a traitor ; our fathers were of a different breed ;' and he would have attacked him on the spot but for the kings intervention.[5] The discussion in Parliament

Parliament at Westminster : royal demands.

Insolence of William of Valence.

---

[1] The Papal commission to Arlot is dated 30 Dec., 1257.
[2] *Ann. Burt.* 412 seq.
[3] ' Forte aliqua cautela mediante.'—*Ann. Tewk.* 163 ; this must refer to the Parliament of Westminster, though referred there to the Parliament of Oxford.
[4] ' Infinitam pecuniam.'—*Matt. Par.* 963.
[5] *Matt. Par.* 963 calls Simons opponent here ' Episcopus Willelmus,

CHAP.
VII.

1258
Discussion
in Parlia-
ment.

first turned on the question of Wales, and it was decided that the army should meet at Chester towards the end of June to attack the Welch. The altercation as to the papal subsidy was not so easily settled. In the debates that ensued Leicester took the lead, demanding reparation for his recent insult, and urging the necessity for reform rather on the barons than on the king.[1] All seem to have joined in accusing Henry of gross partiality, of wasting the revenues, and of such incapacity that he allowed his country to be insulted even by the Welch, 'the very dregs of humanity.'[2] The king attempted to cut short the altercation by issuing, on April 28, an edict demanding one-third of the income of all England, as a subsidy for the Pope. This produced the long-expected outburst.

A days delay was granted, during which the barons considered their position. On the third day, April 30, they appeared in full armour at the Council-hall at Westminster, about nine o'clock in the morning. They laid down their swords at the door, and entering saluted the king with due respect. The king, terrified by their appearance, demanded the cause of their coming armed, and asked whether he was their prisoner. Whereupon Earl Roger Bigod

but Aylmer was the bishop, not William. The whole story is perhaps a mere repetition of the similar scene last year, related on p. 123 ; but this is hardly probable, for there are great differences between the two, especially in the cause given for the quarrel. Hugh of la Marche was father to William of Valence, and had deserted the English cause in 1242.

[1] 'Comes præcipue Legrecestriæ non tamen regi sed universitati præcordialiter est conquestus,' &c.—*Matt. Par.* 968. 'Sicut Simon Machabæus surrexit pro fratre suo Juda, . . sic Simon de Monte-forti pro Anglia erexit se, ut pro legibus et libertatibus ejus usque ad mortis perniciem dimicaret.'—*W. de Hemingb.* i. 304.

[2] 'Hominum quisquiliæ.'—*Id.* 968.

answered, 'Nay, my Lord King, but we ask that the CHAP. VII. Poitevins and all other aliens may be expelled from the country, for this is necessary for the honour and welfare of thy realm.' The king then inquiring how he was to meet their wishes, it was required of him that he and Prince Edward should swear an oath to impose no unusual burden on the country, but by the advice of twenty-four prudent men of England, and should deliver the great seal to the man whom the twenty-four should choose.[1] So firm a front did they show that the king gave way, and swore on the relics of St. Edward to do as they wished. In consideration of his formal promise to reform the state of the country before the end of the year, the barons declared they would do their best with the community to get them to grant an aid for the Sicilian enterprise, if only the Pope would abate his demands. It is to be observed that the barons did not promise for themselves, but made use of the 'community' to leave a loophole for escape if the king should break his word. But, knowing they had a Proteus to deal with,[2] they made matters safer by insisting on the immediate election of the committee,[3]

Marginal notes: 1258 their demands, granted by the king. Promise of aid. Election of the committee of twenty-four.

---

[1] This account, apparently by an eye-witness, is taken from *Ann. Tewk.* 163 ; an examination of the context shows that it must belong to this Parliament, though the history, as given in these annals, is very confused. *W. de Hemingb.* i. 305, amplifies the address of the Barons.

[2] 'Nesciebant quomodo suum Protea tenere voluissent.'—*Matt. Par.* 965.

[3] 'Per xii fideles de concilio nostro *jam* electos,' &c.—*Fœd.* i. 371, writ dated May 2, in which the kings consent to the scheme is given. The words in *Ann. Burt.* 445, seem to show that the twenty-four were elected at this time, not at Oxford ; 'Fuerunt etiam in eodem parliamento apud Oxoniam xxiv electi, &c.:' i.e. 'the chosen were present at Oxford.' The embassy to France consisted of 'Nuncii ex electis Angliæ comitibus et baronibus,' which must refer to the committee.—*Matt. Par.* 968. The manner of their election is not stated, but the two bodies of twelve were doubtless elected separately by the two parties, and either at or immediately after this Parliament of Westminster.

CHAP.
VII.

1258
The com-
mittee
to meet at
Oxford.

twelve from the kings side and twelve from that of the barons—so distinctly were parties divided by this time—by whose advice the king was to act. This committee was to meet at Oxford, within a month after Whitsuntide, and proceed at once to the reform of the realm. The place of meeting was probably chosen as being more central than London, and therefore better adapted both for an assembly of the whole baronial force, with which to overawe the royalists, and also as a rendezvous for the army which was to march against the Welch.[1] The promises of the king and Edward, to reform the realm and to acquiesce in the provisions to be made by the twenty-four, having been published,[2] Parliament broke up.

The committee seem to have taken the government in hand at once, and on which side the power lay was evident from the first. An embassy, consisting of Simon de Montfort and Peter of Savoy, the ambassadors of former years, Geoffrey and Guy of Lusignan, the kings half-brothers, and Hugh Bigod, all but one being members of the committee, was

appointed to go to France, with powers to prolong the truce, but really, as it appears, to beg the king not to interrupt the course of reform, 'which was to tend to the peace and benefit of their own and the surrounding nations.'[3] Meanwhile the ports were

---

[1] Dr. Pauli suggests that it was because Oxford was a neutral spot, but that epithet is more fairly applied to a place in which neither party is represented, than to one like Oxford, in which both parties were so strongly represented as to lead to constant breaches of internal neutrality.

[2] Writs dated 2 May, *Fœd.* i. 370, 371. They are tested only by friends of the king.

[3] So *Matt. Par.* 968 declares ; the writ (dated 8 May) in *Fœd.* i. 371 mentions nothing but the prolongation of the truce. It is possible that Geoffrey of Lusignan was one of the kings twelve : see note 1, p. 193.

occupied, for bitter experience had shown the power
of foreign mercenaries.

The famous assembly which was to earn, with a
strange mixture of justice and injustice, the title
of the Mad Parliament, met at Oxford on the appointed day, June 11, 1258. Not only the committee
came, but a great number of barons and clergy,
followed by all who owed military service. It was
a return to the ancient Teutonic assembly of all
the nation, with arms in their hands. The council
began with the presentation of a long list of grievances,
and a petition for their redress.[1] The grievances, like
those mentioned in the baronial petition of 1215, fall
mostly under two heads, territorial and financial ; it is
the abuse of the royal power, as feudal lord and supreme
judge, against which the barons plead. The first division, affecting especially the barons, had the preced-
ence, as before ; but the second, which regarded the
lower ranks of society more than the upper, was by no
means neglected. The grand principle of alliance
between rich and poor is evident here, though
not so distinctly as it had been forty years before.
Many were the matters requiring redress ; but the
most important point, the most crying need, was the
expulsion of the aliens, and the delivery of the royal
castles and forts into the hands of Englishmen ; the
next, the appointment of a Justiciar to deal equal justice to rich and poor.

The king seems either from fear or from a recognition of the justice of these claims to have been
inclined to yield, but his half-brothers, supported by

[1] Given in *Ann. Burt.* 439. The most important details have been
already given in ch. vi.

CHAP.
VII.

1258
Parliament
of Oxford :
oath of
the barons.

Prince Edward, resisted, vowing they would die before they gave up a foot of land. Their resistance produced fresh defensive measures on the part of the barons. The ports were more closely guarded, and the gates of London were fitted with new bolts, and jealously shut at night. After several days of stormy and apparently fruitless debate, the barons met in the Convent of the Dominicans, and in the most solemn way swore 'they would not for life or death, for love or hate, desist from their resolve, till they had purified from the foreign scum the land in which they and their fathers were born.' [1] It was a meeting to be compared with that more famous one, the meeting of the Tiers Etat in the tennis-court at Versailles ; it would have been well if both bodies had kept their

oath pure. After the oath the Earl of Leicester, as an alien, gave up his castles of Kenilworth and Odiham, and called upon the others to follow. They still refused with vehemence, William of Valence as usual taking the lead. Thereupon Simon cut the matter short by crying, 'The castles or thy head.' Terrified by this threat, and by the attitude of the rest of the baronage, and knowing that 'if the nobles did not carry out their intention, the whole mass of the people would besiege them and pull their castles

about their ears,' [2] they secretly left Oxford and fled without drawing rein to Wolvesey, the stronghold of the Bishop-Elect of Winchester. There we must leave them awhile, and return to the history of the Parliament.

The composition of the original committee of

---

[1] This is probably the oath of the commonalty given in the Provisions of Oxford, though there it does not take exactly this form. The words in the text are taken from *Matt. Par.* 971.
[2] *Ibid.*

twenty-four is somewhat uncertain, owing perhaps to the doubtful attitude of the Earl of Gloucester. Only twenty-three names are given, probably because he was claimed by both parties.[1] On the kings side appear first and foremost his own relations: his half-brothers, Aylmer, Bishop-Elect of Winchester, William of Valence, and Guy of Lusignan, and the Earl of Warenne, his brother-in-law. John Mansel, Provost of Beverley, who had served the Crown for sixteen years at least, and had risen to great wealth but little honour in its service, was one of Henrys staunchest adherents. These were the kernel of the party. Henry of Almaine, the kings nephew, played the part of the bat in the struggle, and can hardly be reckoned to either side. Fulk Basset, the Bishop of London, and John de Plessys, Earl of Warwick, represented the moderates among the clergy and the laity. The rest were royalist clergy, the Abbot of Westminster, Henry Wengham, Friar John of Darlington. It was a most unwise proceeding on the part of the king to elect John Mansel and his own brothers, men who had already drawn all the hatred of the kingdom on themselves, and made the royal cause hopeless. On the barons' side was Walter de Cantilupe, Bishop of Worcester, the friend and follower of Grosseteste. He and Simon de Montfort, with the barons John Fitz-Geoffrey, Richard de Gray,

---

[1] In the report of the Oxford Provisions in *Ann. Burt.* 447, Gloucester appears among the barons; in a writ dated 22 June, 1258 (*Rot. Lit. Pat.* 42 Hen. III, m. 6), quoted in the Lords' *Report*, he is mentioned on the kings side. He undoubtedly acted on the side of the barons at this time. Perhaps Geoffrey of Lusignan was the kings twelfth man, or the Archbishop of Canterbury : see Stubbs, *Const. Hist.*, ii. 82, and Appendix iii.

O

1258
Committee
of twenty-
four : the
baronial
party.

William Bardulf, Hugh Despenser, and Peter de Montfort, Simons cousin, represented the extremes. Fitz-Geoffrey was said by some to come next in importance to the Earl of Leicester, but unfortunately died this year. The Earls of Gloucester, Norfolk, and Hereford, with Hugh Bigod and Roger Mortimer, represented the old baronial party. The first seven held firm to the end ; the Earl of Gloucester died before the reaction which he began had led to a renewed outbreak, but the rest had all taken the kings side in 1264. Roger Bigod was on the winning side again after Lewes ; Bohun and Mortimer were too much infected with the lawless life of the Border to endure the supremacy of Simon de Montfort.

Measures
of the
twenty-
four:

This committee, as has been said, was to take measures for the reform of the realm. They proceeded therefore by a somewhat complicated system of election, to establish a form of government, which should embody both a permanent executive and a regular legislature, and should engraft on the aristocratic *régime* to some extent at least the influence of

appoint-
ment of a
council of
fifteen.

the community. Each party chose two electors out of the twelve representatives of the other side. This arrangement would naturally result in the election of the four men whose opinions most nearly approached each other. The four electors thus chosen were the Earl of Warwick, John Mansel, and the two Bigods. It is hard to see why the reformers picked out John Mansel, unless it was because they hoped to be able to terrify him ; if so, they were probably right. These four had to elect a Royal Council of fifteen ; but, owing to the overpowering influence of the barons, and the flight of the aliens, the two royalist electors were the only members of the kings twelve who were elected into the council. Other members, more or less royalist, were the Archbishop of Canterbury, Peter of Savoy, and John Audley, the last being a very firm adherent to the king. On the other hand nine of the baronial committee were chosen on the council, as well as the Earl of Albemarle, so that they had a majority of two-thirds.[1] The duties of the fifteen were to give counsel to the king on all matters pertaining to the government of the country, to hear and amend all grievances, and to look after the administration of justice. Their authority was in fact almost supreme. They were to attend the Parliaments, which were to be held thrice a year, on stated days, in spring, summer, and autumn; they might also be held on other occasions when the king and his council should think fit.

In addition to the council of fifteen, twelve men were elected by the 'community,' who were to attend the Parliaments and act in conjunction with the fifteen, and what the twelve decided the community were to acquiesce in. The reason given for this arrangement was the saving of expense. So far it

CHAP. VII.

1258
The council of fifteen :

their duties

Representatives of the community.

---

[1] According to the list in *Ann. Burt.* the nine barons were the Bishop of Worcester, the Earls of Gloucester, Leicester, Norfolk and Hereford, R. Mortimer, J. Fitz-Geoffrey, R. de Gray, and P. de Montfort. The writ of 18 Oct., 1258, proclaiming in French the kings adhesion to the Provisions, omits from the list given in the text J. Mansel, but adds the Earl of Winchester and Hugh Despenser, thus making sixteen in all. The corresponding writ in English omits the Earls of Hereford and Winchester, and H. Despenser, but possibly means to include them when it states that others not named were present. The *Lib. de Ant. Leg.* p. 37, omits J. Fitz-Geoffrey, who was probably dead before the list there given was made. It is possible that the Earl of Winchester appeared in the place of J. Mansel, who was especially odious to the barons, or that some members of the twelve representatives of the community were present. Only one new member, called P. de Ballech, (? P. Basset) appears in October 1259. See Appendix iii.

CHAP.
VII.
1258
The twelve
representa-
tives do not
really re-
present
the com-
munity:

was an advance upon the corresponding clause of Magna Carta, by which it was stipulated that a general summons should be sent to all the smaller barons; inasmuch as that clause did not cut at the root of the difficulty, the unwillingness or inability of this class to attend. On the other hand, the names of these twelve representatives seem to show that they can hardly be looked on as a real representation of the whole baronial class, or the community, but only of part of it, for they are men who would have attended a Great Council as a matter of course.[1] They were in no sense representatives of the whole

many
barons lose
power
thereby.

body entitled to a share in government, as those elected in 1265 were. Further, many of the greater barons lost individually by the arrangement; for although their class as a whole gained complete command of the executive, through the permanent council of fifteen, yet it does not seem to have been intended that Parliament should consist of any others but the fifteen and the twelve, and probably the high officers if not already included. Thus many who attended the old Parliament in person would have been cut out. That these limited Parliaments were all that was contemplated appears from the very fact of the appointment

---

[1] The twelve representatives of the community are the Bishop of London, the Earls of Hereford and Winchester, H. Despenser, J. de Gray, J. de Balliol, R. de Monthaut, R. de Sumery, T. de Gresley, Giles de Argentine, P. Basset, J. de Verdun. Of these just half appear on the royal side in 1264; one only was certainly on that of the barons. It is remarkable that the Earl of Hereford appears as a member both of the fifteen and the twelve. It is possible, and on other grounds probable, that H. Bohun, the younger, a staunch adherent of de Montfort, was one of the twelve, and not his father; but this is not supported by documents. W. Bardulf is the only one of the original baronial committee who is not a member of the new Parliament, for H. Bigod, though not of the fifteen or the twelve, would surely have attended as Chief Justiciar.

of the twelve, and the special provision that the fifteen should attend. But it is not actually stated that no others shall attend, and on this point, as on many others, certainty seems to be unattainable. Lastly, in addition to the fifteen and the twelve, and in accordance with the promise made by the barons in the spring, there was elected a council of twenty-four to treat specially of aid to the king. This council was almost entirely composed of members of the other two bodies, and seems therefore to have been meant as a kind of Parliamentary Committee, only appointed for this special occasion.

The result of the whole arrangement was that the royal party were completely worsted, and the barons took the management of affairs into their own hands. But the constitution as it stands is most imperfect. One reason may be that the Parliament broke up too soon to bring it to anything like perfection ; but the real cause is the feudal and oligarchical spirit which animated its framers, and the want of constitutional experience and really liberal principles on which to build. The principles of the political poem were too far advanced for the majority of those who led the revolt of 1258. In the first place, the position of the original committee of twenty-four was entirely anomalous. Their work ought to have ceased with the establishment of the new form of government ; but the power remained with them, or rather, after the expulsion of the aliens, with the old baronial committee under a new name, for they and theirs formed a strong majority in the new Parliament. But there was set no legal limit to the duration or the extent of their power, and they might easily have made the original

CHAP.
VII.

1258
Anomalous
position of
the twenty-
four,
object of their appointment an excuse for retaining office. It was not stated whether the council or the representatives were to be perpetual, or, if not, how they were to be re-elected. That the authority of the original twenty-four was not altogether superseded is evident from the provision, that the state of the Church should be amended by them when they should be able

to do so. The relative positions and powers of the fifteen and the twelve are not defined ; it is not stated how long the council of aid is to sit. On these, and many similar points, we are left quite in the dark, and it is probable that the rulers themselves were equally in doubt.

The
scheme of
govern-
ment a
hopeless
one :
But one thing is certain : it was impossible that such a building should stand. Setting aside the certainty that jealousy and opposing interests would cause disagreement among the leaders, the scheme was a contradiction in itself. It pretended to leave the king as he was before, with all his legal privileges and rights, but with the addition of a wholesome restraint in the shape of a standing council and a representative Parliament. In reality the kings

authority was reduced to a shadow, and this cumbrous and complicated assemblage, without any centre or president, substituted for him as the fount of justice and the head of the State. The king was much more completely deprived of power than John had been by the committee of twenty-five appointed in Magna

Carta. The representation of the lower baronage, though they had a nominal share in the election of the twelve, was left as far in the background as ever, nay, further, for the new arrangement superseded the old general summons. Other tenants-in-chief than those who were actually named, as well as the free-holders and the townsfolk, were entirely neglected. No class could have been honestly satisfied with the form of government; the clergy must have been especially offended by their almost complete exclusion from power. Only the individual members of the government had an interest in keeping it up. It was a system which ran counter to the prevailing notions, whether conservative or liberal, and was sure to meet with opposition on all sides. Further, the existing institutions had been modelled on the assumption of a single and undivided central power; they got out of order at once with the division of leaders. There was no means of preventing a dead-lock, no constitutional mode of changing the government; the twelve representatives were in reality powerless against the council. The constitution was in fact an oligarchy, though with none of the prestige of ancient republican growth. It was a feudal triumph, with a merely nominal concession to constitutional principles. The kings position was insupportable ; he might have reformed all the abuses for which the barons claimed redress, but he could not submit to be superseded in all but the name of king. Yet he had no need to struggle against his bonds ; he had only to wait and the machine would fall to pieces of itself. It was this part of the barons work which gave rise to the nickname of the Mad Parliament ;[1] the experience gained by failure enabled the framers of the constitution of 1264 to make a very great advance upon the first effort. If we are to believe a most competent

CHAP.
VII.

1258
The scheme satisfactory to no one :

it introduced an oligarchy.

---

[1] The name was apparently first used in *Lib. de Ant. Leg.* p. 37, ' Insane parlamentum apud Oxoniam,' written temp. Edward I.

CHAP.
VII.

1258
Hesitaticn
of Earl
Simon.

witness,[1] Simon de Montfort showed great repugnance to the provisions, and seeing their impracticability and knowing the difficulties to which the inconstancy of their framers would give rise, he refused to swear to them. This produced general indignation, and at length Simon was induced to take the requisite oath, which he did with these words, 'By the arm of St. James, though I shall take the oath last of all and against my will, yet will I keep it inviolate, and none shall hinder me.'

The Provisions :

The redeeming points of the work were the regulations issued for the method and business, rather than

elective knights,

the form, of government. In the first place it was provided that knights should be elected in each county, who were to hear all complaints made against the sheriffs, bailiffs, and others, and to take the necessary measures for ensuring justice at the visit of the

the Church,

Chief Justiciar. The Church, as we have seen, was

London,

not to be neglected. The affairs of London and other cities were to be amended, and a special note was added as to the reform of the royal household. More

high officers,

important constitutionally was the provision that a chief justice, or two justices,[2] a chancellor, and a treasurer were to be appointed, the first to hold office only for a year, and all to be responsible at the end of each year to king and council. It is not

sheriffs,

stated by whom these high officers or the sheriffs

---

[1] *Chron. Lancercost*, s.a. 1259, but it must refer to this year. This chronicler has information from one who fought for Simon at Lewes, though the chronicle itself is of a later date.

[2] Two justices had held office together before, e.g. the Earl of Leicester and R. de Lucy under Henry II. Hugh Bigod was appointed Justiciar at Oxford ; no Chancellor was appointed for three years ; but certain persons, called sometimes by the title of Chancellor, acted as custodes sigilli.— See p. 61. note 2.

were to be appointed, but we cannot doubt in whose hands the appointment would be. The original committee of twenty-four were to appoint good men in the Exchequer. Several names of the baronial party appear as wardens of the castles, probably in the place of the banished foreigners, and they were to swear an oath which placed them under command of king and council. An oath binding the justice and the chancellor to observe the provisions to be made by the twenty-four is also given. The sheriffs were to be just and loyal men, to hold office only a year, and to give account afterwards. The authority of the justices, sheriffs, bailiffs, escheators, and other officers was carefully regulated, and bribery and extortion expressly forbidden. The whole was clenched by a confirmation of the Charter of Liberties. To these enactments, and others to be made by the Parliament, called collectively the Provisions of Oxford, the king and Prince Edward in October gave their formal consent.[1] The writ containing the royal consent was pub-

CHAP. VII.

1258

wardens of castles,

sheriffs, &c.

Confirmation of Magna Carta : consent of Henry and Edward.

---

[1] The date of this writ (18 Oct., 1258) shows that the Provisions were not all made at Oxford, but were completed in London after the interruption caused by the flight of the kings brothers. The copy given in *Ann. Burt.* is clearly not a final one, still less is it a formal document. Its order is irregular, part is in Latin, part in French. Its incompleteness is evident, e.g. in the omission of the Provision, undoubtedly passed, that no castles should be in the hands of aliens. It bears rather the appearance of a report of proceedings, resolutions passed, persons appointed, and the like. That the work was still incomplete in October is shown by the words of the kings oath. It is impossible to say with certainty what was done at Oxford, beyond the appointment of the Justiciar, the decrees as to the wardenship of castles, and as to the election of the four knights (cf. *Ann. Burt.*, *Ann. Osney*, *Fæd.* i. 375, &c., for these points). It is observable that the Provision as to the four knights is the only one in Latin, except the names of the twenty-four, and therefore probably the only statute regularly passed at Oxford. It is very doubtful whether a formal copy of the whole, in the shape of a statute, was ever made ; none such exists. Dr. Pauli, (*Simon de Mont.*, 90), referring to *T. Wykes*, p. 52, to show that a formal document

Pursuit of
the kings
brothers;

lished in English as well as in French and Latin, a noteworthy fact in its reference to the newly-arisen consciousness of nationality.

The humiliation of the king and his party was only too complete. When the flight of the kings brothers became known at Oxford, the barons at once broke up the Parliament, and taking with them the king, now a helpless instrument in their hands, they marched on Winchester. The custody of Winchester Castle was handed over to the Earl of Leicester, who from his military fame and experience probably took to some extent the position of general-in-chief.

who are
forced to
leave the
country.

Resistance on the part of the fugitives was hopeless, and, after some vain attempts at reconciliation and equally useless intervention on the part of the king, it was decided they should leave the country, taking with them money enough for their support. At first

embodying the Provisions existed, seems to have misunderstood the words. They merely refer to the fifth article or sentence of the oath taken by Henry, which runs thus, ' And if any man or woman come there against (sc. against the decrees) we will and command that all our faithful hold them as deadly foes.' There are five such articles or sentences in the oath as given in *Fœd.* i. 378. The words of T. Wykes are 'Et ne posteris lateat forma jusjurandi quod subditi regem emittere compulerunt, quinque tantum articulos continebat. Jurabant quod provisiones Oxoniæ factas . . . observarent . . . Isti quatuor articuli si observati fuissent, liciti plurimum et tolerandi fuerunt. Quintus articulus omnino illicitus fuit, et detestandus præcipue, viz. quod si quis dictis provisionibus contraire præsumeret . . . hostis publicus censeretur . . . Articulus iste totum confudit negotium.' The words refer not to the Provisions but to the kings oath. Had a complete copy of the former ever been issued, it could hardly have failed to be either in *Ann. Burt.* or *Matt. Par.* The split in the baronial party was enough to prevent completion, but it is important in judging the character of the revolution to recognise the fact that its authors did not fancy they had completed their work. It is probable that some of the Provisions were made at Winchester, after the expulsion of the aliens, for ' Ibi (sc. Wintoniæ) secundum parliamentum celebraverunt.'—*Ann. Tewk.* 165. W. de Hemingburgh (i. 306) assures us that several statutes were passed there, of a spirit antagonistic to the aliens, but his account is somewhat confused and untrustworthy.

William, as Earl of Pembroke, and Aylmer, as Bishop-   CHAP.
Elect of Winchester, were to be allowed to stay in   VII.
England, but they preferred to go with their brothers.   1258
Their property, including a large sum deposited in the   The kings
Temple, was seized ; and the Warden of Dover suc-   banished :
ceeded later in stopping another treasure which was
being sent over to them. On their arrival in France
they do not seem to have gained any favour, either from
king or people. The feeling against them was very
strong, owing chiefly to the insults they had heaped
on de Montfort, who was always regarded by the
French as one of themselves.[1] They landed at Boul-   they land
ogne, and were followed at once by Henry, Simons   in France.
son, who had crossed without his fathers knowledge, or
possibly with his secret connivance, and did his best to
stir up the French against them.[2] The feeling against
them in England was increased by the report that before their expulsion they had poisoned the Earl of
Gloucester and others at a feast at Southwark. It is certain that several of the guests died of poison, though
it did not transpire whether those accused of it had
been set on by the aliens. The Earl of Gloucester
with difficulty recovered.

From Winchester, where the barons continued   Work of
the session of their Parliament, they removed to   reform
London, where the king again confirmed the power   continued.
of the twenty-four,[3] and they, or at least the council, resumed their work of reform. But in order

---

[1] ' Mirabantur ultramarini quod virum tam nobilem et . . . præ-
commendatum audebant viri multo minus nobiles . . . corde dicto seu
facto improperando deturbare.'—*Matt. Par.* 973.

[2] *Matt. Par. ib.*, says that it was against his fathers will, others that
his father sent him.

[3] *Roy. Letters* ii. 129 ; promise in French, dated 4 Aug., 1258.

CHAP.
VII.

1258
Foreign
affairs :
Wales,

Castile,

Scotland,

Sicily,

France.

Four
knights to
hear
grievances.

to carry out their intended measures it was necessary that they should be free from anxiety abroad. While still at Oxford the united attitude of the barons and the large army there assembled had alarmed the Welch ; they sent envoys, and a truce was made before the king left the town. A conciliatory letter was also sent to the King of Castile, making excuses for the failure to help him in Africa and for Richards candidature for the empire. Shortly after the return to London, an embassy, consisting of Simon de Montfort, Peter of Savoy, and John Mansel, was appointed to make peace between the discordant parties in Scotland, which would have resulted in a cessation of hostilities on the part of the Scotch barons, who had allied with the Welch against their own king and against the English.[1] A letter was sent to the Pope concerning the Sicilian affair, to prepare him for the plainer speech which was to follow ; and he was begged to use his influence to bring about a lasting peace with France, which he was the more likely to do, since it would be indispensable if anything were to be done with regard to Sicily.[2]

Thus secured from immediate danger abroad, and freed from the plague of aliens at home, the barons could begin in earnest the work of reform. The summons to elect four knights to examine into grievances was sent round to the counties immediately on the kings return to London. It was however nearly three months before the kings oath to abide by the Provi-

---

[1] It is hardly probable that this embassy went to Scotland. In Sept. 1258 three ambassadors, the Earls of Albemarle and Hereford, and John Baliol, met the King of Scotland at Melrose, and settled terms of peace.—*Chron. Mailros*, 183.

[2] *Fœd.* i. 372 seq.

sions was published through the counties. At the same time a proclamation was issued, explaining the reasons of the delay that had taken place in the completion of the work, and promising reform as speedily as possible. All men were invited to make their complaints to the four knights, and were encouraged by the regulations which had been already made as to the conduct of sheriffs and other royal officers.[1] Similar edicts were issued to prevent extortion on the part of these persons, and for some time, we are told, the good effects of these lasted.[2] No little compulsion had however to be used. The reluctance of Prince Edward to agree to the provisions had been all this time very great. He was therefore put into a kind of honourable arrest, by the appointment of four so-called counsellors, or tutors, who were to attend him, three of them being among the twelve representatives. A reform of his household was also in contemplation, and regulations were to be made as to all foreigners in England, whether Romans, merchants, or others.[2] Perhaps the most important step, and one which was absolutely necessary to conciliate the Church, was the final repudiation of the papal projects with regard to Sicily. A long letter was written to the Pope,[3] in which the barons stated that since the king had acted without their advice, they repudiated all thoughts of further movement in the matter. To this they added a general defence of their proceedings. They set forth the evils which the kings brothers had inflicted on the country, declaring that the Bishop-Elect of Win-

CHAP.
VII.

1258
Proclama-
tion of the
barons.

Resistance
of Edward.

Repudia-
tion of the
Sicilian
scheme.

[1] *Fœd.* i. 375, 377 ; cf. *Ann. Burt.* 453.
[2] *Lib. de Ant. Leg.* 39.
[3] *Fœd.* i. 373.

chester was the worst of all, and that even if they (the barons) were willing, the people would not allow him to come back : they therefore prayed the Pope to remove him, a proceeding which they declared quite justifiable, since he had not yet been consecrated. To all of this the Pope turned a deaf ear, and no answer was sent till two years later. He shortly afterwards excommunicated those who refused to pay his merchants, and threatened to put the kingdom under an interdict if the aid for Sicily were withheld; and, in contempt of the baronial request, he consecrated Aylmer, who would have returned to take possession of his bishopric had not his death, which occurred in 1260, prevented him.

So far then the barons acted up to their promises, and all went well. The compulsory measures taken, violent as they were, were probably not more violent than necessary. The work the barons had in hand was no light one. How far the present system of government was intended to be permanent it is very hard to say ; but there are no signs that the barons thought of yielding the power they had usurped. They had in fact only just entered upon their greatest difficulty, that of adapting the old administrative system to a parliamentary form of government : and upon this rock more than on any other they were to suffer shipwreck. They set to work however with energy, holding council day by day in the Temple.[1] For a time the country was heartily with them : but it was rather the measures of administrative reform, the healing of great abuses such as those connected

---

[1] *Lib. de Ant. Leg.* 39.

with the sheriffs, the expulsion of the aliens, and the like, which met with popular approval. The form of government was popular, or at least tolerated, only so long as it appeared to be successful. The joy of the country was great, but it was premature. The city of London welcomed the Provisions, and the mayor and citizens swore to observe them. The first measures of the barons, we are told, raised great hopes. The expulsion of the aliens made men hope that a similar end would be put to all papal and legal exactions.[1] The relief was sudden, ' like the waking out of sleep ;'[2] the gratitude to the reformers was proportionate. ' Great and arduous are the matters to be settled, and such as cannot be quickly or easily brought to an end,' writes one to the monks of Burton ; 'the barons go boldly forward with their task : may fortune favour them.'[3] It might have been apprehended that King Richard would make some opposition to the movement ; but it was not in his nature to be irreconcileable. His return to England in January 1259 removed all fears on this head. He was not allowed to land till he had taken the oath to the Provisions, which, after some show of reluctance, removed by a letter from the king,[4] he consented to do. After this concession his arrival in London was a matter of great joy to the citizens,[5] and it was doubtless hoped

CHAP.
VII.

1258-59
Popularity
of the
reforms.

---

[1] 'Bonæ leges constitutæ sunt.'—*Ann. Wigorn.* 445. ' Statuta facta ad utilitatem totius regni.'—*Lib. de Ant. Leg.* 54.

[2] *Ann. Wav.* 350.

[3] *Ann. Burt.* 445. This letter describes the immediate intentions of the barons, and incidentally shows that the words 'de hospitio regis' in the Provisions refer to the household, not the hostelry, of the king. See Mr. Luards translation, *Ann. Burt.* 504.

[4] *Fœd.* i. 380, dated 23 Jan., 1259. A letter had been sent him as early as 4 Nov., 1258, bidding him take the oath.—*Roy. Letters* ii. 132.

[5] *Lib. de Ant. Leg.* 39.

CHAP.
VII.

1258-59
Beginning
of a re-
action: its
causes;
that he would play his old part of mediator with success.

But already there were signs of discontent visible. Every element of royalistic feeling was sure to grow stronger while the monarch was powerless; loyal sentiments, latent conservatism, fear of the untried, sympathy for the conquered, all worked in the same direction. The throb of joy with which the reformers had been greeted in the first flush of victory was followed by a steadily-increasing reaction. Their own violence was probably that which turned the wavering scale. A strange instance of the blind hate with which they pursued the aliens was to be seen in the decree passed at Winchester, by which it was forbidden to sell wool to foreigners.[1] But if the principles of free trade had to wait nearly six centuries for recognition, it is no wonder that in the heat of the conflict such laws were considered the height of wisdom. So bitter was the popular hatred of the very name of alien that a short time after this an Italian, whom the Pope had promoted to a prebend at St. Pauls, was murdered in broad daylight in the streets of London, and not a hand was raised to stop the murderers.[2] More annoying than the ignorance of political economy appear to have been the proceedings of the justices. Hugh Bigod incurred considerable odium in London by holding pleas in the city, which according to the charters were to be held only by the sheriffs, and by the severity and arbitrary nature of his sentences.[3] He seems to have shown too little regard for privileges, probably as having been conferred by

---

[1] *W. de Heming.* 306.   [2] *Ann. Dunst.* 214.
[3] *Lib. de Ant. Leg.* 40.

the king. Complaints of him in this respect were
made both by St. Albans and Dunstaple; in the
latter place he enforced a fine by seizing all the property of the monastery till the fine was paid.[1] On
the other hand, his activity was commendable; he
journeyed with two associates through every county,
and, according to some authorities, did justice well,
hearing the complaints made through the four
knights, and redressing many old wrongs.[2] But the
difficulty of keeping the judicial system in proper
order must have been immense. The unlettered
barons were but poor lawyers, and yet would naturally have avoided employing the officials of the
former *régime*, who, though creatures of the Court,
were probably the only persons sufficiently acquainted
with the law. Nature too increased the trouble.
After the famine in the early part of the year, an
unusually fine crop gave hope of some compensation;
but it was almost entirely destroyed by heavy rains
and floods. Corn in great quantities had to be
brought in from abroad to keep even the wealthier
classes from starvation. A pestilence broke out, which
carried off the Bishop of London and many less
noble victims. There were doubtless many then, as
there would be some even now, to lay the blame of
such calamities on the Government.

But the great difficulty was caused by the disunion which was already creeping in among the
leaders, and the inclination already shown by the

CHAP.
VII.
1258–59
Causes of
the re-
action: pro-
ceedings
of the
justices;

---

[1] *Ann. Dunst.* 212.
[2] *Matt. West.* 283; *Matt. Par.* 977 says that the sheriff of
Northants, who had followed in the steps of his predecessor, was deposed and 'duro ac diro carceri mancipatus.' See p. 163, note 3.

Hostility of
Henry to
de Mont-
fort.

king to break loose from the Provisions. Soon after the Parliament of Oxford, some of the barons, yielding, according to one chronicler, to their own wicked impulses and the promises of the king, deserted their party.[1] The inveterate hostility of Henry towards de Montfort, a feeling certainly not very unnatural, was shown by an incident which took place in the summer of 1258.[2] The king in passing down the Thames from his palace at Westminster was caught in so violent a thunderstorm that he was obliged to land at a spot which happened to be close to the palace of the Bishop of Durham, then occupied by the earl. On hearing of this Simon at once went and offered him shelter, telling him there was no cause for alarm, as the storm would soon be over. The king, by no means in jest, but in grim earnest, replied, ‘Thunder and lightning I fear exceedingly, but, by the head of God, I fear thee more than all the storms in the world.’ To which the earl quietly answered, ‘Sire, it is unjust and incredible that thou shouldst fear me, who am thy true friend, and loyal to thee and thine and to the realm of England ; but thy enemies, those who ruin thee and tell thee lies— them thou oughtest to fear.’ The incident, we are told, caused great anxiety in the minds of all who had their country at heart. The oath, by which the king bound himself to look on every one who opposed the Provisions as a public enemy, must indeed (as Wykes says) have been grievous to many besides himself.[3] The general conviction, that the despotic power of the barons was an usurpation, was

---

[1] *Ann. Tewk.* 175.   [2] *Matt. Par.* 974.
[3] See latter part of note 1, p. 201.

CHAP.
VII.

1258-59
Ambiguous
position
of Earl
Simon :

increased in the case of Simon de Montfort by a glaring anomaly in his position. He, an alien by birth, however true an Englishman at heart, had been foremost in expelling aliens ; he who had threatened William of Valence with death if he did not give up his castles, had only given up his own to receive the custody of the fortress of Winchester.[1] It was noticed, with the suspicion which springs out of mere uncertainty, that he tarried long in France, whither he had gone in the autumn of 1258, on the embassy to which he was so often appointed, and was not present at the council which consulted on the return of King Richard.[2] He had never been on very good terms with his English peers ; his ability and foreign influence made them envious ; his undeniable ambition provoked the old cry of upstart ; his broad constitutional principles made him in their eyes a traitor to his order. These feelings were only temporarily smothered by common effort, and Simons own unselfish acknowledgment of foreign extraction at the Parliament of Oxford.

At first the Earls of Leicester and Gloucester were coupled together in popular estimation as the saviours of their country, but the union of these two leading nobles, the object of so many hopes and fears, was to be of very short duration. The classes whom Simon made it his special object to protect, and among whom his chief power lay, the clergy and the smaller barons, were neglected in the new scheme of government ; thus

---

[1] See Pauli, *Simon von Mont.*, 90.
[2] The ambassadors sent on this occasion to a great council, to be held at Cambray, were the Bishops of Worcester and Lincoln, and the Earls of Leicester and Norfolk. *Matt. Par.* 979 says they were unsuccessful.

CHAP.
VII.

1258-59

Earl
Simons in-
fluence on
the wane.

he was deprived of his main support. This alone
would be sufficient to show how little share he can
have had in the lame attempt at a constitution made
in 1258 ; while at the same time it renders still more
remarkable the constancy with which he supported
the Provisions, having once sworn to them, as at any
rate better than the old state of things. When he
got the power into his own hands, he did not scruple
to replace the old scheme with a far better one. For
a year or two however he suffered from the short-
comings of his allies, and his influence was decidedly
on the wane.[1] He was credited with the disappointment of their hopes by those whom he had encouraged to believe in the possibility of a real reform ;
and it was not till they found that he was after all
their only stronghold that they returned to him. Meanwhile other business took him away from the work of
internal reform ; his special duty was to arrange the
peace with France. He had returned to England
shortly after King Richards arrival, bringing with
him an ambassador from the Council of the French

king. He was present at the Lent Parliament of
1259, at which the chief subject of discussion was the
peace with France. Internal affairs were however
not neglected ; an edict was published, embodying
provisions as to sheriffs and others, almost the same
as those made the previous autumn, and repeating
the promises of justice and redress. But justice
seems rather to have been promised than done. Soon

---

[1] That this however was not yet the case in 1259 is evident from the
words of *Matt. Par.* 984, ' Comes Legriæ, de cujus absentia diuturna
tota condoluerat Anglia ;' and from the attitude taken up by the rest
of the baronage in his quarrel with Gloucester.

after the Parliament Simon returned to France, and with his colleagues determined the preliminaries of a durable peace.[1]

The year seems to have passed in profound quiet. But towards the end a remarkable proof of the discontent that was already pervading the country was given. The knighthood were so disappointed by the non-appearance of that which they had so anxiously expected, that in October 1259 they addressed a remonstrance to Prince Edward and the members of the council, declaring that, as the king had done all that was required of him by the barons, the latter ought to fulfil their share of the engagement; whereas they had done nothing but seek their own advantage, to the detriment of king and country.[2] To this Prince Edward replied that he had sworn to the Provisions, and would keep his oath; and accordingly he warned the barons that, if they did not

---

[1] On 10 March, 1259, the Earls of Leicester and Gloucester, P. of Savoy, J. Mansel, and R. Walerand were appointed to treat of peace; and J. Baliol was afterwards added to their number. A preliminary writ was signed by Simon and two others early in May. On 20 May the first form of peace was published. The embassy then returned to England; and on 28 July Simon and his cousin Peter and another were sent out to settle the final peace, which, with its ratification by the council, bears date October 1259.—*Fœd.* i. 384–390; *Roy. Letters* i. 138.

[2] The ' Communitas bacheleriæ Angliæ' (*Ann. Burt.* 47) sent the protest. Dr. Pauli, following Gneist, *Verw.* i. 305, would place this event in Oct. 1258; but there does not appear sufficient ground for upsetting the order in which it comes in *Ann. Burton,* loose as the reckoning generally is. It is hardly possible that the knighthood should have sent in such a complaint within four months of the Parliament of Oxford, and at a time when the barons were hard at work at their measures of reform. Moreover Prince Edwards oath to the Provisions, alluded to in his answer to the protest, was not published till several days after the protest was on this hypothesis handed in. Stubbs, *Const. Hist.* ii. 81, gives the later of the two dates. Pearson, *Engl. Hist.* ii. 225, would refer it to February, 1259.

CHAP.
VII.

1259
The Provisions of Westminster;
judicial,

and constitutional enactments,

speedily fulfil their promises, he should, in conjunction with the community, compel them to do so. The barons thereupon published a new set of Provisions,[1] called, to distinguish them from those of 1258, the Provisions of Westminster. These enactments regulated the legal procedure in the case of land held on feudal tenure, for the better protection of small tenants, wards, and heirs; they put a stop to a number of abuses that had grown up in the sheriffs' and other courts; they prevented the arbitrary jurisdiction of any but duly qualified persons, and any injustice on the part of the itinerant judges, bailiffs, and others. Besides these regulations, which were meant to be permanent, there were a number of enactments of a more temporary nature, as to enquiry to be made into various abuses, the appointment of justices, and so forth. Certain important regulations were made: that two or three of the council were always to be with the king in the intervals between the Parliaments; that four knights were to keep special watch over the proceedings of the sheriffs; that no one should appear armed or with an armed following at Parliament. Appointments of various necessary officials were made; ecclesiastical property was to be

---

[1] Two records of these Provisions are given (*Ann. Burt.* 476, 480), in French and Latin; that in French appears to be a record of the proceedings in Parliament, of resolutions, votes and appointments, much the same as the report of the Provisions of Oxford; that in Latin seems to be the copy intended to be published, containing what was to be embodied in the law of the land. The copy in the statutes of the realm (i. 8) is nearly the same as the Latin copy in *Ann. Burt.*, but on the whole is less distinct and definite. These Provisions were confirmed in 1262 and 1264, and embodied in the statute of Marlborough. The account in Stubbs, *Const. Hist.* ii. 81, substantially agrees with this.

enquired into, and placed under special protection.
Lastly, all who had suffered wrong during the last
seven years were to make complaint before justices
appointed to hear them, and the sheriff was to cause
to be elected twelve men in each hundred to help the
justices by full enquiry. This arrangement superseded
that of the four knights appointed in 1258, who had
doubtless been found insufficient for the amount of work
put upon them.[1] On the whole the amount of business
got through by Parliament testifies to their desire to
institute a thorough reform, and is a great contrast to
the blank in legislation which had prevailed so long.
The spirit of the regulations is remarkably fair, when
we consider that a great portion of them would have
the effect of limiting feudal power, and that the Parliament that passed them consisted of great feudal
lords. On the other hand, no step was taken to im-
prove the anomalous nature of the constitution ; the
kings power was still further limited, especially in the
choice of his ministers and officials. The council
aimed at taking everything into their own hands ;
the king was reduced to a mere witness, without
voice or vote, useful only to give authority to their
proceedings.

Meanwhile the vigorous attempts which had been
made to settle the second great question of foreign
policy had ended with success. The relations between England and France, a matter only less important than the negotiations with the Pope, were
finally determined. The Sicilian scheme had been
sternly and promptly cut short by the barons ; peace

[1] This last order appears in a writ tested by Hugh Bigod as justiciar,
dated 28 Nov., 1259.—*Roy. Letters* ii. 141.

CHAP.
VII.

1259
Necessity
of peace
with
France.

with France was a more delicate and lengthy affair. It was however urgently needed, for the perpetual state of war, which had lasted since the days of John, and in which hostilities were only staved off by frequent truces, prevented the external quiet which was indispensable for the completion of internal reform. It was moreover very desirable to reconcile the King of France to the new state of things. His feeling on the matter soon became known, and in the end only too fully justified the fears entertained. For the present the danger seemed to have blown over, but this was not enough; a settlement that should go to the root of the matter was wanted. This desirable consummation was at first hindered by a difficulty that cannot however have been unexpected.

Negotia-
tions inter-
rupted by a
quarrel
between
Leicester
and Glou-
cester.

The negotiations for peace and the quiet of the realm were near coming to a violent end, through a quarrel between the two leaders, the outcome of long-standing jealousy. It was during the deliberations of the council, on some questions of immediate policy, after the Lent Parliament of 1259 had broken up, that the dispute broke out. The exact cause is not told us, but so hot did the contest become that Leicester angrily exclaimed, 'With such fickle and faithless men I care not to have aught to do. The things we are treating of now we have sworn to carry out. And thou, Sir Earl, the higher thou art, the more art thou bound to keep such statutes as are wholesome for the land.' Shortly afterwards he left England on his embassy to France. The other barons however, with the Earl of Hereford at their head, compelled the Earl of Gloucester to invite him back, and to allay the anxiety of all by proclaiming his readiness to carry out the necessary measures of reform.[1]

The reconciliation was only a pretence, and the quarrel was renewed in France; for the Countess of Leicester insisted on the recognition of her rights as potential heiress to the English crown. Her claim rested on her descent from Eleanor of Poitou, part of whose dowry, the Agenois, had been granted by Richard I to his sister Joanna, wife of the Count of Toulouse. On the death of Raymond VIII the great fiefs of his family came into the possession of the French crown. The Agenois was claimed by Henry III, and long negotiations on this point had taken place. Eventually Henry gave up his claim on this as on other lands for a money payment. His sister naturally objected to this arrangement, which would have been of little good to her. Henry, always in want of money, was angry at the delay thus caused, and was inclined to ride roughshod over her objections. He wrote to Louis that he would take all the responsibility on himself, and guarantee that Eleanors resistance should do him no harm. This however did not suit the French king, who had higher ideas of morality than his cousin of England, and he refused to conclude the arrangement till Eleanor should be satisfied. Besides these claims she had others too, concerning her right to a share in the property of her former husband, the Earl of Pembroke. From the great possessions of the family of Marshall Henry had been accustomed to pay her a small pittance: the earldom was about this time[2] conferred on William of Valence,

---

[1] *Matt. Par.* 987.
[2] In 1264, says Sir H. Nicolas. Perhaps it was informally conferred upon him before this, which, if true, will account for his permission to

CHAP.
VII.

1259
Conduct of
Henry,

and of
Earl
Simon,
in the
matter.

which may be one reason for the hostility between him and Leicester.

It is probable that Henry was not answerable for the mismanagement of Eleanors inheritance, the original arrangement having been made between her and her husbands brother. Still his treatment of his sister ever since her marriage had been distinguished neither by chivalrous feeling nor brotherly affection ; he owed her money, and regarded her as a debtor does his creditor. It is intelligible enough that she should have insisted at least on the recognition of her rights by a formal request for her consent ; and Simons pride was naturally piqued by this treatment of his wife. Possibly too the idea of securing a possession for the house of Montfort on French soil may have suggested the revival of these claims. The delay has been attributed by the royalist Wykes to the grasping avarice of de Montfort ;[1] but from the whole of his conduct in the matter it is evident the real opposition did not come from him. It is in truth no slight testimony to his generosity and unselfishness that all the claims which really interfered with the completion of peace were before long allowed to drop. At first however there is no doubt they were a great obstacle. Their chief importance to us is the opportunity they unfortunately gave for the renewal of that split between the national leaders which for a time ruined

stay in England with his brother, the Bishop of Winchester, when the other aliens were expelled in 1258 ; see Pearson, *Hist. of Eng.* ii. 223.

[1] *T. Wykes*, 123. The animus with which this was written appears from the fact that he attributes the lengthy and expensive sojourn of the court till Easter 1260 in Paris to the opposition of de Montfort ; while the documents show that peace was finally concluded before the preceding Christmas.

the national cause.　It was on the subject of his wifes
claims that the Earl of Gloucester, while in France,
attacked Simon with remarks which we can imagine
were the reverse of a compliment to his supposed
uxoriousness.　De Montfort was not slow to reply,
and the two were with difficulty separated by their
friends amid the laughter of the French spectators.[1]
The negotiations were temporarily broken off, but
Simon on his return to England seems to have been
persuaded to yield.[2]　In July he went out again with
two others, to carry out the final negotiations, and
when they came back to England, bringing with them
the form of peace for Henrys acceptance, the earl
remained behind in France.

The peace was ratified by the royal council about
the middle of October 1259, and is the last act in
which the baronial government appears in that shape.[3]
The presence of Henry, as well as that of the earl and
countess, was considered necessary at the concluding
ceremony in Paris.　The king therefore went over to
Paris in November for the purpose, and in the December following Simon and his wife set their seals to a

[1] *Matt. Par.* 987.　This is the last event of importance noted by
that great historian, whose loss in the confusion of the following period
we cannot sufficiently deplore.　It seems doubtful whether his work ex-
tends beyond 1253, where his history, as we have it in his own MS.,
ends.　He died in 1259, but the last six years may possibly be by him.
[2] The points in dispute were submitted to arbitration ; and eventually the Countess allowed herself to be bought off by the promise that
part of the money paid by the French king should be paid to her.　At
the same time Simon resigned to Henry the earldom of Bigorre in
Gascony, which he had held as security for his own debt, for a certain
sum, and made a formal renunciation of all claims he might have in the
south of France.　This settlement between the brothers-in-law was only
temporary.　For a full account of all these negotiations, see Greens
Princesses ii. 114 seq.
[3] It was possibly to some extent superseded by the council of regency
in the kings absence.

CHAP.
VII.

1259
Terms of
the peace
with
France.

solemn confirmation made before both kings.[1] By this peace, besides the settlement of feudal difficulties in Gascony, the provinces of Normandy, Anjou, Maine, Touraine and Poitou were ceded to France ; the titles of Duke of Normandy and Count of Anjou were dropped ; and thus the long quarrel between the two nations was brought, at least for a time, to an end. It was one of the most important in that series of events which, after raising French princes to the throne of England, and creating under Henry II a great continental power of which England was the less important part, had since the beginning of the thirteenth century reduced those princes to the position of English kings, whose possessions in France, though still by no means inconsiderable, were only awaiting the inevitable fate which had swallowed up the rest. It is needless to say that to England this peace was as great a boon as the losses of territory she had suffered at the hands of Philip Augustus ; yet there were not wanting those who thought it a disgrace to the country.[2]

With this event ended what may be called the first act of the revolution. The foreign policy of England had been in a year and a half completely reversed, the crying evils of the State redressed, and internal peace to some extent secured. But, by the very performance of this work, the power of those that did it was undermined. The only defence for their anomalous position was removed, jealousy broke out, and men began to ask themselves whether the old form of government should not be restored. It was better perhaps to be ruled, even tyrannically, by a born king, than to be worried with reforms by an upstart and ambitious foreigner.

[1] *Fœd.* i. 392.   [2] 'Facta pudenda concordia.'—*Ann. Mels.* 129.

CHAPTER VIII.

THE REACTION.

OF the reactionary period that followed the peace of 1259 it is very hard to get a clear idea. 'For nearly three years from this time,' says Dr. Shirley, 'the history of de Montfort is worse than a blank : it is a riddle.'[1] Perhaps a key to this riddle may be found in the undecided attitude taken up by the King of France. Simons character was better known and more highly estimated among the great nobles of France than among those of England, and with Louis personally he was on excellent terms ; but the pious and autocratic king could not be expected to sympathise with his revolutionary ideas, however much he may have been disgusted by the duplicity and incapacity of Henry. His monarchical principles eventually carried the day, but the length of time during which he hesitated shows how little was wanting to make him throw his weight into the other scale. The struggle between Simon and Henry takes more and more of a personal character ; and with the political aspect of it, private hostility and private disputes about money matters and the like are strangely mixed up. Each of the combatants strives to win the favour

CHAP.
VIII.

1259–62
Obscurity
of the
period.

Struggle
between
Earl
Simon and
the king.

[1] *Quart. Rev.* vol. cxix. 50.

CHAP.
VIII.
1259
Struggle
between
Earl Simon
and the
king.

of the King of France and the people of England. When one is in Paris, the other attempts to steal a march upon him in London. When Henry returns to England Simon finds it convenient to be in France. The two stand opposite each other not as king and subject, but as two independent princes, in whose private disputes as well as in their political quarrels a king or a queen of France is called upon to arbitrate. A process goes on somewhat similar to that before 1258. De Montfort after a temporary depression regains his hold upon the people, while the Pope and the King of France unite to support Henry, the result being an immediate reunion of the national party and the downfall of the monarchy.

When Henry went to France in November 1259, the royal authority was vested in a Council of Regency, pretty equally composed of the two parties, consisting of the Archbishop of Canterbury, the Bishop of Worcester, the Earl Marshal, Hugh Bigod the justiciar, and Philip Basset.[1] The last three were however already wavering, and their nomination shows that the tide had turned.[2] How far this council may be held to have superseded the Council of Fifteen, or whether it was anything more than a committee chosen from it—since all but Basset were members of the Fifteen—is uncertain. It is not probable that the baronial government lost its power till after the kings return, or even later. Before his departure, Henry took leave of the citizens of London in the Folkmoot, and conferred upon them certain unimportant liberties.

Lib. de Ant. Leg. sub anno.

[2] They are found on the kings side in 1264. P. Basset was the kings justiciar in 1261.

But no sooner did he feel himself somewhat secure,
thinking probably he had made sure of Louis, than he
wrote to the Pope from Paris to say that he hoped
now to renew the negotiations about Apulia ; while on
the same day, 16 January 1260, he sent a studiously
polite letter to the justiciar, explaining the reason of
his delay abroad, asking him to send another arbiter to
France, and bidding him refrain from summoning the
regular Lent Parliament on account of the report of a
Welch invasion. Shortly afterwards he distinctly
informed Hugh Bigod that the Sicilian enterprise was
to be taken up again.[1] Thus did he on the first opportunity return to his old schemes, and break one of the
most important of the Oxford Provisions, by forbidding the assembly of Parliament at the stated time.
A sign of his reviving power, and a more defensible
exercise of it, was an edict he issued at the same time,
bidding the sheriffs look to their duties as guardians
of the public peace. But he was too cautious at once
to assert fully the reactionary policy ; he wrote to the
Pope begging him not to insist on the return of the
Bishop of Winchester.

1260
Henry renews negotiations with the Pope,

and re-assumes power in England.

Meanwhile however, after the conclusion of peace,
Earl Simon, whose absence had been as usual much re-
gretted,[2] had returned with his wife and a large suite
to England.[3] He was not likely to acquiesce in such
a breach of the law as that commanded in the kings
letter. The barons therefore intimated to the king
their desire to hold a Parliament, but received only a

Return of Earl Simon.

---

[1] See throughout this period *Royal Letters* ii. 147 seq.
[2] ' Anglia illius praesentia diutius viduata.'—*Matt. West.* 292.
[3] On 10 Feb., 1260, he was at St. Albans, and presented a costly baldekin to the shrine.—*Ibid.*

still more distinct command not to do so till he returned. If anything had been needed to convince them of the necessity of union, and the danger of yielding a foot to the attempted renewal of Henrys foreign policy, it was supplied by a letter from the Pope, which seems to have arrived about this time in answer to their remonstrances on the effect of the usurpation of lay patronage.[1] In it the Pope lays down the principle that no layman has a right to dispose of ecclesiastical things, although his predecessor had fifteen years before confirmed the right of presentation ;[2] the laity may not even, he declares, call upon the Church to reform her ways. With such a warning as

this before their eyes, and with the kings attitude plainly declared, the barons summoned a Parliament in opposition to his mandate, and informed the king that, if he did not soon return from France, he might find it impossible to return when he wished.[3] Henry had, in fear of another outbreak, begged his brother Richard to hinder an intended invasion of his half-brothers, and the assembling of forces in France ; while he reported to Louis, probably prematurely, that de Montfort was bringing men and arms into England, 'whence his attitude towards the king was plainly visible.' Meanwhile, as he confessed a year later, he was himself collecting forces, and in fact brought them into the country soon after his own return.

Alarmed by the attitude of the barons, and still more by the report that Prince Edward had shown a decided leaning towards them, Henry suddenly re-

---

[1] *Ann. Burt.* 487.   [2] *Fœd.* i. 262.   [3] *Ann. Dunst.* 315.

appeared in London a few days after Parliament had met.[1] There was some ground for the rumours as to his son ; for the old quarrel had burst out again between Gloucester and Leicester, and Edward had taken his uncles side. The king immediately entered London and shut the gates, while the barons held their Parliament in the Temple. The city had decided, on the approach of the disputants with their armed foll- owings, in violation of the Provision of 1259, which forbade the bearing of arms, to obviate the chance of disturbance by shutting both parties out. Henry however admitted Gloucester, who doubtless during his long stay in France[2] had come to a good under- standing with him ; Edward and de Montfort re- mained outside with their partisans.[3] It seems very probable, from Edwards character and general atti- tude at this time, that he preferred Leicester to Glou- cester ; but though the king refused to see him for a whole fortnight, from fear that his Roman sense of justice would give way before parental fondness,[4] he was at the end of that interval reconciled to his father. Henry, having secured his son, gave vent to his long-concealed displeasure in an open attack on Simon, using, according to one account, false wit- nesses against him. What was the ground of the attack we know not, but it probably had something to do with the recent breach of filial duty committed by the prince. Be that as it may, Simon answered everything as he had once before on a similar occa-

CHAP.
VIII.
1260

Prince
Edward.

Henry
attacks de
Montfort.

---

[1] Parliament met on 19 April ; Henry returned on 23 April.
[2] He was still with the king on 19 Feb.—*Roy. Letters* ii. 155.
[3] *Lib. de Ant. Leg.* sub anno.
[4] *Ann. Dunst.* 214.

CHAP.
VIII.

1260
War and
truce with
the Welch.

sion, so that his accusers were powerless. Richard, as usual, acted peacemaker, and Simon seems so far to have been taken back into favour that he was sent, as the most able and prudent general in England,[1] to conduct the war against the Welch. His skill was not however called into requisition, for a truce was made shortly afterwards.

Perhaps it was owing to this that he was not present as high steward at the marriage of the Princess Beatrice, in October 1260, at which Henry of Almaine discharged the duty for him. That this absence is not to be looked on as implying any disgrace, is made more probable by the fact that about the same time de Montforts two sons were knighted by Prince Edward. It may have been owing to the dangerous influence, which the earl seemed at this time to be getting over the chivalrous spirit of the young prince, that the latter was sent to Gascony, of which province t will be remembered he had been made lieutenant five years before. It seems very likely that the thought of making Edward regent had crossed the

mind of de Montfort. The nobility of character and warm impulses of the young prince, the sense of honour which from the first distinguished him, and the sympathy for the oppressed, of which he had already given evidence, were enough to encourage such hopes. But these qualities were at this time overpowered by others—a hot-headed rashness, and a quickness of resentment which made him lose sight of aims requiring patience and forethought, and a fickleness of temper which caused him with reason to be compared

---

[1] ' Bel ator prudentior et validior Angliæ.'—*Matt. West*, 299.

to the leopard. He had as yet but little of that bitter experience which made him afterwards so great a king, and de Montfort, if he ever cherished the idea of raising him into his fathers place, must have soon found it impracticable. Deprived of one possible advocate at Court, Simon soon lost the other too ; for King Richard, obeying the repeated injunctions of the Pope, departed for Germany. Henry was left to his own devices.

He employed his time during the autumn of 1260 in strengthening the Tower of London, whence he expected to command the city. He had already compelled all the citizens, from the age of twelve upwards, to swear a renewed allegiance to him ; and, growing confident in his own strength and the prospect of papal support, he began, according to the confession of his own partisans, to issue ordinances contrary to the spirit of the Provisions.[1] He even ventured to summon Parliament to meet in the Tower, but this the barons refused to do, demanding that they should meet in the usual place of assembly at Westminster.[2] Hugh Bigod, the justiciar appointed by the barons in 1258, had resigned early in 1260, for what reason, unless it were a sense of failure in a task for which a Bigod was hardly likely to be fitted, we do not know. Hugh Despenser, a staunch supporter of de Montfort, had been appointed in his place, and this shows the influence exerted by the earl up to the return of Henry from France. But

Henry recovers his position.

Change of justiciars.

---

[1] *T. Wykes* 125.
[2] On what occasion this was does not appear, but it seems to have been in the spring of 1261, after Henry had fortified the Tower (*Ann. Dunst,* 217). Dr. Pauli thinks it was at the autumn Parliament of 1260.

CHAP.
VIII.

1260
Feeling
against the
baronial
govern-
ment.
now things were changed. An uneasy feeling was abroad. It was evident that the Provisions were no longer valid, that the baronial Government, if not already extinct, was tottering to its fall. Their errors had roused fresh resistance. Several towns had refused to admit the itinerant justices appointed by the barons, since their visit had been repeated after an interval less than that ordained in the Provisions of 1259.[1] Another authority tells us that the justices themselves were subjected to vexatious interference on the part of the barons, probably those discontented nobles through whose territories they passed, not those who held the reins of power in London.

All this confusion produced a feeling of hostility to the baronial *régime.* Meanwhile, like a great undertone of misery, the scarcity of food continued throughout England. Things were probably not worse than they were before 1258, but the fact that they were not much better was enough to condemn a Government which had entered into power with such pretensions. The king had openly announced, as far back as February 1260, that as the barons had not kept their share of the pact, he was not bound to keep his; yet he thought it worth while to allay anxiety by issuing an edict commanding the seizure of all who spread abroad reports that he intended arbitrarily to alter the law of the land. Meanwhile he appeared to be making strenuous efforts to settle his private disputes with the Earl of Leicester.[2] It was certainly to his interest to remove all causes of complaint that might strengthen Simons position. In

---

[1] E.g. Hereford.—*Nic. Trivet* 248 : Worcester.—*Ann. Wig.* 446.
[2] *Roy. Letters* ii. 168-175 ; *Fœd.* i. 407.

March 1261 it was agreed between the king and the earl and countess to submit them to the arbitration of the King of France. Louis was besought to undertake the office; the Queen of France, Henrys sister-in-law, strove to bring about a peaceable solution; King Richard wrote to his brother, bidding him abide by the decision, whatever it might be. But Louis showed no great inclination to involve himself in so delicate a matter; he saw too that it was not a mere private quarrel to be settled, and therefore in April he declined to arbitrate. Thereupon Queen Margaret took it up, according to previous engagement. But a little later, apparently in case the queen too, after nearer examination, should find the claims of the opposing parties irreconcileable, a court of arbitration was appointed, to consist of four members, two chosen by each disputant, with two mediators in addition. Their verdict was to be given by the end of September 1261.[1] The part still taken by the King and Queen of France is obscure, but seems to have been limited at this time to a general supervision. So for a time the question remained undecided, in itself unimportant, but, taken in connexion with existing circumstances, a constant source of irritation.

All this while however Henry had been preparing in secret for a great blow. A second time, as five-and-forty years before, the power of the papacy was called in to absolve the king from his most solemn promises, and by an unwarrantable interference,

CHAP.
VIII.

1261

Arrangement of private differences between Henry and Earl Simon attempted.

---

[1] The arbitrators were, for the king, P. Basset and J. Mansel—for the earl, the Bishop of Worcester and P. de Montfort; the mediators were Hugh, Duke of Burgundy, and P. Chamberlain.

CHAP.
VIII.

1261
The papal
absolution
granted,

against which the national sense revolted, again to revivify those principles which it intended to destroy. The papal absolution, for which Henry had been waiting, was made out on April 13, 1261 ; but he was not ready to use it yet. He prepared for the *coup d'état* by occupying Windsor,[1] and by issuing orders to prevent Leicester from introducing soldiers by the Cinque Ports. At last, all being ready, he went to Dover, which he seems to have occupied without any difficulty, turned out Hugh Bigod from the fortress, as he had already ousted him from the Tower, doubtless with his consent ; and, having probably met the papal messengers at Dover, summoned a Parliament at Winchester at the regular time, and on June 14

and pub-
lished.

produced the absolution before the assembled magnates. By this document the Pope released the king from all his promises, declaring the Provisions to be null and void, and the obligation invalid, ' since the sanctity of an oath, which ought to strengthen good faith and truth, must not become the stronghold of wickedness and treachery.'

Effect of
the absolu-
tion.

The effect was immense ; the suddenness of the blow forestalled opposition. At the same Parliament the king deposed Hugh Despenser, as being the nominee of his opponents, and made Philip Basset justiciar. The great seal was given to Walter de Merton. He then retreated hastily to his stronghold of the Tower, thence to crush his enemies in safety. He first attempted to recover the castles, in which however he was hindered, at any rate in one instance, by the opposition of Hugh Bigod, who refused to

---

[1] He was there during the latter part of March, having been in the Tower till March 14.—*Fœd.* i. 405 seq.

give up Scarborough and other places except by
command of Parliament, although he had already
given up Dover and the Tower. His refusal is a good
instance of the vacillating position taken up by so
many of the barons at this time, it being so worded as
to save his conscience, but to leave open the chance
of surrendering, if the king were supported by the
least parliamentary authority.[1] The baronial sheriffs
were removed, and with the appointment of new men
in their places the royal authority was restored, at
least nominally, to its former strength. Strenuous
efforts were however made against this last and
most important measure. The baronial party, though
scattered and disunited, resisted everywhere the in-
trusion of the new officials, and appointed sheriffs of
their own, whom they called Wardens of the Counties.
To mitigate this opposition the king issued conciliatory proclamations, declaring that he was doing nothing nor would do anything against the law of the
land, and laying all the blame of recent disturbances
on the barons, whose dissensions, he said, had rendered
necessary the introduction of foreign troops last year.
This confession must have gone far to spoil the effect
of the promises that preceded it.[2] Still, in spite of
the outspoken opposition of a few scattered individuals, and doubtless the secret anxiety of man
more, the kings success must have seemed at the
time complete. The universal acquiescence, though it
cannot justify the means he took to shake off the yoke,
shows how much public opinion had changed in the

CHAP.
VIII.

1260
Effect of
the papal
absolution.

Resistance

and
attempts at
concilia-
tion.

Success of
the king.

---

[1] *Fœd.* i. 409. H. Bigod gave up the castles in the autumn of this
year.—*Roy. Letters* ii. 222, note.
[2] *Fœd.* i. 408.

last three years. At the same time it proves how easily Henry might have taken advantage of this change in a constitutional manner, and have restored, nay doubled, his power by an open and legitimate arrangement with Parliament. If violent repudiation of the most solemn engagements provoked so little opposition, it is probable that all classes would have welcomed with heartfelt joy and a fresh burst of loyalty a proposal for a fair and honourable solution of the difficulties. Henry not only neglected this great opportunity, but he hastened to show the country that it was only the first step towards a complete revival of the tyranny.

What the Earl of Leicester had been doing since his appointment as general against the Welch in the previous summer it is impossible to say with certainty. He had probably been engaged in settling the question of arbitration between himself and his brother-in-law, a question which assumed more and more of a political character. It was unfortunate that the two aspects of the quarrel were not kept more

Connexion
of his pri-
vate dis-
pute with
public
questions.

distinct. The political action of de Montfort would have been more free from the possible charge that he used his power to satisfy private interests and to right personal wrongs; but it is almost needless to call the general feeling of the country, as well as the extent and character of the movement, to witness how little weight these interests had in the matter. There was moreover this amount of real connexion between the public and the private quarrel, that the wrongs of which the earl and countess had to complain were merely specimens of Henrys general way of dealing with his subjects, and with the settlement of this particular question was involved the settlement of many others, the sum of which went far to produce the opposition to the king. This was acknowledged by Henry himself when he wrote in July 1261 to Louis, to say that the points submitted to arbitration were those in which he was at variance ' with his barons and especially with the Earl and Countess of Leicester.'[1] The publication of the papal bull showed what were the real issues at stake between de Montfort and the king.

The shock seems for a moment to have reunited the leaders, though the reunion was soon seen to be but momentary. The Earls of Gloucester and Leicester and the Bishop of Worcester took the remarkable step of summoning to the autumn Parliament of 1261 three knights from each county south of the Trent. The Parliament was to meet a fortnight before the time ordained by the Oxford Provisions, and at an unusual place, St. Albans. The intention of this act is obvious ; it was a recognition of the justice of the complaints put forward by the knighthood two years before, and was meant to secure their aid in the coming struggle. The boldness of the move seems to show the same hand which summoned the Parliament of 1265. The king however resolved not to be outbidden, and issued counter-writs commanding the knights to meet him on that day in Parliament at Windsor, where, if we are to believe Henrys words, a meeting had been arranged between him and the opposite party to discuss terms of peace.[2] But a discussion of this sort before the papal absolution was a very dif-

[1] *Fœd.* i. 407.　　[2] *Sel. Chart.* 396 : *Roy. Letters* ii. 179.

CHAP.
VIII.
——,——
1261
Summons
to the
knights.

ferent matter from the same discussion after the chief point in dispute had been violently decided by one of the parties. It appears probable that the meeting spoken of by the king never took place, and it is doubtful whether the knights ever came to Parliament as summoned. But though the barons, we are told, refused to meet the king on this particular occasion, he was successful in his efforts to avoid the immediate

danger. It was not long before he prevailed on the Earl of Gloucester again to desert the opposition, and persuaded him and others to consent to an arbitration on the terms of the Provisions.[1] The arrangement to be made was obviously intended to be final, since the last appeal, in, case of a failure on the part of the future court to decide, was to be made to King Richard, and, if he too failed, to the King of France, than whom no higher authority acceptable to both sides could well be found. It is very doubtful if the court ever sat : according to some accounts the discussion was to be put off till the return of Prince Edward from Gascony. At any rate the arbitrators must have very soon handed it over to Louis, who was from the first looked upon as the only possible judge.

So clearly did the Earl of Leicester perceive this,

that, apparently foreseeing the failure of his last attempt to win back power, he crossed to France towards the end of August 1261. He did not return for a year and a half. His departure was attributed by some to vexation at the conduct of the Earl of

---

[1] The arbitrators were—for the king, the Bishops of Salisbury and Hereford and John Mansel ; for the barons, the Earl of Norfolk, P. de Montfort, and R. Marsh, Dean of Lincoln. Judgment was to be given before next Whitsuntide.

Gloucester ; by others it was put down to his resolution not to submit the Provisions to arbitration. He left the country, it is said, declaring 'he would rather die without a foot of land than live in perjury and falsehood.'[1] His real object, which he concealed under a vow of crusade, was doubtless to make a last effort to win the help of Louis. Terrified by the news of Simons departure, Henry wrote to the King of France to anticipate his efforts ;[2] he was still more alarmed to find that the national party, that is, at the moment, Simon de Montfort, had like himself a regular representative at the Court of Rome, who seems for a short time to have had the ear of the new Pope, Urban IV.[3] The temporary displeasure of Rome, whether real or simulated, was demonstrated by a letter to the king, rebuking the proceedings of his bailiffs in Ireland, and laying to their charge exactly the same things as those of which complaint had been made by Bishop Grosseteste ten years before.[4] But the alienation, such as it was, was of very brief duration, and had no effect, since the absolution had been already published. Simons efforts in that quarter were without any result : Urban continued the policy of his predecessors, and repeated the absolution next spring in yet stronger terms than those of Alexander.[5]

Meanwhile the desultory resistance which had

---

[1] 'Dicens se sine terra malle mori quam perjurus a veritate recedere.'—*Ann. Dunst.* 217. ' Dicens se velle adire Terram Sanctam.' —*Ann. Osn.* 129.

[2] *Fœd.* i. 409. He declares the earl to have gone without his consent, and for unknown reasons, though he evidently guessed them.

[3] *Roy. Letters* ii. 190, 210 ; and see note 2 on p. 239.

[4] *Fœd.* i. 411.

[5] Bull dated 2 Feb., 1262, in *Roy. Letters* ii. 206, dated 26 April in the *Fœdera.*

CHAP.
VIII.

1261

Henry re-
covers his
power,
been made in the counties to the arbitrary appointment of sheriffs, though it appears to have continued
late into the autumn of 1261, was gradually appeased.
The introduction of foreign soldiers on the kings side,
in spite of the opposition of the Cinque Ports, continued. The tenth was collected again, but with some
difficulty, and deposited in the royal castles.[1] Soon
afterwards the barons, who a month or two before had
refused to meet the king, were summoned afresh to
appear, unarmed and under a safe conduct, at Kingston, to discuss terms of peace. It was at this Parliament that the court of arbitration just mentioned was
appointed, and certain new Provisions drawn up, in
the shape of a treaty or form of peace. Of these we
know nothing, beyond that a compromise was effected
on the important question of the appointment of
sheriffs. It was determined that each county should
select four knights for the office, and that the king
should appoint one of these.[2] That some form of
peace was determined is evident from the fact that the
king wrote in December 1261 to several barons, including the Earl of Leicester and others of his party,
as well as more doubtful members, such as the Earls
of Norfolk and Warenne, and Roger Mortimer, bidding
them set their seals to the peace, and offering them
pardon if they would sign within a certain time.[3] The
absence of so many great nobles was alone sufficient

---

[1] *Roy. Letters* ii. 193, 195.

[2] 'Juxta promissionem nuper factam, prout in compositionis forma
continetur,' &c.—*Id.* ii. 198.

[3] First writ dated 7 Dec., 1261, in the *Fœdera* ; second dated 16 Dec.,
1261, not mentioning the pardon, *Roy. Letters* ii. 196. It is remarkable that the Earl of Gloucester, the Bishop of Worcester, and H. Bigod
do not appear on the pardon list, while the Earl of Norfolk, who was
one of the arbitrators appointed at this very peace, appears.

to deprive the decrees of this Parliament of any force ;
and the question seems not to have been settled even
so, for in the early part of next year the sheriffs were
still under discussion. Finally King Richard cut the
matter short by ruling, when the question was referred
to him, that the right of appointment and dismissal
belonged to the king alone.[1] From this it may be
judged what sort of a peace it was that Simon de
Montfort was bidden to sign, and how little he was
likely to sign it, though others weakly acquiesced.
During the winter of 1261–62 he remained in stubborn
silence abroad, occupied partly in negotiations with
Louis, partly perhaps in collecting his forces for
the inevitable struggle. But he did not force it on :
he bided his time. In England the royalist cause was
in the ascendant, and Henry determined on a journey
to France, to destroy the last hopes of his enemies by
securing the consent of Louis to his plans.

So safe did he feel himself that he issued a proclamation, declaring that since the barons had not kept
their side of the engagement, and since the Pope had
absolved him from his, he considered himself free from
all promises made with respect to the Provisions of
Oxford ; still he should not fail to keep all the
statutes of the Great Charter and the Charter of
Forests.[2] At the same time the form of peace lately
made seems to have been published throughout England, with a kind of promise that certain difficulties
should be settled by means of peaceable discussion with

CHAP.
VIII.

1261–62

Settlement
of the
question of
sheriffs.

Earl Simon
remains
abroad.

Henry
declares
himself free
from the
Provisions.

---

[1] *T. Wykes* 130, and *Ann. Osney* 130 seq. are a good deal confused
as to the events of this winter, but they are on the whole corrected and
explained by the writs, &c., in the *Fœdera* and in the *Royal Letters.*
Rishanger (*de Bellis*, &c.) is altogether wrong in his chronology.

[2] *Fœd.* i. 419.

CHAP.
VIII.
1261-62
Reversal of
the baron-
ial policy.

the chiefs of the baronial party.[1] Preparations were even made for taking up anew the mad scheme of conquest in Africa in conjunction with the King of Castile.[2] The work of 1258 was completely upset, with the exception of the peace with France: the baronial party was dissolved, the king to all appearance more firmly seated than ever. The despair felt by those whose hopes, three or four years ago, had been so high

Exhorta-
tion to the
barons.

is expressed in the song which calls on the barons collectively to 'observe that which they had sworn,' and bids several by name to keep their word.[3] The Earl of Gloucester is exhorted ' to finish what he has begun unless he would deceive many.' The Earl of Norfolk is reminded of his military prowess, and bidden as a good knight to use his strength in a just cause. Above all Simon de Montfort is exhorted not to fear, since 'the foreign hounds' are few, and it is he who should take the lead against the common foe.

Popular
estimate of
de Mont-
fort:

No greater testimony could be paid to the manner in which Simon had become an Englishman of the English: he was praised as the ' key of England, who had locked out the aliens for three years ;'[4] his personal

---

[1] This seems to be the meaning of the notices in *T. Wykes* 130, *Lib. de Ant. Leg.* 52, and *Matt. West* 313, though it is hard to combine with much certainty the varying accounts.

[2] *Fœd.* i. 420. This project dates from 1254.

[3] *Polit. Songs*, ed. Wright, 121. Mr. Wright places this song in 1264-65 ; but this is hardly possible, since the Earls of Gloucester and Norfolk have not yet finally deserted the baronial side, and it seems to be the old Earl of Gloucester who is alluded to ; de Montfort is not yet fully recognised as the only leader, and his position in the song is not like that he assumed after the battle of Lewes. Stubbs, *Const. Hist.* ii. So, places this song at about the same period. *Rishanger, de Bellis,* &c., 18, introduces it after the Mise of Amiens, but his account of the events before the outbreak of the war is very confused and untrustworthy.

[4] *Rishanger, de Bellis,* &c., 10.

character, his qualities as a leader of men, moulded others to his will; the younger men, we find, especially followed him, though the older stood aloof.[1] At the same time, the words of the song show that he had not yet reached the position he held three or four years later: it was not thought necessary after the battle of Lewes to exhort him not to fear, but to take the post of leader as his right. He might indeed have said that he never knew fear, but there were doubtless some at this time who attributed his waiting policy to a dread of the seemingly hopeless contest. His attitude was often overbearing, his temper, as we have seen, was sharp; for he knew himself to be true, and did not spare words to express his contempt and hatred of a breach of faith. Add to this a strong individuality, which had in it no small element of personal ambition, and we need not be much surprised that the ruling families of England refused to follow his lead, and looked upon him with a jealousy which deepened into hate. There was however a larger, if not so powerful a class, which regarded him as their only safeguard, and it was this class which on the death of the Earl of Gloucester in the summer of 1262 invited him to return and be their leader. He did not fail to respond to the call. After eighteen months absence in France, broken perhaps by a visit to England in the autumn of 1262,[2] he returned to England

CHAP.
VIII.

1261-62

his waiting
policy :

his character sometimes in
his way :

his own
party.

---

[1] 'Quia omnis caro prona ad malum, cum junioribus Angliæ pueris, scilicet Angliæ nobilibus . . . quos vere et autonomatice pueros nominare possumus, qui tamquam cera liquescens ductiles ad quamlibet formam . . . convenerunt,' &c., says the Royalist, *T. Wykes*, p. 133.

[2] It may be inferred from the letter of the king to P. Basset, in Oct. 1262, in which he warns his justiciar to ·be on his guard against the machinations of the Earl of Leicester, that de Montfort was in England at the time ; and this is supported by a passage in the *Chron.*

1261-62
Earl Simon
summoned
back to
England.

Henry
hopes to
win over
Louis,

and goes to
France.

in the spring of 1263. Thenceforward, since for the present Gilbert de Clare, the young Earl of Gloucester, followed him with heart and soul, he appeared as the undisputed head of the baronial party, knowing whom he had to trust and with whom he had to deal.[1] From this point the struggle takes a new aspect. The hopes of the reformers revive, their action becomes more united, their attitude more firm. A far more earnest and thorough character pervades the whole movement.

But we must return for a moment to the king. If he hoped at once to win over Louis, when he determined on his journey to France in the winter of 1261-62, he was much mistaken. Two years were to elapse before he was successful. Just before his departure from England Louis had announced to him that he saw as yet no way of making peace between him and de Montfort.[2] But this only had the effect of making him more eager for the journey, in order personally to direct the negotiations. He left England in July 1262, and probably met Prince Edward, who had been in Gascony, in Paris. There he fell very ill of a fever, which threw back for some time the progress of his plans. Other obstacles too were in the way, and so fruitless appeared the attempt to win over Louis, that in October Henry wrote to his justiciar, Philip Basset, to say that no further advance had been made toward peace between him and the

---

of St. Augustine, Cant. (quoted by Nichols), in which it is said that the earl came privately to England, and in the October Parliament produced a letter from the Pope, confirming the Provisions, and cancelling the kings absolution. This is hardly possible, though Simon had a proctor at Rome ; see above, p. 234.

[1] 'Symon Leicestriæ comes, capitaneus baronum contra regem insurgentium factus, &c.'—*Nic Trivet,* 250.

[2] *Lettres de Rois,* i. 135.

earl, and that he did not intend to make any more attempts in that direction. At the same time he warned him to be on his guard against the machinations of Simon, without however saying what these machinations were. It is uncertain whether he ever met the earl in France. If, as seems probable, the latter seized the opportunity of Henrys absence to pay a short visit to England this autumn, this will perhaps account for the fact that Henry hastened his return, and arrived at Dover just before Christmas 1262. He found troubles in abundance. The disturbances with Wales had broken out again, and the barons of the Marches were at open war with Llewelyn. It is not impossible that these were the machinations of de Montfort, against which Henry warned his minister. The earl may have encouraged the Welch, in order, under cover of their attack, the more easily to prosecute his own plans. That serious disagreements between the barons engaged in the Welch war had taken place is evident from a letter, in which the king sought to allay these disputes.

Meanwhile however the French king remained the centre of interest. Henry wrote to him shortly after his return to England, begging him to settle the question speedily in his favour, ' since the realm had long been disturbed and damaged by the earl.' [1] He sent fresh envoys over, and besought the queen, his sister-in-law, to use her influence in his behalf. It must have been a sore disappointment when his ambassadors announced to him, in February 1263, that Louis was unwilling to enter further into the matter ;

CHAP. VIII.

1262–63

Henry in France :

his return.

Troubles on the Welch border.

Negotiations with France continue,

but receive a check.

---

[1] *Royal Letters* ii. 234.

R

CHAP.
VIII.

1262-63
Negotia-
tions with
France
receive a
check.
for the Earl of Leicester had told him that the king
meant well enough, but was misled by evil counsellors, special enemies of the earl ; that the latter
therefore had declared he could not in honour agree
to the arbitration, and had begged the King of
France to give himself no further trouble.[1]　To this
request Louis was evidently inclined to accede.　The
hint was obvious ; Henry should dismiss these evil
counsellors and make his peace with the earl.　He
had in fact made a great mistake.　He had, by submitting the question to arbitration, practically recognised Simons equality, in the hope of getting a verdict
against him, but the judge from whom he hoped so
much had as yet refused to decide in his favour.
Time was precious, and this last check went near
destroying his chance, for civil war broke out immediately afterwards.　How far Simon de Montfort had
been in earnest in submitting to the verdict of the
French king is uncertain ; he must have felt that the
questions at stake were such as made the device of
arbitration a mere farce, for the result would certainly
Earl Simon
returns to
England. be rejected by the defeated party.　Yet at this
time it cannot be doubted that he stood at least as
high in the favour of Louis as his adversary, and it
seems likely that he too fancied he could get the
weight of such a verdict on his side.　In the certainty
that he would at least not be opposed by Louis, he
now decided on a bolder policy, and returned to
England to put it into execution.

---

[1] *Royal Letters* ii. 242.

CHAPTER IX.

THE BARONS' WAR.

THE year 1263 saw a great change. The confusion in justice and administration which had so undermined the popularity of the baronial party a few years before was perhaps lessened to some extent by the restoration of monarchical unity, but from the popular point of view the state of things was probably little improved, for the inveterate abuses soon reappeared. The king had already given indications of a return to the old foreign policy, with all its consequent oppression ; the Roman Curia was returning to its former trade, and had demanded a subsidy for the banished Emperor of Constantinople. This the Church refused ; England had other things to do than to restore emperors who could not stand alone.[1] The troubles with the Welch which had begun in the previous October still continued, with the usual accompaniment of frequent and resultless forays, burnings of castles, and the like. Peter de Montfort was on the frontier, and at first had held the position of commander on the English side ; he had been in great need of men and money, and the dissensions among the barons of the Marches, which had not

CHAP.
IX.

1263
Bad state
of the
country.

[1] *Matt. West.* 313.

R 2

Return of
Prince
Edward,

and of
Earl
Simon.

Com-
mencement
of hostili- .
ties.

been allayed by royal intervention, still further emboldened the enemy. The restless and lawless spirits
of that district were a mine ever ready to explode ;
but little was needed to fire it, and that little was
at hand. Prince Edward, who had remained behind
after his fathers departure from Paris,[1] had returned
to England early in February 1263, accompanied by
a body of foreign soldiers, and had marched straight
to the border.[2] A little later Simon de Montfort
also returned from France, according to the royalist
chronicler, in secret.[3] The jealousy of the English
barons was aroused by Edwards use of foreign troops
against the Welch, and many refused to help him.
He therefore failed to accomplish anything, and the
Welch continued to press the border hard.[4] But not
being able to beat the Welch, he seems, in his annoyance at the refusal of aid, and possibly acting under
orders from the king, to have turned his arms against
the recalcitrant barons, and to have threatened if not
actually commenced an attack upon them. Hostilities had apparently broken out between the Marchers
and the hated Bishop of Hereford ; that town had
been entered, and the Jews plundered. In this affair
the young Henry de Montfort had distinguished himself, showing already that rashness which was to be
such an obstacle to his fathers success.[5] At this

---

[1] He was still at Paris on 3 Feb., 1263.—*Royal Letters* ii. 242.
Simon de Montfort was there till ten days or so later (*ibid.*), and must
have returned before the end of the month (*id.* ii. 244), though *Ann.
Dunst.* 221 give the date of his return as April 25.

[2] *Matt. West.* 313.   [3] ' Clanculo rediit.—*T. Wykes* 133.

[4] *Ann. Burt.* 499.

[5] This took place on 28 Feb.—*Ann. Worc.* 448. According to
Robert of Glouc., p. 535, the barons had set up a sheriff of their own,
Sir W. Tracy, who was seized and shamefully beaten by the kings
sheriff, Sir M. de Besile, a Frenchman.

crisis Simon de Montfort appeared on the field, and at once took up the position of an almost independent prince.

His first step was to bring about a truce with Edward, whose hot blood was likely still further to complicate matters. In this he was partially successful, for though the prince remained to the end of March at Bristol, in spite of his fathers summons to return, no further hostilities took place. Perhaps, relying on his former influence, Simon was willing to negotiate more fully with the prince. His proposals were supported by the Bishop of Worcester, a man who left no means untried to bring about a peaceable solution, but when that failed recognised as clearly as Simon the necessity of war.[1] But nothing satisfactory could be done. A royal edict ordering an oath of submission to the king and Prince Edward, to be administered by the sheriffs throughout England, was the only answer vouchsafed by Henry to these pacific advances. The king indeed professed himself willing to submit to a committee, but Simon had had enough of committees. Despairing of success except by force, he now introduced foreign aid, the barons of Dover giving his troops free entrance,[2] which they had refused to the kings men two years before. About Whitsuntide the barons under Simons guidance met at Oxford, without the kings knowledge or consent. The Earl of Warenne, the young Earl of Gloucester, even Henry of Almaine were there. King Richard appears to have attended in order to prevent the outbreak of hostilities. Thence Simon sent his

CHAP. IX.
1263

Earl Simon negotiates with Prince Edward,

but in vain.

Meeting of the Barons at Oxford.

[1] Letter dated 4 March, 1263.—*Royal Letters*, ii. 244.
[2] *Royal Letters* ii. 245.

CHAP.
IX.

1263
Earl
Simons
ultimatum:

he takes
up arms.

Successes
of the
Barons in
the west;

ultimatum—a recognition of the Provisions of Oxford, and the outlawry of any one who opposed them.[1] This was modified, according to some authorities, by the proposal that such portions as were really prejudicial to the country should be omitted, so long as the Provisions relative to the expulsion of aliens were kept intact, since these involved 'nothing but what was the rule in all countries of the world.'[2] Nothing was said as to the authority by which the alterations were to be made ; but it can hardly be doubted, since the French arbitration had for the time been dropped, that Simon contemplated free discussion in Parliament on the matter, as the only possible way of solution.   But the dictatorial tone roused Henry out of his usual bland hypocrisy ; he refused to admit the basis proposed, and Simon took the law into his own hands.

This decided step produced an enthusiastic response.   The noble youth of England streamed together in great numbers.[3] Simon led them first of all westward, to the border country where Gloucesters strength lay, and where the Welch might form a support in case of need.   In the long June days they marched from one stronghold to another, seized and chastised the Savoyard Bishop of Hereford, the most obnoxious of the aliens, expelled the royal sheriffs and castellans, and confiscated the goods of their opponents.[4] Without doubt much needless violence

---

[1] *Ann. Dunst.* 221.

[2] *Lib. de Ant. Leg.* 58, speaking of the 'petition' sent to the king at the opening of the campaign, which seems to refer to this proposal.

[3] 'Cum junioribus Angliæ pueris.'—*T. Wykes* 133 ; 'exercitum innumerabilem.'—*Ann. Dunst.* 221.

[4] Sir M. de Besile was taken at Gloucester, and, with the Bishop of Hereford, confined at Erdsley. J. Giffard and R. de Clifford were most active in these affairs.—*Rob. of Glouc.* 536. Gloucester, Worcester, Hereford, and Bridgnorth fell into the hands of the barons.—*Nic. Trivet,* 251.

was done, though Simon issued orders, under penalty of death, to spare all sacred buildings, which however availed little to stop the wholesale destruction.[1] Here, as often elsewhere, the intemperance of his supporters brought de Montfort into trouble. Even his partisans foresaw that the lawlessness of these proceedings would alienate the friends of law.[2] Still even the royalists were forced to own that the Bishop of Hereford deserved his fate, though his holy office rendered the treatment of him unjustifiable. From the border-counties Simon led his forces eastward. King Richard attempted to meet him at Wallingford, but the earl refused to see him, and pressed on towards Dover. He moved with great rapidity; on June 29 he reached Reading; on the 30th, Guildford; the next day he was to be at Reigate.[3] Soon after he reached Dover, the castle of which however held out against him.

Meanwhile the king had tried to concentrate his forces. Prince Edward held Windsor,[4] and Henry withdrew to the Tower. The temper of the city was so hostile that he failed to obtain a loan of money from the citizens. Edward therefore seized the treasures in the Temple, the money deposited there, as in a bank, being the property of private individuals. The indignation of the Londoners burst forth in open revolt against this high-handed robbery, which affected not the princes enemies, but those who had as yet done him no injury.[5] Richard, expecting a general collision, wrote to his brother, telling of the

their violence does damage to their cause.

Earl Simon marches on Dover.

Conduct of the king and Edward.

---

[1] *Rishanger, Chron.* 29.
[2] The treatment of the Bishop of Hereford was 'contra jus, nec stare potuit.'—*Ann. Dunst.* 222; cf. *T. Wykes* 134.
[3] *Royal Letters* ii. 247, 248.
[4] He was still at Shrewsbury on April 15.
[5] *Ann. Dunst.* 222. It was possibly the store for the crusade.

CHAP.
IX.

1263
Earl Simon
negotiates
with the
king.

failure of his attempt at conciliation, and bidding him prevent Edward from attacking the barons. But Simon, having secured the sea-ports, opened negotiations while lying at Dover with his victorious army. The Bishops of Lincoln, London, and Lichfield brought the message of peace, for which they had, as it appears, been commissioned during Simons march. The Bishop of Worcester had already written to the chancellor, begging him to use his influence in persuading the king to accept the conditions which the envoys would propose.[1]

Terms of
peace
offered.

The first stipulation was, that Henry of Almaine, who appears to have been seized by the royalists abroad on account of his inclination toward de Montfort, should be set at liberty.[2] The barons also demanded that Dover should be given up to them, and that the Provisions should be observed, especially that portion which decreed the expulsion of aliens.[3] In answer to these demands, which it will be observed go further than those made a month or two before,

The king
consents to
treat.

the king sent ambassadors, among whom were some citizens of London, to treat with the barons at Dover. This was a great concession, but his situation was in fact almost desperate at this moment. He was blockaded in the Tower by the populace of the city, which in a public assembly declared its assent to Simons proposals of alliance on the basis of the Provisions John Mansel, the most obnoxious of the

[1] Letter dated 29 June.—*Fœd.* i. 427.
[2] The position taken by this prince was always vacillating and uncertain. On this occasion he is said to have pursued J. Mansel in his flight to France, and to have been arrested by order of the latter there ; *Nic. Trivet,* 252, says it was owing to his adhesion to the barons.
[3] *Ann. Dunst.* 223.

kings creatures, by common report the richest man in
England, fled for his life to France. The queen, in
trying to make her way up the river to Windsor to
join her son, was attacked by the populace with vile
abuse and showers of stones while passing under
London Bridge, and driven back to the Tower. King
Richard, anxious for the release of his son, pressed
the king to yield, and Henry, 'being in a strait,' gave
way at last. It meant little enough that he renewed
his promise to observe the Provisions ; but, upon his
so doing, a truce was made, and the king, in accordance with it, called on his wardens to give up Dover
Castle and other strongholds to the barons.[1] It was
agreed that certain portions of the Provisions should
be remodelled by a council, 'according as the welfare
of the king and the realm demanded.'[2]

Simon thereupon marched to London. He entered the town at once, and was received with all
signs of joy by the citizens.[3] But resistance was not
yet at an end. Prince Edward, having made a rapid
march on the western border, and having failed in an
attempt to seize Bristol, had returned to Windsor, and
seemed inclined to bid defiance to the barons. Simon
marched against him, and, by the advice of the Bishop
of Worcester, whose confidence Edward appears to
have abused, laid hands on him at Kingston, whither
he had come to treat.[4] He was then compelled to

---

[1] · Quia pax inter nos et barones nostros reformata est et firmata.'—
Fœd. i. 427 ; cf. *Ann. Dunst.* 224.

[2] 'Per quosdam electos ad hoc.'—*Ibid.*

[3] · Cum jocunditate et honorifice a civibus receptus.'—*Ibid.*

[4] *Rish. Chron.* 19 ; *Matt. West.* 316. According to *Nic. Trivet*,
252, Edward had induced the Bishop of Worcester to protect him on
his way back to London, and on passing Windsor had suddenly left him
and entered the castle.

CHAP.
IX.

1263
Baronial
govern-
ment
restored.

take a fresh oath to observe the Provisions. The Castle of Windsor was delivered up, and the foreign troops in it sent out of the country.[1] For the moment the baronial party was supreme. Hugh Despenser was reinstated as justiciar instead of Philip Basset ; Nicholas of Ely was appointed chancellor in the room of Walter de Merton. Powers were given to eleven commissioners, of whom de Montfort was one, to treat of peace with Llewelyn.[2] Meanwhile the earl lay at Isleworth, probably in King Richards palace there, through July and August, while Henry resided at Westminster, and submitted for a time to his rivals undisputed supremacy.

Parliament
of Sep-
tember:

The autumn Parliament was summoned nearly a month earlier than usual, at the beginning of September. In the discussions, which doubtless turned on the supreme question of the Provisions, Simon took the lead, and spoke of wide and lofty plans of government, which he appeared to wish to carry into execution.[3] According to one authority it was re-

arbitration
of Louis
discussed.

solved in this Parliament to submit the question of the day to the arbitration of the King of France.[4] Until now, there had been no formal submission of the baronial party to this tribunal : the private difficulties of the king and the Earl of Leicester had been the chief subject of discussion, to the partial exclusion of matters of more general interest. We do not know that Louis had ever yet been asked to decide distinctly on the subject of the Provisions. The subject of the arbitration was probably, at any rate, mooted

---

[1] *Rish. Chron.* 19; *Matt. West.* 316.
[2] Writ dated 22 Aug. in *Fœdera.*
[3] ' Erigit cornua superbiæ, moliendo grandia, cogitando sublimia.' *T. Wykes* 136.   [4] *Ann. Tewk.* 179.

at this Parliament, but was not settled till some months later.

In the interval the Earl of Leicester was to suffer from another turn of fortunes wheel. His haughty attitude and domineering spirit again offended many. He was too sure of victory, though he was far from power yet. The north was, and had been through-out, against him ; and now the fickle Marchers, and certain other barons, were induced by Edward, who was rapidly becoming the centre of the royalists, to desert their side.[1]   Henry of Almaine told Leicester he could not fight against his father and uncle, but he would not draw his sword against the earl ; whereupon the latter declared it was not Henrys sword that he dreaded, but his fickleness, and bade him go and do as he pleased, for he feared him not. ' But I and my four sons,' he continued, ' though all should desert me, will stand fast for the cause I have sworn to defend, for the honour of the Church and the welfare of the realm.'[2]   At this same Parliament many, who had suffered from the random pillage and violence of the spring campaign, complained of the injustice with which they had been treated, since they had not op-posed the Provisions. Even Prince Edward seems to have found it impossible to recover three castles which the Earl of Derby, the worst freebooter of all, had seized.[3] In London the mayor, a strong partisan of Leicester, had alienated many of the upper classes by giving great freedom of action to the city officials, and

[1] ' Omnes Marchienses,' with Roger Bigod and others. — *T. Wykes,* 137 ; R. de Clifford gave up Gloucester Castle to him.—*Robert of Gloucester,* 538.   [2] *Rish. de Bellis,* &c. 17.
[3] R. de Ferrars, Earl of Derby, is especially mentioned as ' fidus nec regi nec baronibus.'—*Rish. Chron.* 13.

CHAP.
IX.

1263
Earl Simon
again loses
ground.

thereby causing much confusion.[1] It was more than Leicester could do to rule at once his open foes and his intractable allies. His power began to ebb. The monarchical predilections of the great barons, though they contained but a small element of loyalty, and did not prevent them from resisting their sovereign whenever it suited them to do so, were called into life by jealousy of their leader. It was but natural that they would not brook from a fellow-subject what they submitted to from their king. With de Montfort now, as it had been before and was to be again, the moment of victory was the commencement of defeat. How far this was inevitable, for how much his own character, for how much his followers, were to blame, it is impossible now to say.

The king
goes to
France,

Had Simon been still in a position to prevent it, it is hardly likely that he would have allowed the king to go again to France. The proposal that Henry should visit Louis had already been made in August, and the barons, knowing the danger, insisted on his making a very short stay abroad. He promised therefore to return before Michaelmas, and, as soon as Parliament was over, set off, having first summoned Simon de Montfort and his cousin Peter, with certain others, to

and is fol-
lowed by
Earl
Simon.

meet him and Louis at Boulogne.[2] Simon, much as his presence was required in England, answered the call, having possibly obliged the king to summon him, in order to get an excuse for watching his movements. While at Boulogne he was attacked by the king in the presence of Louis, and accused of wrongful

---

[1] *Lib. de Ant. Leg.* 58.

[2] Writs dated 15 and 16 Sept. 1263.—*Fœd.* i. 432, and *Royal Letters* ii. 249.

imprisonment, sacrilege, injustice of all sorts. He refuted all the charges, to the apparent satisfaction of the French king,[1] but his vigilance was unable to prevent an arrangement being made between the two monarchs which well-nigh ruined his cause. It is hardly possible not to connect, in some way, the sudden change in the policy of Louis with this meeting at Boulogne. The Mise of Amiens was the immediate result.

Henry returned to England at the end of the month, while the queen remained in France. He shut himself up in his stronghold of Windsor, with Prince Edward, and waited for an opportunity of gaining, by a sudden blow, a position which would enable him to reap to the full the advantage of the favourable verdict he expected to get from Louis. All the circumstances of the crisis seem to show that he had settled matters with the French king, and had secured his aid, but that he expected to have to fight. For this reason probably he left the queen abroad. As yet a hollow truce existed; and, though both parties were armed and only awaited the signal, unusual tranquillity, the ominous calm before the hurricane, prevailed for two months throughout the country. It seems probable that it was during this period that the negotiations took place, which ended in the unanimous agreement to abide by the arbitration of Louis. It can hardly have been settled later

---

[1] *Ann. Dunst.* 225. According to the *Chron. of St. August. Cant.* (quoted by Nichols), J. Mansel and other refugees joined in accusing de Montfort, but the latter declared he was not bound to answer such charges in the Court of the King of France, but only before his own king, and by judgment of his peers.

than the end of November.[1] A council of some kind was held at Reading towards the end of October, at which envoys from Llewelyn were present. The Earl of Leicester, for unknown reasons, did not appear. It was probably only a council of the royalists, and the arbitration and the kings immediate policy may have been discussed. It was important to Henry to settle with the Welch in the event of an outbreak of the civil war; but the absence of Leicester is sufficient to show that the question of arbitration cannot have been decided finally at this council.

Meanwhile Simon de Montfort, who seems to have returned from France with the king, had first secured London, and had found means quietly to get rid of the kings partisans, Hugh Bigod and others, who retired from the city. He then withdrew to Kenilworth, his own stronghold, and waited for the reopening of hostilities. They were not long delayed.

The king and Prince Edward, with many of the leading nobles, suddenly marched on Dover (December 4), but Simons partisans there, under Richard de Gray, held firm and refused to admit them. The disappointed royalists turned to London, which some of the leading citizens had offered to give up to them,

hoping by a rapid march to surprise the town. Simon moved quickly from Kenilworth to its rescue, and a trap was laid for him, which nearly proved successful.

---

[1] The agreements to submit to arbitration are dated 13 and 16 Dec. For the first week or more of December the two parties were almost in open hostility; the arrangement could hardly have been completed in the interval. The necessary discussions and formalities must have taken some time, and the assent of both parties must therefore have been secured before the kings attempt on Dover. It was about this time that J. Giffard and others took the town of Gloucester by a stratagem, but failed to take the castle.—*Robert of Gloucester,* 539.

He was lying in Southwark when the kings forces came up, and, not being strong enough to meet them, he tried to escape into the city. The gates were shut against him by some royalists inside, and, hemmed in between the river and the kings army, he would probably have been taken prisoner, had not his partisans among the citizens, hearing the disturbance outside, overpowered all opposition and opened the gates to their protector. Foiled a second time, the king retreated to Croydon, and thence issued an order to the citizens of London to expel Simon and his partisans. This was naturally useless : Simon kept the city and refused the king admittance. The state of things appeared worse than ever. Simon had gained nothing by the years campaign. At one moment he appeared to be successful; then with bewildering rapidity we find him deserted, and only just able to hold his own. The state of the kingdom during this period can better be imagined than described. From such a position any means of relief were acceptable ; and we can well believe that the whole people consented with joy to the appeal to Louis.[1]

In the middle of December, less than a week after the attempt on London, the letters were issued, in which it was formally arranged to submit to the arbitration. The two documents, one giving the signatures of the royalists, the other those of the national party, to the agreement, show clearly enough, if need were to prove it, the marvellous fickleness of the men with whom Simon de Montfort had to deal. They also show why it was that the lower classes of society, and

CHAP.
IX.

1263
Earl Simon
nearly
taken
prisoner.

Fruitless-
ness of his
efforts.

Formal
agreement
to submit
to arbitra-
tion.

[1] 'Clerus et populus unanimi assensu compromittebant.'— *T. Wykes.*

CHAP.
IX.

1263
The two
parties at
this time :

the men who had most memory, the clergy, looked upon him with an ever-increasing devotion. Of all the men who had been chosen on that committee to represent the Parliament against the king in 1244, he and the Bishop of Worcester were the only two who were still on the same side.[1] Ever since that time he had been before the people, never once swerving from the course he had taken at the first. He had bred

up his sons to follow in his steps. Three others of his family signed their names on his side, but besides him not one earl of note appeared. Younger men there were, staunch adherents to the popular party, Hugh Despenser, young Humphry Bohun, Ralph Basset, Richard de Gray, William Bardulph, and others, men who had made their first appearance in politics seven years before ; but Simon de Montfort was the man who, by his long experience and by his friendship with the great Bishop of Lincoln, formed the connecting link with the men who had won the

great charter. On the other side were the two Bigods, the Earl of Hereford, and Roger Mortimer, all of whom had stood up for the barons seven years before. Fitz-Geoffrey and Richard Earl of Gloucester were dead, so that but half of the baronial twelve of 1258 remained true. Of the twelve representatives of the community not one appears now for the barons, while four or five, together with James Audley, a royalist member of the Fifteen, are for the king. Richard of Cornwall had gradually dropped out of the contest, but his son Henry, and the kings hated brother, Will-

---

[1] Several were dead of course ; the events of 1244 are mentioned to show the length of time —twenty years—during which the earl had been associated with the popular cause : see names in Appendix iii.

iam of Valence, reappear among the royalists ; the wild barons of the Scotch and Welch Marches, with several others, make up the number of the kings partisans. It is remarkable that the young Earl of Gloucester appears on neither side.[1] No less than four of those who had resisted the papal absolution of 1261, and appeared as late as that time on the list of the kings nominal foes, had since then accepted the offered pardon and changed sides. Such was the vacillation, such the want of purpose and principle which made Simons work so hard. Well might he exclaim, 'I have been in many lands and among many nations, pagan and Christian, but in no race have I ever found such faithlessness and deceit as I have met in England.'[2]

It is hard at first to see what can have induced the earl to submit so unconditionally to Louis' arbitration. Despair of finding any other solution of the difficulties seems to have driven him to it. He thought perhaps, owing to his recent successful defence at Boulogne, and the good-will Louis had always shown him, that the verdict would turn out to be in his favour. Such a verdict would have rendered Henry defenceless, and even if so good fortune were not to be expected, a one-sided decision in favour of the king would be almost equally damaging to him. There were many who already suspected his eagerness for arbitration to be occasioned by a wish to introduce active assistance from abroad against his own subjects. He would at once forfeit the good-will of

CHAP.
IX.
1263
Changes in
the two
parties.

Reasons
why Earl
Simon
submitted
to the arbitration.

---

[1] Perhaps this was because he had not yet been knighted ; he was knighted with others by Simon on the morning of Lewes.
[2] *Rish., de Bellis*, &c., 17.

S

such persons, since his success would be certain to prompt him to more arbitrary measures than before. A threat of foreign interference would reunite Simons party and confirm many of the waverers. In the latter expectation he was not disappointed. Although however he must have taken both possibilities into account, he does not seem at all to have expected a decision so completely adverse. Henry was probably

Papal
interfer-
ence.
better informed as to the truth. John Mansel had obtained letters from the Pope bidding Louis decide for the king.[1] Urban had even ordered a crusade to be preached against the English rebels, and had written a letter to the Earl of Leicester, threatening him with excommunication, and contrasting his opposition to the papal see with the enthusiastic devotion of his father.[2] But something more weighty even than the papal command must have occurred to change Louis' opinion.

Possible
motive of
Louis :
To gain his favour it is possible that Henry had made a great sacrifice—a sacrifice, that is, from his point of view. Nearly six months before this the Pope had written finally to break off the engagement with respect to Sicily.[3] At the same time he had offered the crown to Louis' brother, Charles of Anjou. A

resigna-
tion of
Sicilian
claims by
Henry
resignation of all claims by Henry may possibly have influenced the pious, but not altogether unworldly, king, and have turned the scale, already heavily weighted by monarchical feeling. Feudal law, in accordance with which the King of England was the Popes vassal since the pact with John, lent its in-

---

[1] *Ann. Tewk.* 179.
[2] *Urbani IV Epist.* iii. 188, 199, quoted by Pauli.
[3] *Fœd.* i. 428, dated 29 July, 1263.

fluence to Urbans command. This supposition is urged with much force by Dr. Pauli,[1] and appears highly probable, but is perhaps hardly sufficient to account for the extraordinary and sudden change in Louis' policy. The French king might have undertaken the conquest of Sicily without any fear of serious opposition from England. Henrys resignation of hopes he had no chance of realising, if he ever made it, was worth little to Louis. On the other hand the king, in his anxiety to settle once for all with the barons, may have made Louis some great concession, perhaps of land in the south of France, as payment for active aid he hoped to receive, and to which the decision at Amiens would have been only the first step.[2] The sudden attack made upon Dover seems to show that he expected shortly to be able to introduce soldiers from France. However this may be, Louis now completely abandoned the attitude of impartiality which he had hitherto maintained, at all events in the private quarrel. There was no longer any hesitation, no hint of the impossibility of bringing about a satisfactory compromise; the matter was no sooner laid before the judge than he decided, without any reservation, in favour of one of the parties.[3]

Shortly after Christmas, 1263, Henry, after first publishing a manifesto to allay suspicion,[4] in which he declared his willingness to observe the Provisions

---

[1] *Simon de Montfort* 128.

[2] It must be said that there is no documentary evidence either for this supposition or for that of a resignation of the Sicilian claims.

[3] Mr. Pearson (*Hist. of Eng.* ii. 239) thinks that no further reason need be given than Louis' monarchical predilections, and the tendency to autocracy in France, and this interpretation is probably right.

[4] Writ dated 20 Dec. in *Fœdera.*

CHAP.
IX.

1264
Henry and
the barons
at Amiens.

of Oxford, and stated that he never had introduced
nor intended to introduce foreign troops into the
country, left for Amiens. Simon de Montfort was
detained at home by a fracture of the thigh, caused
by a fall from his horse ; but his party was represented by a deputation, consisting of Humphry Bohun
the younger, Peter and Henry de Montfort, and three
other barons, attended by their secretaries.[1] The
formal statement of the case on both sides occupied,
apparently some days, and on January 23, 1264, Louis
gave his verdict, called, from the place of assembly,

the Mise of Amiens. He cancelled, in accordance
with the papal absolution, the Provisions and the constitution dependent on them, on the ground that they
had done nothing but injury to the Crown, the Church,
and the whole kingdom. All castles were to be restored to the king ; he was to have the sole right of
appointing to all offices of State, from justiciar to
bailiff, whomsoever he would, and of removing them
at pleasure. A special clause abolished the statute
providing for the government of the country by natives
only, and empowered the king to call aliens to his
council. Only the charters granted before 1258 were
to be observed. Finally, a general amnesty was to be

proclaimed. The royal power was therefore restored
in all its former supremacy, and the whole labour of
the last six years thrown away. And not only this,
but since the Provisions, with the exception of those
enactments which placed the government in the hands
of an oligarchy, were, as is evident from an examina-

---

[1] *T. Wykes*, 139, gives the names of Adam of Newmarket, Walter
Blount, ' et pauci alii,' as the baronial deputies.

tion of their contents,[1] only the logical outcome and consequence of Magna Carta, the latter, though retained,
was endangered by the entire removal of its super-
structure. The ecclesiastical power, which three years
before had absolved Henry from his oath, could not
but rejoice at so hearty an approval of its policy ; the
Mise, as soon as it was announced at Rome, received
the papal confirmation, and a legate was to be sent to
England to ensure complete success.[2] Thus were the
three greatest powers of Europe, the Pope and the
kings of France and England, leagued together against
Simon de Montfort and the national party.

CHAP.
IX.

1264
approved
by the
Pope.

We need not ask what was the result of the decision in England. London and the Cinque Ports, we
are told, with almost the whole community of the
middle classes, utterly refused to recognise the verdict.[3] Even the royalist chronicler condemns it as
hasty and imprudent.[4] The people put it down to
bribery, or traced it to the influence of the two Provençal queens.[5] The outbreak which followed can
hardly be condemned on the ground that it involved
a distinct breach of faith. It is true that the barons
had sworn in the most sacred manner to submit
themselves unconditionally to Louis' arbitration on
the whole question of the Oxford Provisions. But it
cannot be doubted that such a proceeding as the

General
refusal to
recognise
the Mise.

The barons
justified in
refusing
recogni-
tion.

---

[1] See above, pp. 200, 213.

[2] Confirmation dated 16 March, and again 23 March, in *Fœdera*.

[3] *Lib. de Ant. Leg.* 61.

[4] *T. Wykes* 139, ' Rex Francorum . . . forte minus sapienter
et utiliter quam deceret, eructatione siquidem improvisa suum præcipit-
avit arbitrium.'

[5] Popular opinion is expressed in the song, ' O rex Francorum,
multorum causa dolorum, Judex non rectus, ideo fis jure rejectus,'
quoted by Blaauw. In *Ann. Tewk.* 176 it is attributed to the queens
influence ; in *Ann. Wigorn.* 448, to the queen and Prince Edward.

CHAP.
IX.
1264
The Mise
of Amiens :
complete
abrogation
of the Pro-
visions not
contem-
plated by
the barons ;

complete abrogation of those Provisions was never contemplated by the baronial party. Only a few months before the king had sworn to keep the Provisions ; the frequent proposals of submission to arbitration by elected commissioners or otherwise had pointed to a reform or modification of the Provisions, never to their entire removal. Some portions had been almost universally condemned ; the scheme of government had perished as it deserved. A practicable compromise on the subject of sheriffs had been suggested ; a similar arrangement might have been made for the appointment of the high officers of State. On the other hand, some notice might have been taken of the subject of taxation, so strangely omitted from the Provisions. But the safeguards against the abuse of power by the royal officers, and the statutes concerning the government of the land by Englishmen, were points which touched the root of the whole quarrel. It is as absurd to think that the barons would have submitted to arbitration, had they thought it possible that their decision on these points could be reversed, as to think that Henry would have submitted, had he thought it possible that Louis would reinstate the government of the baronial oligarchy. There can be no doubt that Louis exceeded his moral if not his legal right in giving so sweeping a verdict. The barons declared at once that they had never intended to submit the statutes against aliens to arbitration. It was doubtless a great mistake not to have stated this beforehand ; but a fact which tends to show the truth of their words is that in the petition before the opening of the war, and in the terms of peace proposed in the previous July, the observance of the statutes against aliens was made a *sine qua non*, and these seem therefore to have been exempted from the subjects under discussion. No one can blame the king for resisting the total abolition of his power decreed by the constitutional enactments at Oxford, in spite of his oath to abide by what the twenty-four should decide ; it can hardly be imputed as a crime to the barons that they rebelled against the complete annihilation of their work in the Mise of Amiens, although they had sworn to abide by the verdict of Louis.

CHAP.
IX.

1264
The barons
in the
right.

The event was in itself decisive of the future course of the struggle. The king remained three weeks longer in France, but hostilities broke out at once. Only a fortnight had elapsed when an order was sent from Court to destroy the bridges over the Severn, except that at Gloucester, in order to cut off the barons who had crossed the river, and to prevent others from crossing to join Llewelyn in an attack on Roger Mortimer.[1] There was no need of declaring war ; both parties had been long prepared. The northern barons began to move beyond the Trent, and Robert Nevill wrote to offer his assistance to the king in that quarter.[2] The Welch invasion was all in Simons favour, and he was doubtless, as the king suspected, in communication with Llewelyn.[3] The first collision seems to have taken place between some of the Marchers and the sons of de Montfort. Roger Mortimer had ravaged Simons lands, whereupon, being

Result of
the Mise of
Amiens :

outbreak
of hostili-
ties on the
Welch
border.

[1] Writ dated 4 Feb. 1264.—*Royal Letters* ii. 253. Mortimer began the attack, according to *Nic. Trivet* 254.

[2] This letter is assigned with great probability to this date by Dr. Shirley.—*Royal Letters* ii. 255.

[3] ' Adjuncto sibi principe Walliæ.—*Nic. Trivet* 254.

CHAP.
IX.

1264
Hostilities
on the
Welch
border,

as yet unable to move, owing to his accident, the earl sent his sons to the border. They besieged and took Radnor Castle, and then entered Gloucester. Prince Edward, in hot pursuit, attacked them there, on Ash Wednesday, but failed to force his way into the town, though aided by the royalists in the castle. Foiled on this side, he nevertheless made his way into the castle by means of a boat, and repelled all the attacks of the barons until the arrival of the Earl of Derby with reinforcements obliged him to negotiate. An arrangement was made, through the mediation of the Bishop of Worcester, in accordance with which the barons left the city. Edward then seized many of the citizens, and punished them by fines and imprisonment, after which he made good his escape. Earl Simon was much annoyed at this mistake, and with good cause, for had he captured Edward—as he might have done by blockade—he would have had the king at his mercy. The incompetence shown by de Montforts sons, in military no less than in other matters, is very remarkable, and finally cost their

father his life.[1] From Gloucester Edward proceeded northwards, attacking on his way the earls borough of Northampton, and Robert Ferrars' lands in Derbyshire ; but Kenilworth, which Simons inventive genius had lately fortified with all sorts of engines, previously unknown in England, was not to be taken. Thence he went to join his father at Oxford, in the

---

[1] These events (*Rish.*, *de Bellis*, &c., 20 ; *Nic. Trivet* 254, &c.), ought doubtless to be referred to this point, and are not to be confused with the somewhat similar occurrences last year at Bristol. They explain the reputation for 'vulpecularis astutia,' attributed to Edward. —*Matt. West.* 318. I have mainly followed the account of *Rob. of Glouc.* 542 seq.

early part of March, after burning and pillaging wherever he came.[1]   The campaign was carried on with all
the horrors of civil war, for passions were much embittered by this time; the men of Simons rearguard
at Rochester were killed and cruelly mutilated a little
later, and the Welch archers, taken in Sussex by the
kings forces, were beheaded.[2]   The wilder elements
of Simons party were doubtless not far behind their
enemies in ferocity.

Henry had probably chosen Oxford for his rendezvous, for the same reason as the barons in 1258
and Simon the previous spring, as being an excellent
military centre. The meeting there was in strong
contrast with that of six years before. The spirit of
the University did not look with so much favour on
the object the king now had in view, as on the Provisions which took their name from the town. The
students had given vent to their feelings in a fierce
quarrel with the townsfolk shortly before the kings arrival, and Henry accordingly dismissed the University,
alleging as a pretext the danger to the students of
rough treatment from his soldiery. The students
marched out in a body, it is said, 15,000 strong, and
joined the barons.[3]   What became of the senior part
of the University we are not told. Roger Bacon
perhaps worked on in his cell, and paid little attention to the clang of arms in the street below.[4]

Meanwhile Simon de Montfort had sufficiently
recovered from his hurt to take the field. He col-

---

[1] 'Tres socii, prædatio, combustio, occisio.'—*Matt. West.* 320.
[2] *T. Wykes* 148.
[3] *Rish.. de Bellis*, &c. 22.
[4] See a long and amusing account of the quarrel in *Rob. of Glouc.* 540 seq.

CHAP.
IX.

1264
Negotia-
tions
between
Earl Simon
and the
king,

broken off.

lected his forces, and encamped at Brackley, a few miles north of Oxford. There one more attempt for peace was made. Negotiations were opened through the medium of several bishops on the barons' side, with the French ambassador, then attendant on the king. It did not however promise well for peace that Henry at the same time issued a summons to all the magnates of the country, bidding them meet him in arms within a fortnight. Simon, on the other hand, as was shown by his repeating the attempt on the eve of Lewes, was earnest in his endeavours to maintain the peace. He declared his willingness to recognise the Mise of Amiens, if the king would give up the article admitting foreigners to power in England,[1] and stated that the barons had never meant to submit this article to arbitration. Some advance had been made, and a draught at least of the agreement for the return of the Archbishop of Canterbury made out ;[2] but William of Valence was with

[1] The constant recurrence to this point justifies the statement in *Chron. Mailros*, s. a. 1264, 'Dissensio . . . habuit initium et finem a retentione alienigenarum.' The popular hatred of these persons may be judged from a story told by Rishanger (*de Bellis*, &c. 4). A young man passing through the village of Trumpeton (? Trumpington) threw a stone at a dog that barked at him, but missed the dog and killed a hen belonging to a woman in the village. The lad swore it was done by accident, and offered double the value of the hen, but the woman refused the money and cried out for vengeance. Thereupon a bailiff of Will. of Valence seized the lad and chained him in prison so cruelly that he shortly died. His body was thrown out on a dungheap and then buried. But a steward of W. of Valence passing by some days after, and hearing the story, ordered the body to be exhumed and suspended on the gallows. The story, true or false, shows what the state of feeling must have been. The same steward is said to have answered petitions with the reply, 'If I do you a wrong, who is to grant you justice? The king wills all that my lord wills, but my lord wills not all that the king wills.' John of Oxenedes (p. 175) relates the still more atrocious murder of one of the kings cooks by Geoffrey of Lusignan, and adds that those who brought the matter before the king were jeered at for their pains.

[2] MS. quoted by Blaauw, *Barons' War*, 122. cf. *Fœd.* i. 436 seq.

the king, and he was certain to uproot any lurking wish for peace which Henry may still have cherished. The negotiations were broken off, and the bishops bidden by the king to go about their business.

War was now as good as declared, and de Montfort, anticipating an attack upon London, marched off to secure the city, leaving a strong force, under command of his son Simon, to hold Northampton. No sooner were the royal troops assembled than an attack was made upon that town by the king in person, accompanied by his eldest son and King Richard. The attempt would probably have failed but for the stratagem of the Prior of St. Andrews, a Cluniac monastery, the garden of which abutted on the walls of the town. The monks, many of whom were French, and had strong royalist proclivities, were in communication with the king, and had undermined the walls, putting in wooden props as a temporary support.[1] A feigned assault was made on the other side of the town, under cover of which the royalists made an easy entrance by the breach so caused. The baronial force made a gallant resistance, but their leader, the young de Montfort, having been taken prisoner, the remainder, who had taken refuge in the castle, surrendered next day, to the number of fifteen bannerets and sixty knights, with many of lower rank. The Oxford students, who had fought well on the baronial side, were dispersed. The town was given over to pillage.

---

[1] *Rish., de Bellis,* &c. 23 ; *Ann. Dunst.* 229, 'Muri villæ . . . qui circumdant gardinum prioris Scti. Andreæ, quos idem prior, *ut dicebatur,* malitiose quodammodo debilitaverat.' *W. de Hemingb.* 319, lays it to the charge of ' monachi alienigenæ.'

CHAP.
IX.

1264
London
declares for
the barons.

It was a serious blow, but London had meanwhile declared energetically for Simon. An alliance for twelve years was made between the barons and the city.[1] On March 31 the citizens, under command of Hugh Despenser, and other captains chosen from themselves, sallied out and destroyed the house and property of King Richard at Isleworth, as well as those of William of Valence and other obnoxious persons.

Rising of
London in
favour of
the barons:
attack on
the Jews;

The deposits in the Temple, or what was left of them after Edwards raid upon them last year, were taken, and thus a pernicious example was only too well followed. A fortnight later, on Palm-Sunday, April 12, the Jews, who were plundered by both parties indiscriminately whenever any disturbance gave the excuse, were attacked, and many of them murdered. Much gold was taken from them;[2] and Simons enemies declared he had excited the massacre and shared the spoil. That he had no great liking for the Jews, his own charter to Leicester proves; but there appears to be no reason for connecting him with so wantonly cruel an act, while the fact that after the war he issued special edicts for their protection tends to prove his innocence on this occasion. On the

other hand, the report that the Jews were going to burn the city with Greek fire, and hand it over to the royalists, which seems to have occasioned the attack upon them, is utterly absurd and incredible.[3] They could have had no wish to fall into the clutches of a king who throughout his reign used them as mere

---

[1] *Lib. de Ant. Leg.* 61.
[2] The citizens are quaintly likened in *Chron. Mailros,* to fish 'who snatch all they can.'
[3] *Ann. Dunst.* 230.

money-bags, and oppressed them mercilessly on the paltriest excuses. Probably the affair was a mere outburst of popular suspicion and frenzy ; its objects were doubtless more obnoxious to the popular party, which was composed mainly of the lower classes in London, and therefore suffered more at the hands of the usurers, than to the other side. The political struggle was degraded by the admixture of class hatred, which was intense in the city, and prompted the riotous mob to the seizure of the Temple trea-sures, which probably belonged to their wealthier fellow-citizens. It was but natural to attribute to the leader, as the royalist chroniclers did, the wild deeds of his partisans ; no doubt he must bear the blame of having been the primary cause. The movement doubtless had in it as large an element of violence, brutality, and selfishness as popular movements in all times have been cursed with ; the question is whether the gain justifies the price. At this particular time it was quite impossible to check the outbreak of the evil elements, for fear of losing the whole. Simon was probably at St. Albans,[1] whither he had gone, on his way to relieve Northampton, when this outbreak took place. Had he been in London, it might not have happened.

On hearing of the mishap at Northampton the earl was much moved, but showed no signs of de-spondency ; he was roused into fury by the loss of his son and cousin, and, 'raging like a lion robbed of his whelps,' vowed that before the end of May

CHAP. IX.

1264

Violence of the out-break laid to Simons charge.

Constancy of Earl Simon.

[1] About this time so fine and well fortified a town that it was called 'little London.'

the fortune of war should be reversed.[1] Returning through London, he first made an attempt on Rochester, the capture of which would have been of great advantage for the defence of London. He took the town and part of the castle, having destroyed the water-gate by means of a fire-ship ; but the attack on the strong Norman keep failed, in spite of all the machines which he brought against it. He was however on the point of forcing this last stronghold, so great was his skill in the arts of siege,[2] when he was forced to hasten back to London to ward off an attack on the city, threatened by Prince Edward, which was to have been aided by the royalists within.[3] The king, after the capture of Northampton, had also occupied Leicester and Nottingham, and, having been joined by the northern barons, had sent his son northwards to ravage the lands of the Earl of Derby. The news that Rochester was in imminent peril caused father and son to move hastily to its rescue, and Simon was forced to raise the siege at the moment when success appeared certain. London was too strong for attack : Henry therefore, taking Kingston on his way, marched on Rochester, and dispersed the remainder of Simons forces there. Thence he moved southwards and took Tunbridge, where he showed magnanimity or policy by releasing the Countess of Gloucester, who was in the castle. The Cinque Ports, his next object, contained a small party of royalists ;[4] but the other side were the

---

[1] ' Infremuit nec tamen concidit vultus ejus.'—*W. de Hemingb.* 313 : ' Non præteribit mensis Maii, quin adeo confusi erunt, &c.—*Rish., de Bellis,* &c., 24.

[2] Rishanger (*de Bellis,* &c. 25) says he set an example to all Englishmen how a siege should be carried on, a matter of which they were totally ignorant.

[3] *Ann. Dunst.* 231.   [3] *W. de Hemingb.* 314.

stronger, and on the kings approach they manned
their ships and put to sea, in order to prevent their being used against London. The population of Kent and Sussex is said also to have been hostile. The densely-wooded district through which the kings army passed supplied no food, and the troops suffered much privation. The fleet having been the chief object in the attack on the Cinque Ports, Henry, after the failure of his attempt, and being unable to seize Dover,[1] left the coast and marched to Lewes, in the hope perhaps of receiving foreign reinforcements through Pevensey or Newhaven.

The Earl of Leicester, after consultations held in London with the leaders of his party, had resolved again to offer peace to the king, on condition of the observance of the Oxford Provisions, and with the promise of indemnity to be made for the damage done to royal and other property. Then with a large force of Londoners he set off on his journey southward, with the intention, if peace were again refused, of dealing a decisive blow before foreign assistance arrived. The barons, after a march as rapid as the number of their foot-soldiers allowed, encamped at Fletching, about ten miles north of Lewes, in the Weald of Sussex, the dense forests of which served to conceal their movements. The letter with offers of peace, a letter worded in submissive and respectful style, not accusing the king but his evil counsellors, was signed by the Earl of Leicester, and young Gilbert de Clare, Earl of Gloucester, for the whole

---

[1] Blaauw (*Barons' War*, 117) says that Dover was surrendered to the king after the Mise of Amiens, but he gives no authority for this statement.

CHAP.
IX.

1264
Offer of
peace,

rejected by
the king.

The king
and others
defy Earl
Simon.

The Battle
of Lewes;
the baro-
nial pre-
parations;

army. It was conveyed by those whose holy office made them the rightful peacemakers, but whom a traditional policy and a long alliance bound to their leader. Walter de Cantilupe, Bishop of Worcester, was Simons oldest living friend, and Henry of Sandwich, Bishop of London, was no unworthy follower of his immediate predecessor in that see. But the offer was indignantly and contemptuously rejected, and the idea of submitting to an arbitration of prelates laughed to scorn, as unworthy of those who held their titles by the sword. The king in his answer, and Richard and Edward in their letter of defiance, did not even deign to give the hostile earls their titles; they were saluted as lying traitors, and challenged to do their worst. Richard had put off his old character of mediator, for the destruction of his property had touched him in his tenderest part.[1] Edward was not likely to forget or forgive the insult put upon his mother by the Londoners, and burned with the desire for revenge, which he was enabled to gratify to his own hurt. The negotiation occupied Monday and Tuesday, May 12 and 13. After the royal answer nothing more was to be done, and the earl resolved on losing no time. Next day, Wednesday, May 14, the fate of the country was decided on the battlefield of Lewes.

The soldiers of de Montfort were marked with a white cross on back and front, as a distinguishing sign, and in token that they called themselves, like their ancestors in 1215, the army of God. There was in them a nascent spark of the religious fervour which

---

[1] He is said at first to have offered to mediate on promise of a large indemnity. -- *Polit. Songs*, ed. Wright, 69.

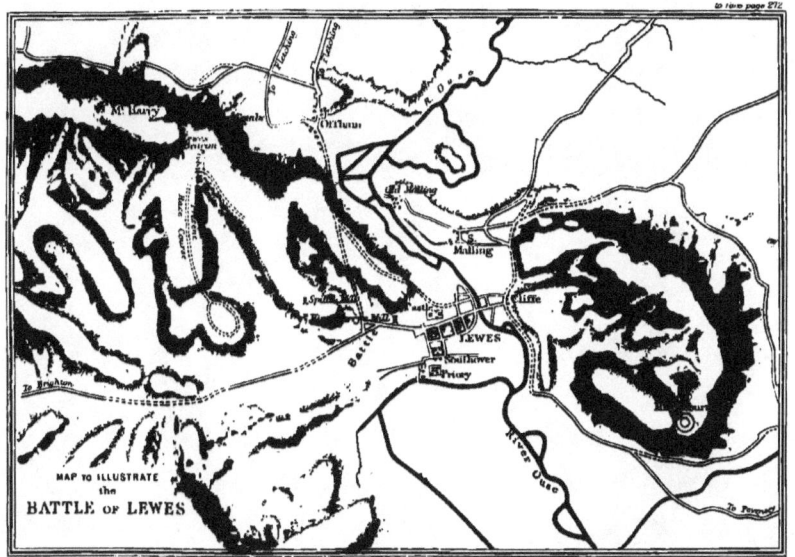

MAP TO ILLUSTRATE
the
BATTLE OF LEWES

London: Longmans & Co.

animated the armies of Cromwell. Simon himself passed the night in prayer and in anxious prepara- tion for the morrow, encouraging all around him, and infusing into them some portion of his own en- thusiasm. His troops were shriven by the Bishop of Worcester, while the royalist army indulged in wine behaviour and pleasure, not scrupling to carry on their orgies of the royalists. even on holy ground. The account of the different preparations of the two armies recalls that given of the night before another battle, fought not very far from the same place two hundred years before, and must be received with equal caution.[1] De Montforts plans were laid with a care and foresight, and executed with a combination of resource and decision, which would be sufficient, even if we knew nothing more of his milit- ary prowess, to support his reputation as the first general of his day. He determined to surprise his foes; as soon therefore as it was light enough to move, the march began. But, before we enter upon the details of the march and the battle itself, a brief description of the locality will be necessary.

The undulating ridges of the South Downs, which Descrip- form the natural bulwark of the coast of Sussex, tion of the battle-field. consist, in the neighbourhood of Lewes, of two main ridges running east and west, both of which are cut by the river Ouse in its course towards the sea at Newhaven. The northern of these ends abruptly, a short way to the east of the town, in the height called Mount Caeburn ; the southern runs on eastward till

[1] It must however be allowed that the account of the debauchery of the royal army on this occasion is supported by several independent witnesses, one of whom, the informant of the Melrose Chronicler, declares he saw it with his own eyes. The same story is told about the night before Bannockburn, as well as of that before Hastings.

CHAP.
IX.

1264
The battle
of Lewes :
description
of the
battle-field.

it ends in the cliffs of Beachy Head. In the gap between the two portions of the northern ridge lies the town of Lewes. On the eastern or left bank of the Ouse the hill rises precipitously from the bed of the stream, leaving but scant space for houses on this side. On the other side of the river this ridge, at a point two miles north-west of the town, just above the hamlet of Offham, makes a sudden curve, and is continued in two or three minor ridges, like the fingers of an outstretched hand, of constantly decreasing elevation, which tend in a south-easterly direction, till they merge in a broad undulating shelf. On this shelf the chief portion of the town is built ; a picturesque old town, consisting mainly of one long street, which runs nearly due east and west, and ends in the open down. In former days the castle, with its double keep, formed its boundary in this direction. Similarly the western portion of the southern ridge sends off one long off-shoot towards the north-east, which nearly meets those from the northern ridge. At the end of this offshoot lies the suburb of Southover, at a lower elevation than the part about the castle ; and at the point where it sinks southward into the marshy flat, which at no very distant period was covered by the sea, are still to be seen the ruins of the Cluniac Priory of St. Pancras. A line drawn from the castle to the priory would cross the intervening depression in a direction almost due north and south.

The direct road from Fletching to Lewes passes through Offham, and skirts round the bend in the ridge above mentioned, entering .the town near the castle. Had Simon followed this route, he would have been seen from the castle at least two miles off, and he would have had to fight on the level, without anything to compensate for his inferiority of numbers.[1] On arriving therefore at Offham, he turned sharp off to the right and ascended the great northern ridge of the downs by one of several tracks which lead slantwise up the steep hill-side, probably at a depression which marks the top of what is called the Combe, just to the east of Lewes Beacon.[2] Thence he followed along what may be called the middle finger of the hand above spoken of, passing close by the present racecourse, and always keeping a little way down the western side of the ridge so as to avoid being seen from the town. But already fortune had begun to favour his bold attempt. The royalists had posted a vedette somewhere on the ridge, probably on the

First success.

---

[1] *Ann. Waverley*, p. 356, make the barons 50,000, the royalists 60,000 ; others make the proportion in favour of the king much larger. Simons army included 15,000 Londoners, very poor troops.

[2] There are three points on this ridge, one without a name immediately above Offham, at the bend of the ridge, then, westward of this, Lewes Beacon, which is higher, and lastly Mount Harry, supposed to be named from Henry III, which is higher still. Mr. Blaauw supposes the barons to have mounted by the Combe, and this is most probable, as there was no reason for them to go further west. I may take this opportunity of saying that I visited Lewes purposely without any knowledge of Mr. Blaauws account, and came to a perfectly independent decision about the battle, which I was glad to find agreed in the main with his. The chief authorities from which my account is compiled, are the Chronicles of Melrose, Lanercost, John of Oxenedes, Walter of Hemingburgh and the two Chronicles attributed to Rishanger, the *Chronicon* edited by Mr. Riley for the Rolls Series, and the *Narratio de Bellis apud Lewes et Evesham*, edited by Mr. Halliwell for the Camden Society, which are however too contradictory to have been written by the same person ; all these appear to have come from independent witnesses, and are more often explanatory of one another than inconsistent. In the second rank come the Chronicles of T. Wykes, Nicolas Trivet. Waverley, and others. Unfortunately the chronicler of Osney was prevented from telling all he knew, because, as he says, 'forte quod placeret regalibus displiceret baronum fautoribus.'—*Ann. Osn.* 149.

T 2

CHAP.
IX.
1264
The battle
of Lewes :
march of
the barons;
height above Offham, whence the whole country as
far as Fletching could be commanded. These men
however had got weary of waiting, and in the course
of the night had returned to the town, leaving one
solitary watcher behind them. He had naturally
fallen ‚asleep, and was roused from his slumbers by
Simons men. From him they doubtless gained useful
information about the enemy, and after this piece of
good fortune proceeded, we are told, with great joy.
When they reached the point where the Spital Mill
now stands, and the ground sinks gently towards the
south and east, they mounted the ridge, and from its
flat top caught sight of the castle to the eastward,
and the bell-tower of the priory below, just tinged by
the rays of the rising sun.

Then Simon, knowing that the struggle would not
be long delayed, dismounted from his horse, the rest
following his example, and addressed his troops as
follows : ‘My brethren well-beloved, both peers and
vassals, the battle we fight to-day we fight for the
sake of the realm of England, to the honour of God
and of the blessed Virgin, and to maintain our oath.
Let us pray the King of all men that, if that is pleasing
to Him which we have undertaken, He may grant us
strength and aid, that we may do Him good service by
our knightly prowess, and overcome the malice of all
our foes. And since we are His, to Him we commend
our souls and bodies.’ Then they all knelt down
upon the ground, and, stretching out their arms, prayed
aloud to God for victory that day. After that the

earl knighted young Gilbert de Clare and others, and
so arranged in three bodies they marched down the hill
upon the enemy. The left consisted of the Londoners,

under the command of Nicholas de Segrave, Henry of
Hastings, and others. Simon appears to have sent
them, knowing they could hardly stand in the open
field against the mounted and well-armed foe, to enter
the town by another way and attack the enemy in
the rear.[1] The centre, probably directed against the
castle, was commanded by the young Earl of Gloucester, eager to show himself worthy of his spurs. The
right was led by Henry and Guy, two of Simons sons,
the eldest, Simon, having been taken prisoner at
Northampton ; it was meant to surprise that portion of
the royal army which was encamped round the priory.
This was the important point, for in the priory lay
the prize of victory, the king. The earl himself seems
to have remained with a fourth body in reserve, to go
wherever the course of the struggle should demand his
presence.

Even yet the advancing army does not seem to
have been perceived, until it came into collision with
a party which had come out in the early morning to
forage, some of whom, rushing back into the town, gave
the alarm. From the point where the barons halted
to the castle is about a mile, to the priory about a
mile and a half, so that the royalists had no time to
lose. Prince Edward, who was in the castle, was
naturally the first to appear, and sallying forth fell

---

[1] *J. of Oxenedes*, p. 221, says that Simon sent 'quosdam ex nobili-
oribus' to fire the town in the rear of the enemy ; these I suppose to
have been the nobles who led the Londoners. This is the only way I
can account for the Londoners being near the castle, so as to meet
Edwards attack, for it seems to me absurd to think, with Mr. Blaauw,
that they had the place of honour, and were sent directly against the
castle, the strongest point. They were, as we know, on the left, and
would naturally have been employed on this sort of service. Edward
must have sallied forth before Gloucester with the centre reached the gates.

CHAP.
IX.
1264
The Battle
of Lewes :
defeat of
the Lon-
doners ;

vigorously upon the first portion of the enemy that he came across. These happened to be the Londoners,. whom he probably took in flank as they were hurrying past the castle to enter the town, and were doubtless in very poor order. They were immediately put to flight, and pursued by the relentless victor for some miles. They appear to have fled along the road to Offham, and their bones have been discovered in pits along the steep hill-side, up which they hoped that the horses of their pursuers could not follow them.[1] When he had sufficiently glutted his sword with the blood of these unwarlike townsmen, and bitterly avenged the insult they had put upon his mother, the prince was returning towards the battle-field, when he descried upon the hill where Simons army had halted a large vehicle, on the top of which the earls standard

was flying. This was the carroccio, or waggon, on which it was the custom of the time to carry the standard of a town to battle.[2] On this occasion however it had been made use of by the earl as a place of confinement for four[3] citizens of the royalist party, whom he had taken with him as hostages on leaving the city. The waggon was very strong and barred with iron. Round it was piled what baggage the army had brought with it. The royalists, seeing the earls standard, and fancying that he was within, as being not yet sufficiently recovered from his fall to be able to mount on horseback, attacked the waggon.

---

[1] Blaauw, *Barons' War*, pp. 354, 356.

[2] As for instance in the Battle of the Standard, where the flags of York, &c, and in the Battle of Legnano, where that of Milan was carried.

[3] This number is given in *Rish.*, *de Bellis*, &c., and *Matt. West.*; others give three or two. Some say they were the citizens who had barred the gates of London against Simon in the previous autumn.

with great vehemence. They lost some time in driving off those who guarded the vehicle, and more in breaking it open, for its strength defied for a long while all their efforts. In vain they shouted, ' Come out, come out, thou devil Simon! come out, thou basest of traitors!' In vain did those within declare that not Simon but friends and allies were there. The royalists, finding all their efforts to burst open the waggon unavailing, at length set fire to it and burnt it with its unfortunate inmates.[1] By this time the day was far advanced, and Prince Edward, the Rupert of his day, returned to Lewes, exhausted with his easy but fruitless victory, to find the main battle lost and won.[2]

For de Montfort no sooner saw the best troops of the enemy engaged in pursuing the least valuable portion of his own force, than he hurled the rest of his army upon that body of the royalists which was led by the two kings in person.[3] The latter were taken completely by surprise, but speedily ranged themselves in the best order they could, and issued from the priory enclosure with the royal standard, the

---

[1] *Chron. Mailr.* p. 194, says that some of the Londoners, in order to deceive the enemy, told them that Simon had pretended he could not ride, and had not wished to come with them ; that they had therefore confined him in the waggon, in fear that if they left him behind he would play them false. But Edward can hardly have been fool enough to believe this story, which sounds as if it had been made up by the Londoners after the event. A good deal of guile has been imported into this affair, which was probably, after all, merely a lucky accident,

[2] Blaauw, *Barons' War*, p. 204, says he returned about 8 o'clock ; but surely ' usque ad octavam horam' (*Chron. Mailr.* 195) means 2 o'clock : even this is hardly possible.

[3] *Ann. Wav.* p. 357, say that the barons paused on the hill, and did not attack at once, so as to give the royalists time to wake ; so too *Rob. of Glouc.* 547 : but this is almost too Quixotic to attribute to them.

CHAP.
IX.

1264
The Battle
of Lewes :
Defeat o
the king ;
dragon of England, flying in their van. The struggle
here was long and stubbornly contested, but eventually the baronial forces, having the advantage of the
position, routed their adversaries at all points. King
Henry, who fought bravely and had his horse killed
under him, was driven back into the priory, round the
walls of which for some time the battle was continued.
Many of the vanquished were left on the field, or
were driven into the marshes, where they were
smothered.[1]   But few of this body can have made
their escape.   King Richard, who seems to have
fought his way some distance up the hill-side, was
surrounded and compelled to take refuge in a windmill.[2]   Here he was assailed with shouts of 'Come
down, come down, thou wretched miller! thou who
didst so lately defy us poor barons, with thy titles
of King of the Romans and "Semper Augustus,"
come down!' It was no place in which to stand a
long siege, and he therefore soon surrendered.   Prince

Edward came back to find his uncle a prisoner, his
father surrounded, without a chance of escape, and
the greater part of the royalist forces routed or slain.[3]
He was however about to renew the conflict, when his

---

[1] *Chron. Lanercost* **74**, says that many were found afterwards sitting
upright in their saddles, with their arms stretched out, and their swords
in their hands, as if they had been alive.

[2] This windmill was for a long time afterwards pointed out as King
Harrys mill, but has long ceased to exist.   The spot in which tradition
fixes it is where a public-house now stands, on the right-hand side of
the street, just below the gaol.—Blaauw, *Barons' War*, p. 202.

[3] The accounts of what happened to the prince after his return are
very confused and inconsistent.   I have taken what seems to be on the
whole the most probable view, which is mainly that of Rishanger (*de
Bellis*, &c.).   Some say he entered the castle, which he could hardly
have done, seeing that if he had he would not have surrendered so easily,
and that the castle was probably taken by this time : others that he

own followers, seeing it was all over, took to flight.
Among them were the Earl of Warenne and William
of Valence, the latter of whom probably expected
small mercy from de Montfort. They succeeded in
cutting their way through the town, and escaping
across the bridge to Pevensey, whence they took ship
for France.[1] The prince, thus deserted, took sanctuary
with the few who were left to him in the church of
the Franciscans, or as others say in the priory itself.
The victory of the barons was now complete, and the
priory, the last stronghold of the royalists, would probably have soon been taken by storm had not wiser
counsels prevailed, or darkness put an end to the
conflict.[2] About nightfall a truce was made. Prince
Edward surrendered himself as hostage for his father,
while Prince Henry of Almaine did the same for
the King of the Romans. Simon de Montfort was
undisputed lord of England.

fought his way into the priory, which is more likely. Some say he
surrendered at once ; others that he did so next day to save his father.
Some say that the king surrendered to Simon ; others that he would only
yield to Gloucester, from hatred of the other.

[1] *Rish. Chron.* is here inconsistent. It first says these nobles were
with Edward, then that they deserted the king. A combination with
Rish. de Bellis, &c. gives what I believe to be the truth : cf. *Walt. de
Hemingb.* 317. There is also an uncertainty about their subsequent fate.
Six months later the sheriffs were summoned to bring several of them
to London, so that they appear not to have escaped to France, but to
have been taken. The next we hear of them is their landing in Wales
in 1265.

[2] Here again the authorities differ as to whether the truce was made
that evening or next day. There are great discrepancies too as to the
number of the slain. The most circumstantial accounts give between
two and three thousand, besides those of the Londoners who were killed
in the flight, perhaps as many more. No nobles of the first rank, and
only two on each side of less repute, lost their lives.

CHAPTER X.

THE GOVERNMENT OF SIMON DE MONTFORT.

CHAP.
X.

1264
The Mise
of Lewes:
arbitrators
appointed:

THE first measure of the Earl of Leicester after the battle of Lewes was to dictate a preliminary edict, declaring the general principles on which the government was to be carried on, and sketching out a new court of arbitration, to which the principal matters in dispute were to be referred. This document was in the form of a treaty, and is called the Mise or Compromise of Lewes. The text is not preserved, but we have a contemporary abstract,[1] by which it is seen that the composition of the court was to be of a mixed nature, English and foreign, lay and clerical, with the addition of the Cardinal-Legate Guido.[2]

points to
be decided;

These commissioners were to discuss everything but the fate of the prisoners; their decision needed not to be unanimous, but whatever the majority should determine was to hold good. On some points however it appears the court was not left to decide. The king, it was declared, was to rule justly, and without respect of persons ; none but Englishmen were to be

[1] *Rish. de Bellis*, &c. 37.
[2] The names are given in Rishanger : the Archbishop of Rouen, the Bishop of London, Peter the Chamberlain, and Hugh Despenser. But the authorities differ.

made councillors, high officers, or bailiffs of any sort. The charters were to be confirmed, and precautions to be taken against the abuse of judicial and minister- ial power. The king was to be kept under a sort of financial tutelage until his debts should be paid, and he should be able to live on his own revenue, without oppression of any one. The Princes Edward and Henry of Almaine were bound over as hostages for the preservation of peace till the arbiters should give their decision. Full indemnity was granted to the Earls of Leicester and Gloucester and their followers. Lastly, the discussion was to be carried on in Eng- land, and to be concluded by Easter 1265.

The spirit of the edict must be regarded as re- markably just and moderate, when we consider that the fate of war had compelled the royalist party to an unconditional surrender. The only point that has any appearance of unfairness is that of the choice of arbiters. We are not told how they were to be chosen, but it is evident that the defeated side could have had but little voice in their selection. That the cardinal-legate was to join in the discussion is how- ever a proof that their interests were not neglected. According to another account,[1] the arbiters were to be selected by the King of France, from French and English prelates and nobles ; but much uncertainty on this point prevailed, and it is hardly likely that Simon can so soon have been willing to submit again to the influence of King Louis. The terms dictated to the conquered were all but identical with those proposed before the war ; nay, they are at first sight

---

[1] *Matt. West.* 336.

CHAP.
X.

1264
The Mise
of Lewes:
form of
govern-
ment not
left to
arbitration,
even more moderate, for no part of the Oxford Provisions or the questions under dispute was exempted
from arbitration, except the statute as to the expulsion of aliens from all offices of State. But this
extreme moderation is rather in appearance than
reality. It does not seem that the question of the
form of government was to be submitted to arbitration ; it was impossible to wait, in the present state
of confusion, till the verdict should be given. Some
form of government was absolutely necessary, and the
nature of this could not be left to the decision of so
narrow a tribunal. It would of necessity remain with
de Montfort to decide what points should be arbi-
trated on, and what these were we cannot with any

certainty say. They would possibly include the exact method of appointing sheriffs and other officers,
the general principles of which were laid down in the
Ordinance of London ; the kings household, a financial committee, and other points not of primary
importance, would be touched on. Constitutional
questions are in fact omitted in the fragmentary
copy of the Mise which we possess ; but since the
Ordinance of London and the constitution therein
adopted were considered to be in accordance with the
Mise, we may conclude that the lost portions included
some general decrees on this most important point. The

document was probably intended to allay mens fears,
and to act as an announcement of peace. For this purpose its moderate and reassuring tone was well adapted,
and marks at once the statesmanlike wisdom and the
honesty of purpose which distinguished its author.

From Lewes the earl, after having deposited his
less noble prisoners in safe places, but taking Henry

with him, moved to London. An universal suspension
of hostilities was decreed, as well as mutual restoration of prisoners without ransom ; breaches of the
peace and even the carrying of arms [1] were forbidden,
under very severe penalties ; instead of the sheriffs,
provisional guardians of the peace, doubtless from
the number of Simons friends, were appointed,[2] and
various other measures taken to restore a state of
quiet to the land.[3] The most urgent necessities
having been provided for, a Parliament was summoned to meet in London, and the thorough nature of
Simons reforms was at once apparent. The guardians
of the peace were instructed to see that four knights
were elected for the purpose of attending Parliament
by and for each county. The exactness of the word-
ing of this clause shows the importance which was
attributed to the measure.[4]

The Parliament met on June 23, and there is no
reason to doubt that the county members were present.[5] The transactions were most important. The

[1] The Earl of Leicester was specially excepted.

[2] That the Custodes Pacis did not altogether supersede the sheriffs
is shown by the proclamation (*Fœd.* i. 455) addressed to ' R. Basset
custodi pacis, *et* vicecomitibus eorumdem comitatuum.' So too in the
writ (*Fœd.* i. 456) addressed to the Custos Pacis *and* the Sheriff of
Yorkshire. On the other hand, the Custodes Pacis alone were bidden
to see to the election of four knights in 1264 ; while the Sheriffs of Sussex
and Hertford alone were bidden to bring their prisoners to the Parliament of 1265.

[3] Edicts as to damage done to property of the Church and the Jews ;
recall of the University of Oxford, &c.

[4] ' Vobis mandamus quatenus quatuor de legalioribus et discretiori-
bus militibus dicti comitatus, per ejusdem comitatus assensum ad hoc
electos, ad nos pro toto comitatu illo mittatis, ita quod sint . . . nobiscum tractaturi de negotiis prædictis,' sc. the ' negotia regni,' to be
treated by the king with the prelates, magnates, and other vassals (*Fœd.*
i. 442).

[5] This seems to be conclusively proved by the words ' voluntate
. . . regis, prælatorum, baronum, ac etiam *communitatis* tunc ibidem

CHAP.
X.

1264
Parliament
of June:
ecclesiasti-
cal legisla-
tion;

difficult question of lay and clerical jurisdiction was handled in a way which, though fragmentary, shows de Montforts ecclesiastical tendencies, and the importance of the aid rendered by the Church to the cause of liberty. At the same time it must be allowed that the regulations now issued tended to perpetuate the evils arising from the dominance and isolation of the priestly class. On the other hand, it may be argued that they placed a bulwark in the way of the extension of royal power, formed out of that body which had from the first been most closely connected with the defence of national rights. In cases of robbery, where both an ecclesiastic and a layman were concerned, the bishop of the diocese was to judge the cause. In cases where there was suspicion of the unlawful imprisonment of ecclesiastics, the bishop was to decide. The distinctness of the clerical profession was guarded by an enactment against the bearing of arms by the clergy. A committee of three

bishops was appointed to enquire into the injuries suffered by the Church within the last year, and their decisions were to be supported, if need were, by the strength of the secular arm. Finally, Archbishop Boniface was commanded to return at once, and perform the duties of his high office.[1] Simon had to repay the confidence and good faith of the Church; his gratitude found expression in these perhaps too favourable provisions.[2]

'præsentis' (relative to acts done in this Parliament); though it is doubted in the Lords' *Report* i. 154; and Dr. Pauli (*Simon de Mont.* 146) says their presence is not 'urkündlich erwähnt.' The 'communitas' can only mean the elected knights.

[1] *Lib. de Ant. Leg.* 65, 70; *Fœd.* i. 443.

[2] Pearson, *Hist. of Eng.* ii. 254, says 'They help to explain de Montforts popularity with the clergy, his place among miracle-workers

In the second place, the general principles enunciated in the Mise of Lewes were confirmed, with more special regulations as to the free entry of foreign merchants, if they came unarmed and in not excessive numbers. But the most important point was the formation of a scheme of the constitution. It is most desirable to know if this constitution was intended to be permanent or not; but from the obscurity of the preamble it is impossible to speak on this point with certainty.[1] It appears most probable that it was to last during the rest of Henrys reign, and for so long a period of that of Edward as the latter should decide; whether his decision was to be made now or when he came to the throne does not appear. That is to say, it was intended to be as permanent as any constitution could be expected to be under the

CHAP.
X.

1264
Scheme of government drawn up: question of its permanence.

---

after death, and his failure in government.' But they do not go very far to explain these facts.

[1] The preamble runs thus, 'Hæc est forma pacis a domino rege &c. . . . communiter et concorditer approbata : videlicet quod quædam ordinatio facta in parliamento Londoniis habito . . . pro pace regni conservanda quousque pax inter dictum dominum regem et barones apud Lewes per formam cujusdam misæ prælocuta compleretur duratura omnibus diebus prædicti domini regis et etiam temporibus domini Edwardi postquam in regem fuerit assumptus usque ad terminum quem ex nunc duxerit moderandum firma maneat stabilis et inconcussa ;' then follows the ' dicta ordinatio.' It is uncertain whether the word ' duratura' agrees with ' ordinatio' or with ' pax ;' if with the latter, then it is merely said that the ' ordinatio' is to remain firm and stable for an indefinite period. At the end we read, ' omnia prædicta faciat dominus rex . . . in forma prædicta (sc. forma regiminis) . . . præsenti ordinatione duratura donec misa apud Lewes facta . . . fuerit concorditer consummata vel alia provisa quam partes concorditer duxerint approbandam.' It seems therefore that the constitution, at the time that it was made, was announced to last until the terms of the Mise should be executed ; that when that result took place, the constitution was confirmed and declared to continue for at least the rest of Henrys reign, as stated in the preamble, which was drawn up in 1265. It is probable that Simon from the first meant it to be permanent, but thought it premature positively to announce so important a change in June 1264.

circumstances. The Ordinance, as this form of government was called, was confirmed the next spring; and in consequence of this the hostages were released. Now the hostages had been given in order that the arbitration might take its course, and that the peace of the kingdom might be placed on a firm basis. That this was considered to have been done in March 1265 is shown by the release of the hostages; and it was done by the acceptance of this constitution of June 1264 and certain other subsequent arrangements. Thus it was on the existence of this constitution that the peace of the country was held to depend; and the constitution was not meant to last,. as might perhaps be inferred from the preamble, only till the permanent arrangements for the preservation of peace were complete. It was itself the most important of these arrangements. That however it did not complete them, but was in reality only the first step, is shown by the fact that the hostages were not released till after many additional arrangements had been made and collectively confirmed in March 1265.

According to this scheme of government there are to be 'chosen and nominated' three persons, called electors. These electors are to receive authority from the king to elect or nominate, on his behalf, nine councillors. By counsel of these nine, three of whom by turn are to be always at Court, the king is to transact all business of State. If any State official, great or small, transgress, the king is at once, by counsel of. the nine, to depose him, and substitute another in his place. If any councillor perform his duty ill, or if there be any other reason for his removal, the king shall, by counsel of the electors, remove him and substitute another. If the councillors cannot agree on any question, the electors or two of them shall decide. If the electors disagree, that which two of them decide shall hold good, provided that in ecclesiastical questions one of the two shall be a prelate of the Church. Finally, if it shall seem good to the whole body of prelates and barons that any one of the electors should be removed, the king shall, by counsel of the aforesaid body, appoint another in his place.

This scheme of government may fairly be regarded as the creation which more than any other marks the genius of Simon de Montfort. Other matters—his courage, constancy, sympathy with the oppressed— may call forth more general admiration. His adaptation of the existing county machinery to parliamentary representation marks his ingenuity and insight into contemporary politics. But that which bears the most unmistakeable stamp of political genius is this constitution of 1264. So far as it goes it is perfect; elaborate, yet simple; a constitution, in the true sense of the word; that is, a form of government which will stand by itself, a building so composed as to exist without any external assistance. It shows an advance upon the crude ideas of six years before, which would be inexplicable were we obliged to believe that Simon had any but the smallest share in the planning of the earlier scheme. The principles on which it rests are almost precisely the same as those of the constitution under which England has been governed for the last century and a half.

First of all, it is a purely electoral system. The electors are to be chosen, though it is not stated by

The constitution of 1264 : its general character ;

and principles.

U

CHAP.
X.

1264
The con-
stitution of
1264 : its
principles :
whom they were to be chosen in the first instance.
They were in fact at first self-elected, though nominally chosen by the king ; but the theory was that
they were chosen by some one ; and, once appointed,
their position depended on the will of the 'community,' who, in conjunction with the king, could
depose any or all of them if they saw fit. The basis
then of government, the ultimate holder of power, is
the 'community of prelates and barons,' including not
only the greater barons but the smaller too, who were
now enabled to attend through their representatives
from town and county ; that is therefore, at any rate, the
whole class of which the old Great Council was theoretically composed. The king is the exponent and
executor of the will of all three bodies—the electors,
the council, the community ; the centre in which they
all meet, the representative by whom they act, the
embodiment of the State, through whom it touches
and becomes visible to the nation. The king has no
absolute will of his own, any more than any other
single officer or collection of officers ; he is but the
highest officer of the State ; the only absolute and
independent will is that of the community. The only
occasion in which it appears that the king is to have
the initiative is in the appointment of the councillors,
for here he, being the centre of the executive, may be
supposed to know best who is fitted for the post.
the elec-
tors; their
position
that of a
prime-
minister.
But even here he is not absolute ; he is to act by
counsel of the electors, the representatives of the
community. The electors stand in the position of a
prime-minister, who is in fact chosen by the force of
public opinion, finding expression in the kings uttered
choice. The means of deposing the electors, as of

deposing the prime-minister, may vary ; it may be the adverse vote of the community, or some other way, but the electors and the prime-minister are in fact equally in the hands of the community. Again, the prime-minister receives authority from the king to appoint his fellow-ministers, and he submits the list for the kings approval : similarly the electors are authorised by the king to appoint the councillors. In neither case is the king the absolute granter of the authority ; that he shares that authority with the community is shown by the fact that the latter have the power of determining with him the person to whom he shall transmit it.

There are, it is hardly necessary to say, differences between our system and that of de Montfort : the power of the community to appoint their own chief ministers is not yet even in our day fully recognised, the theory being that the authority is conferred absolutely by the monarch, however little it may be so in reality. The fact however is there, though it is not formally recognised ; in this respect Simons constitution is more advanced than ours, for he insisted on the co-operation of the king and the community in the actual choice of the ministers, while we have only the practical right of a veto on an appointment disagreeable to the nation. Simon recognised the impracticability of any other system than that which we have gradually adopted, holding that, in any constitution that is to stand, the real rulers must be those who, from whatever cause or in whatever way, have most power. The inevitable result of any other system is an outbreak of the confined forces ; in other words, a revolution. Other differences, such as that between the

CHAP.
X.

1264
Contrast of
the consti-
tution of
1264 with
the modern
system.
triumvirate of electors and the single prime-minister,
are only such in appearance, since in the former case
unity of action was secured by the vote of the majority. Others again, such as the restriction of the
electors to the right of appointing and of acting as a
kind of high court of appeal, in cases where the councillors could not agree, compared with the multi-
farious powers exercised by a prime-minister, are
comparatively unimportant. The 'community' in
Simons constitution was not so wide as in ours;
but in both cases it is limited, in both cases the
electoral right within the electorate is equal. The
ground-principle is the same; that is, the mutual
dependence of all parts of the government, the division and distribution of power, resting finally on the
broadest basis possible, the whole of the electorate.

One must not forget that the constitution of 1264
was incomplete. What we have is a mere sketch,
doubtless intended to be filled in by the teaching of
experience. We have for example no idea as to how
legislation was to be carried on, as to the right of
taxation, what voice Parliament was to have in
foreign affairs, or in the ordinary administration of
government; there was no provision for the regular
summons, no definition of the class to be represented.
We have however what was of paramount necessity,
the ground-plan; the rest could wait awhile. The

constitution broke down before it had had time to
get into working order, because it was premature,
and that in two ways: in the first place, the political
instinct necessary for working it was not yet in existence; in the second, the limits of the franchise were
too wide, and power was granted to those who were not

yet able to hold it. The point at which this constitution drew the line was far below that at which it had been drawn at the Conquest ; and, while in the interval the power of parliament had become real instead of nominal, the difference between the strongest and the weakest of the holders of power had enormously increased. Thus, whereas two centuries ago the baronage had been nearly on the same level of inferiority to the monarch, the powerful few were now almost his equals, and stood as high above the weakest of their peers as the king had stood above them in former years. This change in the relative positions of the greater and smaller barons increased the difficulty of enfranchising the weaker members of the class. They had been unable to hold the power conferred on them by Magna Carta : they were still unable to hold what Simon gave them ; he took the step of enabling them to use their right by means of representation, in order to draw out their power and support himself by it, but it gave way under the strain. Still the gift taught the receiver to use his strength, which grew with the desire to use it : in the next generation the class was strong enough, and the gift granted by Simon was renewed by Edward to a worthier generation, and was not taken away again. Since then, the breadth of the electorate has grown, as each successive class has grown more powerful. Simon, whether consciously or unconsciously, formed a perfect constitution embodying this principle. His constitution died with him ; but England, half consciously, half unconsciously, has been following the same direction ever since.[1]

[1] Mr. Pearson (*Hist. of Eng.* ii. 252) seems to me to have misrepresented the nature of this constitution. He says of it, ' While the

CHAP.
X.

1264-65

Earl Simon
and repre-
sentation :

his chief
object.

The step for which Simon de Montfort is generally renowned, the summoning of four knights from
each county in 1264, and still more the summoning
of members from counties and boroughs in 1265, is
not so great a mark of his genius as this constitution,
though it is perhaps a more remarkable proof of his
statesmanship. He was in fact compelled by the
jealousy of the upper classes to seek for support
elsewhere. The object with which he had grasped the
supremacy was, next to the preservation of England
from foreign influence, the enfranchising of the class
of smaller barons, the 'bachelorhood' of England.
Nominally members of the Great Council since the

general plan of government adopted at Oxford six years before was renewed in this scheme, its details were evidently more oligarchical. It
was no longer felt necessary to admit a royalist element. The result
was a strong government for the moment, but without the broad basis
which alone can withstand the shocks of a revolutionary epoch.' How
a constitution which ensured elective and responsible ministers, with the
representation of a larger class than had yet been practically admitted
to the franchise —for the measures of 1264 and 1265 must of course be
taken together—can be called more oligarchical than a system which
placed absolute power in the hands of fifteen or twenty nobles, self-
elected and irresponsible, with a sham representation and a dummy
king, I am at a loss to understand. The royalist element was not admitted in 1264, it is true, because the victory of the reformers was much
more complete than in 1258 ; but it would have been admitted subsequently by the regular process of election and representation. The
royal power in 1258 was left apparently untouched, but really annihilated ; in 1264 it was utilised as at the present day. In 1264 the phrase
of M. Thiers might have been used, 'The king rules but does not
govern.' Finally the constitution was upset, not because its basis was
not broad enough—for in fact it was still too broad—but because in its
young helplessness it depended on its founder, and with his fall it fell.
Since the account in the text was written, I am glad to find that I am
in general agreement with Prof. Stubbs, who says (*Const. Hist.* ii. 91),
' The provisions of 1258 restricted, the constitution of 1264 extended, the
limits of Parliament. . . . Either Simons views of a constitution had
rapidly developed, or the influences which had checked them in 1258
were removed. Anyhow he had genius to interpret the mind of the
nation, and to anticipate the line which was taken by later progress.'
With the countenance of such an authority I am content to let my
words stand.

days of the Conquest, they had, from a variety of
reasons, dropped out of power, and the rising influence
of Parliament made their exclusion from it the more
bitter.   De Montfort was but redeeming a pledge
and following the spirit of Magna Carta when he
secured their representation.   Without them a victory
of the baronage resulted, as we have seen, in an
oligarchy, just as a victory of the king without the
aid of the greater barons must have ended in a
tyranny.   On the other hand, had the greater barons
enlisted faithfully under de Montforts standard, it
would not have been necessary for him to appeal to
the next class in the social scale ; had he won by
their aid, they would have hampered him in his
endeavours to raise the lower order.   Granting that
his sympathy with that class was deep and true, it is
still possible that, had he been in a position to do so,
he would have considered it sufficient to carry his
administrative reforms, his measures for the welfare
of the people, in an autocratic manner, without any
reference to the wish of those who were to gain by
those measures.   He might, had he had the greater
barons to back him, have followed the maxim of
Frederick of Prussia, and done 'everything for the
people, but nothing through the people.'   But this
was not so ; he had to call in their aid, and they thus
acquired the right to an independent position, the
right to make themselves heard in matters concerning their own welfare.   Thus it was that the popular
cause, in its truest sense, actually gained through its
desertion by those who should have protected it.

But if the people gained by the selfishness of the
greater barons, they also profited by the weakness of

CHAP.
X.

1264-65
Reasons
which
necessi-
tated
popular
representa-
tion :
hostility of
the greater
barons ;

weakness of
the king.

CHAP.
X.

1264–65
Weakness
of the king
a cause of
the growth
of repre-
sentation.

the king. Had Henry been able to rule alone, he might have reduced the greater barons, and therefore still more the lower vassals, to the level at which they stood under his grandfather. Had he even known how to use their divisions, had he understood the support which an able king might have won from what may be called the upper-middle classes of the day, he might have played off one against the other, and our political institutions might have passed by a natural transition from feudalism into the condition to which a despotic monarchy reduced them in France. But the incapable attempt at despotism which was made during the half century after Magna Carta supplied a stimulus to the movement, while it was unable to prevent it from gaining strength and consistency at its most critical period, so that when a strong king appeared the plant was too vigorous to be rooted out. It is the undying honour of Simon de Montfort, not that he sowed the seed, nor that he garnered the crop, but that he fostered and directed its growth in the hour of weakness. With an eye far keener than any of his fellows he saw the only possible cure of the evils which all felt, he perceived the principles which underlay the popular movement, and the way in which they were to be applied ; when others, in cowardly fear for their own interests, shuddered at the spirit which they had raised, and sought to retrace their steps, he went boldly on, knowing that while there was one to lead the spirit would follow, and would be a servant and not a master.

How he applied the principle of self-government to the supreme authority of the country we have seen

in the constitution of 1264. The Parliament of 1264
was the first step in the execution of that idea. The
principle was then applied, though not for the first
time, to the election of members by the people.[1] Popular representation a matter of principle with Earl Simon ;
What is most remarkable in Simons action in this
matter is not however so much this step, as the fact
that what was before merely tentative was in him a
principle and a conviction. The only real novelty in
the Parliament of 1265 was the recognition of a distinction between county and borough, a great advance
indeed, but hardly to be called the introduction of a
new principle. The representative system has been its origin
traced back into the earliest periods of English hist- and early application;
ory, and has its roots in the popular institutions of
the Anglo-Saxon township.[2] Applied by Henry II
to the jury system, extended from civil to criminal
cases, and thence to the assessment and valuation of
land for the purposes of taxation, it was first adapted
by John to purely political affairs. Thus even in
political matters the idea of representation was no
new one ; it was acted on in 1213 ; its unconscious
growth is traceable, though at first sight not ap-
parent, in Magna Carta. In that document the pre- apparent in Magna Carta.
sence of a number of members in the Great Council,
much larger than usually attended, is looked upon as
legitimate ; their attendance is not insisted on, and
the possible results of their non-attendance are carefully guarded against, by the provision that the proceedings of the council are not to be considered null

---

[1] It was probably the first time that we can be sure that these members actually joined in the discussions of Parliament ; see note 5 on p.
285.

[2] Stubbs, *Const. Hist.* i. 585, 608, 620 seq. ; and *Sel. Charters* 24,
36 seq.

CHAP.
X.

1264-65
Popular
representa-
tion
apparent in
Magna
Carta ;
and void if all the members do not appear. So far
then there would seem to be no thought of representation in the charter ; but in this very disregard
for the personal attendance of the smaller barons the
idea is visible ; for the latter do not choose their own
representatives, because they are in fact considered
to be represented by the more powerful members of
their class. Those present speak for the whole body ;
the absent are bound by the vote of the few who
attend, just as if they had elected them. This fact,
though not observed at first, was gradually recognised
by the greater barons ; it was a necessary consequence of the right possessed, or at least claimed, by
the whole body of tenants-in-chief to assent to taxation. In some cases the whole body is said to have
consented to a tax when all could not have attended
to give their consent.[1] Whether in such cases the
greater barons took upon themselves to authorise a
tax levied on the whole body, or whether they in
some way or other conferred with the smaller barons
and gained their consent, is uncertain. But that this
fact of representation and the responsibilities dependent on it were acknowledged by this time is
shown by the action of the barons in 1258, when
they declined to vote an aid on behalf of the whole
body, until they had consulted the 'community,'
whose representatives they regarded themselves. In
the constitution of 1258, the principle of representa-

---

[1] In the charter of 1225, earls, barons, &c., with the 'libere tenentes
et omnes de regno nostro,' are said to have consented to the fifteenth.
In 1232 earls, barons, &c., with the 'libere tenentes et villani de regno,'
voted the fortieth, while in 1237 the 'liberi homines' &c. promised
'pro se et suis villanis,' which explains the former writ. The remonstrance of 1246 is said to have emanated from 'the clergy, barons, &c.,
and the whole people.'

tion, however maimed and imperfect its expression, was through the appointment of the twelve representatives of the community confirmed as a regular and constant element in the supreme tribunal of the nation.

Thus the growth of the idea in general and its gradual application to different parts of the machine of government are plain enough ; but many important details are very obscure. In the first place, what is the 'community' which was represented by the twelve members in the constitution of 1258 ? Who were the persons who chose the four knights in 1264, the borough and county members in 1265 ? From what class were the knights representative taken ? Was every elector also eligible ? These and other questions it is very hard to answer with any confidence. It seems certain however that the word 'community' in the first instance included the whole body of the baronage, the tenants-in-chief of the Crown, or in its narrower sense, when used in distinction from 'the barons,' the rest of that body, the smaller barons who did not personally attend.[1] This is evident from its connexion with what we know of the constitution of the Great Council, the difference between its legal and its actual members, the allusions in Magna Carta, the subsequent appearances of this body on subsequent occasions. It is this class of smaller military tenants-in-chief, and not those below it, which is most prominent among the unrepresented during this whole period. There appears no reason to suppose that the mention of them in Magna Carta, especially as the clause was suppressed, brought about

---

[1] This is the conclusion arrived at by the framers of the Lords' *Report* (i. 140) after consideration of all instances in which the word occurs.

CHAP.
X.

1264-65
Popular
representa-
tion :
the ' com-
munity '
and the
knights
representa-
tive.

any real change in their political position. They were the first of the non-governing classes of the day, so that it is impossible not to connect them with the ' four lawful and discreet knights,' who were to be elected by the counties in 1226, to declare before the magnates their causes of complaint against the sheriffs; with the two knights summoned in 1254 to Westminster, 'to provide an aid in time of need ;' with the four knights elected in 1258 and 1259 by the counties, to report on grievances against the sheriffs. It is probable that many of this class were included in the number of those tenants-in-chief, a hundred or more, who appeared at Oxford in 1258 ; for so large an assembly was very rare, and must have contained other than the usual elements. They did not however appear there as representatives, but only as individual tenants-in-chief. The ' bachelorhood '[1] who were so ill represented by the twelve in 1258 that they complained next year to Prince Edward, must be in the first instance the lords of small manors and owners of knights fees, though others may have, and probably did, join in the remonstrance.

But, if it is probable that the knights representative stood at first for the smaller military tenants-in-chief, and for no others, it is pretty certain that at the time we have reached the class represented by them was far less limited. The smaller barons were at first separated by very vague limits from the greater members of their class, by nothing else in fact than the distinction between the special and the general summons. But as these limits became more strictly

---

[1] The derivation is uncertain. Littré derives it from ' vaccalaria,' a small farm. In Latin it is ' baccalaria ' or ' bachilleria.' In *Matt. Paris.* it is Ritterschaft.

defined through the consequences of that distinction, and by constant usage, those separating the smaller barons from the classes below seem to have become less strict. Through the falling-in of escheats and other causes the number of small tenants-in-chief by military tenure was constantly on the increase. The subtenants, the whole class of freeholders and socage-tenants increased as rapidly. The amalgamation of all these classes is natural enough, and is traceable perhaps to the action of two main causes. Since all freeholders were on certain occasions liable to military service, those who held their land of the king in chief by military tenure, and were therefore legally members of the Great Council, tended to coalesce with those who, though not holding their lands by military tenure, might still be received as members of the same class. Secondly, the want of representation was equally felt by all; and the ancient right of one part of the unrepresented class would naturally be used to further the claims put forward on behalf of the whole body. The military tenants-in-chief by escheat, who seem to have been considered to possess no legal claim to a seat in the council, formed a link between the old tenants-in-chief and the subtenants; while the more important subtenants would be unlikely to acquiesce in the possession of even nominal political rights by the many tenants-in-chief who were weaker than themselves. Thus common military service and common lack of political power tended to obliterate the artificial distinctions of feudalism.

This tendency towards amalgamation is apparent in the fluctuating use of words, and in the usurpation

CHAP.
X.

1264–65

obliteration of ancient distinctions,

owing to the universality of military service,

and common lack of political power.

Changes in the use of titles.

Simon de Montfort.

CHAP.
X.

1264-65
Popular
representa-
tion : usur-
pation of
the title of
baron,

of titles by those not originally possessing them. We have heard Henry revile those 'London boors who styled themselves barons :' the rioters of London called themselves 'bachelors,' seeing clearly enough the advantage of connecting themselves in name at least with their superiors. Municipal dignities would probably be held, at least in the great towns, by some who had a right to a still higher position : we hear of 'Barons of the Cinque Ports,' whose position, as defenders of the coast, gave them military and political importance. Those who shared with them municipal power would probably aspire to share with them political power as well. Moreover, this exten-

and the use
of the
county-
court,
imply an
extension
of the
franchise.

sion of the electorate, which must have been rendered almost necessary by the gradual coalition of classes, appears still more probable when we regard the fact that in all the instances of the election of representatives it is the regular county machinery which is set in motion. It is the sheriff who is bidden to superintend the election ; the knights are elected by and for the county ; the writs place no restriction on the right of election. In after times the knights of the shires were elected at the county courts by the suitors of those courts. We can hardly imagine any other means of electing the members, if, as was provided with such care by Simon de Montfort, the members were to be anything more than mere nominees of the sheriff. It is pretty certain therefore that all who owed suit at the county court joined in the election. An exact definition of those suitors is hard to give ; they cannot however have been limited to the military tenants-in-chief.[1]

[1] I believe that I differ slightly here from Prof. Stubbs, who thinks (*Const. Hist.* ii. 225, seq.) that the knights from the first represented

But supposing the body represented to have been so large as this, it seems impossible that all who composed it can have had the right of being elected as well as that of electing. The definition of the county members, that they were to be ' legal and discreet knights,' shows that they were limited to such military tenants as held sufficient land to qualify them for knighthood. It was indeed hardly possible yet for any but those whose profession was in the first place that of arms to sit in Parliament, even as members for the boroughs. That subtenants were however eligible, is shown by the lists of those who attended the parliaments of Simon de Montfort. It is uncertain how far the sheriff was able to interfere in the election, or to limit the number of those who might act as representatives; but it is evident that he must have had great power in this respect, perhaps to the extent of presenting a certain number of persons to the county court for election. He may have even nominated the knights representative in 1213, for no mention of election is made. The long struggle for the right of appointing sheriffs shows the great influence those officers must have exercised in political matters, an influence similar to that of the prefects under the French empire. It is hardly probable that they would have allowed the election of any one below the rank of a military tenant-in-chief. In 1264 it appears likely that the four knights belonged to the class of barons not personally summoned. The words of the writ for the

CHAP.
X.

1264–65
Limitations of the passive franchise;

influence of the sheriff on elections;

proofs of the limitation in 1264.

the whole body of suitors attending the county-courts ; but it seems improbable that they should have been regarded at once as representing any but those who were legal members of the Great Council. This was no longer the case in 1264.

CHAP.
X.

1264-65
Popular
representa-
tion : the
passive
franchise
more
limited
than the
active.

appointment of guardians of the peace contemplate a settlement of affairs by the king and barons,[1] which shows that the Parliament to be assembled was a Parliament of barons only. But in the same writs the election of the four knights to sit in this Parliament is ordered. These knights were therefore included under the name barons, and can only have belonged to the smaller baronage, the greater members of which attended in person. The passive right of election was therefore probably much more limited that the active. It is unfortunate that the evidence we have is not sufficient to guarantee very positive declarations on these points, but, in leaving this portion of the subject so uncertain, we do but follow the precedent of the Lords' ' Report,' which declares the whole matter ' to be involved in great obscurity.'

First
appearance
of the
knights
representa-
tive in Par-
liament.

There remains the question as to the first occasion on which the representatives actually took part in the discussions of Parliament. We have no documentary proof that they did so till 1264. The knights whom John summoned in 1213 were to consult with him on affairs of State. The words used do not imply more than that they were to appear and to speak with the king ; not necessarily that they were to sit in council with the greater barons. In 1237 mention is made by one authority[2] of ' citizens and burghers ' being ' in council.' But besides the extreme improbability that borough members were present in the kings council at so early a date, the vagueness with which the chroniclers speak makes them most untrustworthy

---

[1] ' Donec per nos et barones nostros . . . fuerit ordinatum.'—*Fœd.* i. 442 ; cf. Lords' *Report* i. 138. This may be however attributing too much weight to an interpretation of the word ' barons.'

[2] *Ann. Tewk.* sub anno, ' civium et burgensium.'

witnesses in such matters. The presence in Parliament of elected knights in 1252 might be inferred
from the words of the writ in which the 'earls, barons,
knights, and others,' tested the confirmation of the
charters ; but we cannot lay much weight on the
expression, for these knights may have been members
of the exchequer, or other high officers, who would
naturally attend a council. The summons for two
knights of the shire to grant an aid, in 1254, is so
carefully worded, and the object for which they met
so distinctly stated, that it is hardly possible to doubt
that they actually appeared. Whether they assembled in the same chamber as the greater barons
of the council is however uncertain. The object of
their summons being restricted to the granting of an
aid, it seems improbable that they took part in the
regular discussions which would have taken place in
the council.[1] It is not likely that the greater barons
in 1258 admitted the large number of tenants-in-chief
who appeared at Oxford to the actual discussions on
the form of government ; their interests would have
obtained more attention had they had a voice. In
1261 the attendance of knights representative was no
doubt contemplated by the Earl of Leicester, but we
have no proof, nor is it on other grounds at all probable, that that meeting, or the one called in opposition to it by the king, ever took place. But in the
year 1264 we are no longer left in doubt. The concluding words of the Ordinance of London, made at
this Parliament, are explicit. 'This Ordinance was
made at London, by consent, will, and command of
our sovereign lord the king, also of the prelates, the

[1] See Stubbs, *Const. Hist.* ii. 67, 221.

X

CHAP.
X.

1264–65
Popular re-
presenta-
tion : the
parliament
of 1265.

barons, and lastly of the community then present in the same place.'[1] The prelates and barons are the ordinary members of the national council hitherto ; the community can mean no other than the elected knights. The presence of the county and borough members in the great Parliament of 1265 is not certified in so distinct a manner, but cannot be doubted. That in the confirmation of the charters,[2] issued in March 1265, this Ordinance is referred to as made 'by assent of king, prelates, earls, and barons,' does not invalidate the above argument ; it does not imply the exclusion of the knights, any more than the former writ implies the exclusion of the earls. Besides the occasions above mentioned, it is not unlikely that they were assembled on others too. They may have been frequently consulted when necessary, without taking part in the discussions of the council, as the assembly of minor ecclesiastics often met when the prelates attended Parliament.

The union of these distinct chambers was one of the great objects of Simon de Montfort. As far as the laity were concerned, he carried out his intention in the Parliament of June 1264. It is not so well known that he intended to apply the same principles to the clergy. He was not content with the system of convocation, to which, if the above supposition is correct, these occasional assemblies of the smaller lay baronage in some measure answered. Neither of these bodies could have any real power as long as they met separately, and were merely consulted at will by the members of the more important assembly. Accord-

---

[1] *Fœd.* i. 443 ; see note 5 on p. 285.
[2] *Sel. Charters,* 407.

ingly he summoned to the Parliament, which was to have met at Winchester in June 1265, two canons from each cathedral chapter.[1] This stroke of de Montforts political genius, which is in itself as remarkable as the summoning of the lay members, though of far less political importance, and was a logical complement of that measure, does not seem to have been sufficiently noticed : the reason probably is that his death prevented the execution of the plan, and it remained therefore, unlike the corresponding measure with regard to the laity, a mere intention.

It was then in the Parliament of 1264 that one great and lasting constitutional advance was made. The other was reserved for the Parliament of 1265. It was in this latter that the distinction between county and borough members first appears. In the ranks of the smaller baronage were included not a few inhabitants of the towns ; the 'nobles of the seaports' joined in the remonstrance of 1246. Especially remarkable in this respect is the appearance of the Mayor of London, who acted as witness to Magna Carta and to the Ordinance of London in 1264. In what capacity he attended does not appear ; he may have been considered a member of the council, or may have been summoned simply to witness an important writ. In both cases he must have attended as representative of the great city which had so largely contributed to the victory of the popular cause. But apart from him there is no trace of

Parliament of 1265 : distinction of county and borough.

[1] *Sel. Chart.* 409. Prof. Stubbs (*Const. Hist.* ii. 222) in speaking of this writ, says, ' It is not impossible that Henry III, after the victory of Evesham, when he summoned proctors for the cathedral chapters, summoned also representatives of the Commons to Winchester.' But the writ is dated 15 May, nearly three months before Evesham, and must therefore have emanated from Simon and not from Henry.

CHAP.
X.

1264-65
Parliament
of 1265 :
distinction
of county
and
borough.

special members for the boroughs till 1265. For the purpose of electing representatives the towns would have been hitherto merged in the counties, and thus faf they were already represented. The representation of Middlesex was doubtless practically the representation of London, since the city had gained municipal freedom, and even become responsible for the county in which it lay. But other towns were not so well off, and it was a remarkable piece of political insight to recognise the justice of their claims on separate representation. What towns were invited to send representatives we are not told ; the number, apart from London and the larger sea-ports, was probably not large.[1] The Cinque Ports were distinguished from the rest by sending four knights each to the Parliament of 1265, while other boroughs sent two apiece. How many members represented London we do not know ; there is, strangely enough, no evidence that a writ was addressed to the city, but that it was represented it is impossible to doubt.

It need hardly be remarked that the Parliaments of 1264 and 1265 were in a sense very incomplete. As Mr. Pearson says, ' It was no longer felt necessary to admit a royalist element.' He might have said, ' It was no longer possible to admit a royalist element.' When the royalists aimed at nothing less than the total destruction of all that the Parliament was summoned to do, it would have been the merest absurdity to ask them to take part in its debates.[2] As well might the National Assembly in 1791 have allowed the *emigrés* to discuss with them on equal

---

[1] We are only told that writs were issued to York, Lincoln, ' et ceteris burgis Angliæ.'

[2] Cf. Stubbs, *Const. Hist.* ii. 92.

terms the groundwork of their new constitution. When the infant State had become consolidated and able to stand alone, then it would have been time enough to admit those who were its sworn enemies. Hence the incompleteness of de Montforts Parliaments. We do not know the names of the members who composed the Parliament of 1264; but in that of 1265, though the Church was very fully represented, summonses were issued to only five earls and eighteen barons. This list however does not include all who were present, for the names of some are mentioned afterwards, who must have attended, but to whom no writs are stated to have been issued.[1] A certain number of counties were also apparently excluded from representation in the Parliament of 1264, though for almost all the omissions reasons can be given; and the omission of any summons addressed to London in 1265 warns us not to depend too much on the correctness of the list.[2]

Thus then there appears in the work of Simon de Montfort, apart from the two most important points

CHAP.
X.
1264-65

members
summoned
to the par-
liament of
1265.

[1] The lists give the names of one archbishop, twelve bishops, 105 abbots, priors, and deans, the masters of the two orders of Knights Templars and Knights of St. John, five earls and eighteen barons: ten of the northern barons received safe conducts a little later (17 Jan.). The number of the clergy is not extraordinary, when we consider that many of them who would not usually have attended were probably regarded as corresponding to the county and borough members. No writs are said to have been issued to Giles de Argentine, P. de Montfort and Simons own sons, who must have been present. The Bishop of Llandaff also attended, but is not mentioned in the list.

[2] Durham, Chester, Lancaster, and Cornwall were under separate and peculiar jurisdiction : Monmouth and Hereford were border-counties and half Welch ; Middlesex was accounted for by London ; Rutland was perhaps too small. The reason for the omission of Surrey, Sussex, Lincoln, and Somerset does not appear. Mr. Pearson however (*Hist. of Eng.* ii. 251) sees in the omission of Cornwall, Surrey, Sussex, and Hereford the fear of royalist influence ; but he includes in his list of omitted counties Gloucestershire, to which a writ was sent: see *Fœd.* i. 442, possibly the list in the *Fœdera* is incomplete.

CHAP.
X.

1264–65
Summary
of Earl
Simons
work.

explained above, hardly so much novelty as he usually receives credit for. He can hardly be called without reserve the 'creator of the House of Commons,[1] though to him doubtless is owing far more than to any other individual. Still less can the famous Parliament of January 1265 be said to 'consist of completely new elements.'[2] Simon would have been the first to repudiate so radical a change as these words imply. His mind was as truly Conservative as it was truly Liberal. It seems therefore useless to guess whether he was influenced by a possible acquaintance with the popular institutions of Aragon, or took hints from the constitution which Frederick the Great set up in his kingdom of Sicily.[3] With a far wiser spirit of reform he worked upon existing materials, and with his adopted country he made her principles his own. His claim to our gratitude is a claim which has hitherto seemed to belong specially to English reformers, a claim which rests on the development and adaptation of popular institutions, on a constant and disinterested pursuit of the truest political education of the people. The constitution of 1264 shows Earl Simon in the light of a far-seeing politician, a man of great ideas. The Parliaments of 1264 and 1265 prove him a wise statesman and a practical reformer. He can afford to have the claim for novelty put in the second place, for greater praise cannot be given to a statesman than that he has clearly perceived and has fostered into a stronger life that which already exists of good.

---

[1] ' Der Schöpfer des Hauses der Gemeinen.'—Pauli, *Simon de Montfort.*
[2] 'Jenes so völlig neu zusammengesetzte Parlament.'—*Id.*
[3] For Aragon, see Pauli, *Simon de Montfort*, 218, and Hallam, *Middle Ages*, ii. 43. For Sicily, see Milman, *Lat. Christianity*, bk. x. ch. 3.

CHAPTER XI.

T.H E   L A S T   Y E A R.

SIMULTANEOUSLY with the formation of a scheme of government in June 1264, the first three electors were appointed, and received the royal authority to select the nine councillors, and to carry on the government.[1] The electors were the Earls of Leicester and Gloucester, and the Bishop of Chichester. Who the councillors were, or whether they were chosen in Parliament, we do not know. Their names do not appear till next year as authorising any writ, and it is possible that the danger of invasion and the disturbances on the Marches prevented the immediate execution of the scheme. The queen assembled in the course of the summer a large army on the coasts of Flanders, apparently with the countenance, if not the active aid, of the King of France. This army, composed of the most heterogeneous materials, and commanded by those who had escaped from Lewes, only waited for a favourable breeze to cross over to England. The danger was very great, and Simon made efforts to meet it, as strenuous as those made three hundred years later to ward off a similar peril. Fortunately the wind continued unfavourable, or

1264
Appoint-
ment of
the electors
and coun-
cillors.

Danger
from
abroad.

---

[1] Writ dated 23 June in *Fœdera*.

CHAP.
XI.

1264
Prepara-
tions to
resist
invasion.

rather, as Mr. Freeman says, the nation held firm,
and the motley array of troops lingered in vain until
with the approach of winter it melted away. For
Simon had not trusted in the wind alone ; he sent
the ships of the Cinque Ports to patrol the seas, and
called upon every county in England to defend the
coast.[1] The people felt the common danger and
flocked together to defend their country. ' Never
would one have thought to see such a multitude,' says
the chronicler, ' as was collected then on Berham-
down.' [2]   The Clergy contributed its tithes for the
same object—an object far nobler than that for which
they had so often had to drain their pockets. Diplo-

macy was not neglected. Letters were written to
Louis, begging him not to allow the assembling of
troops in his dominions for an attack on England,
and requesting him to send ambassadors to Boulogne
to treat with others from Henry.[3] Louis acceded
to the latter request, and did not commit himself to
the policy of his sister-in-law. With the cessation of
immediate danger from abroad came leisure for a
settlement at home.

· The most important business that occupied the
latter part of the summer was the execution of the
engagement about arbitration entered into at Lewes.
Of the arbiters then selected, three still appeared —the
Bishop of London, the Archbishop of Rouen, and
Hugh Despenser ; but there was no further mention

---

[1] ' De singulis comitatibus,' *Lib. de Ant. Leg.* 69 ; 'per universos
comitatus,' *Ann. Dunst.* sub anno ; writ to Cambridge in *Fœdera* ; and
to Northumberland, in *Royal Letters* ii. 271.

[2] *Matt. West.* 325. The place was Barham Downs, near Canterbury.

[3] *Royal Letters* ii. 258–264.

of the papal legate, in whom Henry had trusted, in 1264 as in 1258. The other members of the court, the Count of Anjou and the Abbot of Bec in Normandy, as well as the archbishop, were probably well-disposed towards Simon.[1] The arbiters were empowered to treat of all matters, except the form of government and the retention of castles and public offices in the hands of Englishmen, and the barons swore to abide by their decision. There is a lack of honesty about the composition of this court which, it must be confessed, casts some stain on the uprightness of him who doubtless appointed it. It was a packed tribunal, and Simon can hardly have expected that the King of France would consent to treat with such a court for the purpose of reversing or at least modifying his former decision. Whether the exigencies of the case can be held to excuse such a proceeding, or whether the good effects which a unanimous decision in favour of reform would have had on the peace of the country counterbalanced the bad impression produced by the unfairness of the selection, is very hard to decide.

powers of the court;

its composition.

Simultaneously with the appointment of arbiters, Henry of Almaine was released, though only on very heavy bail given by the bishops, to further the negotiations for peace.[2] But the papal opposition was too strong. The legate vehemently repudiated the arrangement, as contrary to the spirit of the Mise of Lewes, an accusation to a great extent justified by the facts. He

Papal opposition.

---

[1] The Count of Anjou, as Dr. Pauli points out, was the candidate for Sicily, and so well-disposed toward Simon that he was supposed to be his brother (*Matt. West.* 327); the Archbishop was a Franciscan, and had probably entertained Simon once at least (see *Mon. Franc.* 86).

[2] Writ dated 4 Sept. in *Fœdera.*

CHAP.
XI.

1264

Papal opposition,

demanded to be allowed to enter England, but this was refused; he summoned the English bishops before him, but they excused themselves on the plea that the barons would not let them go, and sent proctors instead.[1] The legate refused to recognise the proctors, and, far from showing any wish for reconciliation, bade them publish the papal ban against Simon de Montfort and his followers. From the effects of this the king and Prince Edward were specially exempted, since they were but unwilling parties to the revolution.[2] Whereupon the bishops appealed to the Pope, and their appeal was supported by the whole body of the clergy in their assembly.[3] Clearly there was no want of unanimity between the Church and its great ally. Nor did the people allow them to give way, for when the bishops returned with the bull of excommunication which was to have been published in England, the men of Dover seized it and threw it into the sea. The bishops did not oppose or excommunicate the perpetrators of this sacrilege.

not supported by the English clergy and people.

Disturbances on the Marches,

While the question of peace and arbitration was temporarily suspended by this occurrence,[4] and by the elevation of the legate to the papal see as Clement IV, disturbances had broken out in the West of England. The Marchers, who had been released after Lewes, no sooner found themselves at home

---

[1] The proctors were the Bishops of London, Worcester, and Winchester; with them were appointed as ambassadors Hugh Despenser and P. de Montfort (27–30 Sept.). Two of the five were arbiters already.

[2] Bull dated 29 Sept. in *Fœdera*.

[3] *T. Wykes* 156; *Ann. Dunst.* 234.

[4] That it was not altogether given up is shown by a letter of Henry (*Royal Letters* ii. 278; Oct. 30, 1264), in which he alludes to the sending of fresh envoys.

again, than they broke their plighted word. An attempt was made by some of them to rescue Prince Edward, who was then at Wallingford, but failed owing to the vigilance of the garrison. In their own country they speedily found a pretext for a renewal of the war in the endless feud with the Welch, now embittered by the fact that Llewelyn was an ally of Simon de Montfort. At the same time the Earl of Derby came into collision with the royalists in Chester.[1] The alliance of this lawless baron was far more an obstacle than an aid to the party he pretended to support. He took advantage of the unsettled state of things to rob and plunder in all directions, and had to be treated later as the freebooter that he was. Simon was obliged to interrupt his peaceable settlement of affairs in order to suppress the worst of these disturbances. He marched westward, and with the help of the Welch, who attacked the Marchers in the rear, forced them to surrender. Sentence was passed upon them at a council held at Oxford, towards the end of November, and they were banished from the kingdom for a year and a day, after which they were to return and be tried by their peers.[2] Yet even after these events so much leniency was shown them that several were allowed to visit and converse with Prince Edward, then under the care of his aunt in the impregnable stronghold of Kenilworth.

suppressed by Earl Simon.

Thus was danger apparently warded off both at home and abroad. Tranquillity returned for a brief space to the harassed land. Simon de Montfort

Peace at home and abroad.

---

[1] Perhaps Chesterfield, as in 1266 : see below p. 353.
[2] *Matt. West.* 325 ; *Ann. Dunst.* 235 ; *Lib. de Ant. Leg.* 70.

reigned supreme. 'All things were ordered by him,' we are told; 'the king had but the shadow of royalty.'[1]   The earl was not slow to avail himself of this calm in order to set about the consolidation of the political edifice, the foundations of which had been laid in the Parliament of June.   Even the hostile barons of the North had apparently come round.[2]   Some of those who were against the earl the previous Christmas, as Roger Bigod, were now such strong partisans as to incur with him the papal excommunication.   But the outward calm concealed many angry feelings.   The sight of a captive king, a prisoner in the hands of one who still called himself a subject, and made a cats-paw to further all the plans of his gaoler, could not fail to arouse sympathy even in those who opposed Henry while in power.   But,
more than this, Simon was accused of cruelty to his prisoners, of unfairness to his friends.   It was said he did not divide the confiscated property justly, but took eighteen baronies for himself,[3] and gave too much to his sons.   It is only probable that here again Simons adherence to his principles and his imperious nature made him many enemies.   He was for the time the ruler of England, and did not attempt to hide the fact.   Bitter experience had taught him the evils of a divided party; he seems to have thought it safer to brave the jealousy and

---

[1] *Matt. West.* 328.

[2] It is observable that a summons was thrice sent to these barons to appear in London between 4 June and 5 Aug., 1264, but not after the latter date (*Royal Letters* ii. 256-270).   *Matt. West.* confirms this supposition.

[3] Possibly these eighteen baronies are King Richards, as he held exactly that number.—Pearson, *Hist. of Eng.* ii. 260, note.

hatred of his own side, than to let the reins of government become loose and entangled in other hands. And he was probably right ; it was an almost hopeless undertaking ; in this policy lay his only chance of success.

Much of the odium he incurred was due to jealousy of his power, perhaps still more to the folly of his allies. The men of the Cinque Ports were accused of piracy and violence on the high seas ; the scarcity of provisions and the high prices were attributed, probably with some reason, to the excessive hostility they manifested towards foreigners. These charges, it should be added, are confirmed by independent authority.[1] There were plenty to draw inferences very damaging to de Montfort ; it was said, as had been said before on the occasion of the riots in London, that he received a third of the booty. To these and the like accusations we are probably justified in giving little credence. They were indignantly rejected by the earls friends at the time, by the very men, that is, whom his enemies declared he injured ; there is nothing to prove the charge, and, whatever may have been Simons faults, avarice was certainly not one. That the plunder was taken by him and applied to the uses of government is probable enough, and may explain the charges against him. Moreover, if the folly and perhaps the rapacity of our mariners caused considerable privation, the terrible confusion in which the country had been plunged for the last seven years will account to a great extent for the decay of trade. To remedy this Simon declared, with true insular feeling, if on mistaken principles, that England could

CHAP.
XI.

1264

Violence of Earl Simons supporters,

gives rise to charges against him.

Decay of trade.

[1] *Lib. de Ant. Leg.* 73.

Imprudence of Earl Simons sons.

do without foreign merchandise. Many of his friends, we are told, acted on his advice, and wore clothes made of undyed wool, the produce of the country. Of all his party his own sons seem to have done him as much mischief as any; that this had not escaped his notice is shown by the words he addressed to them on the morning of his death. But he loved them only too well, and probably overlooked acts of violence and imprudence on their part, which it would have been wiser to check with a strong hand. The fact that Henry de Montfort acquired the nickname of the ' wool-merchant,' because he seized the wool which was being exported, gives a great air of probability to these reports.[1]

Opposing views of Earl Simons conduct :

Of Simons own conduct towards his enemies it is, owing to the contradictory verdicts of prejudiced chroniclers, very hard to judge. One side declares he treated the king with the utmost indignity, while the other says he showed him all respect.[2] Henry was in fact a prisoner, and that is enough of itself to account for the discrepancies between two sets of writers, regarding the matter from opposite points of view. It was utterly impossible to give such a king his liberty ; it was fatal to Simons cause that he was obliged to keep him in confinement. Necessity will or will not excuse his action in such matters, according to the political opinions of the judge. It is easier to be definite on other points. As to the estates of the King of the Romans, which had been handed over to the earl after the battle of Lewes, their

Dilemma in which he was placed.

[1] *T. Wykes* (p. 159) calls him ' lanarius.'
[2] Compare *T. Wykes* 153, with the corresponding *Chronicle of Osney*, p. 150.

cession can only have been regarded as temporary, a pledge for Richards good behaviour. The same was not the case with the castles of Chester, Newcastle, and the Peak, which had been in Prince Edwards hands, but were now, as places of primary importance, conferred upon the earl and his heirs, to be held of course, like other castles, of the king. Certain lands were given to the prince in exchange,[1] of equal pecuniary but not political value. The confiscation of Simons property after his death showed that with this exception he had not enriched himself at the expense of others. There is no doubt as to what he would have had to expect had he been beaten at Lewes ; the treatment of himself, his family, and his lands after the battle of Evesham removes all uncertainty on this head. Whether the motive was self-interest or generosity, the policy he adopted in his hour of victory cannot be characterised, under the circumstances, as any other than merciful and conciliatory.

That the Church and the people remained faithful to their champion is plainly shown by the great contemporary poem already referred to.[2] It begins with an elaborate defence of his policy, both before and after the battle of Lewes. After a triumphant allusion to the battle itself, the occurrences which preceded it, and the joy of England at the release from so many evils, the poem proceeds to defend Simon from the charge of deceit and cunning. Far from it, exclaims the writer, he has ever been true and constant, and has maintained the good cause in the

CHAP.
XI.

1264
Earl Simon
does not
abuse his
power.

Opinion of
Earl Simon
in the
poem on
the battle
of Lewes.

---

[1] *Rot. Lit. Pat.* 49, Hen. III, quoted by Pauli.
[2] See p. 178 note 2, and appendix ii.

CHAP.
XI.

1264
Opinion of
Earl Simon
in the
poem on
the battle
of Lewes.

teeth of death ; he alone has kept the oath he swore.
His sense of right appears in his words to the Bishop
of Chichester, who, when attempting to reconcile the
two parties, was bidden by Simon to choose arbiters
from among the best and truest men, those who knew
the Provisions well, and who were learned in the law
of God ; to them he would submit and so avoid
perjury. He would not have acted as he has acted,
continues the poem, had he looked to his own
advantage ; he has sacrificed himself for the good of
others. His is not the cunning which intrigues for a
secret object ; he fights in the sight of heaven, and
gives himself, like his master Christ, unto death for
many. His cause must be favoured of God, or he
could not have won the victory over such foes. With
Simons 'faith and fidelity' is compared the treachery
which Edward manifested at Gloucester and elsewhere ; the prince is like the leopard, beautiful but
faithless. Had he and his won the day, England
had been lost for ever ; but praise be to God who
has given the earl the victory, for his enemies are the
enemies of heaven, the Church, and the country.
Such is the enthusiasm which Simon excited in men
like the author of this remarkable song of triumph ;
and the same strain of praise is kept up in other
songs of the time. His name of Montfort gives occasion for many allusions to 'the strong mount' to
which his friends look for protection ; the feeling
towards him is nothing less than veneration.

Disunion in
Earl
Simons
party.

But, in spite of this support, Simons position with
the greater barons was daily becoming more difficult
and unsatisfactory. No sooner was the victory won
than disunion began to show itself. An interesting

letter,[1] evidently belonging to this period, the author of which calls himself 'a faithful English subject,' warns the barons of the danger to be feared from their divisions. They are in this dilemma, says the writer. If the legate be not admitted, the kingdom will be placed under an interdict, and the barons excommunicated; while if he be admitted, he will speedily overpower them. United action is therefore indispensable. The Earl of Leicester is advised to leave no means untried in order to keep his party together, an object which he has endangered by injustice in giving the confiscated property of John Mansel to his son. The French king is ready to enter England; the Pope is urging him not to tarry. Let the barons therefore beware, let them make alliances with Scotland, Wales, and Ireland, and carefully defend the coasts. Lastly, they ought to choose a leader to take the place of Simon de Montfort, in case he should die. The letter is impartial and prudent, and appears to come from a person of authority. The danger it alludes to is that which always thwarted Simons plans, disunion among his own followers, fostered by his own arbitrary action. The warning was only too well grounded. The majority of the greater barons maintained a policy of sullen opposition, or at least could not be relied upon for active aid. This fact is clearly proved by the composition of the great Parliament of January 1265, writs for which were issued in the preceding December. The small proportion of the lay nobility

Earl Simon has few allies.

---

[1] *Ann. Tewk.* 179. The mention of the legate shows it to belong to this period. The author, from his connexion with Tewkesbury, was probably one of Gloucesters partisans.

Y

CHAP.
XI.

1265
Parliament
of January:
obscurity
of its pro-
ceedings.

Defiant
attitude of
Earl
Simon :

summoned to this Parliament is a disheartening proof of the difficulties with which the earl had to contend.[1] The Parliament assembled about the middle of January, but of its proceedings, and of the light in which they were regarded by the country at large, we know next to nothing. It cannot be doubted that the completion of peace must have been looked upon as a real blessing by the greater part of the population, that all Englishmen must have rejoiced to see the government in the hands of their own flesh and blood. But the great measures, of which we have spoken above, do not appear to have had the effect on the nation which might have been expected, and, whether from apathy or surprise, very slight efforts were made to aid the earl when engaged in his last struggle. The people may have thought he was safe without their aid, for the popular belief in him, as shown in song and legend, was too strong to allow one to think that he reaped the reward of contemporary ingratitude, which has been the lot of so many reformers. He himself showed no sign of fear. His action in this very Parliament of 1265 showed that he was inclined to brave all the consequences of disaffection. So defiant was his attitude that one is forced to blame it as at least injudicious. It was not much that the office of high steward was now restored to him ; a far less justifiable proceeding was the appointment of himself as justiciar.[2] The object of this act is hard to discover, especially as Hugh Despenser was at hand to undertake the duties he had already

---

[1] See note 1 on p. 309.

[2] There is some doubt about this. Foso does not give the earls name as Justiciar, but the evidence from writs signed by him as Justiciar seems too strong to reject. In *Fœd.* i. 450 H. Despenser appears still as Justiciar.

twice before discharged. Such an accumulation of power was most unwise ; it was a needless challenge to the opposition. Acts of this kind form the heaviest indictment against the earl ; they were an imitation of the worst faults of his enemies, and laid him open to the charge that he was aiming at a tyranny. Whether it was that he had begun to distrust even his best friends, or, as is more probable, that he let ambition and the sense of power get the better of his political sense, certain it is that from this time he began to sink towards his final fall.

The discussions in Parliament were at first interrupted by the threat of a tournament, to be held at Dunstable, in which the sons and partisans of de Montfort were to have met the Earl of Gloucester and his followers. It seems to have been a challenge to the latter, and the result would doubtless have been to fan the smouldering embers of civil war, if not to lead to actual bloodshed. Simon peremptorily forbade the meeting, and was so annoyed that he is said to have threatened to imprison his sons. The prohibition was however used by Gloucester as a grudge against the earl, on the ground that all the money spent in the preparations for the affair had been thereby wasted.[1] It was a bad omen too when the old imputation of foreign blood began again to be cast in Simons teeth.[2] The real cause of the growing hostility between the two chief men of the kingdom

Signs of growing hostility towards Earl Simon.

[1] *Rish. Chron.* 32 ; cf. *Op. Chron.* 15. The prohibition was sent by Henry to Leicester as well, probably to avoid any appearance of unfairness. The earl tested the writ as justiciar, in which character he first appears on 17 Jan., 1264. *P. de Langtoft* 145 says the overbearing behaviour of the young de Montforts affronted the Earl of Gloucester.

[2] He was upbraided as an ' alienigena.'—*Rish. Chron.* 32.

CHAP.
XI.

1265
Causes of
the quarrel
between
Leicester
and
Gloucester.

is however said to have been the fact that Simon kept all the royal castles in his own hands, or granted them to his sons.[1]　This proceeding placed in far too strong a light the supremacy of Leicester, and gave the lie to the nominal equality of the three electors. To the young Earl of Gloucester the retention of Bristol Castle[2] was doubtless a special source of irritation, and he is not likely to have borne in patience an assumption of authority, which the Bishop of Chichester, a creature of de Montforts,[3] had not the power, if he had the inclination, to resist. Hampered by these difficulties and deserted by his chief ally, Simon had to curb the insolence of his own partisans. He seized the chief offender, the Earl of Derby, had him tried by his peers in Parliament, and condemned him to imprisonment in the Tower. The notion of some writers[4] that Simon imprisoned him in order to protect him from the kings wrath is evidently absurd.

He also summoned to London his old ally and late enemy, Hugh Bigod, with the Earl of Warenne, William of Valence, and Peter of Savoy. They were ordered to attend as prisoners, and to receive judgment at the hands of Parliament. It does not appear how or when they came into de Montforts power, for they are said to have escaped after the battle of Lewes; nor are we told what punishment they received. That they went abroad soon after this is certain, for we find them landing with troops in May.　It is

---

[1] *Ann. Wig.* 453; *Ann. Wav.* 358; *Ann. Osn.* 162.

[2] According to *Rob. of Glouc.*, the fugitives from Lewes had occupied Bristol. It was probably retaken by Simon in the preceding autumn.

[3] See Stubbs, *Const. Hist.* ii. 91, note 3.

[4] E.g. *Rob. of Glouc.*, who adds that Gloucester feared a like fate, and that Simon put foreigners into the castles—a most improbable statement—who were removed at this parliament.

therefore probable that they were at this time banished from England.[1] To their deadly enmity was now added the hostility of some of Simons own partisans, John Giffard and others, whom he had offended by forbidding them to demand ransom for their prisoners, which was contrary to one of the enactments of the Mise of Lewes.[2] But worst of all was the breach with the Earl of Gloucester, who had now an additional cause of complaint in a similar prohibition. So hot did the quarrel grow that he feared, or pretended to fear, the fate of the Earl of Derby. The split grew daily wider; in vain did the bishops use their influence to reconcile the leaders ; the old experiment of an arbitration is said to have been tried again in vain. De Montfort would not tolerate any resistance ; Gloucester would not recognise the superiority of a fellow-subject. In this very Parliament the latter gave vent to his jealousy by accusing Simon of violating the Compromise of Lewes, of arbitrary and tyrannical action, of aiming even at the Crown. Some of these charges may have been correct, but the real reason of the quarrel could have escaped no ones notice. Between two such men a rupture was inevitable.

Meanwhile however Parliament brought its labours to a close. The session was protracted to an unusual length. The chief business which occupied the attention of the members was the final settlement of the terms of peace, and the confirmation of the measures

CHAP.
XI.

1265

The quarrel
between
Leicester
and
Gloucester
grows
hotter.

Business of
Parliament.

---

[1] This point is very obscure. It seems doubtful whether they were ever in de Montforts hands. Pauli, *Simon de Mont.* 173, says they escaped to France, and were invited on 19 March to the Parliament of June 1. 1265. So too Blaauw, *Barons' War*, 259. But see *Fœd.* i. 449 on this.

[2] *T. Wykes* 160 : so too *Rob. of Gloucester.*

CHAP.
XI.

1265
Business of
Parlia-
ment :

taken by Parliament in the preceding year, with the·
object of releasing the king and the hostages, and
setting the new government fairly in motion. Of the·
debates that took place we know nothing, except that
the bishops seem to have passed some resolutions to·
resist the power of Rome, 'for which,' says a chronicler, 'they had to suffer afterwards;' and that the·
Earl of Leicester, in the course of the discussion,
upbraided the magnates with their inconstancy.[1]
Owing to the disturbing influences spoken of above,
the wished-for result was not obtained till the begin-

acceptance
of the con-
stitution of
1264 ;

ning of March. The plan of Simons constitution was·
then accepted as it stood, and the other enactments·
already mentioned were passed. The kings formal
confirmation of these acts was the sign of the conclusion of peace.[2] The spirit of fairness in which·
Simon acted is shown by the enactment passed with
respect to the outlawry of any one opposing the new·
measures, so different was it from the sweeping condemnation of such persons forced upon the king in·
1258. It was now provided that such declaration of·
treason should not be made without the assent of·
the council and the nobles of the land. The scheme·
of the constitution was probably completed at this
Parliament by the appointment of the Council of
Nine.[3] A fresh confirmation of all existing charters

[1] *T. Wykes* 160.

[2] Writ of confirmation dated 10 March ; Prince Edwards oath, and
the orders for his and Prince Henrys release, 10 March ; the kings oath
to the new statutes, 14 March ; writs for delivery of castles to Leicester,
17 March—2 April.

[3] In several writs subsequent to this Parliament the council is mentioned as authorising their issue, though the whole nine never appear
together, nor can we do more than guess at their names. Prof. Stubbs
says (*Const. Hist.* ii. 92), 'The names of the council do not appear.
It no doubt contained P. de Montfort, Roger St. John, and G. de
Argentine.'

was issued, and an oath taken by all to observe the
new arrangements. No sooner was this done than,
in accordance with the terms of the Compromise, the
hostages were released ; but Edward had to promise
to keep only Englishmen near him, and not to leave
England for three years. King Richard seems already
to have ransomed himself in the previous autumn by
payment of a large sum.[1] The royal castles formerly
in Edwards keeping were handed over to the Earl of
Leicester ; a general amnesty and oblivion of all injuries was decreed ; to call in papal intervention was
declared high treason. To these terms the king and
Edward took the oath with the usual solemnities ;
fresh homage was done by those of their vassals who
had been in arms against them ; and therewith the
new government was formally ushered in.

To a superficial observer the Earl of Leicester must
now have seemed at the height of his power. The land
had apparently recovered its equilibrium ; the monarchy, freed from the bondage temporarily imposed
upon it, took up the position assigned to it in the
new order of things ; the author of these changes had
received the sanction of law and the popular voice.
But the anomaly of Simons position was thereby
only made the more apparent. He was in a hopeless
dilemma. To release Henry even now was to let
slip the dogs of war ; but by keeping him in a confinement which was patent to all, though it was called
freedom, he violated the principles of his own constitution, and placed himself in a false and untenable
position. The inconsistency was too glaring to escape

CHAP.
XI.

1265
Release of
the hos-
tages ;
an am-
nesty, &c.

Earl Simon
apparently
supreme,

really in
great diffi-
culties.

[1] *Chron. Mail.* sub anno 1264.

CHAP.
XI.

1265
Earl Simon
in difficul-
ties.

any ones notice ; it was evident that Simon must fall, or the king. It is a mournful spectacle, a high and noble spirit struggling hopelessly with circumstances into which the principles of justice and aims however honourable, with the aid, it must be confessed, of his own indiscretion, had thrown him, and which he was no longer able to control. Yet 'it was notorious,' we are told, 'that no one ever saw the earl in despair, or even downcast ; he was like a mountain, strong, constant, immoveable ; wherefore he was rightly called de Montfort.'[1] But for all that his fate was inevitable. The man and his principles were an anachronism, and could not survive in the political ignorance of the times.

The end is soon told. Gloucester had left London before the close of Parliament,[2] and had betaken himself to his own county. There he met with the Marchers, who had lurked there instead of departing for Ireland in accordance with their sentence, and with the discontented members of Simons own party. By the middle of March Parliament had broken up, and Simon de Montfort had left London. On March

19 he met the Princes Edward and Henry, whom in spite of their release he still kept near him, at his castle of Odiham. There, attended by a princely retinue, he remained till the end of the month. The disturbances on the western border, and the proclamation of another tournament, this time at Northampton, made an expedition westward a matter of necessity. He left Odiham on April 2, and never

---

[1] *Opus Chron.* 17.
[2] It is evidently Gloucester, not Leicester, as Dr. Pauli supposes, who is referred to in the words of *T. Wykes* 160, 'Juncta sibi turma non modica, spreto parliamento, secessit ad partes occiduas.'

saw his wife or home again.[1] With him went the king and the princes. By this time the Earl of Gloucester had struck an alliance with Roger Mortimer, one of the staunchest royalists, and a renewal of the civil war was evidently impending. To meet this danger Simon marched to Northampton, where he probably put an end to the preparations, if such were being made, for the proposed tournament ; and then to Hereford, the centre of the disaffected district. On his way he visited Worcester and Gloucester, both which towns were most important as holding the bridges across the Severn. At the former place a council was held, which decreed anew the banishment of the rebellious Marchers.[2] While at Hereford he received the news that the Earl of Warenne, William of Valence, Hugh Bigod, and others, had landed with a strong force at Pembroke. He immediately issued edicts commanding the ports to be carefully watched, to prevent assistance being introduced from abroad, and bidding the sheriffs, in accordance with the decrees lately made at Worcester, seize all who should break the peace.[3] At the same time however the negotiations with France were not allowed to fall through ; letters were written to Louis, and Prince Henry sent over again to do what he could for peace ; ships were despatched to fetch the French ambassadors, and the Countess of Leicester made ready to welcome

Margin notes:

CHAP. XI.

1265

Alliance of Gloucester and Mortimer.

Earl Simon goes westward.

Landing of royalists at Pembroke.

Negotiations with France continue.

---

[1] See *Household Expenses*, 13 seq. He had with him at the castle a retinue of 160 knights.

[2] Writ in *Fœd.* i. 456, spoken of in writ issued 20 May. It seems nearly certain that this is not the writ of condemnation referred to on p. 315, which was issued at Oxford. *Rob. of Gloucester* says that the Marchers again seized Bristol, and held it till obliged by letters from Edward to give it up : but this seems to be a confusion with the events of the previous autumn.

[3] *Royal Letters* ii. 282 ; dated 10 May.

CHAP.
XI.
1265
Attempt to
settle the
quarrel
between
Leicester
and
Gloucester.
them at Dover. Her position as warden of the most important stronghold of the realm shows the trust which the earl always placed in that constant and high-souled woman. Lastly, in spite of the hostile bearing of the malcontents, headed by the Earl of Gloucester, the attempt to settle the difficulty by arbitration was renewed, and a proclamation issued, assuring the country that the reports of a quarrel between the two earls were false.[1]

The truth of these reports was however too soon apparent. The Earl of Gloucester had already, it appears, attempted to seize Simon and the king, or to rescue the latter, while on his way through the Forest of Dean from Gloucester to Hereford.[2] In spite of this attempt, which possibly was only projected and therefore remained unknown to Simon, two of the royalist barons, Leyburne and Clifford, were allowed to visit Prince Edward at Hereford. This ill-timed leniency seems to have been the cause of the decisive event which followed, for it was probably at this meeting that a plan for Edwards escape was arranged. Through Thomas de Clare, younger brother of the Earl of Gloucester, his constant attendant, he kept up communication with the Marchers. At length

all was ready. On May 28 Edward went out in the cool of the evening with the companions assigned to him, one of whom was Henry de Montfort, to ride in the flat meadows outside the walls of Hereford. His friends had managed to convey to him a horse of great speed, which he proposed to try with the rest. Mounting his comrades' horses one after another, he

---

[1] *Fœd.* i. 445; dated 20 May. According to *Rob. of Glouc.* negotiations went on between Leicester and Gloucester, ending in a nominal reconciliation on May 12.   [2] *Ann. Wav.* 362.

rode them till they were tired out. At this moment
a horseman appeared on the hill, and waved his hat.
This was the signal agreed on. Edward at once
leapt on his own steed, saluted his gaolers with sarcastic politeness, and rode off, attended by one or two
who were in the secret. Before his guardians had time
to recover their surprise he had disappeared in the
forest, and though they pursued they were owing to
his artifice unable to overtake him. He was soon met
by some of his friends, and made the best of his way
to Roger Mortimers castle of Wigmore. The consequences of his escape were immediately felt. Two
days afterwards the Countess of Leicester left Odiham
and travelled with all speed to Porchester, and thence
soon after to Dover. De Montfort saw his danger,
and at once issued edicts summoning all tenants-in-
chief to march against Prince Edward. Another
week and the desertion of the Earl of Gloucester was
published abroad, and the earl denounced as a rebel.
The bishops were bidden, in accordance with the enactments of the last Parliament, to excommunicate
Prince Edward and his adherents, as violators of their
plighted faith. The garrison of Bristol Castle was
commanded to surrender that stronghold to de Montfort, but refused.[1]

conse-
quences of
this event.

Meanwhile the Earl of Gloucester had met Prince
Edward at Ludlow, and had sworn allegiance to him,
after having however induced him first of all to vow
that he would observe the ancient laws of the land,
and would never introduce aliens to power.[2] Edward
immediately became the centre to which all royalistic
elements streamed. His name united all the dis-

Prince
Edward
takes the
lead of the
opposition.

---

[1] For these events see writs in the *Fœdera*, dated 30 May—9 June.
[2] *T. Wykes* 164.

CHAP.
XI.

1265

Prince
Edward
takes the
lead of the
opposition.

Earl Simon
makes
alliance
with the
Welch.

affected—the old royalists, the unruly Marchers, the moderates under the Earl of Gloucester.[1] Crowds joined him as he marched on Worcester, and occupied it and the neighbouring strongholds of Bridgnorth and Shrewsbury. Gloucester remained, and he lost no time in attacking it. The force which Simon had been able to spare for its protection was not strong enough to hold it. After a brave struggle the defenders gave way, and surrendered the castle towards the end of June. The royalists at once broke down the bridges, carried off the boats, cut the fords, and so hemmed in de Montfort behind the line of the Severn.[2] No help could reach him from the east. Despairing of succour, he had already struck a close alliance with Llewelyn, and to gain his aid he seems to have made concessions scarcely justifiable under any circumstances. He remitted many obliga-tions which the Welch had been bound to fulfil, gave up to them for a nominal sum all the lands and castles which they had lately retaken, and even yielded others that were not in their possession. The terms, we are told, provoked great disgust in London,[3] and doubtless elsewhere, for an alliance with the Welch was generally looked on as little less than monstrous. Simon must have been very hard pressed before he would have been driven to take so extreme a step. Having however thus secured allies in this quarter, he moved down the Wye to Monmouth, and then went on to Newport, whence he tried to escape across the channel to Bristol. He summoned ships

---

[1] Cf. Dr. Hort in *Macmillans Magazine*, June 1864.
[2] *T. Wykes* 161 seq.
[3] *Lib. de Ant. Leg.* 74 ; the alliance was signed 22 June.

from that port, and though the garrison is said to have been hostile,[1] the citizens were friendly and sent them. But Edward, sallying forth from Gloucester, attacked the transport fleet on its way, and dispersed it ; then, landing on the northern side, he drove Simon westward across the Usk into Newport, and was only prevented from entering the town after him by the destruction of the bridge. Under cover of night Simon left the town, and retreated northwards again. His men suffered terribly from privation, not being able to subsist on the goats flesh and milk which formed the only food of the Welch. They were also wearied out by the difficult march through a wooded and trackless country. At Hereford he paused awhile to recruit, and after a vain attempt to cross the Severn, in which he was probably checked by floods, he returned to wait for reinforcements.

So far he had been completely unsuccessful, and every day which he had to spend in wearisome inactivity on the other side of the Severn was so much loss to a cause in which the inspiration of his personal presence was indispensable. Still all would not have been lost, but for the folly of the younger Simon, who was blockading Pevensey Castle when the news of Edwards escape led him to raise the siege. He had since then been engaged in collecting troops in the south and east, and especially in London, to bring to the assistance of his father. The democratic party in the capital had had some difficulty in keeping the upper hand, and the decay of the popular cause was shown by the violent measures resorted to

CHAP.
XI.

1265
Earl Simon tries in vain to cross to Bristol,

and retreats to Hereford.

Earl Simon waits for the arrival of his son,

who collects reinforcements.

---

[1] They were probably temporising, for they were Simons men.

CHAP.
XI.
⌣
1265
Simon the
younger
marches
westward,

in order to keep down its enemies in that stronghold of the reform party.[1] As yet however these measures were successful. Simon, after conducting his mother to Dover, was able to bring together a considerable force of Londoners and other partisans, with which he set out from London early in July. But, instead of marching straight towards the west, he went southward again, and wasted precious time in an attempt upon Winchester, with the object of collecting funds and men. The citizens of that loyal town refused him admittance, whereupon he forced his way in and gave the city over to pillage. Thence he pursued his journey by way of Oxford and North-ampton, both of which towns showed themselves friendly, or at least neutral. Marching thus by easy stages he arrived at Kenilworth in the last days of July.[2]

and arrives
at Kenil-
worth.

Culpable
negligence
of Simon
the
younger.

He reached the castle late one evening, after sunset. His army was too numerous to lie within the enclosure of the walls ; the troops were therefore scattered about the village and in the priory. The younger Simon himself, and many of his most important partisans, lay outside the castle, finding there more comfortable quarters, or, according to other authorities, on account of the greater facilities for bathing.[3] This they appear to have done for two or

[1] Forty men were seized, and were only saved from death by the news of the battle of Evesham.—*Lib. de Ant. Leg.* 114.

[2] There is a doubt about the date. *T. Wykes* says they arrived on July 31, but it was probably a little earlier, since the surprise took place on Aug. 1. *Ann. Wav.* say they were at Kenilworth 'vi dies,' which Dr. Hort would change into ' iii dies.'

[3] So *Chron. Mel.* 199, the chief authority on this affair : the account in this chronicle is very lively and evidently taken from an eye-witness. *T. Wykes, Ann. Wav.* and others are useful. W. de Hemingburgh adds as usual picturesque and not improbable details, having their origin most likely in local tradition.

three nights, in fancied security but with a most

culpable want of vigilance, for they knew that Prince
Edward was hard by, and had in fact been warned by
him, according to the rules of chivalry, that he meant
to pay them a visit.[1] It was Simon de Montforts
plan to surround the royalists as they lay at Worcester,[2] or to effect a junction with his son and then
attack them with a superior force. The prince resolved to anticipate this danger, and to crush his
enemies singly. He saw his opportunity, and having
found out through spies[3] the position of Simons
troops at Kenilworth, he left Worcester with a strong
force on the evening of Friday, July 31.[4] On Satur-
day morning, August 1, at early dawn, they came in
sight of the castle and halted in a neighbouring
hollow, where they had the good fortune to fall in
with some foragers, whom they easily overpowered,
and so were able to exchange their own jaded horses
for fresher animals. Thence they marched into the
village. Edward had given orders to capture all, if
possible, alive, and the enemy were so completely
taken by surprise that they were incapable of making
any resistance. They were roused from their beds
by loud shouts of 'Get up, get up, ye traitors, and

[1] 'Mandavit ei Edwardus . . . quod eum visitaturus veniret.'—
Ann. Wav. 363.

[2] So *Chron. Mel.* 198, and *Ann. Wav.* 364, ' Proposuit Edwardum
et G. de Clare ex uno latere includere, et ut filius suus includeret ex
altero.'

[3] According to *Chron. Mel.*, by means of a certain knight ; *T.
Wykes* says, ' per exploratores callidos ; W. de Hem. says it was
through a female spy named Margot, who was dressed in mans clothes.

[4] 'In aurora die sancti Petri ad vincula,' *Ann. Osn.* 166 ; ' Acta
sunt hæc primo die mensis Augusti.'—*T. Wykes* 171. So too *Rish. de
Bellis. Rob. of Glouc.* however says that Edward left Worcester on
a Lammas night, ' Sater night that was.'

CHAP.
XI.

1265
Simon the
younger
surprised at
Kenil-
worth :
come out, or by the death of God ye are all undone !'
A few made their escape by back ways, and fled,
some stark naked, some with their breeches on, others
carrying their clothes under their arms. Young
Simon himself, having perfect knowledge of the
locality, escaped by way of the large moat or pond,
which he crossed in a boat, and so got safe into the
castle. But far the greater number were taken
prisoners, and among them ten or more bannerets,
including the Earl of Oxford, William de Munchanesy, Richard de Gray, and others of note. The
booty was immense. So many horses were taken
that Edward was able to turn his infantry into
cavalry, and the very grooms paraded themselves
before him in the arms and on the war-horses of

knights. The blow was fatal, for though Kenilworth
itself could not be taken, the larger half of the
baronial army was annihilated, and Edward left free
to attack the remainder with an overpowering force.

Earl Simon
leaves
Hereford,
and crosses
the
Severn,
Meanwhile the Earl of Leicester, weary of waiting
for the aid which never came, or, according to pre-
concerted plan, had at length broken up from Hereford. All unconscious of his sons defeat,[1] he crossed
the Severn in boats, on Sunday, August 2, and passed
the night at Kempsey, a few miles below Worcester,
a manor belonging to his old friend the bishop. He
remained at Kempsey most of the next day, and late
on Monday evening started for Evesham, with the
intention of marching up the Avon to Kenilworth,

---

[1] *Ann. Osney* 167 must be wrong in saying that he knew of it the
same day ; *T. Wykes* and *Ann. Wav.* agree in making him ignorant
of it, and all the circumstances point to the same hypothesis. Most
accounts agree in making him cross the Severn on Sunday.

there to join his son, if he did not meet him on the road. They appear to have arrived at Evesham some time early on the morning of Tuesday, August 4. They had marched some fifteen miles during the night, and were doubtless glad to halt awhile and take rest and refreshment. The king breakfasted and heard mass in the abbey ; the earl however would take nothing. The day wore on, and time was pressing. They made ready therefore to continue their march, and Simon and the king were just about to mount their horses, when some of the vanguard, who had already left the town, ran back and reported that an armed troop was approaching.[1]

The little town of Evesham lies in a bend of the river Avon, which turning sharp to the west and then to the north forms here a complete peninsula, which may be likened to a tightly-stretched bow. Across the arc of this bow runs a line of low hills, which, ending eastward in the Avon itself, are continued westward along the right bank of the river, when it resumes its former course. At the extreme or southern end of this peninsula lay the abbey, on a slight eminence sloping into the stream, and north of the abbey walls is the little town, the chief street of which follows the line of the Alcester road, running due north and south. To the east of the town, just outside the abbey walls, is a bridge over the Avon, by

CHAP.
XI.

1265
He arrives
at Eves-
ham.

Position of
the town of
Evesham.

---

[1] The authorities differ a little in the chronology, but the majority agree in the dates which I have given. Of those that bear on the battle of Evesham, the most useful are those which I have already mentioned in giving an account of the battle of Lewes. T. Wykes relates all the events of this period with a circumstance which shows how truly pleased he was by the result. Rob. of Gloucester and W. de Hemingburgh preserve many interesting details. Some, but not the best, authorities, say that Simon passed the night at Evesham.

z

CHAP.
XI.

1265
Position of
the town
of Eves-
ham, &c.

which the road crosses to the suburb of Bengeworth,
and then turns northward along the left bank of the
river towards Kenilworth. This road however splits
into two at Bidford, one route crossing the river
again and going on by way of Alcester, the other
going by way of Stratford and Warwick. Simon
had therefore three routes by which to make his way
to Kenilworth, the most natural of which was probably the road leading directly northward through
Alcester. Two roads lead from Evesham to Worcester, one of which follows the left bank of the Avon,
and crosses it again when it bends southward at Pershore, while the other follows the right bank of that
stream. But by neither of these did Edward arrive
at the battle-field.

He heard that the earl would start for Kenilworth by way of Evesham on Monday night, and
resolved at once to cut him off from his stronghold at
all hazards, by a flank march which should cross his
line of route. But he had to elude the vigilance of
certain spies whom he suspected to be in his camp.
He started therefore late in the evening of Monday,
August 3, and marched at first northwards up the
left bank of the Severn, as if aiming at Shrewsbury
or Bridgnorth. When he had reached Claines, a
little village about three miles north of Worcester,
he considered he had gone far enough to deceive
· the spies, and turned suddenly towards the east.
Thence he rode without drawing rein, probably by
way of Alcester, and crossed the Avon at Priors
Cleeve, about four miles north-east of Evesham.
This brought him to the Warwick and Kenilworth
road. Finding that Simon had not passed that way,

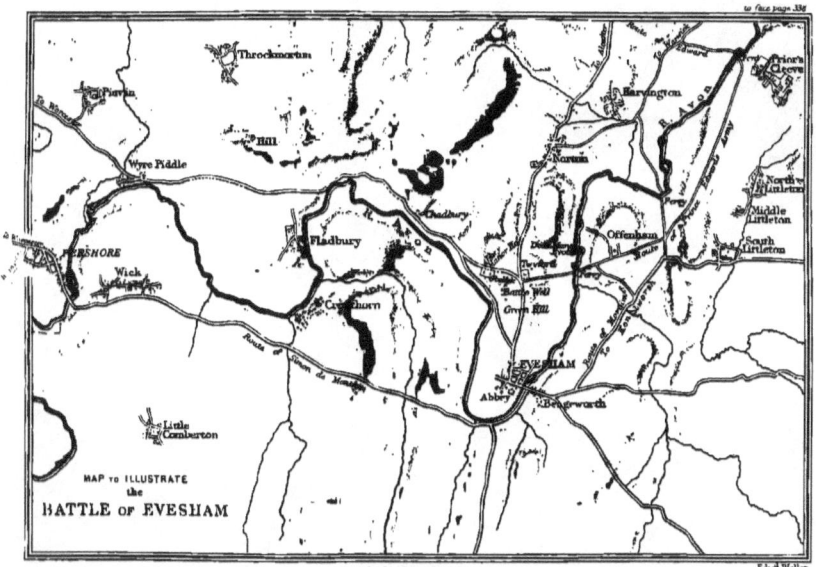

London; Longmans & Co.

Edwd Weller

he concluded he must have taken the direct road by
Alcester, and therefore recrossed the Avon near Dead
Mans Eyot, mounted the elevation now called Green
Hill, and took his station on the summit at a place
where four roads meet. Posting his own men in the
open, he stationed Gloucester with his troop a little
way to the left, out of sight from the town. From
this point they commanded all the outlets, and knew
that Simon could not escape them. For Roger Mortimer, with a third body, had been detached when
the rest recrossed the Avon, to march down its left
bank, and close the only remaining exit, that over
Bengeworth Bridge.[1] But Simon made no attempt

CHAP.
XI.

1265

Position of
Edward at
Evesham.

---

[1] I must take this opportunity of acknowledging my obligations to
Mr. H. New, of Evesham, who gave me most valuable help, in maps
of the country, and in his own publications on this subject. I have
however taken the liberty of differing from him on one or two comparatively unimportant points. He believes Gloucester to have followed
the northern road by the right bank of the Avon, from Worcester to
Evesham, and Mortimer to have advanced by the southern, following
from Pershore the same route as Simon had the day before. But I do
not think there is sufficient authority for this hypothesis, and it is
hardly probable that Edward would have separated his forces till he
knew exactly where Simon was, for had he met him single-handed he
would not have had so many troops as the earl. But we are told that
Edward crossed *a* river at Cleeve, ('transito fluvio juxta oppidum quod
dicitur Clive viam comiti versus, &c.'—*Rish.*, *Chron.* 35, where the editor
has appended a note, 'Clinemam in Wats' text.'). There is some
doubt about the place, and some have thought that Edward crossed the
Severn at Claines ; but Claines is not on the river, nor is there any
reason why he should have crossed the Severn, as he would have had
to do, twice. On the other hand, we know that he left the north road
from Worcester three or four miles from Worcester, that is, at Claines.
Arrived at Priors Cleeve he may, as Mr. Hort suggests, have sent
Mortimer across and marched on himself to Evesham. But there is no
direct road to Evesham from Priors Cleeve on the right bank of the
river, by which he could have gone, and moreover he was yet too far
from Evesham to have known for certain of Simons whereabouts At
the crossing by Dead Mans Eyot he was near enough to have found
out. I am inclined, therefore, to think that he sent Mortimer round
from there. We know he came up in Simons rear, and the only way
he could have done so was by crossing the Bengeworth Bridge.

CHAP.
XI.

1265
Battle of
Evesham ;
Earl Simon
sees the
enemy
approach-
ing.

to fly.   Hemmed in on all sides by his foes, the old
lion turned savagely at bay.

When the earl heard that troops were seen approaching, he cried out with joy, 'It is my son.
But nevertheless,' he added, 'go up and look and
bring me word again.'   His barber, Nicholas, who
was gifted with a long sight and had some knowledge
of heraldry, mounted the bell-tower of the abbey,
and appears to have been followed by his master.[1]
At first Nicholas distinguished the ensigns of young
Simon and his partisans, floating in the van of the
advancing force.   Another minute, and he saw they
were in hostile hands, a bitter proof of the fate of
his friends, and a warning of his own.   From the
tower-roof one can still look out with Simons eyes
upon the beautiful landscape below.   Straight in front
of him, about a mile distant, he looked upon the
slopes of Green Hill, glistening with the weapons of
those who were thirsting for his blood.   A little to
the right, over the shoulder of the hill, his eye followed the course of the winding stream, towards the
place where his home lay.   Between him and the
hill stretched a small plain, over which he would have
to pass to his death, a plain probably then as now
bright with gardens,[2] and golden with the ripening
fruit of autumn.   Beneath him lay the little town,

---

[1] *Rish.*, *de Bellis*, &c., p. 45, says, 'Symon . . . cum montem
quandam vicinam ascendisset, ut ordinem cæterorum consideraret, &c. ;'
but this is hardly possible, for there is no such hill, or even mound,
until you come to Green Hill.   The bell-tower is the only place, and
the most natural place, whence he could have viewed the foe.   The
present bell-tower was built early in the sixteenth century.   *Rob. of
Gloucester* says that young Simon had started from Kenilworth to join
his father, and had stopped at Alcester to dine, but this seems hardly
probable.

[2] The Welch are said to have been cut down in numbers in the
gardens about the town.

and as he glanced at the bridge, while one thought
of escape crossed his mind, he may have seen the
horsemen of Mortimer hastening down to block his
path. Behind him lay the river, before him the foe.
It needed not many moments to show him that all
was over. And bitterer than the thought of his own
fate, with years of life and power yet in him, more
numbing than the vague sense of what had befallen
his son, must have been the conviction that for a
time at least the cause which he had at heart, and for
the sake of which he had looked death in the face,
must perish with him. For a time at least: let us
hope that in his moment of agony he was consoled
by some vision of what was to come, by the faith
that in after years one yet greater and far more
fortunate than he would arise and protect the liberties
of the nation he had adopted for his own. But it
was no time for dreams ; he would sell his life as
dearly as he could. 'May the Lord have mercy upon
our souls,' he said, 'for our bodies are undone.'

Outnumbered as they were by three to one, vic- Earl Simon
tory was out of the question. His friends urged him prepares
for battle.
to fly, but the thought of flight for himself was not
in his mind. A natural flash of anger burst forth in the
remark that it was the folly of his own sons which had
brought him to this pass. Nevertheless he endeavoured
to persuade his eldest son Henry, his old comrade
Hugh Despenser, and others to fly while there was
yet time, and maintain the good cause when fortune
should smile again. But one and all refused to
desert him, preferring not to live if their leader died.
'Come then,' he said, 'and let us die like men ; for
we have fasted here and we shall breakfast in heaven.'

CHAP.
XI.

1265
Battle of
Evesham ;
Earl Simon
prepares
for battle.

His troops were hastily shriven by the aged Bishop of Worcester, who had performed the same office a year before upon a happier field. Then he led them out against the enemy, with the white cross again upon their shoulders,[1] in as close order as he could. In the midst of them was the king, for Simon seems to the last to have cherished a faint hope of cutting his way through his adversaries; and as at Lewes,. the possession of the royal person was everything to him.[2] As they neared the hill, Prince Edwards troops, who had been in no hurry to leave their point of vantage, began to descend upon them. Simons heart was struck with admiration of the fair array before him, so different from that which he had met a year before ; his soldierly pride told him to whom their skill was due. 'By the arm of St. James,' he cried, 'they come on well ; they learnt that not of themselves, but of me.'

On the south-western slope of Green Hill there is a small valley or combe ; in this hollow the chief struggle raged. On the further side, in the grounds of a private house, stands the obelisk, which marks the spot where, according to tradition, Simon de Montfort fell. Towards the higher part of the combe is a spring, still called De Montforts Well, which, on the day of the battle, is said to have run with blood.

Prince Edward began the fray, and while the earl was engaged with him, Gloucester came up with a second body on his left, so that he was soon sur-

---

[1] The royalists were marked here and at Lewes with red crosses.
[2] I think we may fairly reject the hypothesis that Simon placed the king in the midst of his troops, that he might not survive them, as well as the story that he disguised him in his own dress that he might be taken for him. He was, however, very nearly killed in mistake by his own friends.

rounded. The Welch infantry, poor, half-armed troops, fled at once, and were cut down in the neighbouring gardens by Mortimers forces, which must now have been advancing from the rear. / Simons horse was killed under him ; his eldest son was among the first to fall. When this was told him, he cried, 'Is it so ? then indeed is it time for me to die ;' and rushing upon the enemy with redoubled fury, and wielding his sword with both his hands, the old warrior laid about him with so terrific force, that had there been but half a dozen more like himself, says one who saw the fight, he would have turned the tide of battle. As it was he nearly gained the crest of the hill.[1] But it was not to be. For a while he stood 'like a tower,' but at length a foot soldier, lifting up his coat of mail, pierced him in the back, and, with the words 'Dieu merci' on his lips, he fell. Then the battle became a butchery. No quarter was asked or given. The struggle lasted for about two hours in the early summer morning, and then all was over.

Of the horrid cruelties practised by the victors on the body of their greatest foe it is better not to speak. The gallant old man lay, with the few who remained faithful to him and to his cause, dead upon the field,[2] and with him the curtain seemed to fall upon all that was free and noble in the land. The tempests which raged throughout the country that day were remarked as shadowing forth the grief of

Death of Earl Simon ;

complete defeat of his army.

Treatment of the earls body :

portents.

---

[1] *Rob. of Gloucester* says that the royalists turned to fly, and were rallied by W. de Basingburn, who reminded them of their disgrace at Lewes. The obelisk is just at the edge of the flat top of the hill.

[2] According to *T. Wykes*, 160 knights and an infinite number of nobles not yet knighted fell, besides many of less rank. The fragments of Simons body, with those of his son Henry and Hugh Despenser, were buried in the abbey, apparently by the command of Edward.

CHAP.
XI.

1265
Death of
Earl
Simon :
his political
work ;

heaven. The accompanying darkness, which was so thick that in some places the monks could no longer see to chant their prayers, was nothing to that which must have fallen on many when they heard of the death of their protector. But he had not lived in vain. England had learnt a lesson from him, and had seen glimpses of what might be ; and a re-tributive justice brought his principles to life again through. the very hands which had destroyed him. It was probably well for England that he died when he did, for a victory at Evesham would not have relieved him from the dilemma in which he was caught, but would rather have made it worse. Had he established and maintained his power, there was no one to take his place when a natural death should have removed him from the headship of affairs, and a feudal anarchy worse than that under Stephen would have supervened. It is easy enough to find fault with his politics. The party of order will blame his un-constitutional violence, and declare that his end did not justify his means. The party of reform will object to his moderation, and condemn him as an aristocrat after all. His political principles were doubtless in some measure premature, circumstances sometimes drove him into desperate and unjustifiable acts. But for all that, it would have been ill for Eng-land then, and perhaps would be ill now, had he never lived to raise his voice in favour of the oppressed, to curb the power of a would-be absolute monarch and an irresponsible baronage, and to remind his adopted countrymen that the remedy against such things was in their own hands and in the ancient institutions of their country.

His character will be better learnt from his actions than from any analysis. An impartial judge[1] has said, 'Nothing is more difficult than to form a just idea of the character of this illustrious person, who was abhorred as a devil by one half of England, and adored as a saint or guardian angel by the other.[2] He was unquestionably one of the greatest generals and politicians of his age ; bold, ambitious, and enterprising ; ever considered both by friends and enemies as the very soul of the party which he espoused.' These words are true, but they contain only half the truth. He was more than a great general, more than a great politician, far more than a mere party leader, inasmuch as he obeyed to the death that ruling principle which his own words expressed, 'I would rather die without a foot of land than break the oath that I have made.' This was why he was worshipped as a saint and a martyr ; and if we smile at the popular superstition which believed in the miracles wrought at his tomb, we can look up to the popular instinct which recognised in him that rarest of all miracles, a true patriot. The form of government which he set up and the constitutional measures he adopted to strengthen it sufficiently disprove the assertion that he used the pretext of reform to cover the designs of a purely selfish ambition. The fact, that he never aimed at supreme power, in spite of the insults and injuries he received at the hands of Henry, until it became evident that in no other way could justice be done, acquits him of the charge of traitorous

[1] Dr. Henry. See too the character of him in Stubbs, *Const. Hist.* vol. ii.

[2] See the miracles, &c , given in appendices ii. and iv.

CHAP.
XI.

1265
Character
of Simon
de Mont-
fort.

disloyalty to his king.   The fact that he was the only
one of the greater nobles who remained true to his
cause, shows how far he was above the prejudices
of class, and what temptations he had to surmount
before he left the common rut in which his peers were
content to move, and marked out for himself the
nobler and more dangerous course to which duty
called him.   A conviction of his own honesty of purpose, a firm faith that the right would triumph, as
well as an overweening confidence in his own powers,
led him to persevere in that course to the end, and to
essay the impossible.   He failed, but he was fortunate
in that he did not live to feel the bitterness of failure.
If in his public life he cannot be altogether freed from
blame, his private life was beyond reproach.   A blameless husband, a kind, too kind, father, a constant
friend—he was the model of a christian knight and
gentleman.   That he was the best hated, as he was
the best loved, man of his day, is but natural.   His
character was one calculated to offend as many as it
attracted.   In a rough age, one may perhaps say
in political matters in every age, no one can do
great things without some ambition, some im-
periousness, some selfishness, if one is to stamp
with that name the necessary self-assertion of a
strong character.   Who shall say in what proportion
these are to be mingled with other and nobler attributes—sympathy, devotion, uprightness, perseverance,
energy, faith ?   No man is faultless, and he was no
exception to the rule ; but if any faults can be said
to ennoble a character, they are those of Simon de
Montfort.

CHAPTER XII.

CONCLUSION.

STRANGE to say, the civil war was by no means concluded by the battle of Evesham, crushing as that defeat was for the party that followed de Montfort. The hopeless contest was prolonged for more than two years. Still the main interest was at an end. When Earl Simon had breathed his last, there was no further talk of constitutional liberties. His party was utterly disorganised, without union, without leaders, fighting with the energy of despair for one aim alone, that of self-preservation. The arrogance and pitiless severity of the conquerors were in reality the salvation of the conquered. The violence of the measures taken to stamp out the last sparks of rebellion was such that the survivors were compelled to continue the unequal struggle, until one of the victors of Evesham, ashamed of the part he was playing, stepped forward for their deliverance. The character of the war thus undergoes a complete change, and has no longer the same interest for the student of constitutional history as before ; but it may still be worth while to relate the course of events which led to the final pacification, and the mournful fate which overtook the remaining members of the family of Earl Simon.

CHAP.
XII.

1265
Complete change the character of the war.

CHAP.
XII.
1265
Apparent
complete-
ness of the
victory.

Immediately after the victory of Evesham Henry took the government again into his own hands, and lost no time in following up his success. Kenilworth showed no sign of giving way, but Despensers widow gave up the Tower of London, and the city itself, in which the royalists had for some time been gaining strength, made no effort to resist its surrender. The remnants of the baronial party had hardly yet begun to draw together again, and Henry probably fancied that the work of restoration was complete. But instead of healing the wounds of his exhausted country, he had already done his best to make them incurable.[1]

Council of
Winches-
ter; confis-
cations.

Within a few weeks after the death of Earl Simon, not satisfied by the terrible revenge taken upon the field of Evesham, Henry summoned a council at Winchester (September 8), at which punishment was meted out to the survivors with an unsparing hand. In one sweeping act of condemnation, the family of de Montfort and all his partisans were outlawed, and their property confiscated.

Rewards to
the
victors.

The wide estates which thus fell to the Crown were employed in strengthening the hands of the royal family, and in rewarding not only those who had been loyal to them throughout, but those too who had been traitors to the cause for which they had fought a year before at Lewes. Prince Edward received the goods of all the merchants of London who had opposed the king during the late troubles. Edmund, the kings second son, received the earldoms of Leicester and Derby, to console him for the loss

---

[1] ' Rex et sui complices, non sicut decuerat cautiores effecti sed potius stultiores, sic evecti sunt in sublime ut futura regni dispendia contemnerent præmetiri,' says the royalist *T. Wykes*, 183.

of his nominal kingdom of Sicily. Henry of Almaine
received large estates in Nottinghamshire. The Earl
of Gloucester, Roger Mortimer, and others, were not
neglected. London had to pay a heavy fine, its democratical leaders were imprisoned, its privileges at
least temporarily annulled.[1] That all the acts of the
late government, as well as the Provisions of Oxford,
were repealed, was of course a necessary consequence
of the victory. The action taken by the Court-party
was in strong contrast with that of Simon de Montfort after the battle of Lewes, when he brought upon
himself the wrath of his own followers, by setting
bounds to their avarice and their lust of revenge.
Nevertheless the absence of political executions is
remarkable : death, as a penalty for treason or rebellion, was an invention of later times.

The natural result of this violent action on the
part of the king was a revival of the baronial party.
Isolated bands of malcontents, who went collectively
by the name of 'the Disinherited,' made their appearance in different parts of the country, but, having
no unity or organisation, were attacked singly and
dispersed before they had time to unite their forces.
Prince Edward, to whose well-directed energy and
politic clemency the gradual pacification of the
country was mainly owing, made the first step towards
that end by reducing the stronghold of Dover. The
Countess of Leicester, on hearing of Edwards escape
in the previous May, had left Odiham, and made her
way by Porchester and Pevensey to Dover, resolved
to bar the entrance to England against her husbands

---

[1] *Fœd.* i. 461, seq. ; *T. Wykes,* 176 ; cf Blaauw, *Barons' War,* 298
seq.

CHAP.
XII.

1265

Countess of
Leicester
leaves
England.

foes. There she remained till the news of his death showed her that further resistance was not only dangerous but useless.[1] She did not however seek safety in a precipitate flight. Not till the full effect of the battle of Evesham became evident, and the decrees against the Disinherited had been issued at Winchester, did she relax her hold on the fortress. At length, having sent her two younger sons, Amaury and Richard, before her, and taking with her a considerable treasure, she passed over into France.[2]

Shortly afterwards the royalist prisoners in the castle succeeded in making themselves masters of the keep, and held out against the garrison until Prince Edward, who had been informed of the event, hastened from London to their assistance. Placed thus between two fires, the garrison were soon compelled to sur-

render. The fall of Dover was followed, a few months later, by that of the other ports on the south coast.[3] The queen and the Cardinal Legate Ottoboni were enabled to land at Dover, and having been met at Canterbury by the king and his brother, made a sort of triumphal entry into London.[4]

The temporary lull was disturbed by news of fresh outbreaks in the north and east. Simon de Montfort, the eldest surviving son of the great earl, did not allow the grief and remorse, which he naturally

---

[1] See Hudson Turner, *Household Expenses*, &c. ; *T. Wykes*, 179, says : 'Comitissa Leycestriæ . . . maritali simul et filiali nece comperta, deposita purpura, habitum vidualem. . . . reassumens, eorum inconsolabiliter miseranda funera deplorabat, &c.'

[2] Early in October. The last entry in her accounts is dated October 1 ; Amauri and Richard had crossed Sept. 18.—*Household Expenses*, &c.

[3] The Cinque Ports formally admitted Edward next March.—*Ann. Wav.* 369.

[4] *T. Wykes*, 178, seq.

felt at the loss his own folly had caused, long to over-
power him.[1] He first of all released his prisoners,
King Richard and his second son Edmund. Then,
after pillaging the country far and near round Kenil-
worth, and stocking the fortress with arms and pro-
visions enough, it was thought, to last out a siege of
seven years, he himself, with a strong force, marched
eastwards and occupied the island of Axeholme in
Lincolnshire.[2] Tidings of the ravages which he and
his were committing in the surrounding country soon
brought Edward upon him. The natural strength of
the place, increased by artificial means, enabled him
to hold out for some time ; but Edward, by the aid
of bridges and a strict blockade, forced him, before
the end of the year, to surrender.[3]

A council was shortly afterwards summoned at
Northampton, where the king and the larger portion
of his army lay. There Simon presented himself,
under cover of a safe conduct, and a settlement was
effected, apparently through the mediation of the
legate and King Richard. Simon agreed to give
up the castle of Kenilworth, and to leave the king-
dom for an indefinite period, promising to find surety
that he would not disturb the peace. He was to re-
ceive a pension of five hundred marks a year, until
such time as tranquillity should be fully restored.[4]

he occupies
Axeholme,

but sur-
renders.

Council at
Northamp-
ton :
arrange-
ment with
Simon the
younger.

---

[1] 'Mente tam lugubri paternum et fraternum deploravit excidium,
ut putaretur diebus plurimis cibos vel potum non gustasse.'—*T. Wykes*
175. According to the same writer he had set out from Kenilworth to
meet his father, and returned on hearing of his defeat.
[2] About the feast of St. Martin, 11 Nov.—*Id.* 181.
[3] 'Tertio die Nativitatis Dominici (?)'.—*Ibid.*
[4] *Ann. Dunst.* 240 say that the covenant was not observed by
Edward ; this probably refers not to the subsequent arrangement, but to
the promise made, according to the same authority, before the surrender,

CHAP.
XII.

1266

Suspension
of bishops.

Simon the
younger
flies to
France,

followed by
his brother
Guy.

At the same time the legate, whose appearance must
have reminded men of Cardinal Gualos mission fifty
years before, brought the power of the Church to bear
upon the delinquents. The bishops who had supported the cause of freedom were suspended, and
bidden to journey immediately to Rome, there to
purchase pardon for their misdeeds.[1] From Northampton the king returned to London, taking Simon
with him, but the latter having apparently had a hint
that perpetual imprisonment was in store for him,
shortly afterwards made his escape, without finding
the surety he had promised, and crossed to France.[2]
He was soon followed by his brother Guy, who had
been imprisoned at Dover, but was released by his
gaoler from confinement.[3] It is possible that the

that Simon and his followers should receive back their lands and chat-
tels. According to *Rish., de Bellis*, &c., 51, the terms would have been
better but for the violence of the Earl of Gloucester and others : cf. *T.
Wykes* 180, seq.

[1] These were the Bishops of London, Worcester, Winchester, Lincoln,
and Chichester. *Ann. Osn.* 181 ; *Nic. Trivet* 268. The Bishop of Worcester died in 1266. *T. Wykes*, 180, says of him, 'raptus . . . ne
videret dies malos, qui tanta sanctitatis eminentia cæteris præpollebat
·episcopis, quod nisi. . .' comiti Leycestriæ tam familiariter et fortiter adhæsisset, in catalogo sanctorum non immerito fuerat ascribendus.'
The authorities differ as to the exact date and place at which the sentence was given.

[2] *Ann. Dunst.* 240 ; *T. Wykes* 182. Dr. Pauli (*Simon de Mont.*
204) says that he returned to England shortly afterwards and joined
the Disinherited in the fens of Ely ; and (p. 206) that he made his escape
again in 1267. But this seems to be unfounded, and to rest on a confusion between the affair of Axeholme and that of Ely, caused by the
untrustworthy account in *W. de Hemingb.* 328. Mr. Pearson (*Hist. of
Eng.* ii. 270) seems to be equally without authority in saying that he
returned to Kenilworth. He very possibly intended to come back, for
in a writ (*Fœd.* i. 468) dated May 18, the Wardens of the ports are
bidden to be on their guard against 'S. de Monteforti et complices
ejus.' According to *Rish., de Bellis*, &c., 53, he tried to collect troops
in France, but was hindered from crossing by the king.

[3] *Nic. Trivet* 268. According to *Rish., Chron.* 47, he bribed his
guard.

royalists were glad enough to be rid of them both, and connived at their escape.

In spite of these successes, the country was still so disturbed that captains had to be appointed in every county to aid the sheriff in putting down the armed bands which roved about, ravaging and destroying wherever they went.[1] Prince Edward first attacked one of the most noted of these freebooters, Adam Gurdun, who with a force of eighty knights held Farnham Castle, and carried fire and sword throughout Hampshire and the neighbouring counties. He was surprised in the woods near Alton, through the treachery of one of his own men, and captured, according to one account, by Edward with his own hands.[2] Robert Ferrars, the truest representative of feudal anarchy, the enemy of constitutional government as well as of royal despotism, placed himself at the head of a stronger body in his own county of Derbyshire. There he was joined by many who had been with Simon de Montfort at Axeholme, but had rejected the compromise to which he had given way and under the leadership of John d'Eyville preferred continuing the conflict to acquiescing in confiscation and exile. Henry of Almaine was sent against them, and succeeded in surprising them at Chesterfield (May 15). They were dispersed with great loss, and the Earl of Derby himself was taken prisoner and carried to Windsor, whither Adam Gurdun was also brought, as the chronicler says, to 'bear him company.'[3]

[1] *Nic. Trivet* 268.
[2] *Id.* 269 : 'In septimana Pentecostes.'—*T. Wykes* 189.
[3] 'Ne forte comes Ferrariensis ibidem captivus sine comite moraretur.'—*Id.* 190 ; cf. *IV. de Hemingb.* 326. The legend of the chivalrous treatment experienced by Adam Gurdun at the hands of

CHAP.
XII.
—,—
1266
Siege of
Kenilworth
Castle.

D'Eyville and others cut their way through the royalists and made their escape.

But the strongest opposition was offered by Earl Simons own stronghold of Kenilworth. The siege of that fortress was not formally undertaken till June 25, 1266. The garrison had had plenty of time to prepare, and so strongly had the castle been fortified by the military genius of Earl Simon, and provisioned by the care of his son, that all efforts to reduce it were vain. The garrison were summoned to surrender in accordance with the agreement made in the spring with Simon de Montfort. But they rejected the summons, declaring that they held the castle at the will of the Countess of Leicester, and to her alone would they restore it.[1] They had already given proof that they meant to continue the struggle to desperation, by cutting off the hand of a royal envoy whom they had taken in his passage through the district.[2] They showed a more chivalrous feeling when a royalist prisoner of noble birth died of his wounds in the castle. His body was placed upon a bier, and, with lighted candles, carried out of the castle-gates, in order that his friends might receive it and give it honourable burial.[3] Humorous incidents were not wanting. The legate, who was in the royalist camp,

Prince Edward seems to be of doubtful authenticity, and rests on the story in *Nic. Trivet* (p. 269), whose account of this period is confused. According to Wykes, Gurdun was imprisoned in chains at Windsor. From *Ann. Dunst.* 241, one might infer that the place where Gurdun was taken was Halton, in Bucks ; see Pearson, *Eng. Hist.* ii. 271, note 1.

[1] 'Dicentes se nullam a Simone suscepisse castri custodiam,' &c.—*Rish., Chron.* 43.

[2] This happened in March, before the siege began.—*Royal Letters* ii. 300.

[3] *Rish., de Bellis,* &c. 56.

thought to awe the enemy into submission by the sentence of excommunication, whereupon one of the besieged clad himself in ecclesiastical robes, and from the castle-wall solemnly excommunicated the king and the legate and all their followers.[1] Enormous engines were built, and hurled stones into the castle, or battered the walls. They were met by equally powerful machines from the inside. The garrison, numbering, as they did, more than a thousand men, made frequent sallies, and, meeting the besiegers on equal terms, defeated them with loss. The state of the country was by no means favourable to a prolonged siege, and accordingly, after several months of useless effort, the king consented to a compromise.

Three bishops and three lay barons were appointed by the assembled magnates, and these coopted six others, two of whom were the Earls of Gloucester and Hereford.[2] These twelve formed a committee of arbitration, to draw up terms of peace to which the Disinherited might consent. The terms so arranged were called the Dictum, or Ban,[3] of Kenilworth. This lengthy document, consisting of forty-one articles, begins by recognising the complete re-establishment of the royal authority, the restoration of all rights and other matters alienated from the Crown during the late troubles, and the abolition of all promises or charters extorted from the king or Prince Edward by Simon de Montfort and his party. On the other hand, all ancient charters and liberties,

---

[1] This was 'Maister Philip Porpeis, that was a quointe man, Clerc and hardi of is dedes and hor cirurgian.'—*Rob. of Glouc.* 566.

[2] See the names in Stubbs, *Const. Hist.* ii. 96, the document in *Sel. Chart.* 410.

[3] So called in *Rob. of Glouc.* 568.

CHAP.
XII.

1266
The Dic-
tum of
Kenil-
worth :

especially those of the Church, and all royal grants spontaneously made, were to be observed. It was also recommended that the justices should be chosen from among honest and unselfish men, and that no one, be his quality what it might, should seize corn or other goods without consent of the owner. These two stipulations call to mind similar clauses in Magna Carta.[1] The rights thus secured are limited enough.

But the greater portion of the document was naturally taken up with the settlement of the immediate quarrel. A complete amnesty was offered to all those in arms against the king, with certain exceptions, who should submit within forty days, and the legate was begged to absolve all such as should have incurred the sentence of excommunication by violating the charters. The Disinherited were specially dealt with. The confiscation of their estates decreed the year before was now exchanged for a system of redemption, by which the owners could recover their property on payment of five years rental. An exception was made in the case of the Earl of Derby, who had to pay for seven years, and to surrender his castles. Those who had no landed property were to forfeit half their goods ; those who had neither land nor goods were to take an oath and find surety that they would keep the peace. Special stipulations · were made in favour of those who had been forced into the war, or were falsely accused of taking part against the king. Twelve men were to be appointed to assess the value of confiscated property, and to see

---

[1] Cf. §§ 28, 45 of Magna Carta of 1215.

to the execution of the provisions. In these and a number of smaller enactments, the difficult questions of penalty and reconciliation were arranged with scrupulous care and an evident attempt to do justice, though a hard justice, to all. Finally, the legate was to forbid the holding of Simon de Montfort as a saint, and to prohibit, under severe penalties, the reports of miracles done by him, which were already being spread about through the country.[1] Of the sons of the late earl nothing was said, since the king had put their affairs in the hands of the King of France.

The Dictum of Kenilworth shows a considerable advance in point of justice and moderation on the decrees of the previous year. Still the terms were very hard, and must have been equivalent in many cases to confiscation. They were not accepted at once. The Dictum was published at the end of October, but the defenders of the castle held out for several weeks longer. As soon however as it appeared, they placed hostages in the kings hands, promising to surrender if not relieved by Simon de Montfort, who was then in France, within forty days.[2] No help came, and at last, after suffering the extremes of cold, hunger, and wretchedness of all kinds,[3] they accepted the terms offered them, and gave up the place (December 20).[4]

The war was however not yet over, and was shortly to assume a more serious aspect than it had presented since the death of Earl Simon. No

Surrender of Kenilworth Castle.

Continuation of the war.

---

[1] See Appendix II.

[2] *Ann. Dunst.* 244; *Rish., de Bellis,* &c. 59. It was the term allowed in the Dictum.

[3] See the account in *T. Wykes,* 194 seq.

[4] It was immediately conferred on Prince Edmund.—*Id.* 196.

CHAP.
XII.

1266-67
The Disin-
herited in
the Isle of
Ely:

sooner were the Disinherited suppressed in one
quarter than they reappeared in another. John
d'Eyville collected the fragments of the force that
had been defeated at Chesterfield, and, attacking
Lincoln, massacred the Jews and plundered the city.
Thence he marched southwards, and, with the connivance of the inhabitants, occupied the Isle of Ely.
There, in the district where Hereward so long bade
defiance to the Conqueror, the Disinherited fortified
themselves in the midst of impenetrable marshes, and
blocked all the avenues so that none could approach
without their will. As their forces increased they
became bolder, and there was hardly a town in the
eastern counties which did not suffer from their raids.
They even attacked the important city of Norwich,
and, meeting with no opposition, carried off everything of value in the town. As long as the royal
forces were occupied with the siege of Kenilworth
they pursued their trade unchecked, and even after
the conclusion of the siege they successfully defended
themselves some time longer. The king, who had
removed to London from Kenilworth, was obliged,
old and weary as he was, to enter in the depth of
winter upon a new campaign. The Lent Parliament
was summoned to meet at Bury St. Edmunds ;
Henry, with a large army, took up his quarters at
Cambridge, and sought to reduce the defenders of
Ely by blockade. They however showed no inclination to yield, rejected the legates exhortation to
surrender,[1] and defeated with great loss a fleet which

[1] See the, perhaps rather apocryphal, account of their answer to the
legate, in which they defend their orthodoxy and the justice of their
cause, in *Rish., de Bellis,* &c. 62.

had sailed up the Ouse from Lynn, Yarmouth, and other ports to attack them. Difficulties with the clergy, who refused to pay the tenth for three years, and other taxes which Henry demanded for the subjection of the Disinherited, hampered the efforts of the royalists and emboldened their enemies.[1] Meanwhile the attention of Prince Edward was called away by disturbances in the north. He soon succeeded, by combined activity and clemency, in quelling them ; but in his absence nothing could be done.[2]

Matters were in this state when suddenly, without any warning, the Earl of Gloucester took up arms and marched on London. Pretending that he was come to support the just claims of the Disinherited, which he had hitherto been foremost in rejecting, and to secure the fulfilment by Edward of the oath which he had exacted from him when he escaped from Hereford, he entered the city (April 10), and was favourably received by the democratical party, whom fear alone had kept quiet during the past year. What was the real motive which urged the earl to this step it is impossible to say ; but one can hardly refrain from a suspicion that he merely used the cry of justice for the Disinherited as a pretext to cover a change of sides prompted by some personal grievance which he had, or thought he had, against the king.[3] Of honest effort for constitutional reform there is hardly a trace

CHAP.
XII.

1267
their successful
resistance.

Revolt of
the Earl of
Gloucester:

he occupies
London.

---

[1] The kings demand and the reply of the clergy are given in *Rish.*, *de Bellis*, 60.

[2] See throughout the account in *T. Wykes*, 192, seq.

[3] According to *Rish.*, *de Bellis*, &c., 59, a quarrel had broken out at Kenilworth between him and R. Mortimer, and they had retired from the siege. *Ann. Dunst.* 245, imply that he was jealous of Mortimers influence with the king. Cf. Stubbs, *Const. Hist* ii. 297.

CHAP.
XII.

1267
Revolt of
the Earl of
Gloucester:
he occupies
London,

in his whole career, except for the brief space when he was under the influence of Earl Simon. Naturally however he at once became the head of the malcontents, who streamed to him from all sides. John d'Eyville and other chiefs of the Disinherited left their stronghold and joined him in London. He lost no time in fortifying the city, and in summoning the legate to give up the Tower. The legate refusing, he began the siege in regular form ; but the fall of the fortress, which seemed imminent, was prevented by the arrival of the king.

where he is
besieged by
Edward.

Prince Edward, immediately on hearing of the outbreak, had hastened with his usual rapidity from the north, and, joining the king at Cambridge, continued his march upon the capital. He at once released the legate, and threw into the Tower a strong body of troops. Then he withdrew to a short distance from the city, and waited for an opportunity. It was a curious repetition of the events of 1264. The citizens, emboldened by the respite thus allowed them, marched out and pillaged the neighbouring country, wrecked the palace of Westminster, and murdered many who were suspected of royalist proclivities. Meanwhile those who had been left in the Isle of Ely, under the leadership of Henry of Hastings, one of the defenders of Kenilworth, renewed their ravages. The king was in sore want of money, and could neither pay his French mercenaries, nor supply his own troops with food. At length, when both parties had begun to weary of the fruitless struggle, discussion took the place of war, and after some trouble, neither side being willing to yield, a compromise was effected, through the mediation of

King Richard, Henry of Almaine, and others (June
15). The Earl of Gloucester confessed his fault, and
received pardon after taking an oath never again to
make war upon the king, under a penalty of 20,000
marks. John d'Eyville and other chiefs received a
free pardon. The citizens of London were admitted
to favour, and no penalties were exacted. The mercenaries were dismissed, and the king entered the
city in peace.[1]

While Henry rested from his labours in the
capital, Edward, indefatigable as ever, completed the
work of pacification by reducing the last stronghold
of opposition, the Isle of Ely. Bringing together all
the neighbouring population, he prevailed upon them
by promises and good words to set their services
and local knowledge at his disposal. He was thus
enabled to construct causeways over the morass, by
which horse and foot could approach close to the
island itself. The work was made easier by the dry-
ness of the season, and the connivance of Nicolas de
Segrave, who allowed the royalists to pass the out-
posts which he guarded. Edward then, having made
all the preparations necessary to ensure success,
issued a stern proclamation, threatening death to any
one who should offer further resistance. This measure produced the desired result. The defenders
immediately laid down their arms, and placed themselves at his mercy. They received a free pardon,
and the permission to redeem their lands according
to the Dictum of Kenilworth, and were allowed two
days to depart. The conqueror entered Ely amid

---

[1] *T. Wykes*, 198, seq.; *Ann. Dunst.* 245 ; *Rish.*, *de Bellis* 59.

CHAP.
XII.

1267
Llewelyn
makes
peace.

the applause of the inhabitants.   Only one element
of disturbance remained, Llewelyn, Prince of Wales.
An army was sent to Shrewsbury, which compelled
him, towards the end of September, to sue for peace.
Through the intervention of the legate, his lands,
which had been declared forfeit, were restored on
payment of a heavy fine, and peace was made.[1]

Before the winter began the country was again,
after nearly five years of open or secret warfare, and
incessant anxiety and trouble, completely tranquil.
A plentiful harvest went far to repair the damages
caused by the civil war, and universal exhaustion to
some extent allayed the passions to which it had
given rise.   A spirit of compromise had for some

time been gaining the upper hand.   In the Parliament held at Marlborough, in November of the same
year, at which it seems probable that some representative members were present, the Provisions of
Westminster were reenacted with but slight omissions.
The only important difference was that the appointment of the high officers of the Crown and of the
sheriffs was now left in the hands of the king.[2]   It
was an omen of happy augury when the future
monarch, who had recovered his kingdom by the sword,
signalised his victory by granting of his own free will
a part at least of the boon which at one time he had
striven to withhold from his people.

The first part of his work was done, and he was
able, three years later, to carry his victorious arms
to the assistance of the Christians in the Holy Land.

[1] *T. Wykes*, 209 ; *Ann. Dunst.* 246 ; *Nic. Trivet*, 246.
[2] *Statutes* i. 19 ; cf. Stubbs, *Const. Hist.* ii. 97.

At the head of the nobility of England [1] he performed the duty which was still thought to be incumbent on a Christian king, which his father had so often undertaken, but had never been able to fulfil. Five years of almost undisturbed tranquillity remained for Henry, and a sort of twilight happiness overspread the remainder of his long and troubled reign.[2] Free for a time from the restless elements which might have again disturbed the public peace, the nation waited quietly for the rule of one whom they had proved to be strong, and whom they believed to be good. When the old man sank at length into his grave, the sceptre passed, for the first time since the Conquest, without doubt or difficulty, into the hands of his successor. Twenty-five years of prosperity and development at home, of honour and success abroad, followed. Within thirty years after the battle of Evesham there had grown up a younger generation, in whom the evil tendencies of feudalism were weaker, while the instincts of law and order and constitutional government were stronger, than in their fathers. The movement which crowned the edifice of our constitution does not present the same contrasts of light and shade which are so striking in the movements of 1215 and 1258, but it had a direct connection with those earlier efforts. The great Parliament of 1295 and the statutes of 1297 completed and confirmed that which the Great Charter had begun, and for which Simon de Montfort had died.

---

[1] Twenty-two bannerets and over a hundred knights are said to have gone with Edward on crusade.—Pearson, *Hist. of Eng.* ii. 278. The Earl of Gloucester was to have gone but did not go.

[2] The later difficulties between Edward and the Earl of Gloucester, and the riot at Norwich in 1272, were comparatively unimportant.

CHAP.
XII.
──,──
1263-74
Subse-
quent life
of the
Countess of
Leicester.

It remains to trace briefly the subsequent events which led to the extinction, within two generations, of the family of the great earl. The countess, after her escape to France, did not neglect the interests of her family or of those who had been her husbands followers. In this she was supported, to some extent at least, by her brother Richard, and by her nephew, Prince Edward, who presented to the chancellor a list of his uncles adherents, drawn up by the countess, and recommended them to mercy.[1] She had other advocates, perhaps more hearty, in King Louis and in her sister-in-law, the Queen of England. It was probably through them that Henry, who no longer used the title of 'sister' in reference to the countess, so far relented as to allow her a pension of 500*l.*,[2] and even to offer to receive her in England, and to promise that justice should be done her.[3] This pension was confirmed to her by Edward on his return from the east, while at the same time he showed her other signs of favour.[4] But she did not live to reap any of the advantages which a change of rulers might have conferred upon her. She had taken refuge on her first arrival in France in the Dominican Convent of Montargis, and after nine years, passed under the quiet care of the sisterhood,

---

[1] Greens *Princesses* ii. 454.

[2] *Rot. Lit. Pat.* 51 Hen. III, quoted by Pauli. This was probably the money which Henry had been accustomed to pay her from the possessions of the Marshalls ; see above, pp. 217 seq. Henry had already offered to continue the payment ; see *Rot. Lit. Pat.*, 49 Hen. III. quoted by Pauli.

[3] Greens *Princesses* ii. 455.

[4] Pauli, *Simon de Mont.* 218. According to *Ann. Dunst.* 258, Edward restored to her the lands which belonged to her as widow of William Marshall.

CHAP.
XII.
1265–71
Subsequent
life of
Simon and
Guy de
Montfort.

she died at the age of sixty, apparently some time in the year 1274.[1]

It would have been well for her children had they had so peaceful an end. Henry, the eldest son, fell with his father at Evesham. Simon and Guy, after their flight from England, stayed for a short time with their mother in France. Guy however soon tired of inactivity, and went southwards to take service under Charles of Anjou, then engaged in the acquisition of his kingdom of Sicily. His energy and military talents soon raised him to a high position in that quarter, and won him the hand of Margaret, daughter and heiress of Count Aldobrandini Rosso dell'Anguillara.[2] His elder brother followed him to Italy somewhat later, after having stolen across to England and paid a furtive visit to the graves of his father and brother at Evesham.[3] The bitter thoughts that must have gnawed at his heart as he gazed upon their resting-places, and heard from the monks all the story of that terrible day, it is easy enough to conjecture. The sight of the fair lands which might once have been his but were now anothers, the destruction of all his hopes, the ruin of his family, the brutalities perpetrated on his fathers body, his own poverty and exile—all this may well have implanted in him a deeply-rooted yearning for revenge, which found vent in the terrible crime that followed.

Henry of Almaine had accompanied his cousin Edward as far as Sicily, but when the latter set sail for Syria, in the spring of 1271, he returned north-

---

[1] *Rish., Chron.* 87 ; *Ann. Dunst.*
[2] 'Magnus effectus est in partibus illis.'—*Ann. Dunst.* 259 ; cf. Pauli, *Simon de Mont.* 208.
[3] *Bart. Cotton* 146 ; the date of the visit seems uncertain.

CHAP.
XII.
1271
Murder of
Henry of
Almaine.

wards to take command of Gascony, of which province he had been appointed seneschal[1] during Edwards absence. On his way he stopped at Viterbo.
There he met Charles of Anjou and Philip III of
France ;[2] and there too were his cousins, Simon and
Guy de Montfort.[3] Against Henry they had no
peculiar grudge ; on the contrary, he and his father
had been on more friendly terms with them than the
rest of their kin. But considerations of this kind
were powerless against the blind desire of vengeance.
One of the hated family was at their mercy, and the
sight of him roused their passions into fury. Watching their opportunity, they fell upon him one morning (March 13) in a church in the town.[4] Mass was
over, and he had remained behind to pray alone,
when the brothers entered with drawn swords and
cries of ' murderer' and 'traitor.' Henry rose from his
knees and fled to the altar, but his enemies followed
him and stabbed him as he clung to the holy place
and cried in vain for mercy. They even dragged him
to and fro in horrible mockery of the way in which
their fathers body had been insulted at Evesham.
Then they rode off and succeeded in making good
their escape.

The universal horror inspired by the deed[5] never-

[1] *T. Wykes*, 239.

[2] Dr. Pauli (*Simon de Mont.* 209) suggests that he was the bearer
of some message to the cardinals, then engaged at Viterbo in the election of a Pope.

[3] It is implied by *T. Wykes*, 241, that another brother, Amauri,
was there too and was an abettor in the crime.

[4] The authorities differ as to the name of the church.

[5] Witness Dante, *Inferno*, canto xii. 118,

     ' Mostrocci un' ombra dall' un canto sola,
     Dicendo : colui fesse in grembo a Dio
     Lo cor que in sul Tamigi ancor si cola.'
quoted by Pauli.

theless produced for some time little results. The efforts made to bring the murderers to justice were ineffectual, and caused a suspicion that Charles of Anjou was concerned in their safety. The Church interfered with a tardy excommunication of the offenders, but nothing serious was done till Edwards return from the Holy Land. In the interval Simon had died,[1] but Guy and his father-in-law were brought to trial. The latter cleared himself. Guy was outlawed, and, after submitting to the Pope, was imprisoned for ten years. He was then released by Pope Martin IV, who needed his services as a soldier. Five years later he was captured by the Sicilians at sea, and thrown into a dungeon, whence he never emerged alive.[2] He left only daughters, of whom nothing seems to be known.

What Amauri de Montfort had been doing during this time we are not told, but he appears to have returned to England as chaplain—for he was in orders—to the Bishop of Chester about the time of Edwards accession.[3] He must however have left the country again soon after, for he was captured with his sister, while accompanying her to Wales. Some years later he was set free, and passed into Italy, where he turned soldier and subsequently died.[4] What became of Richard de Montfort we do not know.[5]

The fate of Eleanor, Earl Simons only daughter, is better known. The old connexion between the

---

[1] The place of his death is uncertain.
[2] See *Fœdera*, and other authorities quoted by Pauli, *Simon de Mont.* 224.
[3] *Lib. de Ant. Leg.* 159.
[4] See Pauli, *Simon de Mont.* 228.
[5] According to *Ann. Dunst.* 259, he died in France.

CHAP.
XII.

1265–82.
Subsequent
life of
Eleanor de
Montfort,
two families had doubtless brought about her be-
trothal to Llewelyn, Prince of Wales. For some
time however the necessity of submission to England
prevented Llewelyn from endangering peace by a
marriage which Edward was likely to oppose. When
war became imminent, and repeated summons to
Court showed Llewelyn that the English king was
intent on a more than formal homage, there was
no longer anything to be gained by temporising.
Eleanor was then called to add the strength of her
name to the cause of Welch independence, but in
passing over to Wales was captured in the Bristol
Channel by ships which Edward had ordered to
watch for her (1276). During the war that broke out
immediately after, Eleanor was placed in honourable
confinement, but no sooner was it over than the
generous conqueror granted the wishes of his late foe,
and with his own hand gave him his bride (October
1278). Her wedded happiness was but short-lived.
She died in childbirth in June 1282, before the war,
which the folly and treachery of David had renewed,
had ended so disastrously for Wales. It was well for
her that she was saved from the trouble to come.
Her little daughter was, when the war was over,
brought to England with the children of her uncle
David, and well cared for by order of the king. She
was however not allowed to marry, but remained a
nun in the convent of Sempringham till her death.[1]
In her perished the last known scion of the family
of the great earl, Simon de Montfort.

---

[1] She had a pension of twenty pounds a year. Peter Langtoft
gives the date of her death as occurring in June 1337. Cf. *Cont.
Flor. Wig.* ii. 226. Her name was Guenciliana, that is, Guenllian, or
Gwendolen.

APPENDICES.

APPENDIX I.

PEDIGREE OF THE FAMILY OF MONTFORT L'AMAURI.

B B

PEDIGREE OF THE FAMILY OF MONTFORT L'AMAURI.

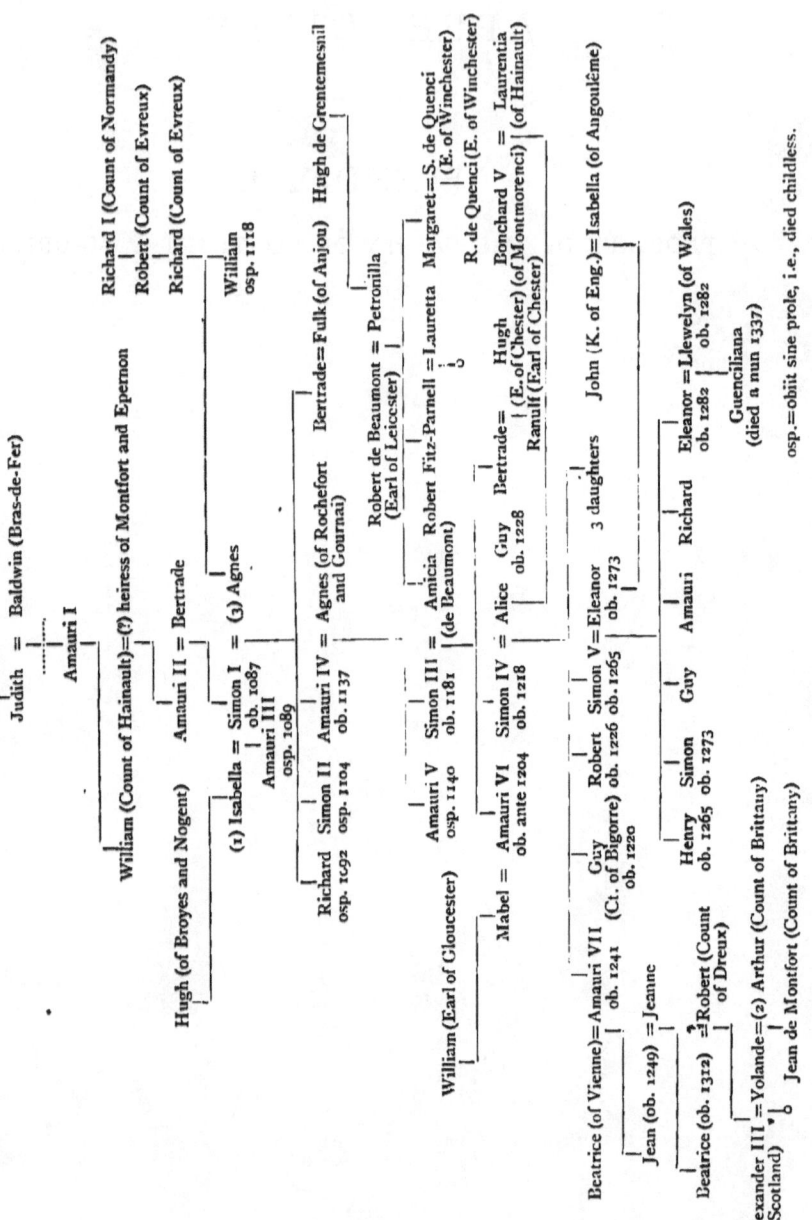

APPENDIX II.

1.—MIRACLES OF SIMON DE MONTFORT.

THE following are a few of the miracles, over two hundred in number, which are related to have been performed by Simon de Montfort after death. They are printed by Mr. Halliwell at the end of his edition of the 'Narratio de duobus bellis apud Lewes et Evesham, &c.,' published for the Camden Society. These miracles are spoken of in the Dictum of Kenilworth, when the Earl had been dead just a year, and are alluded to in several contemporary MSS., e.g. the Chronicle of Evesham and the Brute Chronicle, quoted by Mr. Halliwell on p. xxviii of his preface. The list of miracles was preceded in the MS. by an account of the battle of Evesham, now obliterated, and was compiled by a monk of Evesham. I have thought that they might be found interesting as specimens of the superstition of the time, and have accordingly translated a few of them, as follows:

1. The Countess of Gloucester had a palfrey that had been broken-winded for two years. In returning from Evesham to Tewkesbury, the horse having drunk of the Earls Well[1] and having had its head and face washed in the water,

---

[1] The Earls Well, otherwise called Battle Well, or de Montforts Well, is a small spring in the hollow of the hill where the battle was fought. It is said, in local tradition, to have run with blood after the fight.

recovered. . . . Of this the Countess and all her company are witnesses.

2. A sick woman of Elmley sent her daughter to the Earls Well to fetch water. In returning she met the servants of the castle, who asked her what she had in the pitcher. She answered that it was new beer from Evesham, and they said, 'Nay, but it is water from the Earls Well.' But when they had drawn some forth, they found it as the girl had said, and so they let her go.[1] And when she came to the sick woman, it was again changed into water, and the sick woman having drunk thereof, was healed.

3. It is to be remembered of the hand of Simon,[2] that the bearer of it was journeying by a certain church, and, hearing the bell toll for mass, entered in and prayed ; and when the priest stood up to elevate the body of Christ, the hand moved and stood upright, and adored Jesus, as it was wont while yet alive.

4. William, surnamed Child, had a son who was sick to death, at which William was sore grieved. By chance a certain Friar Preacher, an old companion of his, came to him, and seeing his grief, asked him if he had ever been at enmity with Earl Simon. And he said, ' Yes, for he deprived me of my goods.' And the other answered, 'Ask pardon of the martyr, and thou shalt recover thy child.' Meanwhile the child died, and the father in great grief threw himself upon his bed and slept. And he saw in a dream Christ descend from heaven and touch him, saying, ' Whatever thou askest in the name of my Earl, shall be given thee.' And he rose in haste and measured[3] the boy, and he opened his eyes.

---

[1] It was forbidden by the Dictum of Kenilworth to call Earl Simon a saint, or to spread reports of miracles done by him. The girl would therefore have been liable to certain penalties for drawing water for the purpose of healing from the Earls Well.

[2] This was the hand of Earl Simon that was cut off and sent to the wife of one of the royalists as a trophy.

[3] The word is ' mensuravit.' The custom was to bind round the head or other sick part of the body a piece of riband or cloth which had been steeped in the water of the Earls Well, or applied to his relics.

Of this Clement of London and the father of the dead boy are witnesses.

5. Stephen Hulle and others, citizens of Hereford, relate a wonderful thing about Philip, chaplain of Brentley, who reviled the Earl, and said, ' If the Earl be a saint, as they say, may the devil break my neck, or some miracle happen before I come home.' And as he asked, so it came to pass. For in returning home he saw a hare, and pursuing it fell from his horse. . . . Of this the whole city of Hereford bear witness.

2.—SONGS IN HONOUR OF SIMON DE MONTFORT.

I have thought it best to collect in the shape of an appendix the more important notices of Earl Simon and other interesting pieces in the popular songs of the time, instead of introducing them piecemeal in the notes. The extracts are mostly taken from the book of Political Songs, edited by Mr. Wright for the Camden Society.

1. This extract (Polit. Songs, p. 60), is part of a song made during or shortly after the outbreak in the spring of 1263 :

> Mout furent bons les barons ;
> Mes touz ne sai nomer lur noms,
>   Tant est grant la some :
> Pur ce revenk al quens Simon,
> Pur dire interpretison,
>   Coment hom le nome.
>
> Il est apele de Monfort,
> Il est el mond et si est fort,
>   Si ad giant chevalerie ;
> Ce voir, et je m'acort,
> Il cime dreit, et het le tort,
>   Si avera la mestrie.
>
> El mond est vercement ;
> La ou la comun a ly concent,
>   De la terre loce

C'est ly quens de Leycestre,
Que baut et joius se puet estre
De cele renomee.

2. The following song is on the Battle of Lewes, aimed
especially at King Richard (Polit. Songs, p. 69).

Sitteth alle stille and herkneth to me :
The Kyng of Alemaigne, bi mi leaute,
Thritti thousent pound askede he
For to make the pees in the countree,
    Ant so he dude more.
Richard, thah thou be ever trichard,
    Trichen shalt thou never more.

Richard of Alemaigne, whil that he was kyng,
He spende al is tresour upon swyvyng ;
Haveth he nout of Walingford o ferlyng :
Let him habbe, ase he brew, bale to dryng,
    Maugre Wyndesore.
    Richard, &c.

The Kyng of Alemaigne wende do ful wel,
He saisede the mulne for a castel,
With hare sharpe swerdes he grounde the stel,
He wende that the sayles were mangonel,
    To helpe Wyndesore.
    Richard, &c.

The Kyng of Alemaigne gederede ys host,
Makede him a castel of a mulne post,
Wende with his prude ant is muchele bost,
Brohte from Alemaigne mony sori gost,
    To store Wyndesore.
    Richard, &c.

By God, that is abouven ous, he dude muche synne,
That lette passen over see the Erl of Warynne :
He hath robbed Engelond, the mores, and the fenne,
The gold, ant the selver, ant yboren henne
    For love of Wyndesore.
    Richard, &c.

Sire Simond de Mountfort hath swore bi ys chyn,
Hevede he nou the Erl of Waryn,
Shulde he never more come to is yn,
Ne with shelde ne with spere ne with other gyn,
    To help of Wyndesore.
Richard, &c.

Sire Simond de Mountfort hath swore bi ys cop,
Hevede he nou here Sire Hue de Bigot,
Al he shulde quite here twelfmoneth scot,
Shulde he never more with his fot pot,
    To helpe Wyndesore.
Richard, &c.

Be the luef, be the loht, Sire Edward,
Thou shalt ride sporeless on thy lyard,
Al the ryhte way to Dovere ward ;
Shalt thou never more breke foreward,
    Ant that reweth sore :
Edward thou dudest ase a shreward,
    Forsoke thyn emes lore.
Richard, thah thou be ever trichard,
    Trichen shalt thou never more.

3. The following extracts are from the great political poem written after the Battle of Lewes in defence of Simon de Montfort and of the principles of the baronial party. (Polit. Songs, 72 seq.)

Benedicat dominus Simoni de Monte-Forti,
Suis nichilominus natis et cohorti.
Qui se magnanimiter exponentes morti
Pugnaverunt fortiter, ...
Sed hanc videns populi Deus agoniam,
Dat in fine sæculi novum Matathiam,
Et cum suis filiis zelans zelum legis,
Nec cedit injuriis nec furori regis.
Seductorem nominant Simonem atque fallacem,
Facta sed examinant probantque veracem.
            vv. 65–80.

Comitis devotio sero deridetur,
Cujus cras congressio victrix sentietur.
Lapis hic ab hostibus diu reprobatus
Post est parietibus duobus aptatus.
Angliæ divisio desolationis
Fuit in confinio, sed divisionis
Affuit præsdio lapis angularis,
Symonis religio sane singularis.
Fides et fidelitas Symonis solius
Fit pacis integritas Angliæ totius.

vv. 259–268.

Commodum si proprium comitem movisset,
Nec haberet alium zelum, nec quæsisset,
Toto suo studio reformationi
Regni . . . .
. . . . ad ditationem
Filiorum tenderet, et communitatis
Salutem negligeret, &c.

vv. 325–332.

Non sic venerabilis Simon de Monte-forti,
Qui se Christo similis dat pro multis morti :
Ysaac non moritur cum sit promptus mori ;
Vervex morti traditur, Ysaac honori.
Nec fraus nec fallacia comitem promovit,
Sed divina gratia, quæ quos juvet novit.

vv. 345–349.

En radicem tangimus perturbationis.
Rex cum suis voluit ita liber esse ;
. . . . et habere
Regni cancellarium thesaurariumque,
Suum ad arbitrium voluit quemcunque
Et consiliarios de quacunque gente,
Et ministros varios se præcipiente,
Non intromittentibus se de factis regis
Angliæ baronibus, vim habente legis
Principis imperio, et quod imperaret
Suomet arbitrio singulos ligaret.

vv. 485–504.

Baronum pars igitur jam pro se loquatur.
Quæ pars in principio palam protestatur

Quod honori regio nichil machinatur ;
Vel quærit contrarium, immo reformare
Studet statum regium et magnificare ;
Sicut si ab hostibus regnum vastaretur,
Non sine baronibus tunc reformaretur,
Quibus hoc competeret atque conveniret.

.   .   .   .

Regis adversarii sunt hostes bellantes,
Et consiliarii regi adulantes,
Qui verbis fallacibus principem seducunt,
Linguisque duplicibus in errorem ducunt.

vv. 533–550.

Non omnis arctatio privat libertatem,
Nec omnis districtio tollit potestatem.
Ad quid vult libera lex reges arctari ?
Ne possint adultera lege maculari.
Et hæc coarctatio non est servitutis,
Sed est ampliatio regiæ virtutis.

.   .   .   .

Omnium principium non potest peccare ;
Non est impotentia, sed summa potestas,
Magna Dei gloria magnaque majestas.

.   .   .   .

Ergo regi libeat omne quod est bonum,
Sed malum non audeat : hoc est Dei donum.
Qui regem custodiunt ne peccet temptatus,
Ipsi regi serviunt, quibus esse gratus
Sit, quod ipsum liberant ne sit servus factus.

vv. 667–691.

Si princeps amaverit, debet reamari ;
Si recte regnaverit, debet honorari ;
Si princeps erraverit, debet revocari,
Ab hiis, quos gravaverit injuste, negari,
Nisi velit corrigi ; si vult emendari,
Debet ab hiis erigi simul et juvari.

vv. 729–734.

Si solus [rex] elegerit, facile falletur,
Utilis qui fuerit a quo nescietur.
Igitur communitas regni consulatur,
Et quid universitas sentiat sciatur,
Cui leges propriæ maxime sunt notæ.

Nec cuncti provinciæ sic sunt idiotæ,
Quin sciant plus cæteris regni sui mores,
Quos relinquunt posteris hii qui sunt priores.

. . . .

Ex hiis potest colligi quod communitatem
Tangit quales eligi ad utilitatem
Regni recte debeant ; qui velint et sciant
Et prodesse valeant, tales regis fiant
Et consiliarii et coadjutores.

vv. 763-781.

Nec libertas proprie debet nominari,
Quæ permittit inscie stultos dominari :
Sed libertas finibus juris limitetur,
Spretisque limitibus error reputetur.
Ergo regis ratio de suis subjectis,
Suomet arbitrio quorum (? quocum) volunt vectis,
Per hoc satis solvitur, satis infirmatur.

vv. 833-841.

Legem quoque dicimus regis dignitatem
Regere : nam credimus esse legem lucem,
Sine qua concludimus deviare ducem,
Lex qua mundus regitur atque regna mundi
Ignea describitur ; quod sensus profundi
Continet mysterium : lucet, urit, calet.

. . . .

Ista lex sic loquitur, 'per me regnant reges,
Per me jus ostenditur hiis qui condunt leges.'

. . . .

Dicitur vulgariter, 'ut rex vult, lex vadit :'
Veritas vult aliter, nam lex stat, rex cadit.

vv. 848-872.

Ex prædictis omnibus poterit liquere,
Quod regem (?) magnatibus incumbit videre
Quæ regni conveniant gubernationi,
Et pacis expediant conservationi ;
Et quod rex indigenas sibi laterales
Habeat, non advenas, neque speciales,
Vel consiliarios vel regni majores,
Qui supplantant alios atque bonos mores.

vv. 951-958.

4. The following are extracts from a song (Polit. Songs, 125), written immediately after the Battle of Evesham :

> Chaunter m'estoit, mon cuer le voit, en un dure langage.
> Tut en plorant fust fet le chaunt de nostre duz baronage,
> Que pur la pees, si loynz apres se lesserent detrere,
> Lur cor trencher e demembrer, pour salver Engleterre.
>   Ore est ocys la flur de pris, qe taunt savoit de guere,
>   Ly quens Montfort, sa dure mort molt emplorra la terre.
>
> .   .   .   .
>
> Mes par sa mort le quens Montfort conquist la victorie,
> Come le martyr de Caunterbyr finist sa vie ;
> Ne voleit pas li bon Thomas qe perist seinte Eglise,
> Ly quens auxi se combati, e morust sauntz feyntise.
>   Ore est ocys, &c.
>
> Sire Hue le fer, ly Despencer, tresnoble justice,
> Ore est a tort lyvre a mort, a trop male guise.
> Sire Henri, pur veir le dy, fitz le quens de Leycestre,
> Autres assez, come vus orrez, par le quens de Gloucestre.
>   Ore est ocys, &c.
>
> .   .   .   .
>
> Sire Simoun, ly prodhom, e sa compagnie,
> En joie vont en ciel amount, en pardurable vie.
> Mes Jhesu Crist, qe en croyz se mist, Dieu en prenge cure,
> Qe sunt remis, e detenuz en prisone dure.
>   Ore est ocys la flur de pris, qe taunt savoit de guere,
>   Ly quens Montfort, sa dure mort molt emplorra la terre.

5. The following is a fragment of an office in memory of Simon de Montfort, which concludes the MS. containing the account of his miracles, published with the Chronicle of Rishanger by Mr. Halliwell for the Camden Society. It may be compared with the longer fragment in Appendix IV.

> Anno Domini M.cc.lx.v. octavo Symonis Montisfortis sociorumque ejus, pridie nonas Augusti.
>
>   Salve, Symon Montis-Fortis,
>   Totius flos militiæ,
>   Duras pœnas passus mortis,
>   Protector gentis Angliæ.

Sunt de sanctis inaudita,
Cunctis passis in hac vita,
  Quemquam passum talia ;
Manus, pedes amputari,
Caput, corpus vulnerari,
  Abscidi virilia.
Sis pro nobis intercessor
Apud Deum, qui defensor
  In terris exterritas.

Ora pro nobis, beate Symon, ut digni efficiamus promissionibus Christi.

3.—CHARACTER OF SIMON DE MONTFORT.

' Erat signidem, &c.' *Rish. de Bellis, &c.,* 6. 7.

HE was indeed a mighty man, and prudent, and circumspect ; in the use of arms and in experience of warfare, superior to all others of his time ; commendably endowed with knowledge of letters ; fond of hearing the offices of the church by day and night ; sparing of food and drink, as those who were about him saw with their own eyes ; in time of night watching more than he slept, as his more intimate friends have oft related. In the greatest difficulties which he went through while handling affairs of state, he was found trustworthy, notably in Gascony, whither he went by command of the king, and there subdued to the Kings Majesty rebels beforetime unconquered, and sent them to England to his lord the King. He was moreover pleasant and witty in speech, and ever aimed at the reward of an admirable faith ; on account of which he did not fear to undergo death, as shall be told hereafter. His constancy all men, even his enemies, admired ; for when others had sworn to observe the Provisions of Oxford, and the most part of them despised and rejected that to which they had sworn, he having once taken the oath, like an immoveable pillar, stood firm, and neither by threats, nor promises, nor gifts, nor flattery could he be moved to depart in any way with the other magnates from the oath which he had taken to reform the state of the realm. He commended himself to the prayers of the religious, and humbly, as with brotherly affection, he begged to be allied with them, in the pouring out of prayers to God for the state of the realm and the peace of the church ; and he was constant in supplication that divine grace might keep him spotless from avarice and covetousness of earthly things, knowing for a surety that many in those days were encumbered by such vices, as the issue of things afterwards made clear. To the religious and other prelates of the church, commended by honesty of life, he showed all due reverence ; deserving to be called the perfect disciple of a perfect master ; having been instructed in all good discipline, inasmuch as he clung with hearty affection to the blessed Robert, once Bishop of Lincoln, and gave his children to be brought up by him, and did many things by his wholesome advice. And the said bishop is related to have enjoined upon the Earl, for the remission of his sins, that he should take upon himself that cause for which he fought even unto death ; declaring that the peace of the English church could never be secured without the temporal sword, and constantly affirming that all who died in her and for her should receive the crown of martyrdom. It is related by trustworthy persons, that the bishop once placed his hands on the head of the Earls firstborn son, and said to him, ' My dearest son, thou and thy father shall both die on one day and by one hurt, for the cause of justice.' And of what sort was the life of the Bishop, the miracles, done by the grace of God at his tomb, sufficiently declare. And the Earl, like a second Joshua, worshipped justice, as the very medicine of his soul.

APPENDIX III.

LIST OF THOSE WHO TOOK PART IN EVENTS OF IM-
PORTANCE BETWEEN 1244 AND 1267.

(The names are given in alphabetical order within their respective ranks.)

PARLIAMENTARY COMMITTEE, 1244.

Prelates.

Boniface, Abp. of Canterbury, Robert, Bp. of Lincoln,
William, Bp. of Winchester, Walter, Bp. of Worcester.

Earls.

Richard, E. of Cornwall, Roger, E. of Norfolk,
Simon, E. of Leicester, The Earl of Pembroke.

Barons.

The Abbot of St. Edmunds, John Balliol,
The Abbot of Ramsey, Rich. of Montfichet.

SIGNATURES TO THE LETTER OF REMONSTRANCE TO THE POPE,
1246.

Richard, E. of Cornwall, Earl of Norfolk,
Earl of Derby, Earl of Oxford,
Richard, E. of Gloucester, Earl of Winchester,
Humfrey, E. of Hereford, Earl of Aumâle, and others.
Earl of Leicester,

SIGNATURES TO THE LETTER OF GRIEVANCES TO THE KING, 1258.

Earl of Gloucester,
Earl of Hereford,
Earl of Leicester,
Earl of Norfolk,
Earl of Warwick,
Count of Aumâle,

John of Alditheley,
Hugh Bigod,
John Fitz-Geoffrey,
Peter de Montfort,
Peter of Savoy.

FIRST COMMITTEE OF TWENTY-FOUR, 1258.

Royalist.

Archbishop of Canterbury,[1]
Aylmer, Bp. elect of Winchester,
Fulk, Bishop of London,
Abbot of Westminster,
John of Darlington,
John Mansel,

Henry Wengham,
John, Earl of Warenne,
John, Earl of Warwick,
Henry of Almaine,
Guy of Lusignan,
William of Valence.

Baronial.

Walter, Bishop of Worcester,
Earl of Gloucester,
Earl of Hereford,
Earl of Leicester,
Earl of Norfolk,
William Bardulf,

Hugh Bigod,
Hugh Despenser,
J. Fitz-Geoffrey,
Richard de Gray,
P. de Montfort.
Roger Mortimer.

ELECTORS OF THE COUNCIL OF FIFTEEN, 1258.

Royalist.

John Mansel, | Earl of Warwick.

Baronial.

Earl of Norfolk, | Hugh Bigod.

---

[1] The membership of the Archbishop of Canterbury is uncertain but most probable. The framers of the Lords' *Report* think that the Earl of Gloucester was elected on the kings side ; it is possible he was elected by both parties. See above, p. 193, note, and Stubbs, *Const. Hist.* ii. 75, 82.

THE COUNCIL OF FIFTEEN, 1258.

Royalist.

Archbishop of Canterbury,   J. of Aldithley,
John Mansel,[1]   P. of Savoy. '
Earl of Warwick,

Baronial.

Bishop of Worcester,   Count of Aumâle,
Earl of Gloucester,   J. Fitz-Geoffrey,
Earl of Hereford,   R. de Gray,
Earl of Leicester,   P. de Montfort,
Earl of Norfolk,   Roger Mortimer.

REPRESENTATIVES OF THE COMMUNITY, 1258.

Bishop of London,,   Hugh Despenser,
Earl of Winchester,   John de Gray,
Giles de Argentine,   Thomas de Gresley,
John Balliol,   Roger de Monthaut,
Philip Basset,   Roger de Sumery,
Humfrey Bohun,[2]   John de Verdun.

COUNCIL OF TWENTY-FOUR TO TREAT OF AID FOR THE KING, 1258.

Bishop of London,   Philip Basset,
Bishop of Sarum,   Giles de Erdinton,
Bishop of Worcester,   J. Fitz-Geoffrey,
Earl of Gloucester,   John de Gray,
Earl of Hereford,   Thomas de Gresley,
Earl of Leicester,   Fulk de Kerdiston,
Earl of Norfolk,   John Kyriel,
Earl of Oxford,   P. de Montfort,
Earl of Winchester,   R. de Monthaut,
Count of Aumâle,   Roger Mortimer,
G. de Argentine,   P. of Savoy,
John Balliol,   Roger de Sumery.

[1] The framers of the Lords' *Report*, on the authority of *Fœd.* i. 378, writ dated 18 Oct. 1258, give the name of H. Despenser and the Earl of Winchester instead of John Mansel and the Count of Aumâle. I have given the list of the Fifteen according to the list in Stubbs, *Const. Hist.* ii. 82 : see above, p. 195, note.

[2] I have given the name of H. Bohun the younger instead of his father the Earl of Hereford, as it seems hardly possible that the Earl should have been a member both of the Council and the Representative Body. Professor Stubbs however (l. c.) gives the Earl as one of the latter.

LIST OF THOSE TO WHOM PARDON WAS OFFERED BY THE KING,
1261.

Earl of Leicester,	J. Fitz-John,
Earl of Norfolk,	H. of Hastings,
Earl of Warenne,	Roger Mortimer,
W. Bardulf,	N. de Segrave,
Hugh Despenser,	R. de Vipont.
J. Fitz-Alan,	

LIST OF THOSE WHO PROMISED TO SUBMIT TO LOUIS' ARBITRATION,
1263.

Royalist.

Prince Edward,	R. Fitz-Peter,
Earl of Hereford,	R. Foliot,
Earl of Norfolk,	A. of Geremuth,
Earl of Warenne,	J. de Gray,
Henry of Almaine,	W. de Latimer,
William of Valence,	R. de Leyburn,
J. of Alditheley,	P. Marmion,
John Balliol,	R. Mortimer,
W. of Basingburn,	J. de Muscegros,
Philip Basset,	R. de Nevile,
Hugh Bigod,	H. de Percy,
R. de Brus,	R. de Sumery,
W. de Brus,	J. de Vaux,
R. de Clifford,	J. de Verdun,
H. l'Estrange,	A. de la Zuche.
J. Fitz-Alan,	

Baronial.

Bishop of London,	G. de Lucy,
Bishop of Worcester,	W. Marshall,
Earl of Leicester,	H. de Montfort,
W. Bardulph,	P. de Montfort,
R. Basset (Sapcote),	S. de Montfort (jun.),
W. le Blond,	W. de Munchanesy,
H. Bohun (jun.)	A. of Newburgh,
J. de Burgh,	R. de Ros,
W. de Coleville,	N. de Segrave,
Hugh Despenser,	R. de Toney,
J. Fitz-John,	J. de Vescy,
R. de Gray,	R. de Vipont,
H. of Hastings,	B. Wake.

C C

NAMES OF THOSE KNOWN TO HAVE TAKEN PART IN THE BARONS'
WAR,[1] 1264.

Royalist.

Prince Edward,
Earl of Hereford,
Earl of Warenne,
Henry of Almaine,
William of Valence,
J. of Aiditheley,
D. de Barentin,
Hugh Bigod,

R. de Clifford,
J. de Gray,
R. de Gray,
J. Fitz-Alan,
R. Mortimer,
J. de Vaux,
W. de la Zuche.

Baronial.

Gilbert, Earl of Gloucester,
Earl of Leicester,
H. of Basingburn,
J. of Bracebridge,
R. of Bruton,
P. de Covel,
J. of Craunford,
A. Despenser,
J. Despenser,
H. Despenser,
B. of Drayton,
J. Estormy,
J. l'Estrange,
W. of Eylesford,
W. d'Eyville,
R. Fitz-Walter,

G. de Furnival,
W. de Furnival,
H. of Hastings,
R. de la Hide,
P. de Montfort,
P. de Montfort (jun.),
R. de Montfort,
S. de Montfort (jun.),
H. de Montfort,
G. de Montfort,
H. of Penbregg,
N. de Segrave,
R. of Sutton,
H. de Tywe,
R. de Watervil,
J. de Wiavil.

CUSTODES PACIS APPOINTED BY THE BARONS, 1264.

G. de Argentine,
I. de Aur', (?)
R. Basset (Drayton),
R. Basset (Sapcote),
W. de Beauchamp,
W. de Bovil,
J. de Burgh,
O. de Dunant,
G. of Ellesfend,
H. Engaine.
T. of Estleys,
G. d'Escudemor,
J. d'Eyville,
J. Fitz-John,

R. Fitz-Nigel,
B. de Gowiz,
W. Marshall,
J. de Marevil,
H. de Montfort,
T. of Muleton,
A. of Newmarket,
J. de Plesseys,
R. of Stradeley,
R. de Toney,
W. de Tracy,
R. de Vernon,
J. de St. Waleric.

[1] This list must of course be very incomplete. Many more than are
mentioned in the chronicles must have taken part.

NAMES OF LAY BARONS SUMMONED TO PARLIAMENT, JAN. 1265.

Earl of Derby,
Earl of Gloucester,
Earl of Leicester,
Earl of Norfolk,
Earl of Oxford,
R. Basset (Drayton),
R. Basset (Sapcote),
R. Bertram,
R. de Camoys,
W. de Colville,
Hugh Despenser,
J. d'Eyville,

J. Fitz-John,
G. de Gaunt,
H. of Hastings,
G. de Lucy,
W. Marmion,
W. de Munchanesy,
A. of Newmarket,
R. de Ros,
N. de Segrave,
R. de St. John,
J. de Vescy.

Summoned to receive Judgment.

Earl of Warenne,
William of Valence,

Peter of Savoy,
Hugh Bigod.

Received safe-conduct.

John Balliol,
P. de Brus,
A. of Geremuth,

R. de Nevile,
and ten others from the north.

NAMES OF BARONS KNOWN TO HAVE FOUGHT AT EVESHAM.

Killed.

Earl of Leicester,
R. Basset,
J. de Beauchamp,
Hugh Despenser,

W. de Maundeville,
H. de Montfort,
P. de Montfort (sen.)

Wounded and taken.

H. de Bohun (jun.),
H. of Hastings,
J. Fitz-John,

G. de Montfort,
P. de Montfort (jun.),
J. de Vescy.

ARBITRATORS WHO DREW UP THE DICTUM OF KENILWORTH, 1266.

First elected.

Bishop of Bath,
Bishop of Exeter,
Bishop of Worcester,

R. de Sumery,
R. Waleran,
A. de la Zuche.

Appointed by the above.

Bishop of St. Davids,
Earl of Gloucester,
Earl of Hereford,

J. Balliol,
P. Basset,
W. of Basingburn.

APPENDIX IV.

PORTIONS OF AN OFFICE IN MEMORY OF SIMON DE MONTFORT.

I have thought it worth while to add here an interesting fragment, not hitherto published, illustrative of the veneration in which Simon de Montfort was held after death. It consists of three hymns, and the special portions of a service, in which the memory of Earl Simon was hallowed, by some part of the Church at least, as that of a martyr. It seems that in this commemoration of him, and the setting apart of a day for that purpose, consisted that popular canonisation, which was forbidden by the Dictum of Kenilworth. I am indebted to the kindness of Mr. Bradshaw, of the University Library, Cambridge, for the copy of the MS. It was made from the last leaf but one of MS. Kk, 4, 20, in that Library, a volume which in the fourteenth century was in the Cathedral Library at Norwich. Mr. Bradshaw says : ' The hand-writing is of the time of Edward I, or thereabouts. The three hymns are probably those used at First Vespers, at Matins, and at Lauds, and the *Suffragium* was probably the Commemoration at Lauds.'

HYMN I.

1.

℩ Rumpe celos et descende
   capud ihesu martirum,
Signis sacris et ostende
   comitis martyrium ;
Arma, scutum, comprehende
   contra uires hostium.

2.

Heu dolorum nos mullorum
   torquet infor[tu]nium :
Simon cesus cadit Iesus
   anglie presidium,
Comes fidus regni sidus,
   decus et flos militum.

3.

Est iactura nimis dura
regno et ecclesie :
Simon fortis casum mortis
causa rei pupplice
Sumit, cadit dum inuadit
prelium perfidie.

4.

Juris sator exstirpator
fuit iniusticie,
Effugator et dampnator
fraudis et iniurie,
Pacis dator et seruator
plebis et ecclesie.

5.

Quis anglorum nunc regnorum
tuetur prudencia ?
Militaris expers paris
premitur prestancia.
Plebi cleri forma ueri
cedit sapiencia.

6.

Tu, qui pro salute mundi
crucis pressus pertica,
Da post casum putibundi
fati sit in gloria
Simon celi letabundi
per eterna secula.   Amen.

HYMN II.

I.

❡ Mater syon iocundare,
tantum decus dilatare :
tibi uenit nouus dare
noua martyr gaudia.

2.

Comes symon thomam querit,
causam thome simon gerit,
et cum thoma falsas terit
leges per martyrium.

3.

Thomas tytan orientis,
simon sydus occidentis,
uir uterque pie mentis
pungnat pro iusticia.

4.

Presul thomas, ueritatem
se[r]uans, dampnat prauitatem,
pungnans dedit libertatem
qua floret ecclesia.

5.

Israelis symon murus,
plebi clero profuturus,
pro utroque pungnaturus,
dura passus prelia.

6.

Nunc uterque pugil fortis,
post occasum dire mortis
in agone sacre sortis,
migrat ad celestia.   Amen.

HYMN III.

1.

Ɖ Nequit stare sed rotare
fortuna mutabilis,
Per quam scita mors uel uita
uenit admirabilis.

2.

En iam primus sed nec ymus
flos florem militie
Regnat modo ruit modo,
pacem zelans anglię.

3.

Heu uir fortis montis fortis,
corpus tuum moritur,
Denudatur, mutilatur,
per partes diuiditur.

4.

Amputatur capud, datur,
mulieri mittitur.
Non uilescit nec sordescit,
baptiste coniungitur.

5.

Set mens fortis hora mortis
† morte percutitur :[1]
Sullimatur, coronatur,
in celis recipitur.

6.

Hoc monstrauit, hoc probauit
sol priuatus lumine,
Terre motus, orbis totus
tunc percussus fulmine.

7.

Die martis marce martis
transit in uigilia,
Per amici dominici
cum sua milicia.

8.

Deridebat et pedebat
scutifer ignobilis,
Male sonans quasi plorans
necem plangens comitis.

9.

Laus sit deo nil ab eo
post exisse dicitur :
Tumens uentre gemens mente
derisor confunditur.

10.

Symon ergo mortis ergo
fac ne nos concuciat,
Te tutore te ductore
christus nos suscipiat.

11.

Adhuc rota precor tota
prosterne maliuolos.
Quos leuasti que prostrasti
quam plures beniuolos.

12.

Nonne uides? non est fides
in tota prouincia,
Jura iacent, leges tacent,
mutescit ecclesia.

---

[1] The word 'non' is here omitted in the MS.

13.

Violatur, spoliatur,
nec ligat sentencia.
Quis quid fari quot in mari
nunc fiunt facinora.

14.

Quot dampnantur quot necantur
spiritus et corpora ;
Capiuntur, rapiuntur*
naues mercimonia.

15.

Confundantur, prosternantur
perpetrantes talia,
Nisi cessent et emendent
tot commissa crimina.

16.

Ut hoc fiat et sic fiat
amen dicant omnia.

[*Suffragium de B. Symone.*]

[*Antiphona.*]

O decus milicie
'gentium anglorum,
Comes Leicestrie,
dextra oppressorum,
Sanguine commercio
ius tenes celorum :
posce nobis miseris
uitam beatorum.

[*Vers.*]

Magna est gloria eius
in salutari tuo.
Gloriam et magnum decorem impones super eum.
Psalt. Rom. 20, 5.

[*Oratio.*]

DEUS, qui beatum symonem martyrem tuum uirtute constancie in
agone suo communisti, quique illi ad renouandum britannie
regnum milites inclitos associasti, tribue nos eius precibus adiuuari qui
celebri martyrio meruit consummari. Per.

Explicit
Vita Simonis de Monteforti
Comitis Leicestriæ

INDEX.

LONDON : PRINTED BY
SPOTTISWOODE AND CO., NEW-STREET SQUARE
AND PARLIAMENT STREET

E E

In course of publication, each volume in fcp. 8vo. complete in itself,

EPOCHS OF MODERN HISTORY:

A SERIES OF BOOKS NARRATING THE

HISTORY OF ENGLAND AND EUROPE

At Successive Epochs subsequent to the Christian Era.

EDITED BY

E. E. MORRIS, M.A. Lincoln Coll. Oxford ;

J. S. PHILLPOTTS, B.C.L. New Coll. Oxford ; and

C. COLBECK, M.A. Fellow of Trin. Coll. Oxford.

'This striking collection of little volumes is a valuable contribution to the literature of the day, whether for youthful or more mature readers. As an abridgment of several important phases of modern history it has great merit, and some of its parts display powers and qualities of a high order. Such writers, indeed, as Professor STUBBS, Messrs. WARBURTON, GAIRDNER, CREIGHTON, and others, could not fail to give us excellent work. . . . The style of the series is, as a general rule, correct and pure ; in the case of Mr. STUBBS it more than once rises into genuine, simple, and manly eloquence ; and the composition of some of the volumes displays no ordinary historical skill . . . The series is and deserves to be popular.'
THE TIMES, Jan. 2, 1877.

Ten Volumes now published :—

The ERA of the PROTESTANT REVOLUTION.
By F. SEEBOHM, Author of 'The Oxford Reformers—Colet, Erasmus, More. With 4 Coloured Maps and 12 Diagrams on Wood. Price 2s. 6d.

'Mr. SEEBOHM's Era of the Protestant Revolution shows an admirable mastery of a complex subject ; it abounds in sound and philosophic thought, and as a composition it is very well ordered. . . . This volume, in short, is of the greatest merit.'
THE TIMES, Jan. 2.

The CRUSADES. By the Rev. G. W. COX, M.A. late Scholar
of Trinity College, Oxford ; Author of the 'Aryan Mythology' &c. With a Coloured Map. Price 2s. 6d.

'The earliest period, in point of time, is that of the Crusades, of which we have a summary from the accomplished pen of the well-known Author of one of the best and latest histories of Greece. Mr. Cox's narrative is flowing and easy, and parts of his work are extremely good.'
THE TIMES, Jan. 2.

The THIRTY YEARS' WAR, 1618-1648. By
SAMUEL RAWSON GARDINER, late Student of Ch. Ch. Author of 'History of England from the Accession of James I. to the Disgrace of Chief Justice Coke' &c. With a Coloured Map. Price 2s. 6d.

'The narrative—a singularly perplexing task—is on the whole remarkably clear, and the Author gives us a well-written summary of the causes that led to the great contest, and of the most striking incidents that marked its progress. Mr. GARDINER's judgments, too, are usually just. . . . The Author, we should add, is very skilful in his delineation of historical characters.'
THE TIMES, Jan. 2.

The HOUSES of LANCASTER and YORK; with
the CONQUEST and LOSS of FRANCE. By JAMES GAIRDNER, of the Public Record Office, Editor of 'The Paston Letters' &c. With 5 Coloured Maps. Price 2s. 6d.

Mr. GAIRDNER's Epoch, 'Lancaster and York,' is usually correct and sensible, and the conclusions of the Author are just and accurate.' THE TIMES, Jan. 2.

EDWARD the THIRD. By the Rev. W. WARBURTON,

M.A. late Fellow of All Souls College, Oxford; Her Majesty's Senior Inspector of Schools. With 3 Coloured Maps and 3 Genealogical Tables. Price 2s. 6d.

'This Epoch is a very good one, and is well worth a studious reader's attention. Mr. WARBURTON has reproduced | extremely well the spirit and genius of that chivalric age.'   THE TIMES, Jan. 2.

The AGE of ELIZABETH. By the Rev. M. CREIGHTON,

M.A. late Fellow and Tutor of Merton College, Oxford. With 5 Maps and 4 Genealogical Tables. Price 2s. 6d.

' Mr. CREIGHTON has thoroughly mastered the intricate mysteries of the foreign politics of the whole period : and he has described extremely ably the re- | lations between this country and the other states of Europe, and the character of the policy of the Queen and her counsellors.'   THE TIMES, Jan. 2.

The FALL of the STUARTS; and WESTERN

EUROPE from 1678 to 1697. By the Rev. EDWARD HALE, M.A. Assistant Master at Eton. With 11 Maps and Plans. Price 2s. 6d.

' Mr. HALE has thoroughly grasped the great facts af the time, and has | placed them in a very effective light.'   THE TIMES, Jan. 2.

The FIRST TWO STUARTS and the PURITAN

REVOLUTION, 1603 to 1660. By SAMUEL RAWSON GARDINER, Author of 'The Thirty Years' War, 1618-1648.' With 4 Coloured Maps. Price 2s. 6d.

' Mr. GARDINER'S " First Two Stuarts and the Puritan Revolution " deserves more notice than we can bestow upon it. This is in some respects a very striking | work. Mr. GARDINER'S sketch of the time of James I. brings out much that has hitherto been very little known.'   THE TIMES, Jan. 2.

The WAR of AMERICAN INDEPENDENCE,

1775-1783. By JOHN MALCOLM LUDLOW, Barrister-at-Law. With 4 Coloured Maps. Price 2s. 6d.

' Mr. LUDLOW's account of the obscure annals of what afterwards became the Thirteen Colonies is learned, judicious, and full of interest, and his description of the Red Indian communities is ad- | mirable for its good feeling and insight. ......The volume is characterised by impartiality and good sense.'   THE TIMES, Jan. 2.

The EARLY PLANTAGENETS. By the Rev. W.

STUBBS, M.A. Regius Professor of Modern History in the University of Oxford. With 2 Coloured Maps. Price 2s. 6d.

' As a whole, his book is one of·rare excellence. As a comprehensive sketch of the period it is worthy of very high commendation......As an analyst of institutions and laws Mr. STUBBS is certainly not inferior to HALLAM. His narrative, moreover, is, as a rule, excel- | lent, clear, well put together, and often picturesque ; his language is always forcible and sometimes eloquent ; his power of condensation is very remarkable, and his chapter on the contemporaneous state of Europe is admirable for its breadth and conciseness.'   THE TIMES, Jan. 2.

Volumes in preparation, in continuation of the Series :—

The AGE of ANNE. By E. E. MORRIS, M.A. Original

Editor of the Series.   [*Nearly ready.*

The BEGINNING of the MIDDLE AGES; Charles

the Great and Alfred ; the History of England in connexion with that of Europe in the Ninth Century. By the Very Rev. R. W. CHURCH, M.A. Dean of St. Paul's.   [*In the press.*

The NORMANS in EUROPE. By Rev. A. H. JOHNSON,

M.A. Fellow of All Souls College, Oxford.   [*Nearly ready.*

FREDERICK the GREAT and the SEVEN

YEARS' WAR. By F. W. LONGMAN, of Balliol College, Oxford.

The EARLY HANOVERIANS. By the Rev. J. T.

LAWRENCE, B.A. Downing College, Cambridge.

The FRENCH REVOLUTION to the BATTLE

of WATERLOO, 1789-1815. By BERTHA M. CORDERY, Author of ' The Struggle against Absolute Monarchy.

London, LONGMANS & CO.

JULY 1876.

GENERAL LIST OF WORKS

PUBLISHED BY

Messrs. LONGMANS, GREEN, and CO.

PATERNOSTER ROW, LONDON.

———ᴏᴏᵒᵉᴼᵉᵒᴏ———

History, Politics, Historical Memoirs, &c.

The **HISTORY of ENGLAND** from the Accession of James the Second. By Lord MACAULAY.

STUDENT'S EDITION, 2 vols. crown 8vo. 12*s.*
PEOPLE'S EDITION, 4 vols. crown 8vo. 16*s.*
CABINET EDITION, 8 vols. post 8vo. 48*s.*
LIBRARY EDITION, 5 vols. 8vo. £4.

LORD MACAULAY'S WORKS. Complete and Uniform Library Edition. Edited by his Sister, Lady TREVELYAN. 8 vols. 8vo. with Portrait price £5. 5*s.* cloth, or £8. 8*s.* bound in tree-calf by Rivière.

The **HISTORY of ENGLAND** from the Fall of Wolsey to the Defeat of the Spanish Armada. By JAMES ANTHONY FROUDE, M.A. late Fellow of Exeter College, Oxford.

LIBRARY EDITION, Twelve Volumes, 8vo. price £8. 18*s.*
CABINET EDITION, Twelve Volumes, crown 8vo. price 72*s.*

The **ENGLISH in IRELAND** in the **EIGHTEENTH CENTURY.** By JAMES ANTHONY FROUDE, M.A. late Fellow of Exeter College, Oxford. 3 vols. 8vo. price 48*s.*

JOURNAL of the REIGNS of KING GEORGE IV. and KING WILLIAM IV. By the late CHARLES C. F. GREVILLE, Esq. Edited by HENRY REEVE, Esq. Fifth Edition. 3 vols. 8vo. 36*s.*

RECOLLECTIONS and SUGGESTIONS, 1813-1873. By JOHN Earl RUSSELL, K.G. New Edition, revised and enlarged. 8vo. 16*s.*

On **PARLIAMENTARY GOVERNMENT in ENGLAND**; its Origin, Development, and Practical Operation. By ALPHEUS TODD, Librarian of the Legislative Assembly of Canada. 2 vols. 8vo. price £1. 17*s.*

The **CONSTITUTIONAL HISTORY of ENGLAND**, since the Accession of George III. 1760—1860. By Sir THOMAS ERSKINE MAY. K.C.B. D.C.L. The Fifth Edition, thoroughly revised. 3 vols. crown 8vo. price 18*s.*

DEMOCRACY in EUROPE; a History. By Sir THOMAS ERSKINE MAY, K.C.B. D.C.L. 2 vols. 8vo. *[In the press.*

The **NEW REFORMATION**, a Narrative of the Old Catholic Movement, from 1870 to the Present Time; with an Historical Introduction. By THEODORUS. 8vo. price 12*s.*

A

The **OXFORD REFORMERS** — John Colet, Erasmus, and Thomas More ; being a History of their Fellow-work. By FREDERIC SEEBOHM. Second Edition, enlarged. 8vo. 14s.

LECTURES on the **HISTORY** of **ENGLAND**, from the Earliest Times to the Death of King Edward II. By WILLIAM LONGMAN, F.S.A. With Maps and Illustrations. 8vo. 15s.

The **HISTORY** of the **LIFE** and **TIMES** of **EDWARD** the **THIRD**. By WILLIAM LONGMAN, F.S.A. With 9 Maps, 8 Plates, and 16 Woodcuts. 2 vols. 8vo. 28s.

INTRODUCTORY LECTURES on **MODERN HISTORY**. Delivered in Lent Term, 1842; with the Inaugural Lecture delivered in December 1841. By the Rev. THOMAS ARNOLD, D.D. 8vo. price 7s. 6d.

WATERLOO LECTURES ; a Study of the Campaign of 1815. By Colonel CHARLES C. CHESNEY, R.E. Third Edition. 8vo. with Map, 10s. 6d.

HISTORY of **ENGLAND** under the **DUKE** of **BUCKINGHAM** and CHARLES the FIRST, 1624-1628. By SAMUEL RAWSON GARDINER, late Student of Ch. Ch. 2 vols. 8vo. with two Maps, price 24s.

The **SIXTH ORIENTAL MONARCHY**; or, the Geography, History, and Antiquities of PARTHIA. By GEORGE RAWLINSON, M.A. Professor of Ancient History in the University of Oxford. Maps and Illustrations. 8vo. 16s.

The **SEVENTH GREAT ORIENTAL MONARCHY**; or, a History of the SASSANIANS: with Notices, Geographical and Antiquarian. By G. RAWLINSON, M.A. Map and numerous Illustrations. 8vo. price 28s.

A **HISTORY** of **GREECE**. By the Rev. GEORGE W. Cox, M.A. late Scholar of Trinity College, Oxford. VOLS. I. & II. (to the Close of the Peloponnesian War). 8vo. with Maps and Plans, 36s.

GENERAL HISTORY of **GREECE** to the Death of Alexander the Great; with a Sketch of the Subsequent History to the Present Time. By the Rev. GEORGE W. Cox, M.A. With 11 Maps. Crown 8vo. 7s. 6d.

The **GREEKS** and the **PERSIANS**. By the Rev. GEORGE W. Cox, M.A. (*Epochs of Ancient History, I.*) With 4 Coloured Maps. Fcp. 8vo. price 2s. 6d.

The **TALE** of the **GREAT PERSIAN WAR**, from the Histories of Herodotus. By GEORGE W. Cox, M.A. New Edition. Fcp. 3s. 6d.

The **HISTORY** of **ROME**. By WILLIAM IHNE. VOLS. I. and II. 8vo. price 30s. The Third Volume is in the press.

GENERAL HISTORY OF ROME from the Foundation of the City to the Fall of Augustulus, B.C. 753—A.D. 476. By the Very Rev. C. MERIVALE, D.D. Dean of Ely. With Five Maps. Crown 8vo. 7s. 6d.

HISTORY of the **ROMANS** under the **EMPIRE**. By the Very Rev. C. MERIVALE, D.D. Dean of Ely. 8 vols. post 8vo. 48s.

The **FALL** of the **ROMAN REPUBLIC**; a Short History of the Last Century of the Commonwealth. By the same Author. 12mo. 7s. 6d.

The **STUDENT'S MANUAL** of the **HISTORY** of **INDIA**, from the Earliest Period to the Present. By Colonel MEADOWS TAYLOR, M.R.A.S. M.R.I.A. Second Thousand. Crown 8vo. with Maps, 7s. 6d.

The **HISTORY** of **INDIA**, from the Earliest Period to the close of Lord Dalhousie's Administration. By J. C. MARSHMAN. 3 vols. crown 8vo. 22s. 6d.

The **NATIVE STATES of INDIA** in **SUBSIDIARY ALLIANCE** with the BRITISH GOVERNMENT; an Historical Sketch. By Colonel G. B. MALLESON, C.S.I. With 6 Coloured Maps. 8vo. 15s.

INDIAN POLITY; a View of the System of Administration in India. By Lieutenant-Colonel GEORGE CHESNEY, Fellow of the University of Calcutta. New Edition, revised; with Map. 8vo. price 21s.

The **BRITISH ARMY** in **1875**; with Suggestions on its Administration and Organisation. By JOHN HOLMS, M.P. New and Enlarged Edition, with 4 Diagrams. Crown 8vo. price 4s. 6d.

The **HISTORY of PRUSSIA**, from the Earliest Times to the Present Day; tracing the Origin and Development of her Military Organisation. By Captain W. J. WYATT. Vols. I. and II. A.D. 700 to A.D. 1525. 8vo. 36s.

POPULAR HISTORY of FRANCE, from the Earliest Times to the Death of Louis XIV. By ELIZABETH M. SEWELL, Author of 'Amy Herbert' &c. With Coloured Maps. Crown 8vo. 7s. 6d.

STUDIES from GENOESE HISTORY. By Colonel G. B. MALLESON, C.S.I. Guardian to His Highness the Maharájá of Mysore. Crown 8vo. 10s. 6d.

LORD MACAULAY'S CRITICAL and HISTORICAL ESSAYS. CHEAP EDITION, authorised and complete. Crown 8vo. 6s. 6d.

CABINET EDITION, 4 vols. post 8vo. 24s. | LIBRARY EDITION, 3 vols. 8vo. 36s.
PEOPLE'S EDITION, 2 vols. crown 8vo. 8s. | STUDENT'S EDITION, 1 vol. cr. 8vo. 6s.

HISTORY of EUROPEAN MORALS, from Augustus to Charlemagne. By W. E. H. LECKY, M.A. Second Edition. 2 vols. 8vo. price 28s.

HISTORY of the RISE and INFLUENCE of the SPIRIT of RATIONALISM in EUROPE. By W. E. H. LECKY, M.A. Cabinet Edition, being the Fourth. 2 vols. crown 8vo. price 16s.

The **HISTORY of PHILOSOPHY**, from Thales to Comte. By GEORGE HENRY LEWES. Fourth Edition. 2 vols. 8vo. 32s.

The **HISTORY of the PELOPONNESIAN WAR.** By THUCYDIDES. Translated by R. CRAWLEY, Fellow of Worcester College, Oxford. 8vo. 10s. 6d.

The **MYTHOLOGY of the ARYAN NATIONS.** By GEORGE W. Cox, M.A. late Scholar of Trinity College, Oxford. 2 vols. 8vo. 28s.

TALES of ANCIENT GREECE. By GEORGE W. COX, M.A. late Scholar of Trin. Coll. Oxon. Crown 8vo. price 6s. 6d.

HISTORY of CIVILISATION in England and France, Spain and Scotland. By HENRY THOMAS BUCKLE. New Edition of the entire Work, with a complete INDEX. 3 vols. crown 8vo. 24s.

SKETCH of the HISTORY of the CHURCH of ENGLAND to the Revolution of 1688. By the Right Rev. T. V. SHORT, D.D. Lord Bishop of St. Asaph. Eighth Edition. Crown 8vo. 7s. 6d.

MAUNDER'S HISTORICAL TREASURY; General Introductory Outlines of Universal History, and a series of Separate Histories. Latest Edition, revised by the Rev. G. W. COX, M.A. Fcp. 8vo. 6s. cloth, or 10s. 6d. calf.

CATES' and WOODWARD'S ENCYCLOPÆDIA of CHRONOLOGY, HISTORICAL and BIOGRAPHICAL. 8vo. price 42s.

The **ERA of the PROTESTANT REVOLUTION.** By F. SEEBOHM. With 4 Coloured Maps and 12 Diagrams on Wood. Fcp. 8vo. 2s. 6d.

A 2

The **CRUSADES.** By the Rev. G. W. Cox, M.A. late Scholar of Trinity College, Oxford. With Coloured Map. Fcp. 8vo. 2s. 6d.

The **THIRTY YEARS' WAR, 1618–1648.** By Samuel Rawson Gardiner, late Student of Christ Church. With Coloured Map. Fcp. 8vo. 2s. 6d.

The **HOUSES of LANCASTER and YORK**; with the Conquest and Loss of France. By James Gairdner, of the Public Record Office. With Five Coloured Maps. Fcp. 8vo. 2s. 6d.

EDWARD the THIRD. By the Rev. W. Warburton, M.A. late Fellow of All Souls College, Oxford. With 3 Coloured Maps and 8 Genealogical Tables. Fcp. 8vo. 2s. 6d.

The **AGE of ELIZABETH.** By the Rev. M. Creighton, M.A. late Fellow and Tutor of Merton College, Oxford. With 5 Maps and 4 Genealogical Tables. Fcp. 8vo. 2s. 6d.

The **FALL of the STUARTS**; and Western Europe from 1678 to 1697. By the Rev. E. Hale, M.A. Assistant-Master, Eton. With 11 Maps and Plans. Fcp. 8vo. 2s. 6d.

The **FIRST TWO STUARTS and the PURITAN REVOLUTION,** 1603–1660. By Samuel Rawson Gardiner, late Student of Christ Church. With 4 Coloured Maps. Fcp. 8vo. 2s. 6d.

The **WAR of AMERICAN INDEPENDENCE, 1775–1783.** By John Malcolm Ludlow, Barrister-at-Law. With 4 Coloured Maps. Fcp. 8vo. 2s. 6d.

REALITIES of IRISH LIFE. By W. Steuart Trench, late Land Agent in Ireland to the Marquess of Lansdowne, the Marquess of Bath, and Lord Digby. Cheaper Edition. Crown 8vo. price 2s. 6d.

Biographical Works.

The **LIFE and LETTERS of LORD MACAULAY.** By his Nephew, G. Otto Trevelyan, M.P. 2 vols. 8vo. with Portrait, price 36s.

The **LIFE of SIR WILLIAM FAIRBAIRN, Bart. F.R.S.** Corresponding Member of the National Institute of France, &c. Partly written by himself; edited and completed by William Pole, F.R.S. [*In the Press.*

ARTHUR SCHOPENHAUER, his LIFE and his PHILOSOPHY. By Helen Zimmern. Post 8vo. with Portrait, 7s. 6d.

MEMOIRS of BARON STOCKMAR. By his Son, Baron E. Von Stockmar. Translated from the German by G. A. M. Edited by F. Max Müller, M.A. 2 vols. crown 8vo. 21s.

AUTOBIOGRAPHY. By John Stuart Mill. 8vo. price 7s. 6d.

The **LIFE of NAPOLEON III.** derived from State Records, Unpublished Family Correspondence, and Personal Testimony. By Blanchard Jerrold. 4 vols. 8vo. with numerous Portraits and Facsimiles. Vols. I. and II. price 18s. each. The Third Volume is in the press.

LIFE and LETTERS of Sir GILBERT ELLIOT, First EARL of MINTO. Edited by the Countess of Minto. 3 vols. 8vo. 31s. 6d.

ESSAYS in MODERN MILITARY BIOGRAPHY. By Charles Cornwallis Chesney, Lieutenant-Colonel in the Royal Engineers. 8vo. 12s. 6d.

The **MEMOIRS of SIR JOHN RERESBY,** of Thrybergh, Bart. M.P. for York, &c. 1634–1689. Written by Himself. Edited from the Original Manuscript by James J. Cartwright, M.A. 8vo. price 21s.

ISAAC CASAUBON, 1559–1614. By MARK PATTISON, Rector of Lincoln College, Oxford. 8vo. 18s.

LORD GEORGE BENTINCK; a Political Biography. By the Right Hon. BENJAMIN DISRAELI, M.P. Crown 8vo. price 6s.

LEADERS of PUBLIC OPINION in IRELAND; Swift, Flood, Grattan, and O'Connell. By W. E. H. LECKY, M.A. New Edition, revised and enlarged. Crown 8vo. price 7s. 6d.

DICTIONARY of GENERAL BIOGRAPHY; containing Concise Memoirs and Notices of the most Eminent Persons of all Countries, from the Earliest Ages. By W. L. R. CATES. New Edition, extended in a Supplement to the Year 1873. Medium 8vo. price 25s.

LIFE of the DUKE of WELLINGTON. By the Rev. G. R. GLEIG, M.A. Popular Edition, carefully revised ; with copious Additions. Crown 8vo. with Portrait, 5s.

MEMOIRS of SIR HENRY HAVELOCK, K.C.B. By JOHN CLARK MARSHMAN. Cabinet Edition, with Portrait. Crown 8vo. price 3s. 6d.

VICISSITUDES of FAMILIES. By Sir J. BERNARD BURKE, C.B. Ulster King of Arms. New Edition, enlarged. 2 vols. crown 8vo. 21s.

The RISE of GREAT FAMILIES, other Essays and Stories. By Sir J. BERNARD BURKE, C.B. Ulster King of Arms. Crown 8vo. price 12s. 6d.

ESSAYS in ECCLESIASTICAL BIOGRAPHY. By the Right Hon. Sir J. STEPHEN, LL.D. Cabinet Edition. Crown 8vo. 7s. 6d.

MAUNDER'S BIOGRAPHICAL TREASURY. Latest Edition, reconstructed, thoroughly revised, and in great part rewritten ; with 1,000 additional Memoirs and Notices, by W. L. R. CATES. Fcp. 8vo. 6s. cloth ; 10s. 6d. calf.

LETTERS and LIFE of FRANCIS BACON, including all his Occasional Works. Collected and edited, with a Commentary, by J. SPEDDING, Trin. Coll. Cantab. Complete in 7 vols. 8vo. £4. 4s.

The LIFE, WORKS, and OPINIONS of HEINRICH HEINE. By WILLIAM STIGAND. 2 vols. 8vo. with Portrait of Heine, price 28s.

BIOGRAPHICAL and CRITICAL ESSAYS, reprinted from Reviews, with Additions and Corrections. Second Edition of the Second Series. By A. HAYWARD, Q.C. 2 vols. 8vo. price 28s. THIRD SERIES, in 1 vol. 8vo. price 14s.

Criticism, Philosophy, Polity, &c.

The LAW of NATIONS considered as INDEPENDENT POLITICAL COMMUNITIES; the Rights and Duties of Nations in Time of War. By Sir TRAVERS TWISS, D.C.L., F.R.S. New Edition, revised; with an Introductory Juridical Review of the Results of Recent Wars, and an Appendix of Treaties and other Documents. 8vo. 21s.

CHURCH and STATE: their relations Historically Developed. By T. HEINRICH GEFFCKEN, Professor of International Law at the University of Strasburg. Translated from the German by E. FAIRFAX TAYLOR. [In the press.

A SYSTEMATIC VIEW of the SCIENCE of JURISPRUDENCE. By SHELDON AMOS, M.A. Professor of Jurisprudence to the Inns of Court, London. 8vo. price 18s.

A PRIMER of the ENGLISH CONSTITUTION and GOVERNMENT.
By SHELDON AMOS, M.A. Professor of Jurisprudence to the Inns of Court.
Second Edition, revised. Crown 8vo. 6s.

OUTLINES of CIVIL PROCEDURE. Being a General View of the
Supreme Court of Judicature and of the whole Practice in the Common Law and
Chancery Divisions under all the Statutes now in force. By EDWARD STANLEY
ROSCOE, Barrister-at-Law. 12mo. price 3s. 6d.

The INSTITUTES of JUSTINIAN; with English Introduction, Translation and Notes. By T. C. SANDARS, M.A. Sixth Edition. 8vo. 18s.

SOCRATES and the SOCRATIC SCHOOLS. Translated from the
German of Dr. E. ZELLER, with the Author's approval, by the Rev. OSWALD J.
REICHEL, M.A. Crown 8vo. 8s. 6d.

The STOICS, EPICUREANS, and SCEPTICS. Translated from the
German of Dr. E. ZELLER, with the Author's approval, by OSWALD J. REICHEL,
M.A. Crown 8vo. price 14s.

PLATO and the OLDER ACADEMY. Translated from the German
of Dr. EDUARD ZELLER by S. FRANCES ALLEYNE and ALFRED GOODWIN, B.A.
Fellow of Balliol College, Oxford. Crown 8vo. 18s.

The ETHICS of ARISTOTLE, with Essays and Notes. By Sir A.
GRANT, Bart. M.A. LL.D. Third Edition. 2 vols. 8vo. 32s.

The POLITICS of ARISTOTLE; Greek Text, with English Notes. By
RICHARD CONGREVE, M.A. New Edition, revised. 8vo. 18s.

The NICOMACHEAN ETHICS of ARISTOTLE newly translated into
English. By R. WILLIAMS, B.A. Fellow and late Lecturer of Merton College,
and sometime Student of Christ Church, Oxford. New Edition. 8vo. 7s. 6d.

PICTURE LOGIC; an Attempt to Popularise the Science of Reasoning by the combination of Humorous Pictures with Examples of Reasoning
taken from Daily Life. By A. SWINBOURNE, B.A. With Woodcut Illustrations from Drawings by the Author. Second Edition. Fcp. 8vo. price 5s.

ELEMENTS of LOGIC. By R. WHATELY, D.D. late Archbishop of
Dublin. New Edition. 8vo. 10s. 6d. crown 8vo. 4s. 6d.

Elements of Rhetoric. By the same Author. New Edition. 8vo.
10s. 6d. crown 8vo. 4s. 6d.

English Synonymes. By E. JANE WHATELY. Edited by Archbishop
WHATELY. Fifth Edition. Fcp. 8vo. price 3s.

On the INFLUENCE of AUTHORITY in MATTERS of OPINION.
By the late Sir GEORGE CORNEWALL LEWIS, Bart. New Edition. 8vo. 14s.

COMTE'S SYSTEM of POSITIVE POLITY, or TREATISE upon
SOCIOLOGY. Translated from the Paris Edition of 1851–1854, and furnished
with Analytical Tables of Contents. In Four Volumes, 8vo. each forming in
some degree an independent Treatise :—

VOL. I. General View of Positivism and its Introductory Principles. Translated
by J. H. BRIDGES, M.B. Price 21s.

VOL. II. Social Statics, or the Abstract Laws of Human Order. Translated by
F. HARRISON, M.A. Price 14s.

VOL. III. Social Dynamics, or the General Laws of Human Progress (the
Philosophy of History). Translated by Professor E. S. BEESLY, M.A. 8vo. 21s.

VOL. IV. Synthesis of the Future of Mankind. Translated by R. CONGREVE,
M.D.; and an Appendix, containing the Author's Minor Treatises, translated by
H. D. Hutton, M.A.   [In the press.

DEMOCRACY in AMERICA. By ALEXIS DE TOCQUEVILLE. Translated by HENRY REEVE, Esq. New Edition. 2 vols. crown 8vo. 16s.

ORDER and PROGRESS: Part I. Thoughts on Government; Part II. Studies of Political Crises. By FREDERIC HARRISON, M.A. of Lincoln's Inn. 8vo. price 14s.

BACON'S ESSAYS with ANNOTATIONS. By R. WHATELY, D.D. late Archbishop of Dublin. New Edition, 8vo. price 10s. 6d.

LORD BACON'S WORKS, collected and edited by J. SPEDDING, M.A. R. L. ELLIS, M.A. and D. D. HEATH. 7 vols. 8vo. price £3. 13s. 6d.

On REPRESENTATIVE GOVERNMENT. By JOHN STUART MILL Crown 8vo. price 2s.

On LIBERTY. By JOHN STUART MILL. New Edition. Post 8vo. 7s. 6d. Crown 8vo. price 1s. 4d.

PRINCIPLES of POLITICAL ECONOMY. By JOHN STUART MILL. Seventh Edition. 2 vols. 8vo. 30s. Or in 1 vol. crown 8vo. price 5s.

ESSAYS on SOME UNSETTLED QUESTIONS of POLITICAL ECONOMY. By JOHN STUART MILL. Second Edition. 8vo. 6s. 6d.

UTILITARIANISM. By JOHN STUART MILL. New Edition. 8vo. 5s.

DISSERTATIONS and DISCUSSIONS: Political, Philosophical, and Historical. By JOHN STUART MILL. New Editions. 4 vols. 8vo. price £2. 6s. 6d.

EXAMINATION of Sir. W. HAMILTON'S PHILOSOPHY, and of the Principal Philosophical Questions discussed in his Writings. By JOHN STUART MILL. Fourth Edition. 8vo. 16s.

An OUTLINE of the NECESSARY LAWS of THOUGHT; a Treatise on Pure and Applied Logic. By the Most Rev. W. THOMSON, Lord Archbishop of York, D.D. F.R.S. New Edition. Crown 8vo. price 6s.

PRINCIPLES of ECONOMICAL PHILOSOPHY. By HENRY DUNNING MACLEOD, M.A. Barrister-at-Law. Second Edition. In Two Volumes. VOL. I. 8vo. price 15s. VOL. II. PART I. price 12s. VOL. II. PART II. *just ready.*

A SYSTEM of LOGIC, RATIOCINATIVE and INDUCTIVE. By JOHN STUART MILL. Ninth Edition. Two vols. 8vo. 25s.

SPEECHES of the RIGHT HON. LORD MACAULAY, corrected by Himself. People's Edition, crown 8vo. 3s. 6d.

The ORATION of DEMOSTHENES on the CROWN. Translated by the Right Hon. Sir R. P. COLLIER. Crown 8vo. price 5s.

FAMILIES of SPEECH: Four Lectures delivered before the Royal Institution of Great Britain. By the Rev. F. W. FARRAR, D.D. F.R.S. New Edition. Crown 8vo. 3s. 6d.

CHAPTERS on LANGUAGE. By the Rev. F. W. FARRAR, D.D. F.R.S. New Edition. Crown 8vo. 5s.

HANDBOOK of the ENGLISH LANGUAGE. For the use of Students of the Universities and the Higher Classes in Schools. By R. G. LATHAM, M.A. M.D. The Ninth Edition. Crown 8vo. price 6s.

DICTIONARY of the ENGLISH LANGUAGE. By R. G. LATHAM, M.A. M.D. Abridged from Dr. Latham's Edition of Johnson's English Dictionary, and condensed into One Volume. Medium 8vo. price 24s.

A DICTIONARY of the ENGLISH LANGUAGE. By R. G. LATHAM, M.A. M.D. Founded on the Dictionary of Dr. SAMUEL JOHNSON, as edited by the Rev. H. J. TODD, with numerous Emendations and Additions. In Four Volumes, 4to. price £7.

THESAURUS of ENGLISH WORDS and PHRASES, classified and arranged so as to facilitate the Expression of Ideas, and assist in Literary Composition. By P. M. ROGET, M.D. New Edition. Crown 8vo. 10s. 6d.

LECTURES on the SCIENCE of LANGUAGE. By F. MAX MÜLLER, M.A. &c. The Eighth Edition. 2 vols. crown 8vo. 16s.

MANUAL of ENGLISH LITERATURE, Historical and Critical. By THOMAS ARNOLD, M.A. New Edition. Crown 8vo. 7s. 6d.

SOUTHEY'S DOCTOR, complete in One Volume. Edited by the Rev. J. W. WARTER, B.D. Square crown 8vo. 12s. 6d.

HISTORICAL and CRITICAL COMMENTARY on the OLD TESTA-MENT; with a New Translation. By M. M. KALISCH, Ph.D. VOL. I. *Genesis,* 8vo. 18s. or adapted for the General Reader, 12s. VOL. II. *Exodus,* 15s. or adapted for the General Reader, 12s. VOL. III. *Leviticus,* PART I. 15s. or adapted for the General Reader, 8s. VOL. IV. *Leviticus,* PART II. 15s. or adapted for the General Reader, 8s.

A DICTIONARY of ROMAN and GREEK ANTIQUITIES, with about Two Thousand Engravings on Wood from Ancient Originals, illustrative of the Industrial Arts and Social Life of the Greeks and Romans. By A. RICH, B.A. Third Edition, revised and improved. Crown 8vo. price 7s. 6d.

A LATIN-ENGLISH DICTIONARY. By JOHN T. WHITE, D.D. Oxon. and J. E. RIDDLE, M.A. Oxon. Fifth Edition. 1 vol. 4to. 28s.

WHITE'S COLLEGE LATIN-ENGLISH DICTIONARY (Intermediate Size), abridged for the use of University Students from the Parent Work (as above). Medium 8vo. Third Edition, 15s.

WHITE'S JUNIOR STUDENT'S COMPLETE LATIN-ENGLISH and ENGLISH-LATIN DICTIONARY. New Edition. Square 12mo. price 12s.

Separately { The ENGLISH-LATIN DICTIONARY, price 5s. 6d.
The LATIN-ENGLISH DICTIONARY, price 7s. 6d.

A LATIN-ENGLISH DICTIONARY, adapted for the Use of Middle-Class Schools. By JOHN T. WHITE, D.D. Oxon. Square fcp. 8vo. price 3s.

An ENGLISH-GREEK LEXICON, containing all the Greek Words used by Writers of good authority. By C. D. YONGE, M.A. 4to. price 21s.

Mr. YONGE'S NEW LEXICON, English and Greek, abridged from his larger work (as above). Revised Edition. Square 12mo. price 8s. 6d.

A GREEK-ENGLISH LEXICON. Compiled by H. G. LIDDELL, D.D. Dean of Christ Church, and R. SCOTT, D.D. Dean of Rochester. Sixth Edition. Crown 4to. price 36s.

A LEXICON, GREEK and ENGLISH, abridged from LIDDELL and SCOTT's *Greek-English Lexicon.* Fourteenth Edition. Square 12mo. 7s. 6d.

A PRACTICAL DICTIONARY of the FRENCH and ENGLISH LAN-GUAGES. By L. CONTANSEAU. Revised Edition. Post 8vo. 7s. 6d.

CONTANSEAU'S POCKET DICTIONARY, French and English, abridged from the above by the Author. New Edition. Square 18mo. 3s. 6d.

A NEW POCKET DICTIONARY of the GERMAN and ENGLISH LANGUAGES. By F. W. LONGMAN, Balliol College, Oxford. 18mo. 5s.

NEW PRACTICAL DICTIONARY of the GERMAN LANGUAGE; German-English and English-German. By the Rev. W. L. BLACKLEY, M.A. and Dr. CARL MARTIN FRIEDLÄNDER. Post 8vo. 7s. 6d.

The **MASTERY of LANGUAGES;** or, the Art of Speaking Foreign Tongues Idiomatically. By THOMAS PRENDERGAST. 8vo. 6s.

Miscellaneous Works and Popular Metaphysics.

LECTURES delivered in AMERICA in 1874. By CHARLES KINGSLEY, F.L.S. F.G.S. late Rector of Eversley. Crown 8vo. price 5s.

GERMAN HOME LIFE. Reprinted, with Revision and Additions, from *Fraser's Magazine.* Crown 8vo. 6s.

THE MISCELLANEOUS WORKS of THOMAS ARNOLD, D.D. Late Head Master of Rugby School and Regius Professor of Modern History in the University of Oxford, collected and republished. 8vo. 7s. 6d.

MISCELLANEOUS and POSTHUMOUS WORKS of the Late HENRY THOMAS BUCKLE. Edited, with a Biographical Notice, by HELEN TAYLOR. 3 vols. 8vo. price 52s. 6d.

MISCELLANEOUS WRITINGS of JOHN CONINGTON, M.A. late Corpus Professor of Latin in the University of Oxford. Edited by J. A. SYMONDS, M.A. With a Memoir by H. J. S. SMITH, M.A. 2 vols. 8vo. 28s.

ESSAYS, CRITICAL and BIOGRAPHICAL. Contributed to the *Edinburgh Review.* By HENRY ROGERS. New Edition, with Additions. 2 vols. crown 8vo. price 12s.

ESSAYS on some THEOLOGICAL CONTROVERSIES of the TIME. Contributed chiefly to the *Edinburgh Review.* By HENRY ROGERS. New Edition, with Additions. Crown 8vo. price 6s.

RECREATIONS of a COUNTRY PARSON. By A. K. H. B. FIRST and SECOND SERIES, crown 8vo. 3s. 6d. each.

The **Common-place Philosopher in Town and Country.** By A. K. H. B. Crown 8vo. price 3s. 6d.

Leisure Hours in Town; Essays Consolatory, Æsthetical, Moral, Social, and Domestic. By A. K. H. B. Crown 8vo. 3s. 6d.

The **Autumn Holidays of a Country Parson;** Essays contributed to *Fraser's Magazine,* &c. By A. K. H. B. Crown 8vo. 3s. 6d.

Seaside Musings on Sundays and Week-Days. By A. K. H. B. Crown 8vo. price 3s. 6d.

The **Graver Thoughts of a Country Parson.** By A. K. H. B. FIRST, SECOND, and THIRD SERIES, crown 8vo. 3s. 6d. each.

Critical Essays of a Country Parson, selected from Essays contributed to *Fraser's Magazine.* By A. K. H. B. Crown 8vo. 3s. 6d.

Sunday Afternoons at the Parish Church of a Scottish University City. By A. K. H. B. Crown 8vo. 3s. 6d.

Lessons of Middle Age; with some Account of various Cities and Men. By A. K. H. B. Crown 8vo. 3s. 6d.

Counsel and Comfort spoken from a City Pulpit. By A. K. H. B. Crown 8vo. price 3s. 6d.

Changed Aspects of Unchanged Truths; Memorials of St. Andrews Sundays. By A. K. H. B. Crown 8vo. 3s. 6d.

Present-day Thoughts; Memorials of St. Andrews Sundays. By A. K. H. B. Crown 8vo. 3s. 6d.

Landscapes, Churches, and Moralities. By A. K. H. B. Crown 8vo. price 3s. 6d.

SHORT STUDIES on GREAT SUBJECTS. By JAMES ANTHONY FROUDE, M.A. late Fellow of Exeter Coll. Oxford. 2 vols. crown 8vo. price 12s. or 2 vols. demy 8vo. price 24s.

SELECTIONS from the WRITINGS of LORD MACAULAY. Edited, with Occasional Explanatory Notes, by GEORGE OTTO TREVELYAN, M.P. 1 vol. crown 8vo. [In the press.

LORD MACAULAY'S MISCELLANEOUS WRITINGS :—
LIBRARY EDITION. 2 vols. 8vo. Portrait, 21s.
PEOPLE'S EDITION. 1 vol. crown 8vo. 4s. 6d.

LORD MACAULAY'S MISCELLANEOUS WRITINGS and SPEECHES. STUDENT'S EDITION, in crown 8vo. price 6s.

The Rev. SYDNEY SMITH'S MISCELLANEOUS WORKS; including his Contributions to the *Edinburgh Review.* Crown 8vo. 6s.

The WIT and WISDOM of the Rev. SYDNEY SMITH ; a Selection of the most memorable Passages in his Writings and Conversation. 16mo. 3s. 6d.

The ECLIPSE of FAITH; or, a Visit to a Religious Sceptic. By HENRY ROGERS. Latest Edition. Fcp. 8vo. price 5s.

Defence of the Eclipse of Faith, by its Author ; a rejoinder to Dr. Newman's *Reply.* Latest Edition. Fcp 8vo. price 3s. 6d.

CHIPS from a GERMAN WORKSHOP; Essays on the Science of Religion, on Mythology, Traditions, and Customs, and on the Science of Language. By F. MAX MÜLLER, M.A. &c. 4 vols. 8vo. £2. 18s.

ANALYSIS of the PHENOMENA of the HUMAN MIND. By JAMES MILL. A New Edition, with Notes, Illustrative and Critical, by ALEXANDER BAIN, ANDREW FINDLATER, and GEORGE GROTE. Edited, with additional Notes, by JOHN STUART MILL. 2 vols. 8vo. price 28s.

An INTRODUCTION to MENTAL PHILOSOPHY, on the Inductive Method. By J. D. MORELL, M.A. LL.D. 8vo. 12s.

PHILOSOPHY WITHOUT ASSUMPTIONS. By the Rev. T. P. KIRKMAN, F.R.S. Rector of Croft, near Warrington. 8vo. 10s. 6d.

The SENSES and the INTELLECT. By ALEXANDER BAIN, M.D. Professor of Logic in the University of Aberdeen. Third Edition. 8vo. 15s.

The EMOTIONS and the WILL. By ALEXANDER BAIN, LL.D. Professor of Logic in the University of Aberdeen. Third Edition, thoroughly revised, and in great part re-written. 8vo. price 15s.

MENTAL and MORAL SCIENCE: a Compendium of Psychology and Ethics. By the same Author. Third Edition. Crown 8vo. 10s. 6d. Or separately : PART I. *Mental Science,* 6s. 6d. PART II. *Moral Science,* 4s. 6d.

LOGIC, DEDUCTIVE and INDUCTIVE. By ALEXANDER BAIN, LL.D.
In Two PARTS, crown 8vo. 10s. 6d. Each Part may be had separately:—
PART I. *Deduction*, 4s. PART II. *Induction*, 6s. 6d.

A BUDGET of PARADOXES. By AUGUSTUS DE MORGAN, F.R.A.S.
and C.P.S. 8vo. 15s.

APPARITIONS; a Narrative of Facts. By the Rev. B. W. SAVILE,
M.A. Author of 'The Truth of the Bible' &c. Crown 8vo. price 4s. 6d.

A TREATISE of HUMAN NATURE, being an Attempt to Introduce
the Experimental Method of Reasoning into Moral Subjects; followed by Dia-
logues concerning Natural Religion. By DAVID HUME. Edited, with Notes,
&c. by T. H. GREEN, Fellow and Tutor, Ball. Coll. and T. H. GROSE, Fellow
and Tutor, Queen's Coll. Oxford. 2 vols. 8vo. 28s.

ESSAYS MORAL, POLITICAL, and LITERARY. By DAVID HUME.
By the same Editors. 2 vols. 8vo. price 28s.

The PHILOSOPHY of NECESSITY; or, Natural Law as applicable to
Mental, Moral, and Social Science. By CHARLES BRAY. 8vo. 9s.

UEBERWEG'S SYSTEM of LOGIC and HISTORY of LOGICAL
DOCTRINES. Translated, with Notes and Appendices, by T. M. LINDSAY,
M.A. F.R.S.E. 8vo. price 16s.

FRAGMENTARY PAPERS on SCIENCE and other Subjects. By
the late Sir H. HOLLAND, Bart. Edited by his Son, the Rev. F. HOLLAND. 8vo.
price 14s.

Astronomy, Meteorology, Popular Geography, &c.

BRINKLEY'S ASTRONOMY. Revised and partly re-written, with
Additional Chapters, and an Appendix of Questions for Examination. By J. W.
STUBBS, D.D. Fellow and Tutor of Trinity College, Dublin, and F. BRUNNOW,
Ph.D. Astronomer Royal of Ireland. Crown 8vo. price 6s.

OUTLINES of ASTRONOMY. By Sir J. F. W. HERSCHEL, Bart.
M.A. Latest Edition, with Plates and Diagrams. Square crown 8vo. 12s.

ESSAYS on ASTRONOMY, a Series of Papers on Planets and Meteors,
the Sun and Sun-surrounding Space, Stars and Star-Cloudlets; with a Dissertation
on the Transit of Venus. By R. A. PROCTOR, B.A. With Plates and Woodcuts. 8vo. 12s.

THE TRANSITS of VENUS; a Popular Account of Past and Coming
Transits, from the first observed by Horrocks A.D. 1639 to the Transit of
A.D. 2012. By R. A. PROCTOR, B.A. Second Edition, with 20 Plates (12 coloured)
and 38 Woodcuts. Crown 8vo. 8s. 6d.

The UNIVERSE and the COMING TRANSITS : Presenting Researches into and New Views respecting the Constitution of the Heavens;
together with an Investigation of the Conditions of the Coming Transits of Venus.
By R. A. PROCTOR, B.A. With 22 Charts and 22 Woodcuts. 8vo. 16s.

The MOON; her Motions, Aspect, Scenery, and Physical Condition.
By R. A. PROCTOR, B.A. With Plates, Charts, Woodcuts, and Three Lunar
Photographs. Crown 8vo. 15s.

The SUN; RULER, LIGHT, FIRE, and LIFE of the PLANETARY
SYSTEM. By R. A. PROCTOR, B.A. Second Edition, with 10 Plates (7 coloured) and 107 Figures on Wood. Crown 8vo. 14s.

OTHER WORLDS THAN OURS; the Plurality of Worlds Studied under the Light of Recent Scientific Researches. By R. A. PROCTOR, B.A. Third Edition, with 14 Illustrations. Crown 8vo. 10s. 6d.

The ORBS AROUND US; Familiar Essays on the Moon and Planets, Meteors and Comets, the Sun and Coloured Pairs of Stars. By R. A. PROCTOR, B.A. Second Edition, with Charts and 4 Diagrams. Crown 8vo. price 7s. 6d.

SATURN and its SYSTEM. By R. A. PROCTOR, B.A. 8vo. with 14 Plates, 14s.

The MOON, and the Condition and Configurations of its Surface. By EDMUND NEISON, Fellow of the Royal Astronomical Society, &c. With 26 Maps and 5 Plates. Medium 8vo. 31s. 6d.

A NEW STAR ATLAS, for the Library, the School, and the Observatory, in Twelve Circular Maps (with Two Index Plates). Intended as a Companion to 'Webb's Celestial Objects for Common Telescopes.' With a Letterpress Introduction on the Study of the Stars, illustrated by 9 Diagrams. By R. A. PROCTOR, B.A. Crown 8vo. 5s.

SCHELLEN'S SPECTRUM ANALYSIS, in its application to Terrestrial Substances and the Physical Constitution of the Heavenly Bodies. Translated by JANE and C. LASSELL; edited, with Notes, by W. HUGGINS, LL.D. F.R.S. With 13 Plates (6 coloured) and 223 Woodcuts. 8vo. price 28s.

CELESTIAL OBJECTS for COMMON TELESCOPES. By the Rev. T. W. WEBB, M.A. F.R.A.S. Third Edition, revised and enlarged; with Maps, Plate, and Woodcuts. Crown 8vo. price 7s. 6d.

AIR and RAIN; the Beginnings of a Chemical Climatology. By ROBERT ANGUS SMITH, Ph.D. F.R.S. F.C.S. With 8 Illustrations. 8vo. 24s.

AIR and its RELATIONS to LIFE; being, with some Additions, the Substance of a Course of Lectures delivered at the Royal Institution of Great Britain. By W. N. HARTLEY, F.C.S. Demonstrator of Chemistry at King's College, London. Second Edition, with 66 Woodcuts. Small 8vo. 6s.

NAUTICAL SURVEYING, an INTRODUCTION to the PRACTICAL and THEORETICAL STUDY of. By J. K. LAUGHTON, M.A. Small 8vo. 6s.

DOVE'S LAW of STORMS, considered in connexion with the Ordinary Movements of the Atmosphere. Translated by R. H. SCOTT, M.A. 8vo. 10s. 6d.

KEITH JOHNSTON'S GENERAL DICTIONARY of GEOGRAPHY, Descriptive, Physical, Statistical, and Historical; forming a complete Gazetteer of the World. New Edition, revised and corrected. 1 vol. 8vo. [Nearly ready.

The PUBLIC SCHOOLS ATLAS of MODERN GEOGRAPHY. In 31 Coloured Maps, exhibiting clearly the more important Physical Features of the Countries delineated, and Noting all the Chief Places of Historical, Commercial, or Social Interest. Edited, with an Introduction, by the Rev. G. BUTLER, M.A. Imperial 8vo. or imperial 4to. 5s. cloth.

The PUBLIC SCHOOLS MANUAL of MODERN GEOGRAPHY. By the Rev. GEORGE BUTLER, M.A. Principal of Liverpool College; Editor of 'The Public Schools Atlas of Modern Geography.' [In preparation.

The PUBLIC SCHOOLS ATLAS of ANCIENT GEOGRAPHY, in 25 Coloured Maps. Edited by the Rev. GEORGE BUTLER, M.A. Principal of Liverpool College. Imperial 8vo. or imperial 4to. 7s. 6d. cloth.

MAUNDER'S TREASURY of GEOGRAPHY, Physical, Historical, Descriptive, and Political. Edited by W. HUGHES, F.R.G.S. Revised Edition, with 7 Maps and 16 Plates. Fcp. 6s. cloth, or 10s. 6d. bound in calf.

Natural History and Popular Science.

TEXT-BOOKS of SCIENCE, MECHANICAL and PHYSICAL, adapted for the use of Artisans and Students in Public and Science Schools.

The following Text-Books in this Series may now be had:—

ANDERSON'S Strength of Materials, small 8vo. 3s. 6d.
ARMSTRONG'S Organic Chemistry, 3s. 6d.
BARRY'S Railway Appliances, 3s. 6d.
BLOXAM'S Metals, 3s. 6d.
GOODEVE'S Elements of Mechanism, 3s. 6d.
———— Principles of Mechanics, 3s. 6d.
GRIFFIN'S Algebra and Trigonometry, 3s. 6d. Notes, 3s.6d.
JENKIN'S Electricity and Magnetism, 3s. 6d.
MAXWELL'S Theory of Heat, 3s. 6d.
MERRIFIELD'S Technical Arithmetic and Mensuration, 3s. 6d. Key, 3s. 6d.
MILLER'S Inorganic Chemistry, 3s. 6d.
PREECE & SIVEWRIGHT'S Telegraphy, 3s. 6d.
SHELLEY'S Workshop Appliances, 3s. 6d.
THORPE'S Quantitative Chemical Analysis, 4s. 6d.
THORPE & MUIR'S Qualitative Analysis, 3s. 6d.
TILDEN'S Chemical Philosophy, 3s. 6d.
WATSON'S Plane and Solid Geometry, 3s. 6d.

*** Other Text-Books in extension of this Series are in active preparation.

ELEMENTARY TREATISE on PHYSICS, Experimental and Applied. Translated and edited from GANOT'S Éléments de Physique by E. ATKINSON, Ph.D. F.C.S. Seventh Edition, revised and enlarged; with 4 Coloured Plates and 758 Woodcuts. Post 8vo. 15s.

NATURAL PHILOSOPHY for GENERAL READERS and YOUNG PERSONS; being a Course of Physics divested of Mathematical Formulæ expressed in the language of daily life. Translated from GANOT'S Cours de Physique and by E. ATKINSON, Ph.D. F.C.S. Second Edition, with 2 Plates and 429 Woodcuts. Crown 8vo. price 7s. 6d.

HELMHOLTZ'S POPULAR LECTURES on SCIENTIFIC SUBJECTS. Translated by E. ATKINSON, Ph.D. F.C.S. Professor of Experimental Science, Staff College. With an Introduction by Professor TYNDALL. 8vo. with numerous Woodcuts, price 12s. 6d.

On the SENSATIONS of TONE as a Physiological Basis for the Theory of Music. By HERMANN L. F. HELMHOLTZ, M.D. Professor of Physics in the University of Berlin. Translated, with the Author's sanction, from the Third German Edition, with Additional Notes and an Additional Appendix, by ALEXANDER J. ELLIS, F.R.S. &c. 8vo. price 36s.

The HISTORY of MODERN MUSIC, a Course of Lectures delivered at the Royal Institution of Great Britain. By JOHN HULLAH, Professor of Vocal Music in Queen's College and Bedford College, and Organist of Charterhouse. New Edition. 8vo. 8s. 6d.

The TRANSITION PERIOD of MUSICAL HISTORY; a Second Course of Lectures on the History of Music from the Beginning of the Seventeenth to the Middle of the Eighteenth Century, delivered at the Royal Institution. By JOHN HULLAH. New Edition. 8vo. 10s. 6d.

SOUND. By JOHN TYNDALL, LL.D. D.C.L. F.R.S. Third Edition, including Recent Researches on Fog-Signalling; Portrait and Woodcuts. Crown 8vo. 10s. 6d.

HEAT a MODE of MOTION. By JOHN TYNDALL, LL.D. D.C.L. F.R.S. Fifth Edition. Plate and Woodcuts. Crown 8vo. 10s. 6d.

CONTRIBUTIONS to MOLECULAR PHYSICS in the DOMAIN of RADIANT HEAT. By J. TYNDALL, LL.D. D.C.L. F.R.S. With 2 Plates and 31 Woodcuts. 8vo. 16s.

RESEARCHES on DIAMAGNETISM and MAGNE-CRYSTALLIC ACTION; including the Question of Diamagnetic Polarity. By J. TYNDALL, M.D. D.C.L. F.R.S. With 6 plates and many Woodcuts. 8vo. 14s.

NOTES of a COURSE of SEVEN LECTURES on ELECTRICAL PHENOMENA and THEORIES, delivered at the Royal Institution, A.D. 1870. By JOHN TYNDALL, LL.D., D.C.L., F.R.S. Crown 8vo. 1s. sewed ; 1s. 6d. cloth.

SIX LECTURES on LIGHT delivered in America in 1872 and 1873. By JOHN TYNDALL, LL.D. D.C.L. F.R.S. Second Edition, with Portrait, Plate, and 59 Diagrams. Crown 8vo. 7s. 6d.

NOTES of a COURSE of NINE LECTURES on LIGHT delivered at the Royal Institution, A.D. 1869. By JOHN TYNDALL, LL.D. D.C.L. F.R.S. Crown 8vo. price 1s. sewed, or 1s. 6d. cloth.

FRAGMENTS of SCIENCE. By JOHN TYNDALL. LL.D. D.C.L. F.R.S. Third Edition, with a New Introduction. Crown 8vo. 10s. 6d.

LIGHT SCIENCE for LEISURE HOURS; a Series of Familiar Essays on Scientific Subjects, Natural Phenomena, &c. By R. A. PROCTOR, B.A. First and Second Series. Crown 8vo. 7s. 6d. each.

A TREATISE on MAGNETISM, General and Terrestrial. By HUMPHREY LLOYD, D.D. D.C.L., Provost of Trinity College, Dublin. 8vo. 10s. 6d.

ELEMENTARY TREATISE on the WAVE-THEORY of LIGHT. By HUMPHREY LLOYD, D.D. D.C.L. Provost of Trinity College, Dublin. Third Edition, revised and enlarged. 8vo. price 10s. 6d.

The CORRELATION of PHYSICAL FORCES. By the Hon. Sir W. R. GROVE, M.A. F.R.S. one of the Judges of the Court of Common Pleas. Sixth Edition, with other Contributions to Science. 8vo. price 15s.

The COMPARATIVE ANATOMY and PHYSIOLOGY of the VERTE-BRATE ANIMALS. By RICHARD OWEN, F.R.S. D.C.L. With 1,472 Woodcuts. 3 vols. 8vo. £3. 13s. 6d.

PRINCIPLES of ANIMAL MECHANICS. By the Rev. S. HAUGHTON, F.R.S. Fellow of Trin. Coll. Dubl. M.D. Dubl. and D.C.L. Oxon. Second Edition, with 111 Figures on Wood. 8vo. 21s.

ROCKS CLASSIFIED and DESCRIBED. By BERNHARD VON COTTA. English Edition, by P. H. LAWRENCE; with English, German, and French Synonymes. Post 8vo. 14s.

The ANCIENT STONE IMPLEMENTS, WEAPONS, and ORNA-MENTS of GREAT BRITAIN. By JOHN EVANS, F.R.S. F.S.A. With 2 Plates and 476 Woodcuts. 8vo. price 28s.

The NATIVE RACES of the PACIFIC STATES of NORTH AMERICA. By HUBERT HOWE BANCROFT. 5 vols. 8vo. with Maps, £6. 5s.

The ORIGIN of CIVILISATION and the PRIMITIVE CONDITION of MAN ; Mental and Social Condition of Savages. By Sir JOHN LUBBOCK, Bart. M.P. F.R.S. Third Edition, with 25 Woodcuts. 8vo. 18s.

BIBLE ANIMALS; being a Description of every Living Creature mentioned in the Scriptures, from the Ape to the Coral. By the Rev. J. G. WOOD, M.A. F.L.S. With about 112 Vignettes on Wood. 8vo. 14s.

HOMES WITHOUT HANDS; a Description of the Habitations of Animals, classed according to their Principle of Construction. By the Rev. J. G. WOOD, M.A. F.L.S. With about 140 Vignettes on Wood. 8vo. 14s.

INSECTS AT HOME; a Popular Account of British Insects, their Structure, Habits, and Transformations. By the Rev. J. G. WOOD, M.A. F.L.S. With upwards of 700 Illustrations. 8vo. price 14s.

INSECTS ABROAD; a Popular Account of Foreign Insects, their Structure, Habits, and Transformations. By J. G. WOOD, M.A. F.L.S. Printed and illustrated uniformly with 'Insects at Home.' 8vo. price 21s.

STRANGE DWELLINGS; a description of the Habitations of Animals, abridged from 'Homes without Hands.' By the Rev. J. G. WOOD, M.A. F.L.S. With about 60 Woodcut Illustrations. Crown 8vo. price 7s. 6d.

OUT of DOORS; a Selection of original Articles on Practical Natural History. By the Rev. J. G. WOOD, M.A. F.L.S. With Eleven Illustrations from Original Designs engraved on Wood by G. Pearson. Crown 8vo. price 7s. 6d.

A FAMILIAR HISTORY of BIRDS. By E. STANLEY, D.D. F.R.S. late Lord Bishop of Norwich. Seventh Edition, with Woodcuts. Fcp. 3s. 6d.

The SEA and its LIVING WONDERS. By Dr. GEORGE HARTWIG. Latest revised Edition. 8vo. with many Illustrations, 10s. 6d.

The TROPICAL WORLD. By Dr. GEORGE HARTWIG. With above 160 Illustrations. Latest revised Edition. 8vo. price 10s. 6d.

The SUBTERRANEAN WORLD. By Dr. GEORGE HARTWIG. With 3 Maps and about 80 Woodcuts, including 8 full size of page. 8vo. price 10s. 6d.

The POLAR WORLD, a Popular Description of Man and Nature in the Arctic and Antarctic Regions of the Globe. By Dr. GEORGE HARTWIG. With 8 Chromoxylographs, 3 Maps, and 85 Woodcuts. 8vo. 10s. 6d.

THE AERIAL WORLD. By Dr. G. HARTWIG. New Edition, with 8 Chromoxylographs and 60 Woodcut Illustrations. 8vo. price 21s.

KIRBY and SPENCE'S INTRODUCTION to ENTOMOLOGY, or Elements of the Natural History of Insects. 7th Edition. Crown 8vo. 5s.

MAUNDER'S TREASURY of NATURAL HISTORY, or Popular Dictionary of Birds, Beasts, Fishes, Reptiles, Insects, and Creeping Things. With above 900 Woodcuts. Fcp. 8vo. price 6s. cloth, or 10s. 6d. bound in calf.

MAUNDER'S SCIENTIFIC and LITERARY TREASURY. New Edition, thoroughly revised and in great part rewritten, with above 1,000 new Articles, by J. Y. JOHNSON. Fcp. 8vo. 6s. cloth, or 10s. 6d. calf.

BRANDE'S DICTIONARY of SCIENCE, LITERATURE, and ART. Re-edited by the Rev. GEORGE W. COX, M.A. late Scholar of Trinity College, Oxford; assisted by Contributors of eminent Scientific and Literary Acquirements. New Edition, revised. 3 vols. medium 8vo. 63s.

HANDBOOK of HARDY TREES, SHRUBS, and HERBACEOUS PLANTS, containing Descriptions, Native Countries, &c. of a Selection of the Best Species in Cultivation; together with Cultural Details, Comparative Hardiness, Suitability for Particular Positions, &c. By W. B. HEMSLEY. Based on DECAISNE and NAUDIN'S *Manuel de l'Amateur des Jardins,* and including the 264 Original Woodcuts. Medium 8vo. 21s.

A GENERAL SYSTEM of BOTANY DESCRIPTIVE and ANALYTICAL.
By E. LE MAOUT, and J. DECAISNE, Members of the Institute of France.
Translated by Mrs. HOOKER. The Orders arranged after the Method followed
in the Universities and Schools of Great Britain, its Colonies, America, and
India; with an Appendix on the Natural Method, and other Additions, by
J. D. HOOKER, F.R.S. &c. Second Thousand, with 5,500 Woodcuts. Imperial
8vo. 31s. 6d.

The TREASURY of BOTANY, or Popular Dictionary of the Vegetable
Kingdom; including a Glossary of Botanical Terms. Edited by J. LINDLEY,
F.R.S. and T. MOORE, F.L.S. assisted by eminent Contributors. With 274
Woodcuts and 20 Steel Plates. Two Parts, fcp. 8vo. 12s. cloth, or 21s. calf.

The ELEMENTS of BOTANY for FAMILIES and SCHOOLS.
Tenth Edition, revised by THOMAS MOORE, F.L.S. Fcp. 8vo. with 154 Woodcuts, 2s. 6d.

The ROSE AMATEUR'S GUIDE. By THOMAS RIVERS. Fourteenth
Edition. Fcp. 8vo. 4s.

LOUDON'S ENCYCLOPÆDIA of PLANTS; comprising the Specific
Character, Description, Culture, History, &c. of all the Plants found in
Great Britain. With upwards of 12,000 Woodcuts. 8vo. 42s.

FOREST TREES and WOODLAND SCENERY, as described in Ancient
and Modern Poets. By WILLIAM MENZIES, Deputy Surveyor of Windsor Forest
and Parks, &c. With Twenty Chromo-lithographic Plates. Folio, price £5 5s.

Chemistry and Physiology.

A DICTIONARY of CHEMISTRY and the Allied Branches of other
Sciences. By HENRY WATTS, F.R.S. assisted by eminent Contributors.
Seven Volumes, medium 8vo. price £10. 16s. 6d.

ELEMENTS of CHEMISTRY, Theoretical and Practical. By W. ALLEN
MILLER, M.D. late Prof. of Chemistry, King's Coll. London. New
Edition. 3 vols. 8vo. PART I. CHEMICAL PHYSICS, 15s. PART II.
INORGANIC CHEMISTRY, 21s. PART III. ORGANIC CHEMISTRY, New Edition
in the press.

SELECT METHODS in CHEMICAL ANALYSIS, chiefly INOR-
GANIC. By WILLIAM CROOKES, F.R.S. With 22 Woodcuts. Crown 8vo.
price 12s. 6d.

A PRACTICAL HANDBOOK of DYEING and CALICO PRINTING.
By WILLIAM CROOKES, F.R.S. With 11 Page Plates, 49 Specimens of Dyed and
Printed Fabrics, and 36 Woodcuts. 8vo. 42s.

OUTLINES of PHYSIOLOGY, Human and Comparative. By JOHN
MARSHALL, F.R.C.S. Surgeon to the University College Hospital. 2 vols.
crown 8vo. with 122 Woodcuts, 32s.

HEALTH in the HOUSE; a Series of Lectures on Elementary Physiology in its application to the Daily Wants of Man and Animals, delivered to
the Wives and Children of Working Men in Leeds and Saltaire. By CATHERINE
M. BUCKTON. New Edition, revised. Small 8vo. Woodcuts, 2s.

The Fine Arts, and Illustrated Editions.

A DICTIONARY of ARTISTS of the ENGLISH SCHOOL: Painters, Sculptors, Architects, Engravers, and Ornamentists; with Notices of their Lives and Works. By S. REDGRAVE. 8vo. 16s.

MOORE'S IRISH MELODIES, with 161 Steel Plates from Original Drawings by D. MACLISE, R.A. Super-royal 8vo. 21s.

LORD MACAULAY'S LAYS of ANCIENT ROME. With 90 Illustrations on Wood, from the Antique, from Drawings by G. SCHARF. Fcp. 4to. 21s.

Miniature Edition of Lord Macaulay's Lays of Ancient Rome, with the Illustrations (as above) reduced in Lithography. Imp. 16mo. 10s. 6d.

POEMS. By WILLIAM B. SCOTT. I. Ballads and Tales. II. Studies from Nature. III. Sonnets &c. Illustrated by 17 Etchings by W. B. SCOTT (the Author) and L. ALMA TADEMA. Crown 8vo. price 15s.

HALF-HOUR LECTURES on the HISTORY and PRACTICE of the FINE and ORNAMENTAL ARTS. By WILLIAM B. SCOTT. Third Edition, with 50 Woodcuts. Crown 8vo. 8s. 6d.

The THREE CATHEDRALS DEDICATED to ST. PAUL, in LONDON; their History from the Foundation of the First Building in the Sixth Century to the Proposals for the Adornment of the Present Cathedral. By WILLIAM LONGMAN, F.A.S. With numerous Illustrations. Square crown 8vo. 21s.

IN FAIRYLAND; Pictures from the Elf-World. By RICHARD DOYLE. With a Poem by W. ALLINGHAM. With Sixteen Plates, containing Thirty-six Designs printed in Colours. Second Edition. Folio, price 15s.

The NEW TESTAMENT, illustrated with Wood Engravings after the Early Masters, chiefly of the Italian School. Crown 4to. 63s. cloth, gilt top; or £5 5s. elegantly bound in morocco.

SACRED and LEGENDARY ART. By MRS. JAMESON.

Legends of the Saints and Martyrs. New Edition, with 19 Etchings and 187 Woodcuts. 2 vols. square crown 8vo. 31s. 6d.

Legends of the Monastic Orders. New Edition, with 11 Etchings and 88 Woodcuts. 1 vol. square crown 8vo. 21s.

Legends of the Madonna. New Edition, with 27 Etchings and 165 Woodcuts. 1 vol. square crown 8vo. 21s.

The History of Our Lord, with that of his Types and Precursors. Completed by Lady EASTLAKE. Revised Edition, with 31 Etchings and 281 Woodcuts. 2 vols. square crown 8vo. 42s.

The Useful Arts, Manufactures, &c.

GWILT'S ENCYCLOPÆDIA of ARCHITECTURE, with above 1,600 Engravings on Wood. New Edition, revised and enlarged by WYATT PAPWORTH. 8vo. 52s. 6d.

HINTS on HOUSEHOLD TASTE in FURNITURE, UPHOLSTERY, and other Details. By CHARLES L. EASTLAKE, Architect. New Edition, with about 90 Illustrations. Square crown 8vo. 14s.

B

INDUSTRIAL CHEMISTRY; a Manual for Manufacturers and for use in Colleges or Technical Schools. Being a Translation of Professors Stohmann and Engler's German Edition of PAYEN's *Précis de Chimie Industrielle*, by Dr. J. D. BARRY. Edited and supplemented by B. H. PAUL, Ph.D. 8vo. with Plates and Woodcuts.   [*In the press.*

URE'S DICTIONARY of ARTS, MANUFACTURES, and MINES. Seventh Edition, rewritten and enlarged by ROBERT HUNT, F.R.S. assisted by numerous Contributors eminent in Science and the Arts, and familiar with Manufactures. With above 2,100 Woodcuts. 3 vols. medium 8vo. £5 5s.

HANDBOOK of PRACTICAL TELEGRAPHY. By R. S. CULLEY Memb. Inst. C.E. Engineer-in-Chief of Telegraphs to the Post Office. Sixth Edition, with 144 Woodcuts and 5 Plates. 8vo. price 16s.

TELEGRAPHY. By W. H. PREECE, C.E. Divisional Engineer, P.O. Telegraphs; and J. SIVEWRIGHT, M.A. Superintendent (Engineering Department) P.O. Telegraphs. Small 8vo. with 160 Woodcuts, 3s. 6d.

RAILWAY APPLIANCES; a Description of Details of Railway Construction subsequent to the completion of the Earthworks and Masonry, including a short Notice of Railway Rolling Stock. By J. W. BARRY, Member of the Institution of Civil Engineers. Small 8vo. with 207 Woodcuts, 3s. 6d.

ENCYCLOPÆDIA of CIVIL ENGINEERING, Historical, Theoretical, and Practical. By E. CRESY, C.E. With above 3,000 Woodcuts. 8vo. 42s.

OCCASIONAL PAPERS on SUBJECTS connected with CIVIL ENGINEERING, GUNNERY, and Naval Architecture. By MICHAEL SCOTT, Memb. Inst. C.E. & of Inst. N.A. 2 vols. 8vo. with Plates, 42s.

NAVAL POWERS and their POLICY, with Tabular Statements of British and Foreign Ironclad Navies, giving Dimensions, Armour, Details of Armament, Engines, Speed, &c. By JOHN C. PAGET. 8vo. 10s. 6d.

TREATISE on MILLS and MILLWORK. By Sir W. FAIRBAIRN, Bart. F.R.S. New Edition, with 18 Plates and 322 Woodcuts, 2 vols. 8vo. 32s.

USEFUL INFORMATION for ENGINEERS. By Sir W. FAIRBAIRN, Bart. F.R.S. Revised Edition, with Illustrations. 3 vols. crown 8vo. price 31s. 6d.

The APPLICATION of CAST and WROUGHT IRON to Building Purposes. By Sir W. FAIRBAIRN, Bart. F.R.S. Fourth Edition, enlarged; with 6 Plates and 118 Woodcuts. 8vo. price 16s.

The THEORY of STRAINS in GIRDERS and similar Structures, with Observations on the application of Theory to Practice, and Tables of the Strength and other Properties of Materials. By BINDON B. STONEY, M.A. M. Inst. C.E. New Edition, royal 8vo. with 5 Plates and 123 Woodcuts, 36s.

A TREATISE on the STEAM ENGINE, in its various Applications to Mines, Mills, Steam Navigation, Railways, and Agriculture. By J. BOURNE, C.E. Eighth Edition; with Portrait, 37 Plates, and 546 Woodcuts. 4to. 42s.

CATECHISM of the STEAM ENGINE, in its various Applications to Mines, Mills, Steam Navigation, Railways, and Agriculture. By the same Author. With 89 Woodcuts. Fcp. 8vo. 6s.

HANDBOOK of the STEAM ENGINE. By the same Author, forming a KEY to the Catechism of the Steam Engine, with 67 Woodcuts. Fcp. 9s.

BOURNE'S RECENT IMPROVEMENTS in the STEAM ENGINE in its various applications to Mines, Mills, Steam Navigation, Railways, and Agriculture. By JOHN BOURNE, C.E. New Edition, with 124 Woodcuts. Fcp. 8vo. 6s.

PRACTICAL TREATISE on METALLURGY, adapted from the last
German Edition of Professor KERL's *Metallurgy* by W. CROOKES, F.R.S. &c.
and E. BÖHRIG, Ph.D. M.E. With 625 Woodcuts. 3 vols. 8vo. price £4 19s.

MITCHELL'S MANUAL of PRACTICAL ASSAYING. Fourth Edi-
tion, for the most part rewritten, with all the recent Discoveries incorporated,
by W. CROOKES, F.R.S. With 199 Woodcuts. 8vo. 31s. 6d.

LOUDON'S ENCYCLOPÆDIA of AGRICULTURE: comprising the
Laying-out, Improvement, and Management of Landed Property, and the Cultivation and Economy of Agricultural Produce. With 1,100 Woodcuts. 8vo. 21s.

Loudon's Encyclopædia of Gardening: comprising the Theory and
Practice of Horticulture, Floriculture, Arboriculture, and Landscape Gardening.
With 1,000 Woodcuts. 8vo. 21s.

REMINISCENCES of FEN and MERE. By J. M. HEATHCOTE.
With 27 Illustrations and 3 Maps. Square crown 8vo. price 28s.

Religious and *Moral Works.*

CHRISTIAN LIFE, its COURSE, its HINDRANCES, and its
HELPS; Sermons preached mostly in the Chapel of Rugby School. By the
late Rev. THOMAS ARNOLD, D.D. 8vo. 7s. 6d.

CHRISTIAN LIFE, its HOPES, its FEARS, and its CLOSE;
Sermons preached mostly in the Chapel of Rugby School. By the late Rev.
THOMAS ARNOLD, D.D. 8vo. 7s. 6d.

SERMONS chiefly on the INTERPRETATION of SCRIPTURE.
By the late Rev. THOMAS ARNOLD, D.D. 8vo. price 7s. 6d.

SERMONS preached in the Chapel of Rugby School; with an Address
before Confirmation. By the late Rev. THOMAS ARNOLD, D.D. Fcp. 8vo. 3s. 6d.

THREE ESSAYS on RELIGION: Nature; the Utility of Religion;
Theism. By JOHN STUART MILL. 8vo. price 10s. 6d.

INTRODUCTION to the SCIENCE of RELIGION. Four Lectures
delivered at the Royal Institution; with Two Essays on False Analogies and
the Philosophy of Mythology. By F. MAX MÜLLER, M.A. Crown 8vo. 10s. 6d.

SUPERNATURAL RELIGION; an Inquiry into the Reality of Divine
Revelation. Sixth Edition, carefully revised, with Eighty Pages of New Preface.
2 vols. 8vo. 24s.

NOTES on the EARLIER HEBREW SCRIPTURES. By Sir G. B.
AIRY, K.C.B. 8vo. price 6s.

ISLAM under the ARABS. By ROBERT DRURIE OSBORN, Major in
the Bengal Staff Corps. 8vo. 12s.

RELIGION and SCIENCE, their Relations to each other at the Present
Day; Three Essays on the Grounds of Religious Beliefs. By STANLEY T. GIBSON,
B.D., late Fellow of Queen's College, Cambridge. 8vo. 10s. 6d.

The PRIMITIVE and CATHOLIC FAITH in Relation to the Church
of England. By the Rev. B. W. SAVILE, M.A. Rector of Shillingford, Exeter,
Author of 'Truth of the Bible' &c. 8vo. price 7s.

SYNONYMS of the OLD TESTAMENT, their BEARING on CHRIS-
TIAN FAITH and PRACTICE. By the Rev. R. B. GIRDLESTONE, M.A. 8vo. 15s.

An INTRODUCTION to the THEOLOGY of the CHURCH of
ENGLAND, in an Exposition of the Thirty-nine Articles. By the Rev. T. P.
BOULTBEE, LL.D. New Edition, Fcp. 8vo. price 6s.

An EXPOSITION of the 39 ARTICLES, Historical and Doctrinal.
By E. HAROLD BROWNE, D.D. Lord Bishop of Winchester. New Edit. 8vo. 16s.

The LIFE and EPISTLES of ST. PAUL. By the Rev. W. J.
CONYBEARE, M.A., and the Very Rev. J. S. HOWSON, D.D. Dean of Chester :—
LIBRARY EDITION, with all the Original Illustrations, Maps, Landscapes on
Steel, Woodcuts, &c. 2 vols. 4to. 42s.
INTERMEDIATE EDITION, with a Selection of Maps, Plates, and Woodcuts.
2 vols. square crown 8vo. 21s.
STUDENT'S EDITION, revised and condensed, with 46 Illustrations and Maps.
1 vol. crown 8vo. price 9s.

HISTORY of the REFORMATION in EUROPE in the TIME of
CALVIN. By the Rev. J. H. MERLE D'AUBIGNÉ, D.D. Translated by W. L. R.
CATES. 7 vols. 8vo. price £5. 11s.
*** Vol. VIII. completing the Work, is preparing for publication.

NEW TESTAMENT COMMENTARIES. By the Rev. W. A. O'CONOR.
B.A. Rector of St. Simon and St. Jude, Manchester. Crown 8vo.
  Epistle to the Romans, price 3s. 6d.
  Epistle to the Hebrews, 4s. 6d.
  St. John's Gospel, 10s. 6d.

A CRITICAL and GRAMMATICAL COMMENTARY on ST. PAUL'S
Epistles. By C. J. ELLICOTT, D.D. Lord Bishop of Gloucester and Bristol. 8vo.
Galatians, Fourth Edition, 8s. 6d.
Ephesians, Fourth Edition, 8s. 6d.
Pastoral Epistles, Fourth Edition, 10s. 6d.
Philippians, Colossians, and Philemon, Third Edition, 10s. 6d.
Thessalonians, Third Edition, 7s. 6d.

HISTORICAL LECTURES on the LIFE of OUR LORD. By
C. J. ELLICOTT, D.D. Bishop of Gloucester and Bristol. Sixth Edition. 8vo. 12s.

EVIDENCE of the TRUTH of the CHRISTIAN RELIGION derived
from the Literal Fulfilment of Prophecy. By ALEXANDER KEITH, D.D. 37th
Edition, with Plates, in square 8vo. 12s. 6d.; 39th Edition, in post 8vo. 6s.

HISTORY of ISRAEL. By H. EWALD, late Professor of the Univ. of
Göttingen. Translated by J. E. CARPENTER, M.A., with a Preface by RUSSELL
MARTINEAU, M.A. 5 vols. 8vo. 63s.

The ANTIQUITIES of ISRAEL. By HEINRICH EWALD, late Professor
of the University of Göttingen. Translated from the German by HENRY SHAEN
SOLLY, M.A. 8vo. price 12s. 6d.

The TREASURY of BIBLE KNOWLEDGE; being a Dictionary of the
Books, Persons, Places, Events, and other matters of which mention is made in
Holy Scripture. By Rev. J. AYRE, M.A. With Maps, 16 Plates, and numerous
Woodcuts. Fcp. 8vo. price 6s. cloth, or 10s. 6d. neatly bound in calf.

LECTURES on the PENTATEUCH and the MOABITE STONE.
By the Right Rev. J. W. COLENSO, D.D. Bishop of Natal. 8vo. 12s.

The PENTATEUCH and BOOK of JOSHUA CRITICALLY EXAMINED.
By the Right Rev. J. W. COLENSO, D.D. Bishop of Natal. Crown 8vo. 6s.

An INTRODUCTION to the STUDY of the NEW TESTAMENT,
Critical, Exegetical, and Theological. By the Rev. S. DAVIDSON, D.D. LL.D.
2 vols. 8vo. price 30s.

SOME QUESTIONS of the DAY. By the Author of 'Amy Herbert.'
Crown 8vo. price 2s. 6d.

THOUGHTS for the AGE. By the Author of 'Amy Herbert,' &c.
New Edition, revised. Fcp. 8vo. price 3s. 6d.

**The DOCTRINE and PRACTICE of CONFESSION in the CHURCH of
ENGLAND.** By the Rev. W. E. JELF, B.D. 8vo. price 7s. 6d.

PREPARATION for the HOLY COMMUNION ; the Devotions chiefly
from the Works of JEREMY TAYLOR. By Miss SEWELL. 32mo. 3s.

LYRA GERMANICA, Hymns translated from the German by Miss
C. WINKWORTH. Fcp. 8vo. price 5s.

SPIRITUAL SONGS for the SUNDAYS and HOLIDAYS through-
out the Year. By J. S. B. MONSELL, LL.D. Ninth Thousand. Fcp. 8vo. 5s.
18mo. 2s.

ENDEAVOURS after the CHRISTIAN LIFE: Discourses. By the
Rev. J. MARTINEAU, LL.D. Fifth Edition, carefully revised. Crown 8vo. 7s. 6d.

HYMNS of PRAISE and PRAYER, collected and edited by the Rev.
J. MARTINEAU, LL.D. Crown 8vo. 4s. 6d. 32mo. 1s. 6d.

The TYPES of GENESIS. briefly considered as revealing the Development of Human Nature. By ANDREW JUKES. Third Edition. Crown 8vo. 7s. 6d.

The SECOND DEATH and the RESTITUTION of ALL THINGS ;
with some Preliminary Remarks on the Nature and Inspiration of Holy Scripture. By ANDREW JUKES. Fourth Edition. Crown 8vo. 3s. 6d.

WHATELY'S INTRODUCTORY LESSONS on the CHRISTIAN
Evidences. 18mo. 6d.

BISHOP JEREMY TAYLOR'S ENTIRE WORKS. With Life by
BISHOP HEBER. Revised and corrected by the Rev. C. P. EDEN. Complete in
Ten Volumes, 8vo. cloth, price £5. 5s.

Travels, Voyages, &c.

The INDIAN ALPS, and How we Crossed them: being a Narrative
of Two Years' Residence in the Eastern Himalayas, and Two Months' Tour
into the Interior, towards Kinchinjunga and Mount Everest. By a Lady
PIONEER. With Illustrations from Original Drawings made on the spot by the
Authoress. Imperial 8vo. 42s.

TYROL and the TYROLESE; being an Account of the People and the Land, in their Social, Sporting, and Mountaineering Aspects. By W. A. BAILLIE GROHMAN. With numerous Illustrations from Sketches by the Author. Crown 8vo. 14s.

'The FROSTY CAUCASUS;' An Account of a Walk through Part of the Range, and of an Ascent of Elbruz in the Summer of 1874. By F. C. GROVE. With Eight Illustrations engraved on Wood by E. Whymper, from Photographs taken during the Journey, and a Map. Crown 8vo. price 15s.

A JOURNEY of 1,000 MILES through EGYPT and NUBIA to the SECOND CATARACT of the NILE. By AMELIA B. EDWARDS. With numerous Illustrations from Drawings by the Authoress, Map, Plans, Facsimiles, &c. Imperial 8vo.   [In the Autumn.

OVER the SEA and FAR AWAY; being a Narrative of a Ramble round the World. By THOMAS WOODBINE HINCHLIFF, M.A. F.R.G.S. President of the Alpine Club, Author of 'Summer Months among the Alps.' With 14 full-page Illustrations, engraved on Wood from Photographs and Sketches. Medium 8vo. 21s.

THROUGH BOSNIA and the HERZEGOVINA on FOOT during the INSURRECTION, August and September 1875; with an Historical Review of Bosnia, and a Glimpse at the Croats, Slavonians, and the Ancient Republic of Ragusa. By A. J. EVANS, B.A. F.S.A. With Map and 58 Wood Engravings from Photographs and Sketches by the Author. 8vo. 18s.

DISCOVERIES at EPHESUS, including the Site and Remains of the Great Temple of Diana. By J. T. WOOD, F.S.A. 1 vol. Imperial 8vo. copiously illustrated.   [In the press.

MEMORIALS of the DISCOVERY and EARLY SETTLEMENT of the BERMUDAS or SOMERS ISLANDS, from 1615 to 1685. Compiled from the Colonial Records and other original sources. By Major-General J. H. LEFROY, R.A. C.B. F.R.S. &c. Governor of the Bermudas. 8vo. with Map.   [In the press.

ITALIAN ALPS; Sketches in the Mountains of Ticino, Lombardy, the Trentino, and Venetia. By DOUGLAS W. FRESHFIELD, Editor of 'The Alpine Journal.' Square crown 8vo. with Maps and Illustrations, price 15s.

The RIFLE and the HOUND in CEYLON. By Sir SAMUEL W. BAKER, M.A. F.R.G.S. New Edition, with Illustrations engraved on Wood by G. Pearson. Crown 8vo. 7s. 6d.

EIGHT YEARS in CEYLON. By Sir SAMUEL W. BAKER, M.A. F.R.G.S. New Edition, with Illustrations engraved on Wood, by G. Pearson. Crown 8vo. 7s. 6d.

TWO YEARS IN FIJI, a Descriptive Narrative of a Residence in the Fijian Group of Islands; with some Account of the Fortunes of Foreign Settlers and Colonists up to the Time of the British Annexation. By LITTON FORBES, M.D. F.R.G.S. Crown 8vo. 8s. 6d.

MEETING the SUN; a Journey all round the World through Egypt, China. Japan, and California. By WILLIAM SIMPSON, F.R.G.S. With 48 Heliotypes and Wood Engravings from Drawings by the Author. Medium 8vo. 24s.

UNTRODDEN PEAKS and UNFREQUENTED VALLEYS; a Midsummer Ramble among the Dolomites. By AMELIA B. EDWARDS. With a Map and 27 Wood Engravings. Medium 8vo. 21s.

The **DOLOMITE MOUNTAINS**; Excursions through Tyrol, Carinthia, Carniola, and Friuli, 1861-1863. By J. GILBERT and G. C. CHURCHILL, F.R.G.S. With numerous Illustrations. Square crown 8vo. 21s.

The **ALPINE CLUB MAP** of **SWITZERLAND**, with parts of the Neighbouring Countries, on the Scale of Four Miles to an Inch. Edited by R. C. NICHOLS, F.S.A. F.R.G.S. In Four Sheets, price 42s. or mounted in a case, 52s. 6d. Each Sheet may be had separately, price 12s. or mounted in a case, 15s.

MAP of the **CHAIN** of **MONT BLANC**, from an Actual Survey in 1863-1864. By ADAMS-REILLY, F.R.G.S. M.A.C. Published under the Authority of the Alpine Club. In Chromolithography on extra stout drawing-paper 28in. × 17in. price 10s. or mounted on canvas in a folding case, 12s. 6d.

HOW to SEE NORWAY. By Captain J. R. CAMPBELL. With Map and 5 Woodcuts. Fcp. 8vo. price 5s.

GUIDE to the PYRENEES, for the use of Mountaineers. By CHARLES PACKE. With Map and Illustrations. Crown 8vo. 7s. 6d.

The **ALPINE GUIDE.** By JOHN BALL, M.R.I.A. late President of the Alpine Club. 3 vols. post 8vo. Thoroughly Revised Editions, with Maps and Illustrations:—I. *Western Alps*, 6s. 6d. II. *Central Alps*, 7s. 6d. III. *Eastern Alps*, 10s. 6d. Or in Ten Parts, price 2s. 6d. each.

Introduction on Alpine Travelling in General, and on the Geology of the Alps, price 1s. Each of the Three Volumes or Parts of the *Alpine Guide* may be had with this INTRODUCTION prefixed, price 1s. extra.

Works of Fiction.

HIGGLEDY-PIGGLEDY; or, Stories for Everybody and Everybody's Children. By the Right Hon. E. M. KNATCHBULL-HUGESSEN, M.P. With Nine Illustrations from Original Designs by R. Doyle, engraved on Wood by G. Pearson. Crown 8vo. price 6s.

WHISPERS from FAIRYLAND. By the Right Hon. E. H. KNATCH-BULL-HUGESSEN, M.P. With Nine Illustrations from Original Designs engraved on Wood by G. Pearson. Crown 8vo. price 6s.

NOVELS and TALES. By the Right Hon. B. DISRAELI, M.P. Cabinet Edition, complete in Ten Volumes, crown 8vo. price £3.

LOTHAIR, 6s.	HENRIETTA TEMPLE, 6s.
CONINGSBY, 6s.	CONTARINI FLEMING, &c. 6s.
SYBIL, 6s.	ALROY, IXION, &c. 6s.
TANCRED, 6s.	The YOUNG DUKE, &c. 6s.
VENETIA, 6s.	VIVIAN GREY 6s.

CABINET EDITION of STORIES and TALES by Miss SEWELL:—

AMY HERBERT, 2s. 6d.	IVORS, 2s. 6d.
GERTRUDE, 2s. 6d.	KATHARINE ASHTON, 2s. 6d
The EARL'S DAUGHTER, 2s. 6d.	MARGARET PERCIVAL, 3s. 6d.
EXPERIENCE of LIFE, 2s. 6d.	LANETON PARSONAGE, 3s. 6d.
CLEVE HALL, 2s. 6d.	URSULA, 3s. 6d.

BECKER'S GALLUS; or, Roman Scenes of the Time of Augustus : with Notes and Excursuses. New Edition. Post 8vo. 7s. 6d.

BECKER'S CHARICLES; a Tale illustrative of Private Life among the Ancient Greeks : with Notes and Excursuses. New Edition. Post 8vo. 7s. 6d.

The MODERN NOVELIST'S LIBRARY. Each Work, in crown 8vo. complete in a Single Volume :—

ATHERSTONE PRIORY, 2s. boards ; 2s. 6d. cloth.
MADEMOISELLE MORI, 2s. boards ; 2s. 6d. cloth.
MELVILLE'S GLADIATORS, 2s boards ; 2s. 6d. cloth.
————— GOOD FOR NOTHING, 2s. boards ; 2s. 6d. cloth.
————— HOLMBY HOUSE, 2s. boards ; 2s. 6d. cloth.
————— INTERPRETER, 2s. boards ; 2s. 6d. cloth.
————— KATE COVENTRY, 2s. boards ; 2s. 6d. cloth.
————— QUEEN'S MARIES, 2s. boards ; 2s. 6d. cloth.
————— DIGBY GRAND, 2s. boards ; 2s. 6d. cloth.
————— GENERAL BOUNCE, 2s. boards ; 2s. 6d. cloth.
TROLLOPE'S WARDEN, 1s. 6d. boards ; 2s. cloth.
————BARCHESTER TOWERS, 2s. boards ; 2s. 6d. cloth.
BRAMLEY-MOORE'S SIX SISTERS of the VALLEYS, 2s. boards ; 2s. 6d. cloth.
The BURGOMASTER'S FAMILY, 2s. boards ; 2s. 6d. cloth.
ELSA, a Tale of the Tyrolean Alps. Translated from the German of WILHELMINE VON HILLERN by Lady WALLACE. 2s. boards ; 2s. 6d. cloth.

Poetry and The Drama.

POEMS. By WILLIAM B. SCOTT. I. Ballads and Tales. II. Studies from Nature. III. Sonnets &c. Illustrated by 17 Etchings by L. ALMA TADEMA and WILLIAM B. SCOTT. Crown 8vo. price 15s.

MOORE'S IRISH MELODIES, with 161 Steel Plates from Original Drawings by D. MACLISE, R.A. New Edition. Super-royal 8vo. 21s.

The LONDON SERIES of FRENCH CLASSICS. Edited by CH. CASSAL, LL.D. T. KARCHER, LL.B. and LÉONCE STIÉVENARD. In course of publication, in fcp. 8vo. volumes. The following Plays, in the Division of the Drama in this Series, are now ready :—

CORNEILLE'S LE CID, 1s. 6d.
CORNEILLE'S POLYEUCTE, 1s. 6d.
RACINE'S IPHIGÉNIE, 1s. 6d.
VOLTAIRE'S ZAÏRE, 1s. 6d.

VOLTAIRE'S ALZIRE, 1s. 6d.
LAMARTINE'S TOUSSAINT LOUVERTURE 2s. 6d.
DE VIGNY'S CHATTERTON, 1s. 6d.

BALLADS and LYRICS of OLD FRANCE; with other Poems. By A. LANG, M.A. Late fellow of Merton College, Oxford. Square fcp. 8vo. 5s.

SOUTHEY'S POETICAL WORKS, with the Author's last Corrections and copyright Additions. Medium 8vo. with Portrait and Vignette, 14s.

LAYS of ANCIENT ROME; with IVRY and the ARMADA. By the Right Hon. Lord MACAULAY. 16mo. 3s. 6d.

LORD MACAULAY'S LAYS of ANCIENT ROME. With 90 Illustrations on Wood, from the Antique, from Drawings by G. SCHARF. Fcp. 4to. 21s.

Miniature Edition of Lord Macaulay's Lays of Ancient Rome, with the Illustrations (as above) reduced in Lithography. Imp. 16mo. 10s. 6d.

The ÆNEID of VIRGIL Translated into English Verse. By JOHN CONINGTON, M.A. New Edition. Crown 8vo. 9s.

HORATII OPERA. Library Edition, with Marginal References and English Notes. Edited by the Rev. J. E. YONGE, M.A. 8vo. 21s.

The LYCIDAS and EPITAPHIUM DAMONIS of MILTON. Edited, with Notes and Introduction (including a Reprint of the rare Latin Version of the Lycidas, by W. Hogg, 1694), by C. S. JERRAM, M.A. Crown 8vo. 2s. 6d.

BOWDLER'S FAMILY SHAKSPEARE, cheaper Genuine Editions. Medium 8vo. large type, with 36 WOODCUTS, price 14s. Cabinet Edition, with the same ILLUSTRATIONS, 6 vols. fcp. 8vo. price 21s.

POEMS. By JEAN INGELOW. 2 vols. fcp. 8vo. price 10s.
FIRST SERIES, containing ' DIVIDED,' ' The STAR'S MONUMENT,' &c. Sixteenth Thousand. Fcp. 8vo. price 5s.
SECOND SERIES, ' A STORY of DOOM,' ' GLADYS and her ISLAND,' &c. Fifth Thousand. Fcp. 8vo. price 5s.

POEMS by Jean Ingelow. FIRST SERIES, with nearly 100 Illustrations, engraved on Wood by Dalziel Brothers. Fcp. 4to. 21s.

Rural Sports, &c.

DOWN the ROAD; Or, Reminiscences of a Gentleman Coachman. By C. T. S. BIRCH REYNARDSON. Second Edition, with Twelve Coloured Illustrations from Paintings by H. Alken. Medium 8vo. 21s.

ANNALS of the ROAD; Or, Notes on Mail and Stage Coaching in Great Britain. By CAPTAIN MALET, 18th Hussars. To which are added, Essays on the Road, by NIMROD. With 3 Woodcuts and 10 Illustrations in Chromo-lithography. Medium 8vo. 21s.

ENCYCLOPÆDIA of RURAL SPORTS; a complete Account, Historical, Practical, and Descriptive, of Hunting, Shooting, Fishing, Racing, and all other Rural and Athletic Sports and Pastimes. By D. P. BLAINE. With above 600 Woodcuts (20 from Designs by JOHN LEECH). 8vo. 21s.

The FLY-FISHER'S ENTOMOLOGY. By ALFRED RONALDS. With coloured Representations of the Natural and Artificial Insect. Sixth Edition, with 20 coloured Plates. 8vo. 14s.

A BOOK on ANGLING; a complete Treatise on the Art of Angling in every branch. By FRANCIS FRANCIS. New Edition, with Portrait and 15 other Plates, plain and coloured. Post 8vo. 15s.

WILCOCKS'S SEA-FISHERMAN; comprising the Chief Methods of Hook and Line Fishing, a Glance at Nets, and Remarks on Boats and Boating. New Edition, with 80 Woodcuts. Post 8vo. 12s. 6d.

HORSES and STABLES. By Colonel F. FITZWYGRAM, XV. the King's Hussars. With Twenty-four Plates of Illustrations, containing very numerous Figures engraved on Wood. 8vo. 10s. 6d.

The HORSE'S FOOT, and HOW to KEEP it SOUND. By W. MILES, Esq. Ninth Edition, with Illustrations. Imperial 8vo. 12s. 6d.

A PLAIN TREATISE on HORSE-SHOEING. By W. MILES, Esq. Sixth Edition. Post 8vo. with Illustrations, 2s. 6d.

STABLES and **STABLE-FITTINGS.** By W. MILES, Esq. Imp. 8vo. with 13 Plates, 15s.

REMARKS on **HORSES' TEETH,** addressed to Purchasers. By W. MILES, Esq. Post 8vo. 1s. 6d.

The **HORSE:** with a Treatise on Draught. By WILLIAM YOUATT. New Edition, revised and enlarged. 8vo. with numerous Woodcuts, 12s. 6d.

The **DOG.** By WILLIAM YOUATT. 8vo. with numerous Woodcuts, 6s.

The **DOG** in **HEALTH** and **DISEASE.** By STONEHENGE. With 70 Wood Engravings. Square crown 8vo. 7s. 6d.

The **GREYHOUND.** By STONEHENGE. Revised Edition, with 25 Portraits of Greyhounds. Square crown 8vo. 15s.

The **OX;** his Diseases and their Treatment: with an Essay on Parturition in the Cow. By J. R. DOBSON. Crown 8vo. with Illustrations, 7s. 6d.

Works of Utility and General Information.

The **THEORY** and **PRACTICE** of **BANKING.** By H. D. MACLEOD, M.A. Barrister-at-Law. Third Edition, thoroughly revised. 2 vols. 8vo. price 26s.

The **ELEMENTS** of **BANKING.** By HENRY DUNNING MACLEOD, Esq. M.A. of Trinity College, Cambridge, and the Inner Temple, Barrister-at-Law. Crown 8vo. price 7s. 6d.

M'CULLOCH'S DICTIONARY; Practical, Theoretical, and Historical, of Commerce and Commercial Navigation. New and revised Edition. 8vo. 63s. Supplement, price 5s.

The **CABINET LAWYER;** a Popular Digest of the Laws of England, Civil, Criminal, and Constitutional: intended for Practical Use and General Information. Twenty-fifth Edition. Fcp. 8vo. price 9s.

BLACKSTONE ECONOMISED, a Compendium of the Laws of England to the Present time, in Four Books, each embracing the Legal Principles and Practical Information contained in their respective volumes of Blackstone, supplemented by Subsequent Statutory Enactments, Important Legal Decisions, &c. By D. M. AIRD, Barrister-at-Law. Revised Edition. Post 8vo. 7s. 6d.

PEWTNER'S COMPREHENSIVE SPECIFIER; a Guide to the Practical Specification of every kind of Building-Artificers' Work, with Forms of Conditions and Agreements. Edited by W. YOUNG. Crown 8vo. 6s.

WILLICH'S POPULAR TABLES for ascertaining according to the Carlisle Table of Mortality the Value of Lifehold, Leasehold, and Church Property, Renewal Fines, Reversions, &c.; also Interest, Legacy, Succession Duty, and various other useful Tables. Eighth Edition. Post 8vo. 10s.

HINTS to **MOTHERS** on the **MANAGEMENT** of their **HEALTH** during the Period of Pregnancy and in the Lying-in Room. By the late THOMAS BULL, M.D. Fcp. 8vo. 5s.

The **MATERNAL MANAGEMENT** of **CHILDREN** in **HEALTH** and
Disease. By the late THOMAS BULL, M.D. Fcp. 8vo. 5s.

The **THEORY** of the **MODERN SCIENTIFIC GAME** of **WHIST.**
By WILLIAM POLE, F.R.S. Seventh Edition, enlarged. Fcp. 8vo. 2s. 6d.

The **CORRECT CARD**; or, How to Play at Whist: a Whist Catechism.
By Captain A. CAMPBELL-WALKER, F.R.G.S. late 79th Highlanders; Author of
'The Rifle, its Theory and Practice.' 32mo. 2s. 6d.

CHESS OPENINGS. By F. W. LONGMAN, Balliol College, Oxford.
Second Edition revised. Fcp. 8vo. 2s. 6d.

THREE HUNDRED ORIGINAL CHESS PROBLEMS and **STUDIES.**
By JAMES PIERCE, M.A. and W. T. PIERCE. With numerous Diagrams. Square
fcp. 8vo. 7s. 6d. SUPPLEMENT, price 2s. 6d.

A **SKETCH** of the **HISTORY** of **TAXES** in **ENGLAND** from the
Earliest Times to the Present Day. By STEPHEN DOWELL. Vol. I. to the Civil
War 1642. 8vo. 10s. 6d.

The **NEW CODE** of the Education Department, with Notes, Analysis,
Appendix, and Index, and a Sketch of the Administration of the Grants for
Public Elementary Education (1339-1876). By H. J. GIBBS, and J. W. EDWARDS,
Barrister-at-Law. Second Edition, revised and adapted to the New Code, 1876.
Crown 8vo. 3s. 6d.

A **PRACTICAL TREATISE** on **BREWING**; with Formulæ for Public
Brewers, and Instructions for Private Families. By W. BLACK. 8vo. 10s. 6d.

MODERN COOKERY for **PRIVATE FAMILIES**, reduced to a System
of Easy Practice in a Series of carefully-tested Receipts. By ELIZA ACTON.
Newly revised and enlarged; with 8 Plates and 150 Woodcuts. Fcp. 8vo. 6s.

MAUNDER'S TREASURY of **KNOWLEDGE** and **LIBRARY** of
Reference; comprising an English Dictionary and Grammar, Universal Gazetteer,
Classical Dictionary, Chronology, Law Dictionary, a synopsis of the Peerage
useful Tables, &c. Revised Edition. Fcp. 8vo. 6s. cloth, or 10s. 6d. calf.

Knowledge for the *Young.*

The **STEPPING-STONE** to **KNOWLEDGE**; or upwards of 700
Questions and Answers on Miscellaneous Subjects, adapted to the capacity of
Infant minds. New Edition, revised. 18mo. 1s.

SECOND SERIES of the **STEPPING-STONE** to **KNOWLEDGE**:
Containing upwards of 800 Questions and Answers on Miscellaneous Subjects
not contained in the FIRST SERIES. 18mo. 1s.

The **STEPPING-STONE** to **GEOGRAPHY**: Containing several
Hundred Questions and Answers on Geographical Subjects. 18mo. 1s.

The **STEPPING-STONE** to **ENGLISH HISTORY**; Questions and
Answers on the History of England. 18mo. 1s.

The STEPPING-STONE to BIBLE KNOWLEDGE; Questions and Answers on the Old and New Testaments. 18mo. 1s.

The STEPPING-STONE to BIOGRAPHY; Questions and Answers on the Lives of Eminent Men and Women. 18mo. 1s.

The STEPPING-STONE to IRISH HISTORY: Containing several Hundred Questions and Answers on the History of Ireland. 18mo. 1s.

The STEPPING-STONE to FRENCH HISTORY: Containing several Hundred Questions and Answers on the History of France. 18mo. 1s.

The STEPPING-STONE to ROMAN HISTORY: Containing several Hundred Questions and Answers on the History of Rome. 18mo. 1s.

The STEPPING-STONE to GRECIAN HISTORY: Containing several Hundred Questions and Answers on the History of Greece. 18mo. 1s.

The STEPPING-STONE to ENGLISH GRAMMAR: Containing several Hundred Questions and Answers on English Grammar. 18mo. 1s.

The STEPPING-STONE to FRENCH PRONUNCIATION and CONVERSATION : Containing several Hundred Questions and Answers. 18mo. 1s.

The STEPPING-STONE to ASTRONOMY: Containing several Hundred familiar Questions and Answers on the Earth and the Solar and Stellar Systems. 18mo. 1s.

The STEPPING-STONE to MUSIC: Containing several Hundred Questions on the Science ; also a short History of Music. 18mo. 1s.

The STEPPING-STONE to NATURAL HISTORY: VERTEBRATE OR BACK-BONED ANIMALS. PART I. *Mammalia*; PART II. *Birds, Reptiles, and Fishes.* 18mo. 1s. each Part.

THE STEPPING-STONE to ARCHITECTURE; Questions and Answers explaining the Principles and Progress of Architecture from the Earliest Times. With 100 Woodcuts. 18mo. 1s.

INDEX.

Spottiswoode & Co., Printers, New-street Square, London.

www.ingramcontent.com/pod-product-compliance
Lightning Source LLC
Chambersburg PA
CBHW022022110726
47901CB00006B/1626